SIDNEY SHELDON'S
AFTER THE DARKNESS

Sidney Sheldon was the author of eighteen previous bestselling novels (which have sold over 300 million copies), over 200 television scripts, twenty-five major films and six Broadway plays, ranking him as one of the world's most prolific writers. His first book, *The Naked Face*, was acclaimed by the *New York Times* as 'the best first mystery novel of the year' and subsequently each of his highly popular books have hit No.1 on the *New York Times* bestseller list.

Tilly Bagshawe is the author of four bestselling novels. She divides her time between London and Los Angeles with her husband and children.

TILLY BAGSHAWE

Sidney Sheldon's
After the Darkness

HARPER

This novel is entirely a work of fiction.
The names, characters and incidents portrayed in it are
the work of the author's imagination. Any resemblance to
actual persons, living or dead, events or localities is
entirely coincidental.

Harper
An imprint of HarperCollins*Publishers*
77–85 Fulham Palace Road,
Hammersmith, London W6 8JB

www.harpercollins.co.uk

A Paperback Original 2010
1

A catalogue record for this book
is available from the British Library

ISBN: 978-0-00-730456-1

Set in Sabon by Palimpsest Book Production Ltd,
Grangemouth, Stirlingshire

Printed and bound in Great Britain by
Clays Ltd, St Ives plc

Mixed Sources
Product group from well-managed
forests and other controlled sources
www.fsc.org   Cert no. SW-COC-001806
© 1996 Forest Stewardship Council

FSC is a non-profit international organisation established
to promote the responsible management of the world's forests.
Products carrying the FSC label are independently certified
to assure consumers that they come from forests that are managed
to meet the social, economic and ecological needs
of present and future generations.

Find out more about HarperCollins and the environment at
www.harpercollins.co.uk/green

For Kerstin and Louis Sparr, with love.

Greed is right.
Greed works.
Greed clarifies, cuts through, and captures
the essence of the evolutionary spirit.
Greed, in all of its forms – greed for life, for money,
for love, for knowledge – has marked the
upward surge of mankind.

—Gordon Gekko, in *Wall Street,* 1987

Prologue

New York, December 15, 2009

The day of reckoning had arrived.

The Gods had demanded a sacrifice. A human sacrifice. In ancient Roman times, when the city was at war, captured enemy leaders would have been ritually strangled on the battlefield in front of a statue of Mars, the war god. Crowds of soldiers would have cheered, screaming not for justice but for vengeance. For blood.

This was not ancient Rome. It was modern-day New York, the beating heart of civilized America. But New York was also a city at war. It was a city full of suffering, angry people who needed somebody to blame for their pain. Today's human sacrifice would be offered up in the clinical, ordered surroundings of the Manhattan Criminal Courts Building. But it would be none the less bloody for that.

Normally, the TV crews and hordes of ghoulish spectators only showed up for murder trials. Today's defendant, Grace Brookstein, had not murdered anybody. Not directly anyway. Yet there were plenty of New Yorkers who would have rejoiced to see Grace Brookstein sent to the electric chair. Her son-of-a-bitch husband had cheated them. Worse, he had cheated justice. Lenny Brookstein – *may he rot in hell* – had laughed in the face of the Gods. Well, now the Gods must be appeased.

The man responsible for appeasing them – District Attorney Angelo Michele, representative of the people – looked across the courtroom at his intended victim. The woman sitting at the defendant's table, hands clasped calmly in front of her, did not look like a criminal. A slight, attractive blonde in her early twenties, Grace Brookstein had the sweet, angelic features of a child. A competitive gymnast in her teens, she still carried herself with a dancer's poise, back ramrod straight, hand gestures measured and fluid. Grace Brookstein was fragile. Delicate. Beautiful. She was the sort of woman whom men instinctively wanted to protect. Or rather she would have been, had she not stolen $75 billion in the largest, most catastrophic fraud in U.S. history.

The collapse of Quorum, the hedge fund founded by Lenny Brookstein and co-owned by his young wife, had dealt a fatal blow to the already crippled American economy. Between them, the Brooksteins had ruined families, destroyed entire industries, and brought the once great financial center of New York to its knees. They had stolen more than Madoff, but that wasn't what hurt the most. Unlike Madoff, the Brooksteins had stolen not from the rich, but from the poor. Their victims were ordinary people: the elderly, small charities, hardworking, blue-collar families already struggling to get by. At least one young father made destitute by Quorum had shot himself, unable to bear the shame of seeing his children turned out on the streets. Not once had Grace Brookstein displayed so much as a shred of remorse.

Of course, there were those who argued that Grace Brookstein was not guilty of the crimes that had brought her to this courtroom. That it was Lenny Brookstein, not his wife, who had masterminded the Quorum fraud. District

Attorney Angelo Michele loathed such people. *Bleeding-heart liberals. Fools! You think the wife didn't know what was going on? She knew. She knew everything. She just didn't care. She spent your pension funds, your life savings, your kids' college money . . . Just look at her now! Is she dressed like a woman who gives a shit that you lost your home?*

Over the course of the trial, the press had made much of Grace Brookstein's courtroom attire. Today, for the verdict, she had chosen a white Chanel shift ($7,600), matching bouclé jacket ($5,200), Louis Vuitton pumps ($1,200) and purse ($18,600), and an exquisite floor-length mink handmade for her in Paris, an anniversary present from her husband. The *New York Post* early edition was already on newsstands. Above a full-length shot of Grace Brookstein arriving at Court 14, the front-page headline screamed: LET THEM EAT CAKE!

District Attorney Angelo Michele intended to make sure that Grace Brookstein's cake-eating days were over. *Enjoy those furs, lady. This'll be the last day you get to wear 'em.*

Angelo Michele was a tall, lean man in his midforties. He wore a plain Brooks Brothers suit and his thick black hair slicked back till it gleamed on top of his head like a shiny black helmet. Angelo Michele was an ambitious man and a fearsome boss – all the junior D.A.s were terrified of him – but he was a good son. Angelo's parents ran a pizza parlor in Brooklyn. Or they had run one until Lenny Brookstein 'lost' their life savings and forced them into bankruptcy. Thank God Angelo earned good money. Without his income the Micheles would have been out on the streets in their old age, destitute like so many other hardworking Americans. As far as Angelo Michele was concerned, prison was too good for Grace Brookstein. But it was a start. And he was going to be the man who put her there.

Sitting next to Grace at the defendant's table was the man

whose job it was to stop him. Francis Hammond III, 'Big Frank' as he was known among the New York legal community, was the shortest man in the room. At five foot four, he was barely taller than his tiny client. But Frank Hammond's intellect towered over his opponents like a behemoth. A brilliant defense attorney with the mind of a chess grand master and the morals of a gutter fighter, Frank Hammond was Grace Brookstein's Great White Hope. His specialty was playing juries, uncovering fears and desires and prejudices that people didn't even know they had and turning them to his clients' advantage. In the past year alone, Frank Hammond had been responsible for the acquittals of two murdering Mafia bosses and a child-molesting actor. His cases were always high profile, and his clients always began their trials as underdogs. Grace Brookstein had originally hired another lawyer to represent her, but her friend and confidant John Merrivale had insisted she fire him and go with Big Frank.

'You're innocent, Grace. *We* know that. But the rest of the world doesn't. The m-m-media wants you hanged, drawn and quartered. Frank Hammond's the only guy who can turn that around. He's a genius.'

No one could understand why Big Frank had allowed Grace Brookstein to show up to court every day in such inflammatory outfits. Her clothes seemed designed to enrage the press still further, not to mention the jury. Surely a titanic mistake?

But Frank Hammond did not make mistakes. Angelo Michele knew that better than anyone.

There's a method in his madness. There has to be. I just wish I knew what it was.

Still, it didn't really matter. Today was the last day of the trial and Angelo Michele was convinced he had built an airtight case. Grace Brookstein was going down. First to jail. And then to hell.

* * *

Grace Brookstein had woken up that morning in the Merrivales' guest bedroom suffused with a deep sense of peace. She'd had a dream about Lenny. They were at their estate in Nantucket, always Grace's favorite of their many multimillion-dollar homes. They were walking in the rose garden. Lenny was holding her hand. Grace could feel the warmth of his skin, the familiar roughness of his palms.

'It will be okay, my darling. Have faith, Gracie. It will all be okay.'

Walking into court this morning, arm in arm with her attorney, Grace Brookstein had felt the crowd's hatred, hundreds of pairs of eyes burning a hole in her back. She had heard the catcalls. *Bitch. Liar. Thief.* But she held on to her inner peace, to Lenny's voice inside her head.

It will all be okay.

Have faith.

John Merrivale had said the same thing on the phone last night. Thank God for John! Without him, Grace would have been completely lost. Everyone else had deserted her in her hour of need, her friends, even her own sisters. *Rats on a sinking ship.* It was John Merrivale who had forced Grace to hire Frank Hammond. And now Frank Hammond was going to save her.

Grace watched him summing up now, this fiery little man, strutting back and forth in front of the jury like a farmyard rooster. She only understood a fragment of what Hammond was saying. The legal arguments were way over her head. But she knew with certainty that her attorney would get her an acquittal. Then, and only then, would her real work begin.

Walking free from court is just the start. I still have to clear my name. And Lenny's. God, I miss him. I miss him so much. Why did God have to take him away from me? Why did any of this have to happen?

Frank Hammond finished speaking. Now it was Angelo Michele's turn.

'Ladies and gentlemen of the jury. Over the last five days you have heard a lot of complex legal arguments, some of them from me, and some of them from Mr Hammond. Unfortunately it had to be that way. The scale of the fraud at Quorum: seventy-five *billion* dollars . . .'

Angelo Michele paused to let the impact of the number sink in. Even after so many months of repetition, the sheer size of the Brooksteins' theft never failed to shock.

'. . . means that, by its very nature, this case is complicated. The fact that the bulk of that money is still missing makes it even more complicated. Lenny Brookstein was a wicked man. But he was not a stupid man. Nor is his wife, Grace Brookstein, a stupid woman. The paper trail they left behind them at Quorum is so complicated, so impenetrable, that the truth is, we may *never* recover that money. Or what's left of it.'

Angelo Michele looked at Grace with naked loathing. At least two female jurors did the same.

'But let me tell you what's not complicated about this case. Greed.'

Another pause.

'Arrogance.'

And another.

'Lenny and Grace Brookstein believed they were above the law. Like so many of their kind, the rich bankers on Wall Street who have raped and pillaged this great country of ours, who have taken tax payers' money, *your* money, and squandered it with such shameless abandon, the Brooksteins don't believe that the rules of the *Little People* apply to them. Take a good look at Mrs Brookstein, ladies and gentlemen. Do you see a woman who understands what ordinary people in this country are suffering? Do you see a woman who cares?

Because I don't. I see a woman born into wealth, a woman married into wealth, a woman who considers wealth – obscene wealth – to be her God-given right.'

Up in the gallery, John Merrivale whispered to his wife.

'This isn't a l-legal argument. It's a witch hunt.'

The district attorney went on.

'Grace Brookstein was a partner in Quorum. An equal equity partner. She was not only legally responsible for the fund's actions. She was morally responsible for them. Make no mistake. Grace Brookstein knew what her husband was doing. And she supported and encouraged him every step of the way.

'Don't let the complexity of this case fool you, ladies and gentlemen. Underneath all the jargon and paperwork, all the offshore bank accounts and derivative transactions, what happened here is really very simple. Grace Brookstein stole. She stole because she was greedy. She stole because she thought she could get away with it.'

He looked at Grace one last time.

'She still thinks she can get away with it. It's up to you to prove her wrong.'

Grace Brookstein watched District Attorney Angelo Michele sit down. He'd given a bravura performance, far more eloquent than Frank Hammond's. The jury looked as if they wanted to burst into spontaneous applause.

If he weren't trying to destroy me, I'd feel sorry for him. Poor man, he's tried so hard. And such passion! Perhaps, if we'd met in other circumstances, we'd have been friends?

The general consensus in the media was that the jury would take at least a day to deliberate. The mountain of evidence in the case was so enormous that it was hard to see how they could review it any quicker. In fact, they came back to Court 14 in less than an hour. *Just like Frank Hammond said they would.*

The judge spoke solemnly. 'Have you reached your verdict?'

The foreman, a black man in his fifties, nodded. 'We have, Your Honor.'

'And how do you find the defendant? Guilty, or not guilty?'

The foreman looked directly at Grace Brookstein.

And smiled.

BOOK ONE

Chapter One

'What do you think, Gracie? The black or the blue?'

Lenny Brookstein held up two bespoke suits. It was the night before the Quorum Charity Ball, New York's most glamorous annual fund-raiser, and he and Grace were getting ready for bed.

'Black,' said Grace, not looking up. 'It's more classic.'

She was sitting at her priceless Louis XVI walnut dressing table, brushing her long blond hair. The champagne silk La Perla negligee Lenny bought her last week clung to her perfect gymnast's body, accentuating every curve. Lenny Brookstein thought, *I'm a lucky man.* Then he laughed aloud. *Talk about an understatement.*

Lenny Brookstein was the undisputed king of Wall Street. But he hadn't been born into royalty. Today, everyone in America recognized the heavyset fifty-eight-year-old: the wiry gray hair, the broken nose from a childhood brawl that he'd never gotten fixed (why should he? He won), the sparkling, intelligent amber eyes. All these features made up a face as familiar to ordinary Americans as Uncle Sam or Ronald

11

McDonald. In many ways, Lenny Brookstein *was* America. Ambitious. Hardworking. Generous. Warmhearted. Nowhere was he more loved than here, in his native New York.

It hadn't always been so.

Born Leonard Alvin Brookstein, the fifth child and second son of Jacob and Rachel Brookstein, Lenny had a horrific childhood. In later life, one of the few things that could rouse Lenny Brookstein's rarely seen temper were books and movies that seemed to romanticize poverty. Misery Memoirs, that's what they called them. *Where did those guys get off?* Lenny Brookstein grew up in poverty – crushing, soul-destroying poverty – and there was nothing romantic or noble about it. It wasn't *romantic* when his father came home drunk and beat his mother unconscious in front of him and his siblings. Or when his beloved elder sister Rosa threw herself under a subway train after three boys from the Brooksteins' filthy housing project gang-raped her on her way home from school one night. It wasn't *noble* when Lenny and his brothers got attacked at school for eating 'stinky' Jewish food. Or when Lenny's mother died of cervical cancer at the age of thirty-four because she couldn't take the time off work to see a doctor for her stomach cramps. Poverty did not bring Lenny Brookstein's family closer together. It pulled them apart. Then, one by one, it pulled them to pieces. All except Lenny.

Lenny dropped out of high school at sixteen and left home the same year. He never looked back. He went to work for a pawnbroker in Queens, a job that provided him with more proof, if any were needed, that the poor did not 'pull together' in times of trouble. They ripped one another's throats out. It was tough watching old women handing over objects of huge sentimental value – a dead husband's watch, a daughter's cherished silver christening spoon – in return for a grudging handful of dirty bills. Mr Grady, the pawnbroker, had had heart bypass surgery the year before Lenny went to work for him. Evidently the surgeon had removed his compassion at the same time.

Mr Grady used to tell Lenny: 'Value is not what something is *worth*, kid. That's a fairy tale. Value is what someone is willing to pay. Or *be paid*.'

Lenny Brookstein had no respect for Mr Grady, as a person or a businessman. But the truth of those words stuck with him. Later, much later, they became the foundation for Lenny Brookstein's fortune and Quorum's sensational success. Lenny Brookstein understood what ordinary, poor people were willing to accept. That one person's concept of 'value' was different from another's, and that the market's could be different again.

I owe the old bastard for that.

The story of Lenny Brookstein's rise from pawnbroker's lackey to world-respected billionaire had become an American legend, part of the country's folklore. George Washington could not tell a lie. Lenny Brookstein could not make a bad investment. After a successful run of bets on the horses in his late teens (Jacob Brookstein, Lenny's father, had been an inveterate gambler), Lenny decided to try his luck on the stock market. At Saratoga and Monticello, Lenny had learned the importance of developing a system and sticking to it. On Wall Street, they called a system a 'model' but it was the same thing. Unlike his father, Lenny also had the discipline to cut his losses and walk away when he needed to. In the movie *Wall Street*, Michael Douglas's Gordon Gekko had famously declared: 'Greed is good.' Lenny Brookstein profoundly disagreed with that statement. Greed wasn't good. On the contrary, it was the downfall of almost all unsuccessful investors. *Discipline* was good. Finding the right model and sticking to it, through hell or high water. That was the key.

Lenny Brookstein was already a millionaire many times over by the time he met John Merrivale. The two men could not have had less in common. Lenny was self-made, confident, a walking ball of energy and joie de vivre. He never spoke about his past because he never thought about it. His brilliant amber eyes were always fixed on the future, the next trade, the next opportunity. John Merrivale was upper class, shy, cerebral and prone to depression. A skinny, redheaded young man, he was nicknamed 'Matchstick' at Harvard Business School, where he graduated top in his class, as his father and grandfather had both done before him. Everybody, including John Merrivale himself, expected he would go into one of the top-tier Wall Street firms, Goldman or Morgan, and begin his slow but predictable rise to the top. But then Lenny Brookstein burst into John Merrivale's life like a meteor and everything changed.

'I'm starting a hedge fund,' Lenny told John the night they met, at a mutual acquaintance's party. 'I'll make the investment decisions. But I need a partner, someone with a blue-chip background to help bring in outside capital. Someone like you.'

John Merrivale was flattered. No one had ever believed in him before. 'Thank you. But I'm not a marketing guy. T-t-t-trust me. I'm a thinker, not a s-s-salesman.' He blushed. *Goddamn stammer. Why the hell can't I get over it already?*

Lenny Brookstein thought: *And a stammer, too. You couldn't make this guy up. He's perfect.*

Lenny told John, 'Listen. Salesmen are a dime a dozen. What I need is someone low-key and credible. Someone who can get an eighty-five-year-old Swiss banker to trust him with his mother's life savings. I can't do that. I'm too . . .' He cast around for the right word. 'Flamboyant. I need someone that makes a risk-averse pension fund manager think: "You know what? This guy's honest. And he knows his shit. I like him better than that sharp, cocky kid from Morgan Stanley." I'm telling you, John. It's *you*.'

14

That conversation had been fifteen years ago. Since then, Quorum had grown to become the largest, most profitable hedge fund of all time, its tentacles reaching into every aspect of American life: real estate, mortgages, manufacturing, services, technology. One in six New Yorkers – *one in six* – was employed by a company whose balance sheet depended on Quorum's performance. And Quorum's performance *was* dependable. Even now, in the worst economic crisis since the 1930s, with giants like Lehman Brothers and Bear Stearns hitting the wall, and the government bailing out once untouchable firms like AIG to the tune of billions, Quorum continued turning a modest, consistent profit. The world was on fire, Wall Street was on its knees. But Lenny Brookstein stuck to his system, the same way he always had. And the good times kept rolling.

For years Lenny Brookstein believed he had everything he wanted. He had bought himself homes all over the globe, but rarely left America, dividing his time between his mansion in Palm Beach, his Fifth Avenue apartment and his idyllic beachfront estate on Nantucket Island. He threw parties that everybody came to. He donated millions of dollars to his favorite causes and felt a warm glow inside. He bought a three-hundred-foot yacht, interior-designed by Terence Disdale, and a private Airbus A340 quad jet that he flew in only twice. Occasionally he slept with one of the models who made it their business to be around him, should he suddenly find himself in the mood for sex. But he never had 'girl-friends.' He was surrounded by people, many of whom he liked, but he did not have 'friends' in the traditional sense of that word. Lenny Brookstein was beloved by all who knew him. But he didn't 'do' intimacy. Everybody knew that.

Then he met Grace Knowles.

* * *

15

More than thirty years Lenny Brookstein's junior, Grace Knowles was the youngest of the famous Knowles sisters, New York socialite daughters of the late Cooper Knowles. Cooper Knowles had been a real estate guy, worth a couple of hundred million in his heyday. Never as big as 'the Donald,' Cooper was always far better liked. Even business rivals invariably described him as 'charming,' 'a gentleman,' 'old-school.' Like her elder sisters, Constance and Honor, Grace adored her father. She was eleven years old when Cooper died, and his death left a void in her life that nothing could fill.

Grace's mother remarried – three times in total – and moved permanently to East Hampton, where the girls' lives continued much as they had before. School, shopping, parties, vacations, more shopping. Connie and Honor were both pretty and much sought after by New York's eligible young bachelors. It was generally accepted, however, that Grace was the most beautiful of the Knowles sisters. When she took up gymnastics competitively at thirteen in an attempt to distract herself from her ongoing grief for her father, her elder sisters were secretly relieved. Gymnastics meant training, and traveling out of state, *a lot*. Once *they* were safely married off, it would be fine to have Grace come to parties with them again. But until then, Connie and Honor heartily encouraged their baby sister's love affair with the parallel bars.

By the time she was eighteen, Grace's days as a competition-level gymnast were over. But that was okay. By then Connie had married a movie-star-handsome investment banker named Michael Gray, a real up-and-comer at Lehman Brothers. And Honor had hit the marital jackpot by landing Jack Warner, the Republican congressman for New York's 20th Congressional District. Jack was already being hotly touted as a candidate for the Senate, and perhaps even one day for the presidency. The Warners' wedding was all over Page 6, and photographs of the honeymoon appeared in a number of national tabloids. As the new Caroline Kennedy, Honor could afford to be gracious to her little sister. It was Honor who invited Grace to the garden party where she first met Lenny Brookstein.

In later years, both Lenny and Grace would describe that first meeting as the proverbial thunderbolt. Grace was eighteen, a child, with no experience of the world outside her cosseted, pampered East Hampton existence. Even her friends from gymnastics were wealthy. And yet there was something wonderfully unspoiled about her. Lenny Brookstein had grown used to what his mother would have called 'fast' women. Every girl he'd ever slept with wanted something from him. Jewels, money . . . something. Grace Knowles was the opposite. She had a quality that Lenny himself had never had and wanted badly. Something so precious and elusive, he had almost given up believing it existed: *innocence*. Lenny Brookstein wanted to capture Grace Knowles. To hold that innocence in his hands. To *own* it.

For Grace, the attraction was even simpler. She needed a father. Someone who would protect her and love her for herself, the way that Cooper Knowles had loved her when she was a little girl. The truth was, Grace Knowles wanted to *go back* to being a little girl. To go back to a time when she was totally, blissfully happy. Lenny Brookstein offered her that chance. Grace grabbed it with both hands.

They married on Nantucket six weeks later, in front of six hundred of Lenny Brookstein's closest friends. John Merrivale was best man. His wife, Caroline, and Grace's sisters were the matrons of honor. On their honeymoon in Mustique, Lenny turned to Grace nervously one night and asked: 'What about children? We never discussed it. I suppose you'll want to be a mother at some stage?'

Grace gazed pensively out across the ocean. Soft, gray moonlight danced upon the waves. At last, she said: 'Not

17

really. Of course, if *you* want children, I'll gladly give them to you. But I'm so happy as we are. There's nothing missing, Lenny. Do you know what I mean?'

Lenny Brookstein knew what she meant.

It was one of the happiest moments of his life.

'Do you know what you're wearing yet?' Lenny pulled some papers out of his briefcase and put on his reading glasses before climbing into bed.

'I do,' said Grace. 'But it's a secret. I want to surprise you.'

Earlier that afternoon Grace had spent three happy hours in Valentino with her elder sister Honor. Honor had always had an amazing sense of style and the sisters loved to shop together. The manager had closed the store especially so that they could peruse the gowns in peace.

'I feel quite the rebel.' Grace giggled. 'Leaving it to the last minute like this.'

'I know! We're kicking over the traces, Gracie.'

The Quorum Ball was *the* society event of the season. Always held in early June, it marked the start of summer for Manhattan's privileged elite, who decamped en masse to East Hampton the following week. Most of the women attending tomorrow night at The Plaza would have begun planning their outfits like generals before a military campaign months ago, ordering in silks from Paris and diamonds from Israel, starving themselves for weeks in order to look their flat-stomached best.

Of course, this year there would be some belt tightening. Everyone was talking about the economy and how dire it was. People in Detroit were rioting, apparently. In California, thousands of homeless people had pitched tents along the banks of the American River. The headlines were dreadful. For Grace Brookstein and her friends, nothing compared to the shock they'd felt the day they heard that Lehman Brothers had gone bankrupt. Lehman's collapse was a tragedy far

18

closer to home. Grace's own brother-in-law Michael Gray had seen his net worth decimated overnight. Poor Connie. It really was too awful.

Lenny told Grace, 'We have to strike a different tone this year, Gracie. The Quorum Ball must go ahead. People need the money that charities like ours provide now more than ever.'

'Of course they do, darling.'

'But it's important we aren't too ostentatious. Compassion. Compassion and restraint. Those must be our watchwords.'

With Honor's help, Grace had picked out a *very* restrained black silk shift from Valentino, with almost no beading whatsoever. As for her Louboutin pumps? *Simplicity itself.* She couldn't wait for Lenny to see her in them.

Slipping into bed beside him, Grace turned off her bedside lamp.

'Just a second, sweetie.' Lenny reached over and turned it on again. 'I need you to sign something for me. Where is it now?' He fumbled through the sheets of paper littering his side of the bed. 'Ah. Here we are.'

He handed Grace the document. She took Lenny's pen and was about to sign it.

'Whoa there!' Lenny laughed. 'Aren't you going to read it first?'

'No. Why would I?'

'Because you don't know what you're signing, Gracie. That's why. Didn't your father ever tell you not to sign anything you haven't read?'

Grace leaned over and kissed him. 'Yes, my darling. But *you've* read it, haven't you? I trust you with my life, Lenny, you know that.'

Lenny Brookstein smiled. Grace was right. He did know it. And he thanked God for it every day.

* * *

On the corner of Fifth Avenue and Central Park South, a battalion of media had gathered in front of The Plaza's iconic Beaux Arts façade. Lenny Brookstein was having a party – *the* party – and as always, the stars were out in force. Billionaires and princes, supermodels and politicians, actors, rock stars, philanthropists; everyone attending tonight's Quorum Ball had one crucial thing in common, and it wasn't a burning desire to help the needy. They were all *winners*.

Senator Jack Warner and his wife, Honor, were among the first to arrive.

'Go around the block,' Senator Warner barked at his driver. 'Why the hell did you get us here so early?'

The driver thought, *Ten minutes ago you were on my case for driving too slow. Make your goddamn mind up, asshole.*

'Yes, Senator Warner. Sorry, Senator Warner.'

Honor Warner studied her husband's angry features as they turned onto West Fifty-seventh Street. *He's been like this all day, ever since he got back from his meeting with Lenny. I hope he isn't going to ruin this evening for us.*

Honor Warner tried to be an understanding wife. She knew that politics was a stressful profession. It had been bad enough when Jack was a congressman, but since his elevation to the Senate (at the remarkably young age of thirty-six), it had gotten worse. The world knew Jack Warner as the Republican's messiah – a conservative Jack Kennedy for the new millennium. Tall, blond and chiseled, with a strong jaw and a steady, blue-eyed gaze, Senator Warner was adored by voters, especially women. He stood for decency, for old-fashioned family values, for a strong, proud America that many people feared was crumbling daily beneath their feet. Just watching Senator Warner on the news, hand in hand with his beautiful wife, their two towheaded daughters skipping along beside them, was enough to restore people's faith in the American Dream.

Honor Warner thought, *If only they knew.*

But how could they? Nobody knew.

Tentatively, she turned to her husband. 'Do you like my dress, Jack?'

Senator Jack Warner looked at his wife and tried to remember the last time he had found her sexually attractive. *It's not that there's anything wrong with her. She's pretty enough, I guess. She's not fat.*

Honor Warner, in fact, was much more than pretty. With her wide-set green eyes, blond curls and high cheekbones, she was widely considered a striking beauty. Not as striking as her sister Grace, perhaps, but gorgeous nonetheless. Tonight Honor was poured into a skintight, strapless Valentino gown the same sea green as her eyes. It was a pull-all-the-stops-out dress. To any impartial observer, Honor Warner looked sexy as hell.

Jack said brusquely. 'It's fine. How much did it cost?'

Honor bit her lower lip hard. *I mustn't cry. My mascara'll run.*

'It's on loan. Like the emeralds. Grace pulled some strings.'

Senator Jack Warner laughed bitterly. 'How generous of her.'

'Please, Jack.'

Honor touched his leg in a conciliatory gesture, but he shrugged away her hand. Knocking on the glass partition, he said to the driver: 'You can turn the car around now. Let's get this evening over with.'

By nine P.M., The Plaza's cream-and-gold Grand Ballroom was packed to bursting. On either side of the room, beneath the splendidly restored arches, tables gleamed with brilliantly polished silverware. Light from the candelabras glinted off the women's diamonds as they mingled in the center of the room, admiring one another's priceless couture dresses and swapping horror stories about their husbands' latest financial woes.

'There's no way we can afford Saint-Tropez this year. Ain't happening.'

'Harry's going to sell the yacht. Can you believe it? He *loved* that thing. He'd sell the children first if he thought anyone would buy them.'

'Did you hear about the Jonases? They just listed their town house. Lucy wants twenty-three million for it, but in this market? Carl thinks they'll be lucky to get half that.'

At nine-thirty exactly, dinner was served. All eyes were on the top table. Surrounded by their inner circle of Quorum courtiers, Lenny and Grace Brookstein sat in regal splendor, with eyes only for each other. Other, lesser hosts might have chosen to seat the most glamorous, famous guests at their table. Prince Albert of Monaco was there. So were Brad and Angelina, and Bono and his wife, Ali. But the Brooksteins pointedly kept close to their family and close friends: John and Caroline Merrivale, the vice president and second lady of Quorum; Andrew Preston, another senior Quorum exec, and his voluptuous wife, Maria; Senator Warner and his wife, Grace Brookstein's sister Honor; and the eldest of the Knowles sisters, Constance, with her husband, Michael.

Lenny Brookstein proposed a toast.

'To Quorum! And all who sail in her!'

'To Quorum!'

Andrew Preston, a handsome, well-built man in his mid-forties with kind eyes and a gentle, self-deprecating smile, watched his wife stand up, champagne glass in hand, and thought: *Another new dress. How am I supposed to pay for that?*

Not that she didn't look wonderful in it. Maria always looked wonderful. A former actress and opera star, Maria Preston was a force of nature. Her mane of chestnut hair

22

and gravity-defying, creamy white breasts made her beautiful. But it was her manner, the sparkle in her eye, the deep, throaty vibration of her laugh, the flirtatious swing of her hips, that made men fall at her feet. No one could understand what had possessed a live wire like Maria Carmine to marry an ordinary, standard-issue businessman like Andrew Preston. Andrew himself understood it least of all.

She could have had anyone. A movie star. Or a billionaire like Lenny. Perhaps it would have been better if she had.

Andrew Preston loved his wife unreservedly. It was because of his love, and his deep sense of unworthiness, that he forgave her so much. The affairs. The lies. The uncontrollable spending. Andrew earned good money at Quorum. A small fortune by most people's standards. But the more he earned, the more Maria spent. It was a disease with her, an addiction. Month after month, she charged hundreds of thousands of dollars to their Amex card. Clothes, cars, flowers, diamonds, eight-thousand-dollar-a night hotel suites where she spent the night with God knows who . . . it didn't matter. Maria spent for the thrill of spending.

'You want me to look like a pauper, Andy? You want me to sit next to that smug little bitch Grace Brookstein in some off-the-rack monstrosity?'

Maria was jealous of Grace. Then again, she was jealous of every woman. It was part of her fiery Italian nature, part of what Andrew Preston loved about her. He tried to reassure her.

'Darling, you're twice the woman Grace is. You could wear a sack and you would still outshine her.'

'You want me to wear a sack now?'

'No, no, of course not. But, Maria, our mortgage payments . . . Perhaps one of your other dresses, darling? Just this year. You have so many . . .'

It was the wrong thing to say, of course. Now Maria had

punished him by not only buying a new dress, but buying the most expensive dress she could find, a jewel-encrusted riot of feathers and lace. Looking at it, Andrew felt his heart tighten. Their debts were getting serious.

I'll have to talk to Lenny again. But the old man has already been so generous. How much further can I push him before he snaps?

Andrew Preston reached into the inside pocket of his tuxedo jacket. When no one was looking, he slipped three Xanax into his mouth, washing them down with a slug of champagne.

You always knew Maria would be hard to hold on to. Find a way, Andrew. Find a way.

'Are you all right, Andrew?' Caroline Merrivale, John Merrivale's wife, noticed Andrew Preston's ashen face. 'You look like you have the weight of the world on your shoulders.'

'Ha ha! Not at all.' Andrew forced a smile. 'You look ravishing tonight, Caro, as always.'

'Thank you. John and I both made an effort to be low-key. You know, given the current economic circumstances.'

It was a deliberate dig at Maria. Andrew let it pass, but thought again how much he loathed Caroline Merrivale. Poor John, being pussy-whipped through life by that harridan. No wonder he always looked so downtrodden.

It was obvious to anyone with eyes in their head that the Merrivale marriage was an unhappy one. Anyone, that is, other than Lenny and Grace Brookstein. Those two were so nauseatingly in love, they seemed to assume that everybody else had what they had. *Easy to keep the love alive when you have billions of dollars to throw at it.* But perhaps Andrew was being unfair? The young Mrs Brookstein was no gold digger. She was naive, that was all, and clearly believed that Caroline Merrivale was her friend. Grace never saw the envy that blazed in the older woman's eyes whenever her back was turned. But Andrew Preston saw it. Caroline Merrivale was a bitch.

Caroline had always bitterly resented Grace's position as first lady of Quorum. She, Caroline Merrivale, would have been *so* much better suited to the role. Handsome rather than beautiful, with strong, intelligent features and a sharply cut bob of black hair, Caroline had once had a flourishing career as a trial lawyer. Of course, that was years ago now. Thanks to Lenny Brookstein, her husband, John, had become an immensely wealthy and successful man. Caroline's working days were over. But her ambition was far from extinguished.

John Merrivale, by contrast, had never been ambitious. He worked hard at Quorum, accepted whatever Lenny chose to give him, and was grateful. Caroline would taunt him: 'You're like a puppy, John. Curled up at your master's feet, loyally wagging your tail. No wonder Lenny doesn't respect you.'

'Lenny d-d-does respect me. It's you who d-d-doesn't.'

'No, and why would I? I want a man, John, not a lapdog. You should demand more equity. Stand up and be counted.'

Andrew Preston glanced across the table at John Merrivale now. Lenny was in the middle of an anecdote, with John hanging on his every word. Andrew thought: *He's brilliant. But he's weak.* There was only room for one king at Quorum. Caroline Merrivale might wish it weren't so, but she could keep on wishing. They were all hanging off of Lenny Brookstein's coattails. And they were the lucky ones. Poor old Michael Gray was sitting on Maria's right, also listening to Lenny's story. The Grays were like a walking cautionary tale. One minute they were partying up a storm all over Manhattan, living it up in their Greenwich Village brownstone, summering in the South of France and wintering at their newly remodeled chalet in Aspen. The next minute – *poof* – it was all gone.

Word was that every cent Mike Gray owned had been leveraged against Lehman stock. Their kids, Cade and Cooper, were only still in their private schools because Grace Brookstein, Connie Gray's sister, had insisted on covering the tuition.

Maria whispered in Andrew's ear: 'The auction starts in a few minutes, Andy. I've got my eye on the vintage Cartier watch. Will you bid for it, or shall I?'

Grace Brookstein smiled and clapped throughout the bidding, but she was secretly relieved when the auction ended and it was time for dancing.

'I hate these things,' she whispered in Lenny's ear as he whisked her around the floor. 'All those fragile male egos trying to outspend each other. It's chest beating.'

'I know.' Lenny's hand caressed her lower back. 'But those chest beaters just raised fifteen million for our foundation. In this economy, that's pretty good going.'

'Do you mind if I cut in? I've barely spoken to my favorite brother-in-law all night.'

Connie, Grace's eldest sister, slipped her arm around Lenny's waist. Lenny and Grace both smiled.

'Favorite brother-in-law, eh?' Grace teased. 'Don't let Jack hear you say that.'

'Oh, *Jack*.' Connie waved her hand dismissively. 'He's been in such a funk all evening. I thought being a senator was supposed to be fun. Anyone would think he was the one who'd just lost his house. And job. And life savings. Come on, Lenny! Cheer a girl up, would you?'

Grace watched has her husband dance with her sister, holding Connie close so he could offer words of comfort. *I love them both so much,* she thought. *And I* admire *them both so much. The way Connie can make jokes and laugh at herself when she and Mike are going through hell. And Lenny's incredible, inexhaustible compassion.* People were always talking about how 'lucky' Grace was to be married to Lenny. Grace agreed. But it wasn't Lenny's money that made her blessed. It was his kindness.

Of course, there was a downside to being married to the nicest man in the world. So many people loved Lenny, and relied on him, that Grace almost never got him all to herself. Next week they were flying to Nantucket, Grace's favorite place in the world, for a two-week vacation. But of course, being the gracious host that he was, Lenny had invited everyone at the table tonight to join them.

'Promise me we'll get at least *one* night alone,' Grace begged, when they finally crawled into bed that night. The ball had been fun, but exhausting. The thought of even more socializing filled Grace with dread.

'Don't worry. They won't all come. And even if they do, we'll get more than one night alone, I promise. The house is big enough for us to sneak away.'

Grace thought, *That's true. The house is enormous. Almost as big as your heart, my darling.*

Chapter Two

It was the morning after the Quorum Ball, a Saturday. John Merrivale was in bed with his wife.

'Please, C-C-Caroline. I don't want to.'

'I don't care what you *want*, you pathetic little worm. *Do it!*'

John Merrivale closed his eyes and moved down beneath the sheets till he was eye level with his wife's neatly trimmed black bush.

Caroline taunted him. 'If you weren't such a limp dick, I wouldn't *need* you to do it. But since you've failed to get it up yet again, it's the least you can do.'

John Merrivale began to do what was asked of him. He hated oral sex. It felt disgusting and wrong. But the days had long passed when he was allowed to follow his own desires. His sex life had become a series of nightly humiliations. Weekends were the worst. Caroline expected a morning performance on Saturdays, and sometimes even a Sunday matinee. It was incredible to John how a woman who so patently despised him could still have such a rampant sex drive. But Caroline seemed to get off on degrading him, bending him to her whim.

28

Feeling her writhe with pleasure against his tongue, John fought the urge to gag. Sometimes he fantasized about escape. *I could go to the office one day and never come home. I could drug her, then strangle her in her sleep.* But he knew he would never have the balls to do it. That was the worst part of his miserable marriage. His wife was right about him. He *was* weak. He *was* a coward.

In the beginning, when they first met, John had hoped that he might draw strength from Caroline's dominant personality. That her confidence and ambition would compensate for his shyness. For a few blissful months, they had. But it wasn't long before his wife's true nature emerged. Caroline's ambition was not a positive force, like Lenny Brookstein's. It was a black hole, an envy-fueled vortex that sucked the life out of any human being who came near it. By the time John Merrivale realized what a monster he'd married, it was too late. If he divorced her, she would expose him to the world as a sexual cripple. That would be more humiliation than even John could bear.

Thankfully it only took a couple of minutes for Caroline to reach orgasm. As soon as she had her pleasure, she got up and marched into the shower, leaving John to strip the bed and put on fresh sheets. There was no need for him to perform such a menial task. The Merrivales had a small army of maids and housekeepers on permanent call at their palatial town home. But Caroline insisted he do it. Once, when she considered his hospital corners to be less than perfect, she'd smashed a glass perfume bottle into his face. John had needed sixteen stitches, and still bore the scar on his left cheek. He told Lenny he'd been mugged, which as he saw it was not far from the truth.

If it hadn't been for Lenny Brookstein, John Merrivale would have killed himself years ago. Lenny's friendship, his warm, easy manner, his readiness with a joke, even when

29

business was going badly, was the most important, treasured thing in John Merrivale's life. He lived for the office and his work at Quorum, not because of the money or the power, but because he wanted to make Lenny proud. Lenny Brookstein was the one and only person who had ever *believed* in John Merrivale. Awkward and physically unattractive, with red hair and pale, gangly limbs, John had never been popular at school. He had no brothers and sisters growing up with whom to share his troubles, or toast his modest successes. Even his parents were disappointed in him. They never said anything, of course. They didn't have to. John could *feel* it just by walking into a room.

At his wedding to Caroline, he overheard his mother talking to one of his aunts. 'Of course, Fred and I are absolutely delighted. We never thought that John would marry such a bright, attractive girl. To be perfectly honest, we'd rather given up hope of his marrying at all. I mean, let's face it, he's a sweet boy but he's hardly Cary Grant!'

The fact that his own wife despised him hurt John, but it did not surprise him. People had despised him all his life. It was Lenny Brookstein's friendship, the huge trust Lenny had placed in John, that was the great surprise of John's life. He owed Lenny Brookstein everything.

Of course, Caroline didn't see it that way. Her envy of Lenny and Grace Brookstein had grown over the years to the point where she now struggled to conceal it in public. In private, John had grown used to hearing her refer to Lenny disparagingly as 'the old man,' and to Grace as 'that bitch.' But recently Caroline had taken to wearing her loathing on her face. For John, this made events like last night's Quorum Ball a terrifying experience. His love for Lenny Brookstein was immense. But his fear of his wife was even greater. And Caroline Merrivale knew it.

* * *

30

At breakfast, John tried to make small talk.

'We made a r-r-respectable total last night, I thought, all things considered.'

Caroline sipped her coffee and said nothing.

'I know L-Lenny was pleased.'

'Fifteen million?' Caroline laughed scornfully. 'That's nothing to the old man. He might as well just write a check himself and be done with it. But of course, that would mean missing out on all the adulation. All the great and the good telling him what a terrific, philanthropic guy he is. And we couldn't have his darling Gracie go without getting her picture taken *six thousand times,* could we? Heaven forbid!'

John spread a thin layer of butter on his toast, avoiding his wife's eye. He knew from experience that Caroline's anger could turn on a dime. One wrong move and it would be directed at him. Once again he cursed himself for his cowardice. *Why am I so afraid of her?*

Hoping to get back into her good graces, he mumbled, 'Lenny invited us to Nantucket next week, by the way. Don't worry. I said no.'

'What the hell did you do that for?'

'I . . . well, I . . . I assumed you . . .'

'You *assumed*?' Caroline's eyes bulged with rage. 'How dare you assume anything!' For a moment John wondered if she was going to hit him. To his great shame, he heard his coffee cup rattle against its saucer. 'Who else is invited?'

'Everybody, I th-th-think. The Prestons. Grace's s-sisters. I'm not sure.'

'And you want to let Andrew Preston spend a week sucking up to Lenny, pushing himself ahead of you at Quorum while you sit by and do nothing? Good God, John. How stupid are you?'

John opened his mouth to protest, then shut it again. The business didn't work like that. Andrew Preston could never hope to usurp John's position and he wouldn't try. He wouldn't dare. But there was no point trying to reason with Caroline.

'So you want to go, then?'

'I don't *want* to go, John. Frankly I can't think of anything worse than being cooped up with Lenny Brookstein's inane child bride on some godforsaken island for seven days. But I *will* go. And so will you.' She swept imperiously out of the room.

Once she'd gone, John Merrivale allowed himself a small smile.

I did it. We're going. We're actually going!

The reverse psychology had worked like a charm. All it took was a little courage. *Perhaps I'll try it more often?*

Chapter Three

Senator Jack Warner woke up on Saturday morning with a crushing hangover. Honor had left early for her yoga class. Downstairs, in the playroom of their idyllic Westchester County farmhouse, Jack Warner could hear his daughters, Bobby and Rose, screaming blue murder at each other.

What the fuck is Ilse doing?

The family's new Dutch au pair gave an excellent blow job, but her nannying skills left much to be desired. So far Jack had resisted Honor's requests to be allowed to fire Ilse. But this morning, he changed his mind. An uninterrupted Saturday morning in bed was worth much more than a good blow job. In Senator Jack Warner's world, good blow jobs were easy to come by. Peace and quiet, on the other hand, were priceless.

Jack Warner first knew he wanted to become president of the United States when he was three years old. It was August 1974. His parents were watching Richard Nixon's resignation on television.

'What's that man doing?' little Jack asked his mother. It was his father who answered.

'He's leaving the best job in the world, son. He's a liar and a fool.'

Jack thought about this for a minute.

'If he's a fool, how did he get the best job in the world?'

His father laughed. 'That's a good question!'

'Who's going to do his job now?'

'Why d'you ask, Jacko?' Jack's father pulled him up onto his lap and ruffled his hair affectionately. 'Do you want it?'

Yes, thought Jack. *If it's the best job in the world, I rather think I do.*

So far, Jack Warner's path to the White House had been straight as an arrow. First in his class at Andover? Check. Steady record of volunteer work and public service? Check. Yale undergrad, Harvard Law, partnership in a prestigious New York law firm? Check, check, check. After two brief internships working on senatorial campaigns, Jack Warner ran for Congress, winning the 20th Congressional District seat by a landslide at the astonishingly young age of twenty-nine. Jack Warner never made a friend, took a job, attended a party, or got laid without first thinking, *How will this look on my record?* On the rare occasions when he slept with a less- than-suitable girl, he made sure that the event took place well away from the prying eyes of any potential voters. But such slip-ups were rare. Jack made it his business to be in the right place at the right time with the right people. He knew that his appeal lay in his all-American good looks, the air of confidence and down-home *goodness* that he seemed to project so effortlessly.

Like everything else in Jack Warner's life, his marriage to Honor Knowles had been a carefully choreographed political decision.

Fred Farrell, Jack's campaign manager, sat him down. 'Our data shows you're still perceived as too young to run for the Senate. We need to "mature" your image.'

Jack was frustrated. 'How? Should I grow a beard? Start wearing vests?'

'Actually the beard's not a bad idea. But what you really need to do is get married. A couple of kids wouldn't hurt either. The single women all love you, but you need to work on the family vote.'

'Fine. I'll ask Karen over the weekend.'

Karen Connelly was Jack's girlfriend of the past ten months and his first really serious love. The only daughter of a respected, political family – Karen's father, Mitch, had once been White House chief of staff – Karen was also beautiful, intelligent and kind. She adored Jack unconditionally. The two of them had spoken often about starting a family together one day, when Karen finished grad school and Jack's congressional schedule got less hectic. Evidently 'one day' was now.

Fred Farrell frowned. 'I'm not so sure Karen's the best choice. She's a sweet girl and all. But for your wife . . .'

Jack bristled. 'What's wrong with her?'

'There's nothing wrong with her. Don't take it personally, Jack. I'm merely saying that ideally I'd prefer someone with a little more "wow" factor. Not *too* pretty, of course. That's a big turnoff for your base.'

'But prettier than Karen?'

'Higher profile than Karen. It wouldn't hurt if she were independently wealthy, too.'

'Why?'

'For the future, dear boy.' Fred Farrell shook his head despairingly. 'I'm assuming your political ambitions don't end with the Senate?'

'Of course not.'

'Good. Then start thinking practically. Have you any idea how much a presidential run costs these days?'

Jack had a pretty good idea. Many a wealthy man had lost everything pursuing his White House fantasies. Even so, marrying for money seemed distasteful.

'Look, I have a girl in mind. Meet her, see what you think. No pressure.'

Three months later, Congressman Jack Warner got over his distaste and married society heiress Honor Knowles in a blaze of publicity. The day they left for their honeymoon, Karen Connelly committed suicide, slitting her wrists in the bathtub. Out of respect for Karen's father, the press never ran the story.

For Honor Knowles, her whirlwind romance with the most eligible, dashing congressman in the country was easily the most exciting thing that had ever happened to her. Ever since she was a little girl, Honor had felt overlooked. Her elder sister, Constance, was the brains of the family and their mother's clear favorite. Grace, Honor's younger sister, was drop-dead beautiful and had been the apple of their father's eye when he was alive. All of which left *Honor* pretty much nowhere. The fact that she was bright and attractive in her own right didn't seem to matter to anyone. *I'm the fifth wheel. The backup singer no one ever notices. I'm only popular by association.*

For a handsome man to single her out (and not just any handsome man but Jack Warner, a possible future president!) was so thrilling, so deliciously unexpected, that it never occurred to Honor to question Jack's motives. Or the speed with which he hustled her down the aisle. Jack, she soon learned, did everything at speed. No sooner had he asked her out on a date than he proposed. No sooner had she accepted than he'd booked the church. No sooner had they gotten back from honeymoon than he was on her case about getting pregnant.

'What's the rush?' Honor laughed, stroking his sleek blond head in bed one night. She still had to pinch herself sometimes when she woke up next to Jack. He was so perfect. Not just perfect-looking but perfect on the inside, too. Noble, courageous, visionary. He wanted so many good things for

America. 'We've only been married five minutes. Can't we just enjoy being together for a little while, first?'

But Jack was insistent. He wanted a family and he wanted it now. On their honeymoon in Tahiti, Honor had been worried. Jack got a phone call from home on their first morning at the resort that had clearly upset him. He canceled their snorkeling trip ('You go. I have to work') and barely spoke to Honor for the remainder of the day. That night, he kept calling out 'Karen!' in his sleep. When Honor questioned him the next day, he was defensive. 'Jesus, Honor. You're cross-examining my dreams now?'

After that, he was withdrawn and morose the entire week, refusing to talk about what was troubling him and avoiding all of Honor's attempts at closeness. He didn't even want to make love. But when they got back to New York, to Honor's immense relief, the black mood lifted. Suddenly he was all over her again.

He wouldn't want to start a family if he didn't love me, she reasoned. *This is his way of saying sorry for Tahiti. And really, why should we wait? What could be sweeter than having a mini-Jack running around?*

Their first daughter, Roberta, was born nine months later, followed within a year by her sister, Rose. Because the pregnancies were so close together, Honor was still carrying weight from Roberta when she conceived Rose. As a result, when Jack took her out for dinner to celebrate their second anniversary, Honor was almost fifty pounds heavier than she had been on her wedding day.

'Why don't you start running again?' Jack suggested bluntly over the pan-fried scallops. 'You could go with your sister and her trainer. Grace is looking fantastic at the moment. That guy must be doing something right.'

It was as if he'd stuck a pin in Honor's eyeball. *Grace. Why did everything always have to come back to Grace?*

When Honor married Jack Warner, she felt like the star of the show for the first time in her life. Growing up, Grace had *always* stolen her thunder. The worst part was, she'd done it without even trying. Just by walking into a room, Grace owned it, shining with a light so blinding it obliterated Honor's presence altogether. Honor tried hard to stamp down her feelings of jealousy and resentment. She knew Grace loved her, that she thought of Honor as her best friend. And yet there were times when Honor Knowles fantasized about her sister having an 'accident.' She pictured Grace falling from the high bars, her perfect little doll's body contorted and broken on the gym floor. Or a car accident in which Grace's exquisite, model features were ravaged by flames. *The flames of my hatred.* The fantasies were shameful, but they felt good.

When Honor married Jack, she thought, *All that's behind me now. Now that I'm happy and famous, now that someone wonderful loves me, I can be the big sister Grace always wanted me to be.*

It didn't work out that way. Ironically, it was Honor who had introduced Grace to Lenny Brookstein, at one of Jack's fund-raisers. Two weeks later, Grace announced they were in love.

At first, Honor thought she was kidding. When she realized her mistake, she felt sick to her stomach. 'But, Gracie, you're eighteen years old. He's old enough to be your grandfather.'

'I know. It's crazy!' Grace laughed, that sweet, tinkling laugh that made all men melt like butter on a stove. 'I never thought I could feel this way about someone like Lenny but . . . I'm so happy, Honor. Truly. And so's Lenny. Can't you be happy for us?'

'Darling, I *am* happy. If it's what you really want.'

But Honor wasn't happy. She was furious.

38

It wasn't enough for Grace to settle down with some normal, rich investment banker, like Connie had done. *Oh no. Madam has to go and ensnare the biggest billionaire in New York.* Honor Knowles's brief moment in the sun was already fading. While she was stuck at home, fat and exhausted like a mother hen, Grace was once more the talk of the town. And now here was Jack, her own beloved husband, comparing her unfavorably to her little sister because she'd gained a few pounds giving birth to *his* children! It was not to be borne.

And yet Honor did bear it, stoically and in silence. The same way she bore Jack's neglect of her and the children, his selfishness, his rampant ambition, and most recently, his infidelities. She lost the weight, every last pound of it. As far as the public was concerned, Senator Warner and his wife had a fairy-tale marriage. Honor was not about to disillusion them. The pretense was all she had left, and she kept it up, smiling at Jack loyally during his speeches, giving magazine interviews about her homemaking tips and Jack's brilliance as a 'hands-on' father. Of course, Honor knew full well that the only thing Jack had had his hands on lately were the au pair's breasts, but she would have died rather than admit it.

The same went for her loathing of her sister. On the surface, Honor Warner remained close to both her sisters, but particularly to Grace. The two women ate lunch together twice a week, in addition to their regular shopping trips and vacations *en famille*. But beneath the loving, sisterly façade, Honor's resentment bubbled like scalding magma.

Jack encouraged his wife to strengthen her ties to the Brooksteins. 'It's win-win, darling. You get to spend time with Grace. I know how much you love her. And I get some face time with Lenny. If Lenny Brookstein endorses my run for the White House in four years' time, I'll be unstoppable.'

Honor thought about it. *If Jack runs for president, he'll*

have to stop chasing tail. It's too risky. Plus, if he becomes
president, with Lenny Brookstein's money, I'll be first lady.
Not even Grace can trump that.

Recently, however, Jack's fervor for his billionaire in-laws
had inexplicably cooled. It started with bitchy comments
about Grace's clothes and Lenny's ever-growing paunch. In
the days leading up to the Quorum Ball, it spilled over into
something more overt. Jack was drinking heavily. At home,
when drunk, he would rant at Honor about Lenny
Brookstein's 'disloyalty,' his 'arrogance.'

'Fucking prick, who does he think he's talking to? One of
his employees?' he rambled. 'If Lenny wants his dick sucked,
he should ask John Merrivale or that ass-kisser Preston. I'm
a fucking United States senator!'

Honor had no idea what Jack was talking about. She
longed to ask, but she was too afraid. Despite everything,
Honor Warner still loved her husband. Deep down she was
convinced that if she helped Jack's career – said the right
things, wore the right dress, threw the right parties – he
would eventually fall in love with her again.

She could not know that Jack Warner had never been in
love with her in the first place.

Jack came downstairs in his bathrobe, hunting for some Alka-
Seltzer. Roberta, known to her parents as Bobby, flew into
his arms like a whirlwind.

'Daddy!' Blond and chubby, like a Renaissance cherub,
Bobby had always been a very affectionate child. 'Ilse says
if we're not good, we won't go to In-tuck-it. That's not right,
is it?'

Jack set his daughter back down on the floor.

'Don't pester your father, Roberta,' said Ilse.

'But we *like* In-tuck-it. Even Rose does, don't you, Rosie?'

Four-year-old Rose was pulling Dior lipsticks out of

Mommy's makeup bag and snapping them in half, rubbing waxy pink mess all over the hardwood floor. Ilse was too busy making eyes at her boss to notice.

'Can I help you with anything, Senator Warner?'

'No,' Jack snapped. *Nantucket. I forgot about that. That bastard Brookstein invited us all to his estate last night. Like we're all such good buddies.*

It had cost Jack Warner's pride dearly for him to go to Lenny Brookstein for help. He'd never have done it if he hadn't been desperate. But he *was* desperate, and Lenny knew it. It had started as a sort of stress relief. A few innocent bets here and there, on the horses or the blackjack tables. But as his losses crept up, so did the size of Jack's positions. Gambling had unleashed a reckless side to Jack Warner that he had never before been aware of. It was exciting, exhilarating and addictive. Recently, his addiction had started to cost him dearly in financial terms. But the real risk was political. Jack had built his entire career on his reputation as an upstanding, Christian conservative. Compulsive gambling might not be illegal, but it would lose him the family values vote in a heartbeat.

Fred Farrell gave it to him straight. 'You have to stop this, Jack. Right now. Pay off your debts and wipe the slate clean.'

As if it were that easy! Pay off my debts? With what? Honor's inheritance had all been blown on the house and the children's education. As a senator, Jack earned $140,000 a year, a fraction of what he used to make as an attorney, and an even smaller fraction of what he now owed – in some cases, to some deeply unsavory characters.

There was no way around it. He would have to tap his brother-in-law. It would be embarrassing, sure. But once he explained the situation, Lenny would help him out. *Lenny's a long-term thinker. When they make me president, I'll pay him back a thousandfold. He knows that.*

It turned out Lenny Brookstein did not know it. Instead of writing a check, he'd given Jack a lecture.

'I'm sorry for you, Jack, truly I am. But I can't help. My father was a gambler. Put my poor mother through hell. If it hadn't been for the enablers, the friends who bailed him out time after time, the nightmare might have ended a lot sooner. As it was, he lost the money that could have paid for Ma's medical treatment.'

Jack tried to keep his cool. 'With all due respect, Lenny, I don't think I have much in common with your father. I'm a United States senator. I'm good for this money, you know that. It's just a small cash-flow problem.'

Lenny smiled amiably. 'In which case I'm sure you'll solve it on your own. Now, was there anything else?'

Patronizing bastard! It wasn't just a refusal. It was a dismissal. Jack Warner would not forget the slight as long as he lived. His first thought last night had been to tell Lenny Brookstein to stick his invitation to Nantucket where the 'moon don't shine.' But on reflection, perhaps that was a mistake. The truth was, he was still in urgent need of a significant injection of cash. Honor and Grace were close. Maybe if Honor worked on her little sister, Grace could make her besotted husband see sense? Of course, such a policy would mean Jack coming clean to Honor about his gambling debts. Not an appealing prospect. But at the end of the day, what was she going to do? *Leave me? I don't think so.*

Turning to Ilse, he said, 'We'll leave for Nantucket first thing Monday morning. Please make sure the girls are packed and ready.'

Bobby shot her au pair a look of purest triumph. 'See. I *told* you we were going.'

'Yes, sir. Is there anything . . . *special* . . . you'd like *me* to pack?'

Ilse gave him a lascivious wink. Her meaning could not have been clearer.

Neither could Jack's.

'No. You won't be coming with us. As of Monday, you're fired.'

Grabbing the Alka-Seltzer from the kitchen cupboard, he went back upstairs to bed.

Chapter Four

Connie Gray stood in the playground, watching her sons on the monkey bars.

Look at them. So innocent. They have no idea their world is crumbling around them.

Cade was six and the spitting image of his father, Michael. Dark-haired and olive-skinned, he had the same open, happy, guileless face as Mike. Cooper had more of Connie in him. His coloring was fairer, his features more feminine. And he was altogether a more complex child. Sensitive. Anxious. Both the boys were highly intelligent. With parents like Connie and Michael, how could they not be? But four-year-old Cooper was the deeper thinker.

I wonder what he'd think if he knew what his mommy has been up to? Perhaps one day, when he's older, he'll understand? How desperate times called for desperate measures?

The eldest of the Knowles sisters, Connie had been a straight-A student since first grade. Her mother's pride and joy, Connie had had to make do with her father's respect and affection. Cooper Knowles's heart was already spoken for. It belonged to his youngest daughter, Grace.

Like Honor, Connie recognized early on that the baby of the family was 'special,' a uniquely compelling, lovely child. Unlike Honor, however, Connie had no intention of taking a backseat to little Grace, or of giving up the limelight. She played her role as the brains of the family brilliantly, graduating top of her class in high school and getting accepted into all the premier Ivy League colleges. Though she feigned a lack of interest in beauty and fashion, Connie knew she was attractive, albeit in a strong-featured, masculine sort of way. She did all she could to maintain her flawless alabaster complexion and the trim, long-legged figure that men so admired. She might not be able to compete with Grace in terms of looks, but at eight years older, she didn't have to.

By the time Grace is old enough to come out in society, I'll be happily married. She'll be Honor's problem then.

And of course, she was. Like all the Knowles sisters, Connie married for love. Michael Gray was a knockout in those days. He was still pretty gorgeous, but back then he still had his football player's physique, as well as the chiseled, Armani-model features that made all the secretaries at Lehman Brothers swoon.

Connie kept working as a lawyer until Cade was born. After that, there didn't seem much point. Michael was a partner at Lehman, earning millions of dollars a year in bonuses. Of course, most of that came in the form of stock options. But back then, who cared about that? Bank stocks were only moving one way – up. If the Grays spent multiples of Mike's basic salary every year, they were only doing what everybody else was doing. If you wanted something expensive, like a Hamptons beach house or a Bentley or a $100,000 necklace for your wife on her anniversary, you borrowed against your stock. It was a simple, tax-efficient system and one that no one questioned.

Then Bear Stearns collapsed.

In hindsight, the failure of that venerable old New York institution in March 2008 was the beginning of the end for Michael and Connie Gray, and for thousands like them. But of course, hindsight is 20/20. At the time, Connie remembered, it still felt as if something seismic and awful and unimaginable was happening to *someone else*. Those were the best kind of tragedies. The kinds that were close enough to give you a frisson of terror and excitement, without actually affecting your life.

It was nine months now since the awful September day when Connie's *own* world had collapsed. She still woke up some mornings feeling happy and content for a few blissful seconds . . . until she remembered.

Lehman Brothers went bankrupt on September 16, 2008. Overnight, the Grays saw their net worth drop from somewhere around $20 million to about $1 million – the equity in their heavily mortgaged New York town house. Then the housing market dropped through the floor, and that million dollars fell to $500,000. By Christmas they'd sold everything but Connie's jewelry and pulled the kids out of school. But the real problem was not so much the financial catastrophe itself, but Connie and Michael's polar opposite responses to their predicament.

Michael Gray was a good man. *A trouper.* And you couldn't keep a good man down. 'Just think how many millions of people are worse off than we are,' he would tell Connie constantly. 'We're lucky. We have each other, two terrific little boys, good friends, and some savings. Plus we're both young enough to get out there and start earning again.'

Connie said, 'Of course we are darling,' and kissed him.

Inside, she thought, *Lucky? Are you out of your mind?*

Connie Gray didn't *want* to 'get out there and start earning.' She didn't *want* to dust herself off and try again. She didn't want to pack up her troubles in her old kit bag and smile, smile, smile, and if Michael spouted one more inane fucking platitude, so help her she would strangle him with his one remaining silk Hermès necktie.

Connie had no interest in becoming one of the credit crunch's stoic, plucky survivors. The American Dream wasn't about *surviving*. It was about *winning*. Connie Gray wanted to be a winner. She had married a winner, and he had let her down. Now she must find a new protector, someone who could provide a decent life for her and her children.

The affair with Lenny Brookstein had not been planned.

Affair! Who am I kidding? It was a two-night stand. Lenny made that very clear last night.

Connie had always gotten along well with Grace's illustrious husband. In happier times, she and Mike would have dinner with the Brooksteins regularly. Inevitably, it was Connie and Lenny who ended up screaming with laughter at some private joke. Grace used to tell Connie all the time, 'You know, it's funny. You and Lenny are so similar. You're like two peas in a pod. Whenever he talks to me about Quorum and business, I have no idea what he's going on about. But you? You know everything! It's like you're really *interested.*'

And Connie would always wonder, *How on earth did those two get married?*

Lenny Brookstein was brilliant and engaging, tough and ambitious and *alive,* the most alive person Connie had ever met. Grace was . . . sweet. It made no sense to Connie. But she didn't dwell on it too much. Back then she and Michael were happy and rich, albeit in a modest way.

Back then . . .

The first time it happened was in Lenny's office, late at night. Connie had gone to see her brother-in-law privately, to talk to him about a bridge loan, and the possibility of his helping Michael find another position. The Lehman MDs had become Wall Street's lepers, tainted by failure, untouchable. Michael was a good banker, but no one was prepared to give him a second chance.

Connie had started to cry. Lenny put his arm around her. Before they knew it, they were on the floor, tangled in each other's arms, and Lenny was making passionate love to her.

Afterward, Connie whispered, 'We're so alike, you and I. We both have the hunger. Michael and Grace aren't like that.'

'I know,' said Lenny. 'That's why we have to protect them. You and I can protect ourselves.'

It was not the response Connie had hoped for. But she did not leave Quorum's offices that night disheartened. On the contrary, a new and interesting door had just been opened. Slipping into bed beside Michael an hour later, she wondered excitedly where it might lead.

It led nowhere.

Two weeks later, Connie slept with Lenny again, this time at a cheap hotel in New Jersey. Lenny was crippled with guilt.

'I can't believe we've done this. *I've* done this,' he corrected himself. 'It's not your fault, Connie. You and Michael are under terrible stress. But I have no excuse.'

Connie whispered huskily, 'You don't need an excuse, Lenny. You're not happy with Grace. I understand that. She was never right for you.'

Lenny's eyes widened. He looked at Connie with genuine incredulity.

'Not right for me? Grace? My God. She's *everything* to me. I love her so much, I . . .' The sentence tailed off. He was too choked to finish it. Eventually he said, 'She must never know about this. Never. And it must never happen again. Let's put it down to a moment of madness and move on, okay?'

'Sure,' said Connie. 'If that's what you want.'

Driving home to Michael, she could barely contain her rage. *Move on? MOVE ON? To what? What have I got to move on to? A life of middle-aged penury with my formerly successful husband, living off scraps from my little sister's table? Fuck you, Lenny Brookstein. You owe me. And now you can pay me. You think I'm going to let you walk back into Grace's arms scot-free?*

'Mommy, watch me!'

Cade was on the swing. He rocked his skinny legs back and forth to gain momentum, then leaped into the air, landing with a satisfied thud on the sand.

'Did you see how high I went? Did you see?'

'I saw, honey. That was awesome.' Connie drew her finely woven summer shawl more tightly around her shoulders. Cashmere, from Scotland, it had been a birthday present from Grace. *Soon everything we own will be a present from Grace. The food on our table, the shirts on our backs.*

The thought of spending next week with Lenny and Grace at their magnificent beachfront estate was enough to make Connie feel nauseous. Especially after her little tête-à-tête with Lenny on the dance floor at the Quorum Ball last night. The bastard had actually had the temerity to get angry with her. With *her*! As if *she* were the one who'd pursued *him*. Lenny had led her on, then dropped her like a piece of trash, scuttling back to her baby sister and their oh-so-perfect life together. And now Connie was supposed to be *grateful* to have her airfare paid so she could sit in their $60-million home and watch the two of them canoodling?

It was Michael who forced the issue.

'I'd like to go. It was generous of Lenny to invite us, and I could use a break from New York. Some sailing, some sea air.'

Michael had always liked Lenny. But that was Michael. He liked everyone. When Lenny extended the invitation last night, Mike practically bit his hand off.

If he knew where Lenny Brookstein's hands have been – on my breasts, my ass, between my thighs – he might not be so quick to bite.

But Michael Gray did not know.

As long as Lenny Brookstein did the decent thing and gave Connie what was coming to her, he would never have to.

Chapter Five

Lenny and Grace Brookstein's Nantucket estate was an idyllic, sprawling, gray-shingled mansion set just off Cliff Road on the north side of the island. The main house boasted ten bedroom suites, an indoor swimming pool and spa, a state-of-the-art movie theater, a chef's kitchen and an enormous, gabled roof terrace (known on Nantucket as a 'widow's walk,' because in the olden days, sailors' wives used to climb up to their rooftops and gaze out to sea, hoping to spot their husbands' long-lost ships returning). Formal gardens, planted with lavender, roses, and box hedges in the European style, cascaded down the hillside to Steps Beach, one of the quietest and most prestigious beaches on the island. At the bottom of the garden were four guest cottages, charming, wisteria-clad dollhouses in white wood, each with its own miniature front yard and white picket fence. Anywhere else the cottages would have looked impossibly twee. But here, on this magical island frozen for all time in some simpler, bygone era, they worked.

At least Grace Brookstein thought so. It was she who had built and designed them, down to the very last Ralph Lauren pillowcase and antique Victorian claw-foot tub.

Grace adored Nantucket. It was where she and Lenny got married, without question the happiest day of Grace's life. But it was more than that. There was a simplicity to the island that did not exist anywhere else. Of course, there was money on Nantucket. Serious money. Tiny, three-room fishermen's cottages in Siasconset changed hand for upward of $2 million. During the summer, Michelin-starred restaurants like 21 Federal and the Summerhouse charged more for their lobster thermidor than Georges V in Paris. Upscale boutiques on Union and Orange streets in town showcased thousand-dollar cardigans in their windows. Galleries representing local artists regularly sold pieces for six figures, sometimes even seven, to the island's wealthier residents. And yet, somehow, Nantucket remained determinedly low-key. In all the years she'd been coming to the island, Grace had never seen a sports car. Billionaires and their wives strolled around town in khaki shorts and white cotton shirts from the Gap. Even the yachts in the harbor were conservative, *far* less flashy than the ones at East Hampton or Saint-Tropez or Palm Beach. Lenny never moored anything but a modest, forty-seven-foot bareboat in Nantucket. He would have *died* of shame before he showed up in the three-hundred-foot *Quorum Queen,* even though in Sardinia, Grace could hardly get him off the thing.

Nantucket was a place where rich people pretended to be poor. Or at least poor*er.* It made Grace nostalgic for her childhood, for a simpler time in her life, a time of innocent pleasures. It thrilled her that Lenny loved the island just as much as she did. Other than Le Cocon, their *bastide*-style retreat in Madagascar, there was nowhere else on earth where Grace felt so totally relaxed. The Brooksteins were happy everywhere, but they were happiest of all here, in this house.

Grace and Lenny arrived three days before their guests. Lenny still had some work to catch up on (*didn't he always?*)

and Grace needed time to talk to the staff and make sure that everything was perfect for her visitors.

'Give Honor and Connie the larger two cottages because they've got kids. Andrew and Maria can have the one right on the sand, and the Merrivales can go in the smallest one. Caroline's been here before, so I'm sure she won't mind.'

There was so much to do! Planning menus, ordering flowers, making sure the bikes and fishing rods were ready for her nephews and nieces. Grace felt like she'd barely seen Lenny.

The night before the hordes descended, the two of them had a romantic dinner at the Chanticleer, a pretty, intimate restaurant in the fishing village of Siasconset. At least it would have been romantic if Lenny hadn't spent the entire evening glued to his BlackBerry.

'Is everything all right, darling? You seem so stressed.' Grace reached across the table and squeezed his hand.

'Sorry, honey. Everything's fine. I'm just a little . . . there's a lot going on at the moment. Nothing for you to worry about, my angel.'

Grace tried not to worry, but it was hard. Lenny never brought his work problems home with him. *Never.* This morning a perfectly harmless homeless man on the wharf had asked Lenny for change, and Lenny had flown at him, lecturing him on alcoholism and taking responsibility for ten straight minutes. Later, Grace had been picking raspberries in the garden when she overheard Lenny shouting out of their bedroom window. He was on the phone with John Merrivale. Grace didn't catch everything he said, but one phrase had stuck in her mind:

'They all want a piece of me, John. The bastards are bleeding me dry. If you're right about Preston, after everything I've done for him . . . I'll cut his fucking hand off.'

What did he mean, 'bleeding him dry'? And who were the

53

bastards? Surely not Andrew Preston? Andrew had worked for Lenny since year one. He and Maria were practically family, like the Merrivales.

Grace's only comfort was that at least Lenny was talking to John. She knew he trusted him and relied on him like a brother. Whatever the problem was, Grace felt sure that John would know what to do. He'd be here tomorrow. Then, hopefully, Lenny would feel a little more relaxed.

The vacation got off to a smooth start. Once the houseguests arrived, Lenny was more relaxed, quite his old self again in fact. With the exception of Jack Warner, who still seemed out of sorts, everyone appeared happy to be there and determined to have a good time.

Michael Gray appointed himself Pied Piper to all four of the children, taking his nieces, Bobby and Rose, fishing for crabs with their cousins, and treating them all to ice creams at Jetties Beach. Grace was delighted. Poor Mike and Connie had been through so much this past year. You could *see* the vacation doing Mike good. As for Cade and little Cooper, they were in seventh heaven, outdoors all day on their bikes or up to their necks in sand.

During the days the other four men – John, Andrew, Jack and Lenny – sailed or played golf while their wives indulged in some serious retail therapy. Grace loved treating her sisters to little gifts. Nothing gave her more pleasure than spending her good fortune on others, especially Connie and Honor. She would happily have splurged on Caroline and Maria, too, but neither of them would let her.

It probably feels weird for them, because I'm so much younger. They think of me like a daughter. Still, Caroline especially had always been so kind. Grace was determined to find some way to show her appreciation.

'I was thinking of having a special dinner tomorrow night

at home.' Grace accosted Lenny in his study. She was bursting with excitement. 'I'm going to ask John all of Caroline's favorite dishes and I'll have Felicia make them. What do you think?'

Lenny looked at her fondly. 'I think it's a great idea, Gracie.'

Grace started to walk away but he reached out and grabbed her hand. 'I love you. You do know that, don't you?'

She laughed and threw her arms around him.

'Of course I know it. Honestly, Lenny! What a funny thing to say.'

'I'm not sitting next to her. Or Lenny. And don't expect me to clap my fins together like a performing seal and bark in gratitude either. I'll leave the groveling up to you, John.'

Caroline Merrivale was in a foul mood. Despite the fact that it was she who insisted they accept Lenny's invitation to Nantucket, she now blamed John for everything. The dull excursions, the dreary company, the fact that they'd been relegated to the meanest and shabbiest of the dreadful little guesthouses. She refused to see Grace's 'special dinner' as anything other than yet another patronizing slight.

'Just d-d-don't make a scene, Caro, all right? That's all I'm asking.'

'*All you're asking?* And what do you think gives you the right to ask anything? Have you spoken to Lenny? About the raise?'

John looked pained. 'Not yet. It's not as s-s-simple as you seem to think it is.'

'On the contrary, John. It's very simple. Either you talk to him or I will.'

'No! You c-can't! Please, you must leave L-Lenny to me.'

'Fine. But you'd better grow some balls and talk to him before the end of this vacation. If I have to listen to his vacuous wifelette gush one more time about how *grateful* she is for my *incredible friendship,* I can't be held responsible for my actions.'

John Merrivale thought sadly, *Grace is grateful for your friendship. Poor, misguided girl.*

Lenny was a lucky man. Wives like Grace were one in a million.

'Please, don't stand on ceremony everyone. Dig in!'

Grace felt unaccountably nervous. The dinner itself looked fabulous. Felicia had excelled herself as usual. The lobster bisque smelled exquisite and was the perfect shade of pale pink, the roast lamb looked mouthwateringly succulent on its bed of organic greens and the raspberry Pavlova was as much a sculpture as a dessert, a towering triumph of snow-white meringue and bloodred berries. Caroline couldn't fail to be delighted.

And yet Grace could not enjoy her triumph. Earlier that day she'd seen Connie talking heatedly with Lenny on the beach, then storming off close to tears. When Grace caught up with her sister and asked her what was wrong, Connie had shrugged her away angrily.

'It's Michael,' Lenny explained. 'He's depressed. They're going through so much stress right now, honey, you mustn't take it personally.'

But Grace did take it personally. Not four hours earlier, Honor had bitten her head off, too. All Grace did was ask if she wanted to come to the spa.

'Not everything in this life can be fixed by a fucking massage, Gracie, okay? Christ, is that your answer to everything? To spend more money pampering yourself?'

Grace was deeply hurt. She wasn't a materialistic person. Honor, of all people, should know that. In fairness, Honor *had* apologized afterward. 'It's Jack. He's got so much on his

mind lately, I think some of the stress is rubbing off on me.'
Grace forgave her and they made up. But still, a lingering
anxiety remained. Perhaps she was imagining it, but it seemed
to Grace that there was an almost palpable tension around
the dinner table tonight.

*They're all unhappy. Even Lenny. I want to make them
happy, but I can't.*

'The soup's ambrosial, Grace. Nice job.' Mike Gray grinned
at his sister-in-law.

'Thanks.' She smiled back. *He doesn't look depressed to
me.*

Maria Preston said snidely, 'Indeed, your chef is to be
congratulated. He must have worked like a slave all day to
produce this feast.'

Andrew Preston blushed. Not even Grace Brookstein was
stupid enough to miss a blatant dig like that. He wished
Maria would get a grip on herself, but after a few glasses of
wine she was lethal. It was bad enough that she'd insisted
on coming to dinner in a lavish Roberto Cavalli evening
gown, slashed to the thigh and wildly inappropriate for the
occasion.

'Maria, *cara*. Everyone else will be in jeans or simple
sundresses. You look stunning, my angel, as always. But
couldn't you . . .'

'No, Andy. I couldn't. I am not "everyone else." 'Aven't
you learned this by now?'

Grace was too polite to rise to Maria's bait. Lenny had
no such qualms.

'Our chef is a "she" actually, Felicia.' His tone was measured. 'And she does work hard, though I'd hardly call her a
slave. Last year I paid her considerably more than I paid
your husband, Maria.'

Andrew's blush deepened. Maria glared at him in silent
fury.

Grace wished the ground would open up and swallow her. She hated confrontation. Lenny, on the other hand, had grown tired of walking on eggshells.

'Senator Warner,' he said brightly. 'You're awfully quiet this evening. What's the problem, Jack? Not in the party spirit?'

If looks could kill, Lenny Brookstein would have dropped dead at the table.

'Not really, Lenny, no. Unemployment rates in my constituency are about to reach ten percent. While we're sitting around your table, enjoying this fine food and wine, the people who voted for me are having their homes repossessed. They're losing their jobs, their health insurance, their hope. And they're relying on *me* to try to fix things for them. So, no, I'm not really in a party mood. If you'll excuse me.'

Honor watched in horror as Jack got up from the table and left the room. He'd finally come clean about his gambling debts last night. As a result, Honor hadn't slept a wink. It was exhaustion that had made her lose her temper with Grace earlier, something she'd been kicking herself about all day. Not because she gave a damn about Grace's feelings. But because the entire purpose of this trip was to try to get closer to Grace so she could use her influence with Lenny to get him to clear up Jack's debts.

Last night Jack had yelled at her. 'I *need* Lenny Brookstein! Without that money, I'm finished, do you understand? *We're* finished.'

Honor did understand. But now here was Jack, storming off like a spoiled child, embarrassing them both in front of everyone.

'I'd better go after him,' she said meekly. 'Sorry, Grace. Lenny.'

The dinner party limped on. After the Warners' departure,

everyone made an effort to be upbeat, but Jack and Honor's empty chairs were like two ghosts at the feast. John Merrivale made a toast, thanking Grace for the meal, but his stammer got so bad halfway through that Caroline had to finish it for him. Connie left before dessert, citing a headache. By the time the maid brought the coffee, the forced smiles of the remaining guests were beginning to look like lockjaw.

In bed with Lenny afterward, Grace broke down in tears.

'It was a disaster, wasn't it? Why does everything come back to the stupid economy? Connie and Michael losing their house, Jack stressed out about unemployment.'

'I don't think that's all he's stressed about, sweetheart.'

'Even Caroline and Maria were moaning at the hairdressers about how much less John and Andrew are making this year. I hate it.'

Lenny was furious. 'Maria and Caroline were bitching to you? Are you kidding me? They're lucky their husbands still have jobs. The SEC is all over us like lice.'

Grace gasped. 'You're under investigation?'

'Don't worry, honey, it's nothing. A shit storm in a teacup. They're looking at all the big hedge funds right now. The point is, these are tough times, and Quorum's survived them because of *me*. Which means those ungrateful bitches' husbands have survived it because of me.'

'Please, darling,' Grace sobbed. 'Don't get angry. I shouldn't have said anything. I can't take any more fighting tonight. Really, I can't take it.'

Lenny took her in his arms.

'I'm sorry,' he whispered. 'I've been a bit of a Grinch on this trip, haven't I?'

Grace nestled closer to his body. She always felt safe and happy pressed against him.

'I tell you what. Tomorrow morning, I'll get up early and take the boat out by myself. Sailing always clears my head.

By the time I come home, I'll be so relaxed, you won't recognize me.'

'Sounds good.' Grace began drifting off to sleep.

Later, she would try to remember the exact words that Lenny had said next. It was so hard to untangle dream from reality. What she *thought* she heard was, 'Whatever happens, Gracie, I love you.' But maybe she dreamed it. All she knew for sure was that she'd fallen asleep that night happy.

For the last time.

Chapter Six

John Merrivale tightened his seat belt and closed his eyes as the six-seater, twin-engine plane shuddered its way up through the clouds. A nervous flier at the best of times, he was terrified of these little puddle jumpers. It was like trusting your life to a lawn mower.

'Don't worry.' The woman next to him smiled amiably. 'It's always bumpy first thing in the morning, before the sun burns through the clouds.'

John Merrivale thought, *Can sun burn through clouds?* then smiled at himself for being so philosophical, today of all days.

If the lawn mower didn't fail them, they would land in Boston in twenty-five minutes.

It was 6:15 A.M.

At 8:15 A.M., Andrew Preston took his seat on a different airplane. The hundred-seater Fokker 100 was only two-thirds full. *I guess not a lot of people fly to New York from Nantucket on a Tuesday morning. They all left yesterday.*

He had mixed feelings when he got the call late last night, telling him he was needed urgently back at the office. Peter

Finch, the head of the SEC investigative team looking into Quorum's accounts, wanted some 'face time.' Andrew dreaded the meeting. He could think of no good reason why Finch would summon him back to New York, and quite a few bad ones. On the other hand, being away from the office made him feel hideously out of control. He believed he'd covered his tracks, but these SEC bastards were like bloodhounds.

In any case, he needed to get out of Nantucket. That guest cottage was starting to feel like a prison. After her public humiliation at dinner last night, Maria had flown into a hysterical fury, swearing and screaming at Andrew, even attacking him physically. Rolling up his sleeve now, he could still see the livid red scratch marks from her nails.

'How *dare* you allow Lenny Brookstein to treat us like that! He made a complete fool of me, and you sat by and did nothing.'

Andrew fought back the urge to tell Maria that it was she who had started it, by trying to make a fool of Grace. Instead, he said, 'What would you have me do? He's my *boss*, Maria. He pays our bills.'

'Barely! He pays you less than his goddamn cook. Didn't you hear what he said? Doesn't that bother you?'

Andrew had heard. And it did bother him. He was 90 percent sure that Lenny was joking. If the chef was making more than he was, she was certainly overpaid. But it wasn't unheard of for Lenny's generosity to prompt some peculiar decisions. He tried to reason with himself. *Why should I care what Lenny pays somebody else? It's his money, after all. He can do what he likes with it.* But it still rankled. Perhaps, on some subconscious level, it justified what Andrew had done.

Maria was passed out cold when he left her this morning, exhausted from her drunken rage. When she woke up, she'd have a horrific hangover. Andrew didn't want to be within a hundred miles of her when that happened. Now he wouldn't have to be.

'Cabin crew, please be seated for takeoff.'

Closing his eyes, Andrew Preston tried to relax.

Grace met her sisters for lunch at the Cliffside Beach Club.

After their awkward encounter the day before, Connie went out of her way to be solicitous to Grace, even presenting her with a beautiful guava-pink seashell she'd discovered on the beach that morning.

'I know it's not much, but I thought it would look pretty on your dressing table.'

Grace was touched. She knew how difficult Connie found apologies. The shell said more than any words.

Honor asked, 'Are Caroline and Maria joining us?'

In a cream J.Crew sundress that washed her out, with her hair scraped back in a ponytail, Honor looked exhausted. Grace wondered if she and Jack had fought last night after Jack stormed out of the dining room, but was too tactful to ask.

'I don't think so. Caroline's in town looking at a painting. And Maria's still asleep, I believe.'

The sisters exchanged glances. 'I wonder what she wears to bed?' Connie giggled. 'Spun-gold Versace pajamas?'

It was a nice, light moment. Grace finally started to relax.

The waitress came and took their order. They were sitting at an outdoor table, right on the beach, but by the time their appetizers arrived, storm clouds had begun to gather.

The manager appeared. 'Would you like to move indoors, Mrs Brookstein? I have a lovely table by the window I can offer you ladies.' At that instant a loud clap of thunder made everyone jump. Seconds later, the first heavy drops of rain began to splash onto the table.

'Yes, please,' said Grace, laughing. She thought about

63

Lenny, out on the boat. *I hope he's safe and dry in the cabin, not out on deck catching his death of a cold.*

It was almost four by the time the three sisters arrived home. By that time, the storm was in full force. Michael Gray met them at the front door.

'Thank goodness you're back,' he said, hugging Connie tightly.

'We only went for lunch at the club, honey.' She laughed. 'Why so panicked?'

'I didn't know where you were, that's all. I thought you might have gone sailing with Jack. The conditions are awful out there.'

'Jack's gone sailing?' Honor's white face turned even whiter. 'Are the girls with him?'

'No,' said Michael. 'Don't worry. Bobby and Rose are playing Chutes and Ladders with our boys in the kitchen. They're a little bored, but other than that, they're fine.'

'And Jack? Has anyone heard from him?'

'His radio's down.'

Honor's knees started shaking. Jack had been an avid sailor since his teens, but a storm like this would test anybody's skill, even his.

'It's okay,' said Michael. 'The coast guard thinks they've located him. We should hear more soon. It's been crazy out there, you can imagine, but they're trying to get everybody back to harbor. Come on in out of the rain.'

'What about Lenny?'

Connie and Honor had moved inside, but Grace stood frozen on the front path. Rain dripped from her hair and the tip of her nose. She looked about twelve years old.

Michael Gray frowned. 'Lenny? I thought he was at the golf club. That's what he told the staff here when he left this morning.'

Because he wanted to be alone. He didn't want you or Jack to invite yourselves along.

'No.' Grace was shaking. 'He's on the boat.'

'Did he take any crew?'

'No. I don't think so.'

Michael tried to hide his concern. 'Do you have any idea where he was going, Grace? What his plans were?'

Grace shook her head.

'All right, sweetheart. Don't worry, we'll find him. Come on in and I'll call the coast guard. Those guys are the best. He'll be back home in no time, you'll see.'

Jack Warner got to the house at six P.M., soaked to the skin and badly shaken.

'I've never known a storm to close in that fast. Never.' Honor hugged him. Without thinking, Jack hugged her back.

Connie and Michael were upstairs, putting the children to bed. Downstairs in the kitchen, Grace, Honor, Caroline and a still-green-looking Maria Preston sat waiting for news. Lenny's yacht was still missing.

John Merrivale had gotten back from his business trip in Boston half an hour earlier. Walking over to Grace, he put his arm around her, ignoring Caroline's dagger stares.

'Try not to w-w-worry. Lenny's an experienced sailor.'

Grace barely registered that he'd spoken. She was too busy praying.

I lost one father, Lord. Please, don't let me lose another.

At 8:17 P.M. exactly, the phone rang. Grace pounced on it.

'Hello?'

Ten seconds later, she hung up. Her teeth were chattering.

'Grace?' Caroline Merrivale moved toward her. 'What is it? What did they say?'

'They've found the boat.'

A chorus of 'Thank Gods' and 'I told you sos' echoed round the room. When they'd all stopped hugging her, Grace said softly, 'Lenny wasn't on it.'

Then she passed out.

Chapter Seven

Later, the period after Lenny's disappearance blurred in Grace's memory into one long, unbroken nightmare. Hours became days, days became weeks, but none of it seemed real. She was living in a trance, a hideous half-life from which only one person could awaken her. And that person was gone.

After three days, Sea Rescue called off its search. Around the globe the headlines screamed:

LEONARD BROOKSTEIN MISSING, PRESUMED DEAD

HEDGE FUND GENIUS LOST AT SEA

NEW YORK'S RICHEST MAN FEARED DROWNED

Grace had never read anything so awful in her life. Had anyone told her at the time that worse was to come, she would not have believed them. How could anything be worse than life without Lenny?

It was John Merrivale who brought her home to New York. Her sisters and the others had all gone back when the search was called off, but Grace couldn't bring herself to leave Nantucket.

'You can't stay entombed on this island forever, Gracie. All your friends are in the city. Your f-family. You need a support network.'

'But I can't leave Lenny, John. It's like I'm abandoning him.'

'Darling Grace. I know it's hard. T-t-terribly hard. But Lenny is gone. You have to accept that. No one could survive a day in those w-waters. It's been two weeks.'

With her rational mind, Grace knew John was right. It was her heart she had trouble convincing. Lenny wasn't gone. He couldn't be gone. Until she saw his dead body with her own two eyes, she could not give up hope.

Miracles happen. They happen all the time. Perhaps he was rescued by another fishing boat? Maybe a foreign boat, simple people who don't know who he is? Maybe he's lost his memory? Or found his way to an island somewhere?

It was all nonsense, of course. Voices in her head. But in those early days, Grace clung to the voices for dear life. They were all she had left of Lenny and she wasn't prepared to give them up. Not yet.

When she got back to their Park Avenue apartment, Grace found hundreds of bouquets of flowers waiting for her. She could have piled the condolence cards up to the ceiling.

'See?' said John. 'Everybody l-loves you, Grace. Everybody wants to help.'

But the cards and flowers didn't help. They were unwanted, tangible reminders that as far as the world was concerned, Lenny was dead.

Three miles away, in the FBI's New York offices at 26 Federal Plaza, three men sat around a table:

Peter Finch from the SEC was a short, amiable man, completely bald except for a thin tonsure of ginger hair that made him look like a monk. Normally, Finch was known for his good humor. Not today.

'What we're looking at here is the tip of the iceberg,' he said grimly.

68

'Pretty big fucking iceberg.' Harry Bain, the FBI's assistant director in New York, shook his head in disbelief. At forty-two, Bain was one of the Bureau's highest fliers. Handsome, charming and Harvard educated, with jet-black hair and piercing green eyes, Harry Bain had foiled two of the most significant domestic terror plots ever attempted on U.S. soil. Those had both been pretty huge cases. But if what Peter Finch was saying was true, this one could be even bigger.

'How much money are we talking about? Exactly?' Gavin Williams, another FBI agent who reported to Bain, spoke without looking up. A former SEC man himself, Williams had left the agency in disgust after the Bernie Madoff fiasco. A brilliant mathematician with higher degrees in modeling, statistics, data programming and analysis, as a young man he had dreamed of becoming an investment banker himself, joining the J.P. Morgan training program straight out of Wharton. But Gavin Williams had never quite made it. He lacked the killer commercial instincts necessary to take him to the top, as well as the political, people skills that helped his far-less-intellectually-gifted classmates amass private fortunes in the tens of millions. Tall and wiry with close-cropped gray hair and a military bearing, Williams was a loner, as dour and emotionless as a statue. Brilliant, he might be. But in the clubby world of Wall Street, nobody wanted to do business with him.

Deeply embittered by this rejection, Gavin Williams made the decision to devote the rest of his life to the pursuit of those who *had* made it to the top, cataloging their misdemeanors with crazed zeal. In the early days, working at the SEC had given him a tremendous sense of purpose. But all that changed after Madoff. The agency's failings in that case were catastrophic. Gavin himself hadn't worked on the case, but he felt tainted by collective embarrassment. *Blinded by a simple Ponzi scheme!* The thought of it still gave Gavin Williams sleepless nights, even now in his new dream job as the FBI's top man on securities fraud.

Peter Finch said, 'It's not yet clear. On the surface the accounts looked clean. But after Brookstein disappeared, all Quorum's investors wanted their money back at once. It's those redemptions that have revealed this black hole. And it's growing by the day.'

'But there are *billions* of dollars missing here.' Harry Bain scratched his head. 'How can that kind of money just evaporate?'

'It can't. Maybe it got spent. Or lost, siphoned off into speculative, unprofitable private businesses controlled by Leonard Brookstein and his cronies. More likely Brookstein stashed it away somewhere. That's what we've got to find out.'

'Okay.' Harry Bain's quick mind was working. 'How long before this gets into the press?'

Finch shrugged. 'Not long. A few days, a week at most. Once investors start talking, it'll be out there. I don't need to tell you the implications this could have on the wider economy. Quorum was bigger than GM, almost as big as AIG. Every small business in New York had exposure. Pensioners, families.'

Bain got the picture. 'I'll handpick a task force of our best men to work on this today. The instant new information comes in, you pass it to Gavin. Gavin, you report directly to me. None of the information discussed today is to leave this room. Understood? I want to keep the media out for as long as possible. The NYPD, too. The last thing we need is those idiots running around, sabotaging our case.'

Peter Finch nodded. Gavin Williams sat frozen, his face impassive, inscrutable. Harry Bain thought, *I feel like Jim Kirk, working with Spock*. He felt the familiar rush of adrenaline

70

at the prospect of spearheading such a vital operation. *If I track down that money, I'll be a hero. I might even get a shot at the directorship.* Harry thought about his wife, Lisa, and how proud she'd be. *Of course, if I fail . . .*

But Harry Bain wouldn't fail.

He had never failed in his life.

'There's a trustees meeting next month, Grace, on the twenty-sixth. I think it's important that you be there. If you can b-b-bear it.'

It had been two weeks since Grace's return to Manhattan, and John and Caroline Merrivale had invited her over for supper. When she declined the invitation, Caroline drove over to her apartment and frog-marched her into a waiting cab.

Grace looked pained. 'Can't you deal with it, John? I won't understand a word they say anyway. Lenny always handled all the legal things.'

'You must go, Grace,' said Caroline. 'John will be there with you. But you're the sole beneficiary of Lenny's estate. There'll be things you need to approve.'

'Am I? The sole beneficiary?'

Caroline gave a short, derisory laugh. 'Of course you are, dear. You were his wife.'

Grace thought, *I'm still his wife. We don't know he's dead yet. Not for sure.* But she didn't have the energy to fight about it. Grace couldn't help but notice that Caroline had gotten rather bossy since Lenny . . . since the accident. Whenever John spoke to Grace, he was firm, but deferential. *I really feel so and so. If you can, you should try to do such and such.* Caroline was much more autocratic. *Do this. Say that.*

Still, perhaps that's what I need right now? God knows I don't seem able to make any decisions for myself.

Grace agreed to meet the trustees.

*　　*　　*

71

It was hard to pinpoint exactly when the change started. Like all these things, it began almost imperceptibly. First the flowers stopped coming. Then the calls. Invitations to lunch or dinner began to dry up. On the one day that Grace tried to make an effort and drag herself out of the apartment – she went to the tennis club for coffee – she noticed many of her old girlfriends avoiding her. Tammy Rees practically broke into a run when she bumped into Grace in the powder room, mumbling the quickest of 'How are yous' before scuttling out the door.

Grace tried to talk to her sisters about it, but both Honor and Connie were distracted, distant almost. Neither had time to chat. Grace even called her mother, Holly, a sign of desperation if ever there was one.

It was a mistake.

'You're probably imagining it, darling. Why don't you go on a lovely cruise somewhere? Take your mind off things. I met Roberto on a cruise, you know. One never knows when Cupid might strike.'

A cruise? I won't set foot on a boat again as long as I live.

The next day, Grace's platinum Amex card was declined at Bergdorf Goodman. Grace felt herself blushing scarlet as the women in line behind her stared.

'I think there must be some mistake,' she said meekly. 'I have unlimited credit.'

The salesgirl was kind. 'I'm sure it's just a mix-up, Mrs Brookstein. But you'd best take it up with American Express. I'll be happy to keep the bag on hold for you if you'd like.'

I don't want the stupid bag! I only came here to try to distract myself for five minutes. To forget about Lenny. As if I could ever do that!

'Thank you, that's okay. I'll, er . . . I'll go home and sort this out.'

Grace called Amex. A drone told her that Lenny's account had been 'terminated.'

'What do you mean, "terminated"? By whom? I didn't terminate it.'

'I'm sorry, ma'am, but I can't help you. Your husband's account has been closed.'

Worse was to come. Bills started arriving for unpaid services. An unpleasant man rang the apartment and informed Grace curtly that her mortgage payments were five months in arrears.

'I'm sorry, sir, but I think you must have me confused with someone else. We don't have a mortgage.'

'Mrs Brookstein. It *is* Mrs Brookstein I'm speaking to, right?'

'Yes.'

'The outstanding balance on your mortgage is sixteen million seven hundred and sixty-two thousand dollars and fourteen cents. That's in your and your husband's joint names. Would you like me to resend you the statements?'

It wasn't until Conchita, Grace's loyal maid, quit over unpaid wages – 'I'm sorry, Mrs Brookstein. But my 'usband, he won't let me keep coming here. Not unless you pay me' – that Grace finally overcame her embarrassment and confessed her money worries to John Merrivale.

'It's insanity,' she sobbed on the phone. 'Lenny's worth billions, but suddenly I'm getting all these bills. No one will take my cards. I don't understand it.'

There was a long silence on the other end of the line.

'John? Are you there?'

'I'm here, Gracie. I think perhaps you'd better come over.'

John Merrivale was nervous. Even more nervous than usual. Grace noticed the way he kept scratching at his neck and his eyes rarely met hers. She sat opposite him on the couch in his study as he began to explain.

73

'There have been rumors for s-some time now, Grace. Rumors on Wall Street and among our investors. After Lenny . . . after what happened, the FBI became involved.'

Grace's eyes widened. 'The *FBI*? Why? What sort of rumors?'

'Lenny was a b-brilliant man. An uncannily shrewd investor. One of the reasons for Quorum's success is that he never d-divulged his strategy. Like most of the best hedge fund managers, his model was a c-closely guarded secret.'

Grace nodded. 'He told me it was like inheriting your grandmother's recipe for spaghetti sauce. Everyone who eats it tries to figure out the secret ingredient, but you can never tell.'

'Exactly.' John Merrivale smiled. *She really is a child.* 'My job was to raise f-funds for Quorum. With Lenny's performance, that was easy. We were t-turning away money. It was Lenny's job to invest those funds. No one – n-not even me – knew exactly where he put the money. Until his disappearance, it had never really mattered.'

'But afterward?'

'Despite its size and huge success, Quorum was still f-fundamentally a one-man show. When Lenny disappeared, people w-wanted to withdraw their capital. A lot of people. All at the s-s-same time.'

'And that was a problem?'

John Merrivale sighed. 'Yes. A lot of the money is . . . well, we don't know where it is exactly. It's unaccounted for. It's complicated.'

'I see.' Grace thought about this for a few moments. 'So is that why the FBI is involved? To try to sort out the confusion?'

John's scratching intensified. 'In a way, yes. But I'm afraid there are some unpleasant sides to this. Because the amount of money involved is so large – tens of billions of d-dollars, at a minimum – the police believe that Lenny m-may have deliberately st-stolen it.'

'That's ridiculous! Lenny would never steal. Besides, why would he rob his own fund?'

'I d-don't believe he did, Grace. I want you to know that.' John took her hand. 'But other people – the FBI, investors, the n-newspapers, are jumping to conclusions. They say that once the SEC started investigating, Lenny knew Quorum would collapse and that he would be exposed. G-Grace, they're saying that Lenny might have c-committed suicide.'

Grace felt sick.

Suicide? Lenny? No. Never. Even if he had stolen some money, he would never leave me. He would never take his own life.

She struggled to keep her voice steady.

'Whatever happened on that boat, John, it was an accident. Lenny was happy when he left me that morning. Why hasn't the FBI spoken to me? I would have told them that!'

'I'm sure they will want to talk to you eventually. Once a d-death certificate is issued, there'll likely be an inquest. Right now the p-primary focus is on locating the m-missing money. Until that happens, all Quorum's assets have been frozen, as well as your p-personal accounts.'

Grace looked so small and lost, perched on the edge of the couch. Had John Merrivale been a more tactile man, he'd have gone over and hugged her. As it was, he said, 'Try not to worry. I know it's hard. But you and I b-both know Lenny wasn't a thief. The truth will come out eventually. Everything will be okay.'

No it won't. Not without Lenny. Nothing will ever be okay again.

It was the next morning that the storm erupted. Angry investors marched on Quorum's offices, demanding their money back. CNN showed images of a near riot, with mounted police forcing back the mob. Within hours, the likely scale of what was now being called the Quorum Fraud was making headline news around the world.

Grace watched the television in shock. *'Leonard Brookstein, once one of New York's best-loved philanthropists and an American icon, was today being exposed as perhaps the greatest thief in U.S. history. Furious investors in Brookstein's Quorum Hedge Fund burned effigies of the fifty-eight-year-old, presumed dead after a freak sailing accident last month, outside his former offices.'*

The phone rang. It was John. Grace broke down.

'Oh, John! Have you seen what they're saying about Lenny? The news . . . I can't watch.'

'Grace, l-listen to me. You're not safe. I'm c-coming to pick you up.'

'But that's crazy. Why would anyone want to hurt me?'

'People are angry, Grace. Lenny's n-not here. You're the next best thing.'

'But, John . . .'

'No b-buts. You must stay with us. Pack a bag. I'll be there in t-ten minutes.'

Ten minutes later, Grace was in the back of an armored Town Car. As she left her building, a small group of hecklers was already gathered outside. They jeered at her.

'Where's the money, Grace?'

'Where'd Lenny hide it?'

'Is that seventy billion in your suitcase, baby, or are you just glad to see us?'

By the time John bundled her into the car, she was hyperventilating.

She never set foot in her apartment again.

'No. I won't sell it. I can't.'

Grace was in the boardroom of the law firm Carter Hochstein. Around the table were six forbidding-looking men in dark suits. John Merrivale introduced them as Lenny's trustees, the men responsible for overseeing his estate.

'I'm afraid you have no choice. Put simply, Mrs Brookstein, you do not have the money to continue paying the mortgage on the apartment. We're going to have to put *all* your assets on the market. Historically, your husband funded his lifestyle by borrowing large sums of money against the value of his stake in Quorum. Those loans have now been called in, and you have no immediate means of paying them.'

Grace turned to John Merrivale in bewilderment.

'But how can that be? Can't I, I don't know, sell some shares or something?'

John looked pained. 'The thing is, Grace, until this mess is sorted out at Quorum, you d-don't have any shares to sell.'

'Mrs Brookstein.' Kenneth Greville, the most senior partner, spelled it out in black and white. 'You must understand. *Vast* sums of money remain unaccounted for at Quorum. Hundreds of thousands of your husband's investors have been financially ruined. They've lost everything.'

Grace thought, *And I haven't?*

'Until your husband is determined to be legally dead and the criminal investigation is completed, we can't draw any firm conclusions. But it does look increasingly likely that Mr Brookstein was involved, to some degree at least, in fraudulent activity of a most serious nature. The amounts that were stolen – '

'No.' Grace stood up. 'I'm sorry, but I won't sit here and listen to this. My husband never stole anything. Lenny is not a thief! He's a good man and he built Quorum up from nothing. Tell them, John.'

Kenneth Greville thought, *She still refers to him in the present tense. The poor child's delusional.*

'Your loyalty is admirable, Mrs Brookstein. But it is my

77

unpleasant duty to inform you of the facts with regard to your current, and probably future, financial circumstances. You will not be able to continue living at the Park Avenue apartment. I'm sorry.'

Tears rolled down Grace's cheeks. She felt as if she were manacled to a runaway train. Her life was collapsing around her, and she had absolutely no power to stop it.

That evening at dinner, Caroline Merrivale watched Grace staring listlessly at the dining-room wall. She'd barely touched her soup and looked thin and drawn.

'Eat up, Grace. In this house we make it a rule never to let good food go to waste. Don't we, John?'

John saw the triumphant flash of cruelty in his wife's eyes. *She's loving every second of this. Turning the tables on Grace at last. She's like a cat with a mouse, playing with it before the kill.*

'Caroline's right, Grace. You must try to k-keep your strength up.'

Grace brought a spoonful of soup to her lips. It was cold. She fought down the urge to gag. 'I'm sorry. I really don't feel very well. If you don't mind, I think I'd like to go to bed.'

The sooner today was over, the better. After the meeting with the lawyers, she'd felt lower than she had since the day the coast guard told her the awful news. The whole world was talking about this stupid money. *As if I care about the money! All I want is for Lenny to walk back through the door.*

A maid appeared in the doorway. 'I'm sorry to interrupt, Mrs Merrivale. But there's a policeman at the door. He says he has urgent business with Mrs Brookstein.'

Instinctively Grace panicked. 'No! Tell him to go away. It's late. Tell him to come back in the morning.'

Caroline laughed. 'Don't be silly, Grace. It's the police, not a social call. You must go out and meet him.'

'No, please, Caroline. I can't.'

Caroline was unmoved. 'Melissa, show the officer in. Tell him Mrs Brookstein will be with him momentarily.'

A few minutes later, Grace walked nervously into the entryway. She expected to find an aggressive FBI agent there to interrogate her. Instead, she was greeted by a shy young man in uniform. As soon as he saw Grace, he took off his cap politely. Grace felt the tension in her shoulders begin to ease.

'Good evening, Officer. You wanted to see me?'

'Yes, Mrs Brookstein. I, er . . . I have some news for you. It's about your husband. Perhaps you'd like to sit down?'

Irrationally, Grace's heart soared.

He's alive! Lenny's alive! They've found him! Oh, thank God. Lenny will come back and everything will go back to the way it used to be. We'll have our homes again and our money, no one will hate us anymore . . .

'Mrs Brookstein?'

'Oh, I'm fine, thank you. I've been sitting all day. You say you have some news for me?'

'Yes, ma'am.' The young man looked at his shoes. 'I'm sorry to have to tell you this. But this afternoon the Massachusetts coast guard recovered a body. We believe the remains to be those of your husband, Leonard Brookstein.'

Chapter Eight

Donna Sanchez enjoyed her work at the city morgue. Her friends and family couldn't understand it. 'All those dead people. Aren't you creeped out?' Their reactions made Donna smile. A heavyset Puerto Rican woman with fat, sausagelike fingers and a round, doughy face, Donna had grown up in a big noisy family before starting a big noisy family of her own. Outside of work, the sound track to Donna Sanchez's life was screaming children, smashing crockery, beeping car horns, blaring television sets. Donna liked the dead because they were silent. The city morgue on Clarkson Avenue in Brooklyn was white, clean and orderly. It made Donna feel peaceful.

Of course, she still had bad days. Even after eight years, the sight of small children's bodies could make Donna choke up. Some of the accident victims were pretty gruesome, too. And the suicides. The first time Donna saw a 'jumper,' she had nightmares about the mangled corpse for weeks afterward: bones erupting through the skin, skull collapsed like a rotten melon. Normally, drowning victims were among the easiest to deal with. Immersion in cold, deep water tended to delay decomposition. Donna also noticed that many of the water-dead had a happy, almost beatific look on their faces.

Not today's body, though. The revolting, waxy hulk lying on the slab had no face. The fish had seen to that. All that was left beneath the ravaged stump of a neck was a great, bloated midsection. The left arm and hand were miraculously intact, but the rest of the limbs had gone, snapped off like crab claws. It was, as Donna's friends would have said, creepy.

'Are they really dragging his poor wife in here?' Like everyone else at the morgue, Donna Sanchez knew that the cops believed the body was Lenny Brookstein's. That's why it had been brought back to New York, almost two hundred miles from where it washed up on the Massachusetts coast. 'No one should have to see their loved one like this.'

Duane Tyler, the technician, sneered. A handsome black kid, fresh out of high school, Duane was a born cynic. 'Save your sympathy, Donna. One thing Grace Brookstein ain't is poor. You know what they saying? This son of a bitch ripped off thousands of people. Ordinary people.'

'I know that's what they're *saying,* Duane. It doesn't mean it's true. Besides, so what if he did? It's not his wife's fault.'

Duane Tyler shook his head pityingly. 'Don't you believe it, girl. You think the wives don't know? Those rich white bitches? They *know*. They all know.'

Harry Bain and Gavin Williams were in the district attorney's office.

It was common knowledge that Angelo Michele's parents were two of the many New Yorkers facing ruin because of Lenny Brookstein. Angelo was the best legal brain in New York City, but Harry Bain wondered whether, in this case, his judgment might be clouded. The D.A.'s opening words did not reassure him.

81

'Well, I wanted Brookstein's head on a plate. Looks like I got the next best thing. His torso on a slab.'

'It might not be him,' said Harry Bain. 'His wife's on her way to identify the body. What's left of it. Then we can conduct the autopsy.'

'Good.'

It was the job of the FBI task force to find the missing Quorum money. But it was Angelo Michele's job to prosecute those responsible for the theft. Part of him was pleased they'd found a body. The possibility, however remote, that Lenny Brookstein might have somehow escaped and be living the high life on a private atoll in the South Pacific had been keeping Angelo awake at night for weeks. But another part of him felt robbed. If Lenny Brookstein was dead, he couldn't be punished. Somebody had to be punished.

'Have you got any further with Merrivale or Preston?'

'No.' Harry Bain frowned. 'Not yet.' He had personally interviewed the two senior Quorum execs a total of six times, but was no closer to untangling the mystery of how Lenny Brookstein had managed to spirit away such insane amounts of money. Instinct told him that both men knew more than they were telling. But so far, he couldn't prove it. 'Agent Williams has uncovered something interesting, though.'

Angelo Michele looked at Gavin Williams. The man gave him the creeps. He was more like a robot than a human being. When he spoke, it was in a monotone, studiously avoiding eye contact.

'It appears that in the week before his death, Leonard Brookstein changed the company structure at Quorum. Effectively, he arbitrarily stripped John Merrivale of his partnership status.'

'Damn it.' Angelo Michele shook is head.

Harry Bain cocked his head to one side. 'That's bad?'

82

'Sure. If Lenny Brookstein was the only legal partner, it'll be almost impossible to indict, much less prosecute, the other players. Short of seventy billion showing up sewn into Merrivale's suit pants, we're fucked.'

'He wasn't the only partner.'

'But I thought you said . . .'

Gavin Williams sighed, like a grade-school teacher explaining something painfully simple to a seven-year-old. 'I *said,* Lenny stripped John of his shares. I didn't say he was the only partner. He didn't keep that equity. He transferred it.'

Angelo Michele's heart was racing. 'To who, for God's sake?'

Gavin Williams smiled.

'To his wife.'

Donna Sanchez said gently, 'Are you sure you're ready, Mrs Brookstein?'

Grace nodded. *It doesn't matter. This is all a dream, a nightmare. When she pulls back the sheet, I'll wake up.*

'We'll do this very quickly. Try to focus on the hand. If you recognize the wedding ring, that's all we need.'

Donna pulled back the sheet.

Grace threw back her head and screamed.

John Merrivale stared at the documents in front of him, rubbing his eyes with exhaustion.

'There must be some m-m-mistake.'

Harry Bain lit another cigarette. The smoke made John Merrivale feel nauseous. 'No mistake, John. This is Lenny's signature. And this is Grace's. You don't think we had them checked?'

The documents were legal instructions, changing Quorum's ownership structure. They transferred John's entire equity

83

stake in the fund to Grace. They were dated June 8, the day before the Quorum Ball. Both Lenny and Grace had signed them.

'Face it, John. The Brooksteins ripped you off. They were planning to grab what was the left of the money and run.'

'No. Lenny wouldn't d-do that. N-n-not to me.'

'*Read it,* John! It's right there in black and white. He did it. *They* did it, together. Don't you think it's time you stopped protecting them?'

John squeezed his eyes shut tight. It was so hard to think. *How long have I been in this room? Three hours? Four?* He thought about Grace, alone at the morgue. The police had refused to let him go with her. The poor girl would be terrified.

'Lenny had a l-legal right to restructure the company any way he chose. Quorum was his business.'

Harry Bain looked at him in disbelief. 'You're saying you *don't mind* that Lenny Brookstein robbed you blind?'

'I'm saying he didn't rob me.'

'But he did. It's right here in black and white.'

'He m-must have had his reasons then. Lenny's dead. He's not here to explain, to d-defend his good name.'

'His *good name?*' Harry Bain laughed out loud. 'Lenny Brookstein? The man was a crook, John. So was his wife. That much we know. The question is, what *don't* we know? What are you hiding from us?'

'I'm not h-hiding anything.'

'Why are you protecting him?'

'He was my friend.' *My only friend.*

'He wasn't your friend. He *used* you, John. He used you from the beginning. Why do you think a brilliant guy like Lenny needed a schmuck like you on the team, huh? D'you ever ask yourself that question?'

All the time.

'Because you gave him legitimacy, that's why. Because you were dumb and adoring and blindly loyal. Like a dog.'

John looked up. It was Harry Bain's face sneering at him, but the voice was Caroline's. *You're a lapdog, John. You're pathetic! Stand up and be counted!*

'No. I wasn't Lenny's d-d-dog. It wasn't like that.'

'No? What were you, then? Because the way I see it you're either a fucking moron who couldn't see what was going on right under your nose. Or you knew.'

'No. I d-didn't know anything.'

'I don't believe you. Where's the money, John?'

'I don't know.'

'Where'd you stash it, huh? You and your *good friend* Lenny Brookstein. The guy who trusted you so much. Who relied on your advice. Where'd you put the cash?'

'I've told you. I don't – '

'Maybe it's Andrew Preston we should be talking to. Was Preston was the one Lenny *really* trusted?'

'Of course not. Lenny was always much c-closer to me than to Andrew. '

'So close that he gave your shares to Grace?'

A high-pitched whistle in John's head was getting louder, like a boiling kettle.

'Where is it, John? Where's the money? If you weren't Lenny's little dog, prove it.'

The whistle was so loud, he thought his eardrums would shatter.

'WHERE'S THE *FUCKING* MONEY, JOHN?'

'I DON'T KNOW!' Slumped over the table, John Merrivale broke down in sobs. 'For G-God's sake, what's the matter with you? I don't know.'

On the other side of the two-way glass, Angelo Michele turned to the psychologist.

'What do you think?'

'I think he's telling the truth. He doesn't know anything. When he saw that partnership document, it blew him away.'

Angelo Michele nodded. *I agree.*

I wonder if that automaton Williams is having any more success with Grace?

'Where were you when you signed these documents?'

Grace tried to focus. Still reeling from the shock of seeing Lenny's body, she found it hard to remember where she was. The gruff, gray-haired man sitting opposite her was from the FBI. He'd arrested her as she left the morgue and driven her somewhere, but she couldn't remember where, or how long it had taken. Now she was in a white, windowless room. Images of Lenny's mutilated corpse flashed through her mind like a horror movie. The man kept talking.

'They're dated June eighth.'

Lenny's skin, waxy and white, like the stuff that covers the skin of a newborn baby.

'Mrs Brookstein, these documents prove that you knowingly made yourself a partner in Quorum International LLC, with a view to profiting illicitly from illegal trades, made between 2004 and 2009.'

Lenny's swollen finger, the skin bursting around his wedding ring.

'What do you know about the whereabouts of the profits from the following transactions: 2005, Innovation Management's six-year fund of funds, executed in Grand Cayman?'

'I don't know anything.' Grace's voice was barely a whisper.

Gavin Williams leaned across the table till his face was millimeters from hers. Grace smelled his sour breath. 'Don't lie to me, Mrs Brookstein. You will regret it.'

Grace looked up and saw the compassionless void in his eyes. A cold stab of fear ran through her. 'I'm not lying.'

'You were a partner in your husband's fund.'

86

'A partner? No. You're mistaken. I was never a partner. I don't know anything about business. It was Lenny and John.'

'Do you deny this is your signature?'

Angrily, Gavin Williams shoved a piece of paper across the table. Grace recognized her own writing. But she couldn't for the life of her remember what the document was, when she'd signed it or why. Lenny handled all of that.

'I don't deny anything. I . . . I'm confused.'

Gavin Williams was shouting. 'Two thousand and five, Inspiration, Grand Cayman!'

'I want my attorney present.' Grace was shocked to hear the words come out of her own mouth. *I sound like a bad episode of* Law & Order.

'What?'

'I . . . I said I need a lawyer.'

Gavin Williams seethed with frustration. He'd hoped that by catching Grace at such a vulnerable moment, he'd be able to bully her into a confession, get her to break down. But if she wanted a lawyer, he could not deny her one. *Bitch*.

'Interview terminated. Turn off the tape.'

With a look of disgust, Gavin Williams left the room.

The following morning, news of Grace Brookstein's arrest and the recovery of Lenny Brookstein's body was splashed all over the papers.

Honor Warner shook as she read the report. 'They've found Lenny's body.'

'Yes, I know,' said Jack, deadpan. 'I can read.'

'How can you be so calm about it? The FBI has arrested Grace. Have you seen the list of charges? The things they're accusing her of: securities fraud, money laundering . . . Grace can barely add two plus two! What are we going to do?'

Jack smiled. '*Do?* We're not going to *do* anything.'

'But, Jack . . .'

'But Jack, what? We're going to wash our hands of your little sister and walk away.'

Honor looked horrified. Jack laughed at her.

'Oh, please. Don't try to pretend to me that you *care* about Grace. It's a little late for that, darling. Did you think I couldn't see through you all these years?'

'What do you mean?'

'You think I don't know how much you hate your sister? How much you've always hated her?'

Honor looked away, ashamed. *It's true. I do hate her. But to let her go to jail?* She tried another tack. 'All right. Let's forget about Grace. What about us, Jack? If Grace goes on trial, there'll be questions. Questions about Lenny's business affairs, his associates, what happened the day he disappeared. What if the police find out?'

'They won't.'

'But what if they do?'

Jack looked at her coldly. 'Do you want to be first lady, Honor?'

Honor did want it. More than anything.

'Do you want to see me in the White House?'

'Of course. You know I do.'

'Then stop panicking. Keep your mouth shut and your head down. Lenny's dead. He can't hurt us anymore. But Grace could. God knows how much the old man may have told her.'

Honor shivered. She hadn't thought of that.

'Your sister going to jail could be the best thing to happen to us. Now pass me the coffee, would you? It's getting cold.'

Michael Gray was horrified when he heard the news. Instinctively he put his arms around Connie. 'I'm so sorry, honey. Is there anything I can do?'

Connie shook her head. 'What can anyone do, Mike? Obviously, Lenny and Grace were not who we thought they were.'

Michael Gray looked surprised. 'You don't seriously think Grace is *guilty* of these charges, do you?'

Connie shrugged. 'I don't know what to think anymore. The world's gone mad.'

'Yes, but *money laundering*? *Grace*?'

'I don't see what's so impossible about that. After all, look at Lenny. We all loved and respected him. But it turns out he was nothing but a thief and a coward.'

There was a venom in Connie's voice that Michael had never heard before. It frightened him.

'We all know Grace was obsessed with Lenny. Who knows what she might have done to protect him, or to help him?'

Maria Preston treated Grace's arrest like an exciting episode in one of her soap operas.

'The police are saying that Grace stole John Merrivale's partnership. That she and Lenny were planning to rip him off as well as the investors and run off with all the money! *"Grace Brookstein is the Quorum Fund's only living partner,"* that's what it says here. *"That makes her legally responsible for all of Quorum's losses."* Can you believe that?'

Andrew couldn't believe it. He couldn't believe any of it. Since that fateful trip to Nantucket, he'd barely slept.

I've been lucky so far. The FBI has bigger fish to fry. But the knock on the door will come eventually. I know it will.

It wasn't exposure itself that scared him, or even prison. It was losing Maria. Everything he'd done, he'd done for her. *And she thinks the whole thing's a game!*

'I think I'll wear my new Dior to the trial. The fuchsia one.'

'We're not going to the trial.'

'Not going? But, Andy, everyone will be there.'

'Jesus, Maria, it's not a fucking Broadway show!' It was so rare for Andrew to lose his temper, Maria just stared at him. She rather liked this new, macho Andrew. 'Billions of dollars are missing. The feds are all over us like a rash. Everyone at Quorum's under suspicion.'

'Well, they won't be anymore,' said Maria cheerfully, cutting herself another slice of panettone. 'It looks like the FBI has found its sacrificial lamb. Sweet little butter-wouldn't-melt Gracie is going to jail.'

Andrew thought, *I hope so*, then realized what a terrible thought that was.

When had he become so callous, so coldhearted?

I don't recognize myself anymore. Oh, Maria! What have you done to me?

'You're not going to jail, Grace. Let's get that straight from the get-go. You're innocent, and you're going to plead innocent. Okay?'

Grace nodded weakly. It was all so confusing.

Frank Hammond seemed so upbeat. Not like her first lawyer, Kevin McGuire. Kevin was an old friend of Grace's parents from East Hampton. Grace called him the day she was arrested. She wanted him to rescue her from the bullying agent with the dead eyes, and he had. But once they were alone, he didn't pull his punches.

'As a full partner in Quorum, you're legally liable for Lenny's actions, whether you actually made any decisions or not,' Kevin told her. 'You have to plead guilty.'

'But I never even knew I *was* a partner.'

Kevin McGuire was sympathetic, but firm. Ignorance might be a moral defense, but it wasn't a legal one. 'You signed the contract, Grace. If you don't take responsibility, the judge may be even harsher at sentencing.' He was firm about bail, too. 'My advice is not to seek it.'

Grace couldn't believe it. 'You mean . . . you want me to stay in jail? But it could be months before the case gets to court.'

'It will be months. And I know it's tough. But believe me, Grace, you're safer in there. I don't think you fully appreciate the anger people feel toward you and Lenny.'

He was right. Grace didn't. Apart from the small crowd who heckled her when she left her apartment to stay with the Merrivales, she'd had little or no direct contact with the outside world since she returned to New York. John refused to let her watch the TV reports, and did not allow newspapers in the house. The day after the coroner officially ruled Lenny's death a suicide, Kevin McGuire had shown Grace some of the headlines she'd been shielded from.

BROOKSTEIN TOOK COWARD'S WAY OUT

'DESPICABLE' CON MAN COMMITS SUICIDE, CHEATS JUSTICE

BROOKSTEINS 'MOST HATED COUPLE IN AMERICA'

A week ago, the headlines would have shocked her. Now, having been through the horror of identifying Lenny's body, Grace doubted anything would have the power to shock her ever again. Instead she felt numb. Dissociated.

Are they talking about Lenny? About me? How can people hate us? We haven't done anything wrong.

As for the idea of Lenny committing suicide, well, that was just ludicrous. Anyone who had ever met him knew that Lenny loved life. He would have clung to life to the bitter end, no matter what. *It was an accident, a freak storm. No one could have predicted what happened that day.*

Kevin McGuire kept trying to get her to focus on the present, to acknowledge the fact that she may well be sent to prison. But Kevin didn't understand. Prison didn't frighten Grace. It didn't matter what happened to her. Without Lenny, nothing mattered anymore. The world could hold no joy for

Grace, no hope. *They may as well lock me up. My life's already over.*

Once again, it was John Merrivale who had ridden to her rescue and made her see sense. The whole world was accusing Grace of betraying him, of conspiring with Lenny to 'steal' his stake in Quorum, but John's loyalty remained unwavering. 'It's a mistake, Grace, all right? A mistake. I don't know why Lenny d-did it, but he must have had his reasons.'

'You know he would never have tried to cheat you John. Neither of us would.'

'Of c-course I do, sweetheart. Of course I do.'

When John heard the advice Kevin McGuire was giving Grace, he forced her to fire him on the spot.

'But Kevin's an old friend,' Grace protested.

'I daresay. But he's talking nonsense. P-plead guilty indeed! That's insanity. We need to get you Frank Hammond. He's the best.'

John was right, as usual. Frank Hammond burst into Grace's life like a cyclone. From the moment she met him, Grace felt her hope returning. She began to see light at the end of the tunnel. Here, at last, was her champion, a strong man, an advocate, someone who believed her and would fight for her. Just being in Frank Hammond's presence made Grace feel better.

She asked shyly, 'What about bail? Do you think there's any chance . . . ?'

'I've already applied. The hearing's tomorrow. I'm going to get you out of here.'

'You do realize I . . . I don't have any money. I can't pay you.'

Grace was embarrassed, but Frank Hammond was unfazed.

'Forget it. It's taken care of. Now I want you to listen to me. Can you do that?'

Grace nodded.

'Forget about the charges against you. Forget about the trial, forget about what people out there are saying. It's *my* job to straighten all that out. Understood?'

'Understood.' *He's so reassuring. I feel like I'm talking to Lenny.*

'*Your* job is to hold on tight to the truth. You did not steal any money. Lenny did not steal any money. The fact that a whole bunch of money has gone missing means that *someone* must have stolen it. Whoever that person is *framed* you and your husband. That's our case.'

'But who would do that?'

Frank Hammond smiled, revealing a row of jagged, yellowing, old man's teeth. Clearly he did not spend any of his astronomical fees at the dentist's office.

'Who would steal seventy billion dollars? Ninety-nine percent of Americans, if they thought they could get away with it.'

'All right, then. Who *did* steal it?'

'I have no idea. It doesn't matter. All we need to do is establish reasonable doubt. The D.A. has to *prove* that you and your husband were responsible.'

Grace was silent. After a few moments, she asked, 'Mr Hammond, do you believe my husband killed himself?'

Frank Hammond looked his client directly in the eye. 'No, Mrs Brookstein. I do not.'

From that moment on, Grace knew she could trust Frank Hammond implicitly. *He's going to win the case. He's going to set me free. And when he does, I'm going to find out who stole that money and clear Lenny's name.*

Chapter Nine

Grace Brookstein played with the buttons on her Chanel bouclé jacket as the jury filed back into Court 14. She was nervous, but not about the verdict. She knew she would be found innocent. Frank Hammond had told her so.

'Just do exactly what I tell you, Grace, and leave the rest to me. The jury will acquit you.'

When Frank spoke, it was like listening to the voice of the prophet. Grace had followed his instructions to the letter, even down to her courtroom attire.

'It's not your job to look contrite. You're innocent. I want you to walk into that courtroom proudly, with your head held high. Remember, you're representing Lenny as well as yourself.'

Lenny. Darling, Lenny. Are you watching, sweetheart? Are you proud of me?

No, Grace's nerves were not about the verdict. They were about what would happen once the case was over. *How am I going to find out who framed Lenny?* So far the FBI had conspicuously failed to track down more than a few million of the missing Quorum money. *If they can't find that money, what hope do I have?* But she had to do it. She had to clear

Lenny's name. He'd been gone six months now. It was already December, almost Christmas. *My first Christmas as a widow.* Despite being Jewish, Lenny had always loved Christmas, the present giving, the parties. *He had such a generous spirit.*

The judge's voice sounded distant, unreal. He addressed the foreman of the jury.

'Have you reached your verdict?'

I suppose I'll spend Christmas with the Merrivales.

Christmas was a time for family, but both Grace's sisters had let her down badly. Neither of them had called or visited since she'd been arrested. Grace had half hoped, half expected to see them in the public gallery when the trial started, but Connie and Honor were both conspicuous by their absence.

Once I'm found innocent, I'm sure they'll come back to me. When they do, I'll forgive them. I'm going to need their support if I'm going to put things right. If I'm going to find out who really stole that money. Who framed my darling Lenny.

The foreman looked at Grace and smiled. Grace smiled back. He seemed like a nice man.

'How do you find the defendant, on the charge of securities fraud?'

'Guilty.'

District Attorney Angelo Michele punched the air. *So there wasn't a strategy! Big Frank Hammond just screwed this thing up. He's not so invincible after all.*

Grace started to feel the first stirrings of panic. She looked at Frank Hammond, but his eyes were fixed on the judge.

'And on the charge of money laundering?'

'Guilty.'

No! I'm not guilty. This is a mistake! I did everything Frank told me to.

'On the charge of perjury . . . wire fraud . . . mail fraud . . .'

The words tore into Grace like razor blades.

95

'Guilty . . . guilty . . . guilty.'

'This is wrong! Please, Your Honor. This is all a mistake. I'm innocent and so is my husband! We were framed!'

The boos and catcalls from the public gallery were so deafening, Grace could barely hear her own words. It took a full minute for the judge to restore order. When he did, he turned to Grace with chilling anger.

'Grace Brookstein. Between you, you and your husband robbed your investors of an almost unimaginable sum of money. The human suffering brought about by your actions has been profound. Yet at no point have you shown the slightest remorse. You seem to have taken a view that because of your privileged position in society, the laws of this great nation do not apply to you. They do.'

The gallery roared their approval. Grace could hear the muffled cheers from the crowds gathered outside, watching the proceedings on specially erected screens.

'Your decision to plead not guilty in this courtroom, knowing the overwhelming evidence against you, compounds an already despicable crime. It is this utter disregard for the law, as well as for the pain your victims have suffered, that has informed my decision with regard to your sentence. I do not doubt that your denial of any knowledge of your husband's business practices is a lie, a lie you have shamelessly repeated both to this court and to the authorities struggling to repay your husband's victims. For this, I intend to see to it that you spend the remainder of natural life deprived of your freedom.'

The judge was still speaking, passing sentence, but Grace no longer heard him. *What the hell happened? What went wrong?*

Frank Hammond sat beside her slumped over the table, his head in his hands.

As she felt the bailiff's grip tighten on her arm, Grace

looked up at John Merrivale. He mouthed the words 'Don't worry,' but his stricken face said it all. Even Caroline, who'd been cold and unsupportive in the run-up to the trial, looked shocked.

Grace felt sick, not for herself but for Lenny.

I've failed him. I've let him down.

How am I ever going to prove his innocence now?

On the steps of the courthouse, Angelo Michele was being mobbed. Throngs of people pressed forward to shake his hand and pat him on the back. He had avenged them, avenged New York, avenged the poor, the dispossessed, the homeless, avenged all the victims of the Brooksteins' avarice and greed.

A reporter pulled Harry Bain aside. 'Look at Michele. They love him. It's like he's Joe DiMaggio back from the dead or something. The guy's a rock star.'

'He's more than that,' Harry Bain said. 'He's a hero.'

For Angelo Michele, the show was over. But for Harry Bain and Gavin Williams, it had barely begun.

They still had to find that money.

Chapter Ten

Grace Brookstein's conviction and life sentence – the cumulative punishment for all five charges was over one hundred years in jail – was the lead item on news reports around the globe. Grace was no longer a woman, an individual with thoughts and hopes and regrets. She was an emblem, a symbol of all that was greedy and corrupt and rotten in America, of the forces of evil that had brought the country to the brink of economic collapse and caused so much suffering and anguish. When Grace was taken from the courtroom to await transfer to the Bedford Hills Correctional Facility for Women, she was jostled and jeered by a bloodthirsty mob. One woman managed to scratch her face, her talonlike acrylic nail slicing into Grace's flesh. Images of Grace Brookstein clutching her bleeding cheek as she was bundled into a police van were beamed across America. The mighty had truly fallen.

After a terrifying night alone in a cell, Grace was allowed to make a phone call at five A.M. On instinct, she reached for her family.

'Gracie?' Honor's voice sounded groggy with sleep. 'Is that you?'

Thank God. She's home. Grace could have wept with relief.

'Yes, it's me. Oh, Honor, it's terrible. I don't know what happened. My attorney told me it would all be okay, but – '

'Where are you now?'

'I'm in jail. I'm still in New York, I . . . I don't know where exactly. It's awful. They're transferring me tomorrow. Somewhere near you. Bedford, I think? That might be better. But, Honor, you have to help me.'

There was a long silence. Eventually, Honor said, 'I don't see how I can, Gracie. You've been found guilty in a court of law.'

'I know, but – '

'And you didn't exactly help yourself during the trial. Your *clothes*. What were you thinking?'

'Frank Hammond told me to wear them!'

'You see, there you go again. Connie was right.'

'What do you mean?' Grace was close to tears. 'Connie was right about what?'

'About you. Listen to yourself, Grace: "*Lenny* told me. *My attorney* told me. *John* told me." When are you going to start taking responsibility for your own actions? Your own life? You're not Daddy's little princess anymore, Gracie. You can't keep expecting me and Connie to fix everything for you.'

Grace bit her lip till it bled. She'd needed her sister's support so desperately but all Honor wanted to do was lecture her. Clearly, Connie felt the same way.

'Please, Honor! I don't know where to turn. Can't you ask Jack? He's a senator, he must have some influence. This is all a terrible mistake. I didn't steal any money. And Lenny would never – '

'I'm sorry, Grace. Jack can't possibly get involved. This sort of scandal could ruin us.'

'Ruin *you*? Honor, they're locking me up! Lenny's dead, accused of a crime you *know* he didn't commit.'

'I don't know that, Grace. For God's sake, wake up! That money didn't just vanish. Of course Lenny took it. He took it, and he left you holding the bag.'

The words were like a knife in Grace's heart. It was bad enough that strangers thought Lenny was a thief. But Honor knew him. She *knew* him. How could she possibly believe it?

Honor spoke her next words with chilling finality. 'You made your own bed, Gracie. I'm sorry.' The connection was broken.

You're sorry?

So am I.

Good-bye, Honor.

The ride on the prison van to Bedford Hills was long and uncomfortable. The van was freezing and smelly, and the women inside huddled together for warmth. Grace looked at their faces. These women had nothing in common with her. Some were frightened. Some defiant. Some despairing. But all wore the haggard lines of poverty and exhaustion on their faces. They looked at Grace with naked, murderous hatred.

Grace closed her eyes. She was nine years old, in East Hampton with her father. It was Christmas Eve and Cooper Knowles was lifting her up on his shoulders to put the star on the top of the tree.

'You can do it, Grace. Just stretch a little farther!'

She was on the podium, aged fifteen, surrounded by her gymnast friends. The judges were placing a gold medal around her neck. Grace scanned the crowd for her mother's face, but she wasn't there. Her coach told her, 'Forget it, Grace. If you want to be a winner, you have to win for yourself, not for others.'

It was her wedding night. Lenny was making love to her,

softly, tenderly. 'I'm going to take care of you, Grace. You'll never have to worry about anything ever again.' And Grace replied, 'I love you, Lenny. I'm so happy.'

'Get out!'

The female guard grabbed Grace roughly by the arm. Grace hadn't even noticed that the van had stopped. Moments later she was shivering in a desolate courtyard with the other women prisoners. It was late afternoon, already dark, and there was snow on the ground. In front of Grace was a depressing gray stone building. Behind her, and to the left and right, were row after row of barbed-wire fences, jutting violently into the purple night sky. Grace was ashamed to find herself crying.

'Welcome to Bedford Hills, ladies. Enjoy your stay.'

It was three hours before Grace reached the cell she was to share with two other women. By that time, she knew she would not survive a week at Bedford Hills, never mind the rest of her life.

I have to get out of here! I have to reach John Merrivale. John will get me out.

The physical examination was the worst part. A brutal, degrading experience, it was designed to strip prisoners of all human dignity. It worked. Grace was forced to strip naked in a room full of people. A prison doctor inserted a speculum into her vagina and took a Pap smear. Next Grace was made to bend over while a latex-gloved finger probed her anus, presumably for hidden drugs. Her pubic hairs were pulled painfully in search of lice. Throughout the procedure prison guards of both sexes laughed and made disgusting, lewd comments. Grace felt as if she'd been raped.

After that, she was herded like an animal into a tepid shower and told to wash with antiseptic soap that burned her skin. Next, still naked, she stood in line to have her long hair

101

cropped boy-short. The haircut took all of fifteen seconds but it was a harrowing procedure, robbing Grace of her femininity, her entire identity as a woman. Grace never saw her own clothes again. They were gone, along with every other vestige of the person she had been on the outside. They even took her wedding ring, wrenching it painfully off her finger. In place of her old clothes, Grace was given three pairs of underwear, a bra that didn't fit and a scratchy orange prison uniform two sizes too big for her.

'In here.'

A stocky, female prison guard opened the door of a cell and pushed Grace inside. Two Latina women lay on bunks in the grim, twelve-by-nine-foot box. They muttered something to each other in Spanish as Grace staggered in, but otherwise ignored her.

Screwing up her courage, Grace turned to the guard. 'There's been a mistake. I'd like to see the warden, please. I believe I've been transferred to the wrong facility.'

'Is that so?'

'Yes. This is a maximum-security prison. I was convicted of fraud, not murder. I don't belong here.'

The Latina women's eyes widened. But if the guard was shocked, she didn't show it. 'You can see the warden in the morning. Now you sleep.' The cell door closed.

Grace lay back on her bunk. She couldn't sleep. Her mind was racing.

In the morning I'll see the warden. I'll be transferred to a better prison. That's the first step. Then I can call John Merrivale and start my appeal.

She should have called John in the first place. She didn't know what stupid, childish impulse had made her turn to Honor instead. It was a hard thing to admit that she couldn't trust her own family, but that was the reality. Grace had to face it.

Lenny looked on John as a brother. John's my family now. He's all I've got.

Clearly, hiring Frank Hammond had been a titanic mistake. But Grace couldn't blame John for that. The point now was to move forward

Tomorrow. Things will be better tomorrow.

Frank Hammond sat alone in his car in a deserted parking lot. He watched the familiar figure of his client making his way toward him through the shadows. Every few seconds the man glanced over his shoulder nervously, afraid he was being watched.

Big Frank thought, *He looks so pathetic. So weak. Like a deer caught in the headlights. No one would suspect a man like that of doing something this audacious. I suppose that's how he got away with it.*

The man got into the car and thrust a piece of paper into Frank Hammond's hands.

'What's this?'

'It's a receipt. The wire transfer went through an hour ago.'

'To my offshore account?'

'Of course. Just as we agreed.'

'Thank you.'

Twenty-five million dollars. It was a lot of money. But was it enough? After he'd publicly screwed up Grace Brookstein's defense, Frank Hammond's reputation was in tatters. He might never get hired again. Still, it was too late for regrets.

'I trust you were happy with the job?'

His client smiled. 'Very happy. She trusted you completely.'

'Then our business is concluded.'

Frank Hammond started the engine. His client put a hand on his arm.

'There are no grounds for appeal, are there?'

'None whatsoever. Unless, of course, the FBI happens to find that missing money. But that's not going to happen, is it, John?'

'No. It isn't. N-not in this lifetime.'

John Merrivale allowed himself a small smile. Then he got out of the car and quietly disappeared back into the shadows.

Warden James McIntosh was intrigued. Like everybody else in the country, he knew who Grace Brookstein was. She was the woman who'd helped her husband embezzle billions of dollars, then inexplicably shown up for her trial channeling Marie Antoinette, alienating the vengeance-crazed American public even further.

Warden McIntosh was a tired, disillusioned man in his early fifties with balding gray hair and a matching thin mustache. He was intelligent and not without compassion, although Grace Brookstein did little to inspire it. Most of the women who wound up at Bedford Hills had had lives straight out of a Dickens novel. Raped by their fathers, beaten by their husbands, forced into prostitution and drugs while still in their teens, many of them never stood a chance at living normal, civilized lives.

Grace Brookstein was different. Grace Brookstein had had it all, but she'd still wanted more. Warden McIntosh had no time for that sort of naked greed.

James Ian McIntosh joined the prison service because he genuinely believed that he could do good. That he could make a difference. *What a joke!* After eight years at Bedford Hills, his aims had grown more modest: to make it to retirement with his sanity and his pension intact.

James McIntosh did not want Grace Brookstein at Bedford Hills. He'd argued with his superiors about it.

'C'mon, Bill, give me a break. She's white collar. Plus she's a walking incitement to riot. Half of my prisoners have family members who lost their jobs after Quorum collapsed. And the other half hate her for being rich and white and wearing that goddamn mink coat to trial.'

But it was no use. It was *because* Grace was so hated that she was being sent to Bedford Hills. Nowhere else would she be protected.

Now, less that one full day into her sentence, she was already stirring up trouble, demanding to see him as if this were some sort of hotel and he were the manager. *What's the problem, Mrs Brookstein? Sheets not soft enough for you? Complimentary champagne not quite chilled?*

He gestured for Grace to sit down.

'You asked to see me?'

'Yes.' Grace exhaled, forcing the stress out of her body. It was nice to be sitting in an office, talking to an educated, civilized man. The warden had family photographs on his desk. It felt like a tiny, much-needed dose of reality. 'Thank you for seeing me, Warden McIntosh. There seems to have been a mistake.'

The warden raised an eyebrow.

'Does there?'

'Well . . . yes. You see, this is a maximum-security facility.'

'Is it? I hadn't noticed.'

Grace swallowed. She felt nervous all of a sudden. Was he laughing with her, or at her?

This is my chance to explain. I mustn't screw it up.

'My crime . . . the crime that I was convicted of . . . it wasn't violent,' she began. 'I mean, I'm innocent, Warden. I didn't actually do what they *said* I did. But that's not why I'm here.'

Warden McIntosh thought, *Thank heaven for small mercies.* If he had a dollar for every inmate who'd sat in front of him protesting her innocence, he'd have retired to Malibu Beach years ago. Grace was still talking.

'The thing is, even if I had done it, I don't think . . . what I'm trying to say is, I don't belong here.'

'I couldn't agree more.'

Grace's heart soared. *Thank God! He's a reasonable man. He'll sort this mess out, move me out of this cattle farm.*

'Unfortunately my superiors feel differently. You see, they feel that it's the state's responsibility to see to it that you aren't lynched. They're concerned your fellow inmates might want to, oh, I don't know . . . beat you to death with a crowbar. Or strangle you with bedsheets. Pour acid on your face while you sleep, perhaps? Something of that nature.'

Grace went white. She felt her insides liquefy with fear. Warden McIntosh went on.

'For some reason, my bosses believe you're less likely to come to physical harm at Bedford than anywhere else. A misperception, in my opinion. But tell me, Grace, what do you suggest we do about it?'

Grace couldn't speak.

'Perhaps if some harm actually *did* come to you here, they'd reconsider their decision? D'you think that's possible?'

Warden McIntosh looked Grace in the eye. That's when she knew for sure.

They're going to try to kill me. And he doesn't give a damn. He hates me as much as the rest of them.

'I'm moving you to a different wing. You'll have to let me know whether your new cell is more to your liking. Now, if you'll excuse me . . .'

The guard led Grace away.

Grace's new cell mates were a two-hundred-pound black cocaine dealer named Cora Budds and a slim, pretty brunette in her early thirties. The brunette's name was Karen Willis. The guard told Grace that Karen had shot and killed her sister's boyfriend. 'They both got life. Like you. You'll have plenty of time to get to know each other.' He smiled knowingly. Grace wondered if he was making a sexual innuendo, but was too frightened to ask. *I mustn't fight shadows. I'm sure it's a myth that all women prisoners are lesbians.*

Grace eyed Karen and Cora warily, climbing onto her bunk in silence.

Warden McIntosh sent me here as a punishment. These women may be violent. They might try to hurt me. I have to stay on my guard.

Cora Budds heaved her great bulk off of her own bunk and sat down next to Grace. 'Whas yo' name, honey?' She stank of bad breath and sweat. Grace instinctively recoiled.

'Grace. My name is Grace.'

For some reason, Cora Budds seemed to find this amusing. 'Grace. Amazing Grace!' she cackled. 'What you in for, Amazing Grace?'

'Um . . . fraud,' Grace whispered. It still felt strange and embarrassing saying the word. 'But it's a mistake. I'm innocent.'

Cora laughed even harder. 'Fraud, huh? You hear that, Karen? We got us an innocent con artist. We comin' up in the world!' Suddenly the smile died on Cora's lips. 'Hey, wait a minute. Wha'd you say yo' name was again?'

'Grace.'

'Grace who?'

For a minute Grace hesitated. *Grace who?* It was a good question. This whole situation was so unreal, it was as if her identity had already slipped away from her. *Who am I? I don't know anymore.* At last she said, 'Brookstein. My name is Grace Brookstein. I – '

Grace didn't even have time to flinch. Cora's fist slammed into her face so hard, she heard her nose crack.

'Bitch!' Cora yelled. She hit Grace again. Blood gushed

everywhere. Karen Willis continued reading her book as if nothing had happened.

'You the bitch that stole all that money!'

'No!' Grace spluttered. 'I didn't – '

'My brother lost his job because o' you. All them old folks out on the streets while you and your old man were eatin' caviar? You oughta be ashamed of yo'self. I'm gonna make you wish you wuz never born, Grace Brookstein.'

Grace clutched at her nose. Whimpering, she said, 'Please. I didn't steal any money.'

Cora Budds grabbed her by her orange prison shirt and yanked her to her feet. With one hand she slammed Grace's back against the wall, lifting her as easily as she would a rag doll. 'Don't you speak! Don't you fucking speak to me, you rich white bitch.' With each word, Cora banged Grace's skull against the wall, driving her point home. Warm blood seeped into Grace's newly short hair. She began to lose consciousness.

Karen Willis said in a bored voice, 'Cool it, Cora. Denny'll hear you.'

'You think I give a fuck?'

Sure enough, a few seconds later the cell door opened. Hannah Denzel, known to the inmates as 'Denny' (among other things), was the most senior guard in A Wing. A short, dumpy white woman with beetle brows and an incipient mustache, she reveled in her authority and enjoyed making the prisoners' lives as miserable and degrading as possible. She surveyed the scene in front of her. Grace Brookstein lay slumped on the floor in a pool of blood. Cora Budds stood over her like King Kong with Fay Wray, only without the ape's tenderness. Grace was conscious but barely, mumbling something incoherent.

Denny said, 'I want this mess cleaned up.'

Cora Budds shrugged. 'Tell her. It ain't my blood.'

'Fine. She can do it. But make sure she does. I'll be back in an hour.'

That night, Grace lay awake, rigid with fear, waiting for Cora Budds to fall asleep.

Earlier, she had mopped up her own blood, sluicing the floor on her hands and knees while Cora watched and Karen read her book. After an hour Denny returned, nodded a curt approval, and left Grace to her fate. Grace cowered on her bunk, waiting for Cora to launch another attack, but nothing happened. In a way, she wished it would. Nothing was worse than the waiting, the gut-twisting terror of anticipation. Finally, twenty minutes before lights-out, the cell door opened and Grace was summoned to the prison doctor. After a perfunctory cleanup she was given six stitches for the gash to her head and an ineffectual Band-Aid to help set her broken nose, then sent right back to Cora.

Grace pulled the blankets tightly around her. It had been a long time since she'd prayed, but she closed her eyes tight and opened her heart to the heavens.

Help me, God! Please help me. I'm surrounded by enemies. It's not just Cora. They all hate me, the other prisoners, the guards, Warden McIntosh, those people outside the court-house. Even my own family has deserted me. I don't ask for myself, Lord. I don't care what happens to me anymore. But if I die, who will clear Lenny's name? Who will uncover the truth?

Grace tried to make sense of it all. But every time she found a piece of the puzzle, the other pieces drifted away from her.

Frank Hammond's voice. 'Someone framed Lenny.' *But who, and why?*

Why did Lenny make me a partner in Quorum and cut John out?

Where are the Quorum billions now?

The pain Cora's fist had inflicted was nothing compared with the pain of Grace's inner anguish. Being here, in this awful place, felt like a bad dream. But it wasn't. It was reality.

Maybe it was my life before that was the dream? Me and Lenny, our happiness, our friends, our life. Was it all a mirage? Was it all built on lies?

That was the greatest irony of all. Here Grace was, branded a fraud and a liar. But it wasn't Grace who had lied. It was everyone else: her sisters, her friends, all the people who had eaten at her and Lenny's table, who had slapped them on the back during the good times, holding out their hands, vying with one another to pay homage to the king. Their affection, their loyalty, *that* was the lie. Where were those people now?

Gone, all of them. Scattered on the wind. Vanished into thin air, like the missing Quorum billions.

All except for John Merrivale.

Dear John.

Grace woke up screaming. Karen Willis clamped a hand over her mouth.

'Shhhh. You'll wake Cora.'

Grace was shaking. Her bedsheets were drenched with sweat. She'd been having a nightmare. It started off as a beautiful dream. She was walking down the aisle on Nantucket, on Michael Gray's arm. Lenny was waiting at the altar with his back to her. John Merrivale was there, smiling, nervous. There were white roses everywhere. The choir was singing 'Panus Angelicus.' As Grace got closer to the altar, she became aware of a strange smell. Something chemical like . . . formaldehyde. Lenny turned around. Suddenly his face began to collapse, melting like a doll's head in an oven. His torso started to swell till it burst through his shirt, the skin ghostly white and goose-bumped. Then, limb by limb, the hideous corpse fell to pieces. Grace opened her mouth to scream but it was full of water. Great waves of seawater had flooded the church, sweeping away the wedding guests, destroying everything in their path, flowing into Grace's lungs, choking her. She was drowning! She couldn't breathe!

'You'll wake Cora.'

It took a couple of seconds for Grace to register that Karen was real.

'She gets mad when her sleep is disturbed. You wouldn't like Cora when she's mad.'

After what had happened earlier, Karen's statement was so ridiculous Grace laughed. Then the laugh turned into a cry. Soon Grace was sobbing in Karen's arms, all the loss and terror and pain of the last six months flooding out of her body like pus from a lanced boil.

Finally Grace asked, 'Why didn't you do something this afternoon?'

'Do something? About what?'

'About the attack! When Cora tried to kill me.'

'Honey, that was nothing. If Cora'd tried to kill you, you'd be dead.'

'But you didn't even move. You just sat there and let her assault me.'

Karen sighed. 'Let me ask you something, Grace. Do you want to survive in here?'

Grace thought about it. She wasn't sure. In the end she nodded. She had to survive. For Lenny.

'In that case, you better get one thing straight. Ain't no one gonna rescue you. Not me, not the guards, not your appeal lawyer, not your mama. *No one*. You are *alone* here Grace. You gotta learn to rely on yourself.'

Grace remembered her phone call to Honor.

111

When are you going to start taking responsibility? You're not Daddy's little princess anymore. You can't expect me and Connie to fix everything.

Then she remembered Lenny.

I'll take care of you, Grace. You'll never have to worry about anything again.

'The advice is free,' said Karen, creeping back to her own bunk. 'But when you remember where you hid all that money, maybe you can send me a little token of your appreciation.'

Grace was about to protest her innocence again, but changed her mind. What was the point? If her own family didn't believe her, why on earth would anybody else?

'Sure, Karen. I'll do that.'

Grace took her cell mate's advice. For the next two weeks she kept her head down, her wits about her, and her thoughts and fears to herself. *No one's going to help me. I'm on my own. I have to figure out how life here works.*

Grace learned that Bedford Hills was admired across the country as a model for its progressive outreach programs aimed at helping incarcerated mothers. Of the 850 inmates, more than 70 percent were mothers in their thirties. Grace was astonished to learn that Cora Budds was one of them.

'Cora's a mom?'

'Why d'you look so shocked?' said Karen. 'Cora's got three kids. Her youngest, Anna-May, was born right here. Baby came two weeks early. Sister Bernadette delivered her on the floor of the prenatal center.'

Grace had read an article once about babies being born in prison. Or had she heard something on NPR? Either way, she remembered feeling appalled for the children of these selfish, criminal mothers. But that was in another life, another time. In *this* life, Grace did not find the children's center at Bedford Hills remotely appalling. On the contrary, staffed by

112

inmates and local Roman Catholic nuns, it was the one bright spot of hope in the otherwise unremittingly grim regime of the prison. Grace would have dearly loved to get a job there, but there was no chance.

Karen told her, 'New blood always gets the worst jobs.'

Grace was put to work in the fields.

The work itself was backbreaking, chopping wood to build the new chicken coops, clearing swaths of weed-covered ground to make way for the bird runs. But it was the hours that really killed Grace. The Bedford Hills 'day' bore no relation to light and darkness, or to the rhythms of the outside world. After lights-out at 10:30 P.M., prisoners got only four hours of unbroken sleep before low lighting came on again at 2:30 A.M. This was so that the fieldworkers could eat breakfast and be outside in the bitter cold, working, by four. 'Lunch' was served in the communal mess hall, at nine-thirty. Dinner was at two, eight and a half long, boring hours before lights-out. Grace felt like she was permanently jet-lagged, exhausted but unable to sleep.

'You'll get used to it,' said Karen. Grace wasn't so sure. The worst part of all was the loneliness. Often, Grace would go entire days without speaking to a single soul other than Karen. Other prisoners had friendships. Grace watched the women she worked with lean on one another for support. During breaks, they would talk about their kids or their husbands or their appeals. But nobody spoke to Grace.

'You're an outsider,' Karen told her. 'You're not one of us. Plus, you know, they figure you and your old man stole from people like us. So there's a lot of anger. It'll pass.'

'But you're not angry,' Grace observed.

Karen shrugged. 'I used up all my anger a ways back. Besides, who knows? Maybe you really are innocent? No offense, but you don't come across as no criminal mastermind to me.'

113

Grace's eyes welled with tears of gratitude. *She believes me. Someone believes me.*

She clung to Karen's words like a life raft.

'Brookstein. You got a visitor.'

'Me?' Grace was coming in from the chicken runs. It was two days after Christmas and a heavy snow had fallen overnight. Grace's hands were red raw with cold and her breath plumed in front of her like steam from a boiling kettle.

'I don't see no other Brookstein. Visiting hours almost over, so you better get your ass inside now or you'll miss her.'

Her? Grace wondered who it could be. *Honor. Or Connie, perhaps. They've realized they were too tough on me. They're going to help me file an appeal.*

The guard led her into the visitors' room. There, sitting at a small wooden table, was Caroline Merrivale. In an over-size fox-fur coat, her fingers glittering with diamonds like Cruella de Vil, she looked uncomfortable and laughably out of place in the dismal box of a room, a visitor from another world. Grace sat down opposite her.

'Caroline. This is a surprise.'

During the trial, when she had stayed with the Merrivales, Grace had sensed a growing hostility in Caroline. John, darling John, had been staunch in his support from first to last. But Caroline, whom Grace had once thought of as such a dear friend, almost a surrogate mother, had been aloof, even cruel at times, as if she were enjoying Grace's suffering. She had not bothered to hide her irritation about the unwelcome press attention Grace's presence in the house attracted. 'It's intolerable, like living in a cage at the zoo. When is all this going to end?' The deference she had once shown Grace as Lenny's wife had been replaced by a haughty coolness. Grace tried not to resent it. After all, if it weren't for Caroline and John, she'd have been out on the streets. She wouldn't have had the great Frank Hammond to defend her. She wouldn't have had a thing. But Caroline's bitterness still stung. She was the last person Grace expected to see at Bedford Hills.

Caroline looked around, like a nervous flier searching for the nearest emergency exit. 'I can't stay long.'

'That's okay. It was good of you to come at all. Did John get my letter?'

Grace had written to John a week ago asking him about next steps: What should she do about an appeal, should she hire a new attorney, how long did he think it would be before they agreed to review her case, etc.? He had yet to reply.

'He did, yes.'

Silence.

'He's been very busy, Grace. The FBI is still looking for the missing money. John's been helping them as best he can.'

Grace nodded meekly. 'Of course. I understand.' She waited for Caroline to say something else, to ask her how she'd been holding up, perhaps, or if she needed anything. But she didn't. Desperate to prolong the encounter, her first with the outside world in weeks, Grace started babbling. 'It's not too bad in here. I mean, of course it's *bad,* but you try to get used to it. The worst thing is how tiring the days are. It makes it hard to focus on anything. I keep thinking about Lenny. About how any of this could have happened. I mean, *someone* framed us, that much is obvious. But after that it all gets so tangled. Hopefully, once John starts my appeal, there'll be some light at the end of the tunnel. But at the moment it's so dark. I feel lost.'

'Grace, there won't be any appeal.'

Grace blinked, like a mole in the to sunlight. 'I'm sorry?'

Caroline's voice grew harsh. 'I *said* there won't be an appeal. At least, not with our help, or our money. Look,

John stuck with you for as long as he could. But he's had to face the truth now. We all have.'

'The truth? What do you mean? What truth?' Grace was shaking.

'You can stop with the Little Girl Lost act,' Caroline spat. 'It won't wash with me. Lenny ripped off his investors *and* his partners. He betrayed poor John. You both did.'

'That's not true! Caroline, you must believe me. I know Lenny changed the partnership structure, and it's true I don't know why. But I know he would never have done anything to hurt John intentionally.'

'Oh, come on, Grace! How stupid do you think people are? Why don't you come clean and tell the FBI where the money is?'

This was a nightmare. A sick joke.

'I don't know where the money is. John knows that. John believes me!'

'No,' Caroline said brutally. 'He doesn't. Not anymore. He wants nothing more to do with you. I came here today to ask you to stop contacting him. After everything you and Lenny have done to him, to all of us, you owe us that much at least.'

She stood up to leave. Grace fought down the urge to throw herself into her arms and plead for mercy. Inside, her throat was hoarse from screaming: *Don't leave me! Please! Don't take John away from me. He's my only hope!* Outwardly she kept her mouth clamped shut, afraid that if she opened it the screams would never stop.

'Here.' Caroline pressed a small, tissue-wrapped package into Grace's hand while the guard's back was turned. 'John wanted me to give you this, weak, sentimental fool that he is. I told him you're hardly likely to get much wear out of it rotting your life away in here!' She laughed cruelly. 'But given that it's hideous and of no earthly use to me, I suppose you may as well take it.' She turned on her heel and was gone.

Numbly, Grace followed the guard back to her cell. She'd slipped the package inside her sleeve and kept it hidden till she was safely back on her bunk. Her hands trembled as she opened it, carefully unfolding the tissue paper. John Merrivale had been Grace's last true friend. *My only friend.* Whatever this package contained, he had wanted her to have it.

It was a brooch. A butterfly brooch, in rainbow-colored glass. Grace's eyes welled up with tears. Lenny had bought it for her last Christmas from a secondhand store in Key West. When the police froze Quorum's assets, they'd seized all of Lenny's personal effects, including Grace's jewelry. The brooch must have slipped through the net, perhaps because it was valueless. But it could not have been worth more to Grace if it had been made of solid diamonds.

It was a last piece of Lenny. A last symbol of happiness, of hope, of everything that she had lost forever. It was her passport to freedom.

Eternal freedom.

Gently, lovingly, Grace released the brooch's pin from its clasp and started slashing her wrists.

Chapter Eleven

She was surrounded by brilliant white light. Not the peaceful kind. The blinding, painful kind that burned her eyes, shining into the darkest recesses of her memory, leaving her nowhere to hide.

She heard voices.

Frank Hammond: *'Someone framed Lenny and set you up to take the fall. Someone with inside information on Quorum.'*

John Merrivale: *'Trust Frank. D-do everything he tells you and you'll be fine. Don't worry about the FBI; I'll d-deal with them.'*

The light faded.

Warden McIntosh felt beads of sweat trickle down his back as he watched the flat green line on the heart monitor.

Please, God, let her live.

If Grace Brookstein succeeded in killing herself on his watch, his career would be over. He could wave good-bye to his pension, his retirement, to everything he'd worked so hard for these past eight years. None of his achievements, his good intentions, would count for a damn. In that moment,

James McIntosh hated Grace Brookstein more than he had ever hated another human being.

The doctors applied shock paddles to Grace's heart. Her tiny body leaped off the bed. The green line flickered, then jumped to life, pulsing in a slow but steady rhythm.

'She's back.'

The head of the New York State Department of Corrections took the call at his golf club.

'I should be firing you, James. No questions asked. You do realize that?'

'Yes, sir.'

'If word got out we'd allowed Grace Brookstein access to a sharp object *in her own cell . . .*'

'I know, sir. It won't happen again, sir.'

'Damn right it won't! And what was she doing on A Wing in the first place? We sent her to Bedford Hills so she could be protected.'

Warden McIntosh fought down his irritation. Grace Brookstein didn't deserve to be protected. Even now that she was in jail, she was getting special treatment. It stuck in his craw.

'When she's well, I want her on twenty-four-hour suicide watch. She gets psychotherapy, she gets decent food. What's her work detail?'

Warden McIntosh braced himself. 'She's been on the farm, sir. Early shifts.'

'She's been *what*? Are you out of your fucking mind, James? I want her in the children's center, with the nuns, as soon as she's well enough. *Capisce?* Whatever you may feel about her personally, from now on I want you walking on eggshells with Lady Brookstein. Am I clear?'

'Yes, sir. Clear as crystal.'

*   *   *

Grace woke up to a world of pain. It came in waves.

The first wave was physical: the throbbing in her wrists, the parched dryness of her throat, the dull ache in her limbs. Whoever had inserted the needle in her arm had clearly done so in a hurry. Whichever way Grace turned, she felt a sharp stabbing in her vein. The entire surrounding area was badly bruised.

The second wave was emotional: she'd tried to kill herself, and she had failed. She was not in heaven with her darling Lenny. She was here, in Bedford Hills, living the nightmare. Depression washed over her.

But it was the third wave – the mental anguish – that made Grace sit bolt upright in bed and tear at her hair until the doctors came and sedated her. Somewhere deep in her unconscious mind, between death and life, darkness and dawn, the truth had jumped out and grabbed her by the throat. In her mind, she heard Caroline Merrivale's voice, smug and spiteful. *There will be no appeal. John wants nothing more to do with you.*

At the time, Grace had thought, *No, not John. It's you. You're the one who wants nothing more to do with me. You've poisoned him.* But now, finally, she realized. Caroline was just the messenger.

It was John. It was John all along!

John was the one who'd betrayed Lenny. He'd betrayed them both. The more Grace thought about it, the more obvious it was. John was the only person close enough to Lenny to have been *able* to steal that money. When the SEC started looking into Quorum, he must have panicked. Somehow he persuaded Lenny to change the fund's partnership structure so that he, John, wouldn't be liable when the money was discovered missing. Of course, Lenny's sudden death must have raised the stakes dramatically. Exposure was always likely, but after Lenny disappeared it became a certainty. Quorum investors started asking for their money back and the fraud was exposed. But by then it was easy for John to shift the blame to Grace. She was Lenny's partner now, not him. Better still, Grace trusted him. He'd made sure of that. When everyone else had deserted her, John Merrivale stayed close. *Not because he cared for me. Because he wanted to stage-manage the whole thing! The FBI investigation. My trial.* It was John who had dealt with the police, 'protecting' Grace from their questions. It was John who had insisted she fire Kevin McGuire and hire Frank Hammond, the attorney who had let her down in court. Now that she was safely behind bars, John had washed his hands of her. *He wasn't even man enough to come himself. He sent Caroline to do his dirty work for him.*

Looking back, Grace was astonished at her own naïveté. The way she'd begged John to believe her about the partnership, to believe that she knew nothing about Lenny cutting him out and transferring his shares to her. *How could I have been so stupid? It was in his* interest *not to be a partner! If John had been a partner, he'd have been legally liable for what happened at Quorum. He'd be in jail now, not me.*

Grace had no idea how John had done it. How he'd managed to dupe Lenny into changing the company structure, never mind how he'd stolen all that money and kept it hidden. But she knew that he *had* done it somehow. If it took her the rest of her life, Grace Brookstein was going to find out how.

I'll discover the whole truth and nothing but the truth. And when I do, I'll tell the world. I'll clear Lenny's name and my own. I'll get out of the hellhole.

Grace slept.

Gavin Williams felt dirty.

Just being here, inside a prison, surrounded by deviants,

was enough to make his flesh creep. Of course, the fact that the wrongdoers were women made it all the more disgusting. It was unnatural. Women should be chaste and clean and subservient. They should be good and loving, like his mother. Gavin Williams's mother had adored him. *'You're so handsome, Gavin,'* she used to say. *'You're so smart. You can be anything you want to be.'*

Gavin bolted into the men's room and washed his hands for a third time, scalding them under the faucet until his skin was red raw.

Women should be like his mother. But they weren't. In the real world, women were greedy, dirty bitches, whores who only wanted to have sex with you if you were rich or powerful. Hedge fund guys, billionaires like Lenny Brookstein, they spent their lives *drowning* in pussy. How Gavin Williams loathed those men, with their flashy cars and their model girlfriends and their beach houses and their private jets. He, Gavin Williams, was better than the Lenny Brooksteins of this world. He was an incorruptible patriot, a modern-day Robespierre. He was a revolutionary, bringing justice to America.

I am the righteous sword of the law.

The Lord Almighty says, 'I will punish them. The young men will die, their sons and daughters starve. Not one of these plotters will survive, for I will bring disaster upon them . . .'

'Mr Williams?'

Gavin stood in the hallway of Bedford Hills infirmary. A pretty young nurse looked at him strangely.

'Yes? What is it?'

'Mrs Brookstein is awake. You can talk to her now.'

Gavin Williams was certain that Grace Brookstein held the key to finding the stolen Quorum money. The rest of the FBI task force had given up on her as a potential witness. Harry Bain told him, 'Forget about Grace, Gavin. She's a dead end. If she were going to tell us anything, she'd have done it by now.'

But Gavin could not forget about Grace. Her dirty whore's face haunted his dreams at night. Her voice mocked him during his long days spent poring over the complex paper trail that Lenny had left behind: *I know*, she taunted him. *I know where that money is, and you don't.*

The press continually compared the Quorum fraud with the Madoff case, but the two could not have been more different. Madoff's returns were so ludicrously consistent. It was plain to anyone with the brains to look that he was a fraud. Either he was doing insider trading, or running a Ponzi scheme. Those were the only two logical possibilities. Given the fact that *nobody* traded with Madoff, none of the major banks, no brokerages, nobody, it had to be a Ponzi.

Quorum was different. *Everybody* had traded with Lenny Brookstein. There wasn't a firm on Wall Street that had seen through the guy, not a whisper of the scandal that was to engulf him and his fund so spectacularly. The missing Quorum billions were not just the figment of some creative accountant's imagination. They were real. But Brookstein had been so secretive about his trades, even flying paper records to Cayman and Bermuda to be burned, it was virtually impossible to follow any transaction to its end point. Not unless you were an insider. Not unless you *knew*.

When Gavin Williams got word of Grace Brookstein's suicide attempt, he knew it was an opportunity not to be missed. Like the last time he interviewed her at the morgue, she would be in a weakened state. But this time there would be no lawyers to protect her, no phone calls, no escape. *This* time, Gavin Williams would squeeze her till she couldn't breathe. He would get the truth from Grace Brookstein if he had to make her vomit it out.

For today's interview Gavin had dressed as he always dressed: dark suit and tie, his short, gray hair neatly parted, black shoes so shiny he could see his own reflection in the leather. Discipline, that was the key. Discipline and authority. Gavin Williams would *make* Grace Brookstein respect him. He would bend the deviant to his will, and expose Harry Bain, his so-called boss, for the shortsighted fool that he was.

When Grace saw Gavin Williams, her pupils dilated with fear.

Gavin Williams smiled. Her terror aroused him. 'Hello again, my dear.'

She looked weak. Dwarfed by her white prison nightgown, still pale from blood loss, she seemed as insubstantial as a ghost or a wisp of smoke.

'What do you want?'

'I'm here to make a deal with you.'

'A deal?'

Yes, a deal, you greedy bitch. Don't pretend you don't understand the concept. You're as corrupt as hell and one day you will rot in hell for your sins.

'It's a deal you can't refuse. The procedure is simple. You will provide me with three account numbers. All refer to funds held in Switzerland. You are familiar with all of them.'

Grace shook her head. She didn't know any account numbers. Hadn't they been through this the last time?

'In return, I will see to it that you are moved to a mental health facility.'

'Mental health? But I'm not crazy.'

'I assure you, the conditions at penal sanatoriums are considerably superior to those at correctional facilities such as this one. The account numbers, please.' He handed Grace a piece of paper with a Credit Suisse letterhead. Grace glanced at it and sighed, closing her eyes. The drugs made her sleepy. As frightened as she was of this man, it was a struggle to stay awake.

'John Merrivale,' she croaked. 'It's John Merrivale. He took the money. He knows where it is. Ask him.'

Gavin Williams's eyes narrowed. *How typical of a woman! To try to shift the blame, just as Eve blamed the serpent when she polluted the world with her sin. How stupid did Grace think he was? Did she think the FBI hadn't looked into Merrivale, into all the staff at Quorum?*

'Don't play games with me, Mrs Brookstein. I want those account numbers.'

Grace was about to reason with him, but then she thought, *What's the point? He won't listen. He's insane. If anyone needs the sanatorium, it's this guy, not me.*

'I know what you're doing. You're holding out for more.' Gavin Williams positively glowed with rage. 'Well, you won't get it, do you understand me? You won't get it!'

Grace looked around for the nurse but there was no one. *I'm alone with this nutcase!*

'There will be no appeal. No parole. It's the sanatorium or you will *die* in this place. *Die!* Give me those account numbers!'

'I told you! I. Don't. Know. Them.' Exhausted, Grace fell back on the pillow. She was losing the battle for consciousness. Sleep engulfed her.

Gavin Williams watched her eyes flicker and close.

Her neck is so tiny. So fragile. Like a willow twig. I could reach out and snap it. Just like that. Put my hands around her lying, thieving throat and crush the devil inside.

There were no other patients. No staff. He and Grace were alone.

No one would know. I could do it in a split second. Smite the wicked, purge the evildoer of sin.

In a trance, Gavin Williams reached his hands out in front of him, flexing his long, bony fingers open and closed, open and closed. He imagined Grace's windpipe collapsing beneath them, felt his excitement building.

'I know what you're thinking.'

The nurse's voice made him jump physically out of his seat.

'Your fingers. I know what you're thinking.'

Gavin was silent.

'You're a smoker, aren't you? I was the same when I gave up. You never stop thinking about it, do you? Not for a second.'

It took Gavin a moment to register what she was saying. *She thinks I'm grasping for an imaginary cigarette.* As if he, Gavin Williams, would ever be so weak as to succumb to an addiction. Out loud he smiled and said, 'No. You never do.'

'Believe me, I get it,' chirped the nurse. 'It's like an itch you can't scratch. There's a courtyard outside if you're desperate.'

Gavin Williams retrieved the Credit Suisse paper from Grace's sleeping fingers and slipped it back into his brief-case.

'Thank you. I am not desperate.'

But he was.

After two weeks Grace returned to her cell on A Wing. Warden McIntosh had intended to transfer her back to her original cell with the Latinas on the less austere C Wing, but Grace became so agitated that the psychiatrists recommended the prisoner be allowed to have her way. The warden was baffled.

'But Cora Budds assaulted her. She's one of our most violent inmates. I don't understand. Why would Grace want to go back to that?'

The psychiatrist shrugged. 'Familiarity?'

Not for the first time, James McIntosh reflected on how little he understood the workings of the female mind.

Grace's fellow inmates viewed the situation more crudely. 'No wonder Cora and Karen look so excited. Did you hear? Grace is comin' back to A Wing. Looks like the oyster bar has reopened, ladies!'

In fact, when the time came, Cora Budds greeted Grace coolly. Something had changed about Grace. The old fear, the wariness, had gone. In its place was a calmness, a confidence that made Cora uneasy.

'So you made it, huh?'

'I made it.'

Karen Willis was more demonstrative, flinging her arms around Grace and hugging her tightly. 'Why didn't you talk to me? If things were that bad? You shoulda talked to me. I could've helped.'

Karen Willis did not know what it was that drew her to Grace Brookstein. Part of it she put down to her stubborn streak. Grace was the underdog at Bedford Hills, a pariah, hated by screws and inmates alike. Karen Willis did not believe in running with the herd. Besides, Karen knew what it felt like to be an outsider, betrayed by one's own friends and family. When she shot her sister Lisa's abusive boyfriend, a bully and a rapist who had terrorized Lisa for six torturous years, Karen expected her family to rally around. Instead they'd turned on her like a pack of hyenas. Lisa played the grief-stricken widow: *We had our problems, but I loved Billy.* She even testified against Karen in court, making her out to be an angry, violent person who had a 'vendetta' against men, implying that she'd acted not out of sisterly love but out of sexual rejection. *Karen always wanted Bill. I could see it. But Billy wasn't interested.* The prosecutor changed the charges against Karen from manslaughter to second-degree murder. Karen never spoke to any of her family again.

But Karen Willis's affection for Grace Brookstein ran deeper than their shared abandonment. Lisa had been right about one thing. Karen had never been much of a fan of men. Short, weasel-faced rapists like her brother-in-law Billy had never been Karen's type. Fragile, innocent blondes like Grace Brookstein, on the other hand, with her wide-set eyes and slender, supple gymnast's limbs, her soft skin and smattering of girlish freckles across the nose, that was another matter entirely. Karen Willis was as far removed from the stereotypical predatory prison dyke as it was possible to get. Jokes about 'oyster bars' made her want to gag. She had no intention of forcing herself on Grace. The girl was quite clearly (a) straight and (b) grieving. Unfortunately, neither of those things changed the fact that Karen Willis was in love with her. When she heard Grace had tried to kill herself, Karen collapsed. When they told her Grace was going to live, that the worst was over, Karen wept with relief.

Grace hugged her friend.

'You couldn't have helped, Karen. Not then. But perhaps you can help now.'

'How? Tell me what you need Grace. I'm here for you.'

'I know who framed me and my husband. What I don't know is how he did it. I need evidence. Proof. And I don't know where to begin.'

A smile lit up Karen's face. Perhaps she could help Grace after all?

'I have an idea.'

Davey Buccola looked at his watch and stamped his feet against the cold. *I must be crazy, coming out to this godforsaken place on some wild-goose chase for Karen.*

Davey Buccola was tall, dark and, if not quite handsome, certainly better-looking than the vast majority of his

128

profession. He had olive skin, faintly scarred from acute teenage acne, intelligent hazel eyes and strong, masculine features dominated by an aquiline nose that gave him a hawklike, predatory look. Women were attracted to Davey. At least, they were until he took them home to the shoddy two-bedroom apartment in Tuckahoe he still shared with his mother, or picked them up in his twelve-year old Honda Accord, the same car he'd been driving when he graduated from high school. Private investigation was interesting work, dangerous and challenging. But it didn't make anybody rich. It wasn't like *Magnum*, *P.I.*

Davey Buccola had had a crush on Karen Willis since they were kids. He felt bad when they locked her up and her family turned their backs on her. The shit-for-brains Karen killed had had it coming. But Davey wasn't here just for Karen's sake. He was here for his own. He needed money, pure and simple. And Grace Brookstein had money.

At last the gates of the prison opened and the visitors were taken through security. Davey Buccola had visited numerous correctional facilities, so he knew the drill. Coat off, shoes off, jewelry off, scanner, metal detector, dogs. Kind of like catching a plane, only without the luggage and the duty-free stores. Better for people watching, though. You could tell the moms right away, the tired slump of the shoulders, the resignation in the faces, aged from years of sacrifice and pain. There were a couple of husbands, deadbeats most of 'em, overweight, long-haired, telltale signs of drug use. But overall there were very few men in the visiting line. It was all women, women and children, braving the cold to make the depressing journey to Bedford Hills in hopes of keeping their families together.

Davey thought, *Women are a lot less selfish than men.*

Then he thought, *They're also a lot more conniving. Men lie when they have to. Women do it for kicks.* He would

129

listen to Grace Brookstein. But he would take nothing she said at face value.

Davey walked into the visitors' room and sat down at a wooden table. A scrawny little kid came and sat down opposite him.

'I think you have the wrong seat. I'm here to meet Mrs Brookstein.'

The kid smiled. 'I'm Grace Brookstein. How do you do, Mr Buccola?'

Davey shook her hand and tried not to look shocked. 'I'm good, thanks.'

Jesus H. What happened to her? She's only been in here a month. The Grace Brookstein he'd expected to meet was the fur-clad vixen from the courtroom, glamorous, groomed, dripping in diamonds and disdain. The girl in front of him now looked about fourteen, with close-cropped hair and a pale urchin's face. She had a broken nose, deep shadows under the eyes, and she looked like she hadn't eaten in weeks. The orange jumpsuit she was wearing swamped her tiny frame. When Davey shook her hand, he noticed the skin was almost transparent.

'Karen said you need some help.'

Grace dispensed with the pleasantries. 'I want you to help me prove that John Merrivale framed me and my husband.'

Karen hadn't mentioned anything about *this*. 'She needs you to do a little digging,' those had been her exact words. Nothing about Grace Brookstein being a total fucking fruit loop who'd convinced herself her old man was framed. Jesus. Every man and his dog knew that Lenny Brookstein was as crooked as a two-dollar bill.

'John Merrivale. Wasn't he the number two at Quorum? The guy the FBI has been working with.'

Reading his thoughts, Grace said, 'I understand your

130

skepticism. I don't expect you to believe me. All I'm asking is that you look into it. I'm doing as much research as I can from the library here, but I'm sure you appreciate my resources are limited.'

'Look, Mrs Brookstein.'

'Grace.'

'Look, Grace, I'd like to help you. But I gotta be honest. The FBI has been through Quorum's finances with a fine-tooth comb. If there were any evidence that Merrivale had framed your husband, any evidence at all, don't you think they'd have found it?'

'Not necessarily. Not if they trusted him. John's been working *with* the FBI, Mr Buccola. He's part of the investigative team. Don't you see? He's convinced them he's one of their own. Believe me, John Merrivale can be very plausible.'

'Plausible's one thing. Stealing seventy *billion* dollars and stashing it where no one can find it, not the SEC, not the smartest brains at the Bureau, *no one* . . . some might say that's impossible.'

Grace smiled. 'I believe that's what my attorney told the jury. And yet here I am.'

Davey Buccola smiled back. *Touché.*

'I've never even opened a bank statement, Mr Buccola. John Merrivale's a financial wizard. If I could do it, couldn't he?'

Davey Buccola thought, *I underestimated her. She's not a fruit loop. Misguided, maybe. But she's nobody's fool.* 'All right, Mrs Brookstein. I'll do some digging for you. But I'm warning you now, don't believe in foregone conclusions. They're against my religion.'

'I understand.'

'If I take this case, I'll take it with an open mind. I'm digging for the truth. You might not like what I find.'

'I'll take my chances.'

'Another thing you should know: nothing's going to happen quickly. This is a complicated case. A lot of the information is classified. I have FBI sources, guys in the police and the SEC who'll talk to me, but it's slow work.'

Grace looked at the four walls around her. 'Time's about the one thing I have left, Mr Buccola. I'm not going anywhere.'

Davey Buccola shook her hand. 'In that case, Mrs Brookstein, I'm your man.'

'Where are you going, honey? Come back to bed.'

Harry Bain looked at his wife's voluptuous naked body sprawled out across the sheets. Then he looked at his watch. *Six A.M. Fucking Quorum.*

'I can't. We've got a team meeting at seven.'

'Can't you say you're sick?'

'Not really. I called the meeting.'

The whole of America hated Lenny Brookstein. But at that moment no one hated him quite as much as Harry Bain.

I can outsmart a street fighter like Brookstein, Bain had reasoned, when he first took the case. *It's not like we're looking for a pair of cuff links. Seventy-five* billion *dollars is missing. That's like trying to hide a country.* 'Excuse me, but has anyone seen Guatemala? Some dead Jewish guy from Queens mislaid it last June.'

Of course he would find the money. How could he not?

Yet here he was, a year later, with nothing. Harry Bain, Gavin Williams, and their team had commandeered Quorum's old offices as a base for their investigation. With John Merrivale's help, the task force had spent millions, chasing leads all over the world, from New York to Grand Cayman to Paris to Singapore. Between them, Harry Bain, Gavin Williams, and John Merrivale had clocked more air miles than a migrating flock of Canadian geese, produced enough paper to wipe out an entire rain forest, conducted thousands of interviews, and seized countless bank records. If Lenny Brookstein took a shit between January 2001 and June 2009, the FBI had a record of it. But still no goddamn money.

Their failure wasn't from lack of effort. Gavin Williams might be a card-carrying weirdo but you couldn't fault the guy for commitment. As far as Harry Bain could tell, Williams had no friends or family, no personal life at all. He lived and breathed Quorum, following the impenetrable, circuitous paper trail of trades Lenny Brookstein had left behind him with the dogged bloodlust of a fox hound. Then there was John Merrivale, the Quorum insider-turned-police-asset. John was an odd bird, too. So shy he was almost autistic, the guy still teared up whenever Lenny Brookstein's name was mentioned. In the beginning, Harry had wondered whether John might be implicated in the fraud himself. But the more he learned about Lenny Brookstein's business practices, the less he suspected John Merrivale, or Andrew Preston, or any of the other employees. Brookstein was so secretive he made the CIA look indiscreet. Surrounded by people, a social animal to the last, at the end of the day Lenny had trusted no one. No one except his wife.

Rumors on the team were that John Merrivale was unhappy at home. Harry Bain had met Caroline Merrivale once and could well believe it. That bitch probably wore stilettos and a whip to bed. Or a gestapo uniform. No wonder John was happy to put in long hours on the task force. *So would I be if I was married to Madam Whiplash.*

'Okay, folks. What have we got?'

The elite group of FBI agents who formed the Quorum task force stared at their boss dejectedly. One joker piped up, 'Gavin's thinking of heading out to Bedford Hills again, right, Gav? He's gonna use his legendary charm with the *laydeez* to get Mrs B to sing like a bird.'

The rest of the group sniggered. Gavin Williams's obsession with 'breaking' Grace Brookstein had become a running joke. Either Grace didn't know where Lenny had stashed the cash, or she knew but she wasn't telling. Either way, Williams was beating a dead horse and everyone could see it but him.

Gavin didn't join in the laughter. 'I have no plans to return to Bedford, Stephen. Your information is incorrect.'

The joker murmured to his partner, '"Your information is incorrect." Is he human? He sounds like R2 fucking D2.'

'No kidding,' his partner replied more loudly. '"Help me, Obi-Wan Brookstein. You're my only hope!"'

More laughter.

Gavin Williams glanced around the table at his so-called colleagues. If he could, he would have ripped every one of their hearts out with his bare hands and stuffed them down Harry Bain's smug, self-satisfied throat till he choked. What did any of them have to laugh about? They were all part of the biggest, lamest operation in FBI history. If he, Gavin, were running the show, things would be different.

Harry Bain said. 'Okay, then, so it's all on this trip to Geneva.'

John Merrivale had spent the last three weeks researching a huge swap trade from 2006. The trail led as far as a numbered account in Switzerland, then went cold.

'Gavin, I'd like you and John to make the trip together this time. Two heads may prove better than one.'

John Merrivale failed to hide his surprise. He and Gavin Williams usually worked independently, following up on separate leads. This was the first time Bain had asked them to travel together.

'I'm f-fine to handle the Geneva trip alone, Harry.'

134

'I know you are. But I'd like the two of you together on this one.'

John Merrivale's relationship with Harry Bain had come a long way since Harry's 'bad-cop' interview with him, before Grace's trial. It had taken months to persuade not just Bain, but the entire task force, that he was on their side, that he was as much a victim of Lenny Brookstein as anyone else. But slowly, with the steady, quiet patience on which he'd built his entire career, John Merrivale had won them over. He was no longer frightened of Harry Bain. But at the same time he didn't want to cross him. John still loathed confrontation. As much as Gavin Williams's dour, monosyllabic presence was bound to ruin the Switzerland trip, John didn't want to fight about it.

Harry Bain said, 'We need to build some more team spirit. Bounce ideas off each other more. Somehow we've got to break this deadlock.'

John Merrivale tried to imagine a scenario in which anyone might 'bounce an idea' off Gavin Williams. *Bain really must be getting desperate.*

The flight from New York was bumpy and unpleasant. John Merrivale felt his stomach flip over with nerves. He tried to make small talk with his companion. 'Of course, legally we can't force the Swiss to cooperate with us. But I know the g-guys at the Banque de Genève pretty well. I may able to p-persuade them to stretch a point.'

Silence. It was like talking to a corpse.

Gavin Williams closed his eyes. *'Persuade them?' 'Stretch a point?' They're criminals who laundered Brookstein's dirty money. They should be stretched on a rack till their limbs are wrenched out of their sockets and their screams can be heard from the Statue of Liberty.*

'Have you spent m-much time in Geneva, Gavin?'

'No.'

'It's a beautiful city. The m-m-mountains, the lake. Lenny and I used to love coming here.'

Gavin Williams pulled on his sleep mask. 'Good night.'

The plane rattled on.

John Merrivale was booked into Les Amures, an exclusive five-star hotel in Geneva's old town. In the old days, he and Lenny had enjoyed many fine meals in Les Amures' famous restaurant, which had been built in the thirteenth century and decorated with exquisite frescos, painted façades and art treasures. Lenny used to say it was like eating in the Sistine Chapel.

Gavin Williams refused to join him, preferring the more modest Hotel Eden. It was right on the lake, but Gavin purposely chose a room with no view that was closer to the gym and business center. 'We're not here to enjoy ourselves,' he told John tersely.

Heaven forbid.

John thought again how much Lenny would have despised Gavin Williams. His joylessness. His anger. Wandering alone around Geneva's chilly, medieval streets after dinner, he thought how much more fun the trip would have been had Lenny been with him.

'What do you mean I'm not coming?'

Gavin Williams looked fit to be tied. He and John were breakfasting together at Gavin's hotel, prior to the meeting with the people from the Banque de Genève.

'I have a r-relationship with the bankers. They're more likely to trust me if I g-go alone.'

'Trust you?' Gavin Williams balled up his napkin in his fist.

'Yes. Banking, especially in Switzerland, is all about t-trust.'

Gavin Williams thought furiously, *You were the right-hand*

*man to the biggest thief of all time, and you have the nerve
to pontificate about trust? Even now, even after Quorum's
disgrace, it's still an old boys' club, isn't it? You're still one
of them – a banker – and I'm not.* Out loud he snapped,
'Don't patronize me, John. I've written textbooks on Swiss
banking.'

'Marvelous. Then you know what I'm talking about.'

'These *people* you claim to have a relationship with are
money launderers. They are scum and their trust is worth
nothing. I will attend the meeting, whether they like it or not.'

John Merrivale could not resist a fleeting, triumphant
smile. 'I'm afraid you won't, Gavin. You see, I already cleared
it with Harry Bain. I'm g-going alone. You're to follow up
on any information I get out of them. Take it up with Harry
if you're not happy.'

'How can I take it up with Harry?' Gavin spluttered. 'It's
three in the morning in New York.'

'Is it?' John smiled again. 'What a pity.'

Three days later they flew back to the states.

John Merrivale reported to Harry Bain: whatever money
Lenny had stashed in Geneva was long gone. Some of it was
paid out to investors in returns. The rest was siphoned into
property deals in South America. Gavin Williams would fly
to Bogotá tomorrow to see what he could uncover.

Harry Bain put his head in his hands. *Bogotá. And so it
goes on.*

'I'm s-sorry about Geneva, sir. I really thought that might
be a breakthrough.'

Harry Bain hated the way John Merrivale insisted on
calling him 'sir.' Nobody else did. He'd told Merrivale to cut
it out months ago, but it was like a verbal tic with the guy.
Subservience was second nature to him. Not for the first
time, Harry wondered what on earth had attracted a type A

137

man's man like Lenny Brookstein to this weak, mealymouthed number cruncher. It didn't make any sense.

'It's okay, John. You did your best. The Bureau appreciates your efforts.'

'Th-thank you, sir. I'll keep trying.'

Yeah. We're all trying. But there are no prizes for effort. Not in this life.

'John, do you mind if I ask you a personal question?'

John looked momentarily taken aback.

'Does it ever get to you?'

'Does what ever get to me?'

'You must have lost millions because of Lenny Brookstein, right? Tens of millions.'

John Merrivale nodded.

'You see your entire life's work destroyed, your good name dragged through the mud. Doesn't it, I don't know . . . test your faith in humanity?'

John Merrivale smiled. 'I'm afraid I've never had much f-faith in humanity.'

'Okay, then. In friendship.'

In a flash, the smile was gone.

'Let me tell you something about friendship, Mr Bain. Friendship is everything. *Everything.* It's the only thing that really m-m-matters in this world. People can say what they like about me. But I'll tell you this. I'm a loyal friend.'

He turned and walked away. Harry Bain watched him go.

He felt uneasy, but he had no idea why.

In a hotel bathroom in Bogotá, Gavin Williams stood under a cold shower, scrubbing his body with soap. It was so hard to stay clean in this filthy world. Colombia was the greatest cesspool of all. Every aspect of life here was diseased, tainted by greed, infected with corruption. It made Gavin sick.

As he scrubbed away, cleansing his soiled body, Gavin's

thoughts turned to John Merrivale. John had humiliated him in Switzerland. No doubt he thought he'd had the last laugh. But Gavin Williams knew better.

John Merrivale had patronized the wrong man.

He would live to regret it.

Chapter Twelve

Grace's first year at Bedford Hills passed quickly.

Most long-term prisoners looked back on the first twelve months of their sentence as the worst. Karen described it to Grace as 'like cold turkey, except you're not withdrawing from drugs, you're withdrawing from freedom.' It was a good analogy, but Grace didn't feel that way. For Grace, the first year of prison was like awakening from a lifelong slumber. For the first time, she was seeing life as it really was. She was surrounded by women from ordinary backgrounds, poor backgrounds. Women who had grown up less than twenty miles away from where Grace grew up, but who lived in a world as foreign and alien to her as the rice paddies of China or the deserts of Arabia.

It was wonderful.

In her old life, Grace now realized, friendships had been a mirage: fragile, hollow alliances based solely on money or status. At Bedford Hills, she observed a different kind of female friendship, one born of adversity and strengthened through suffering. If someone said a kind word to you here, they meant it. Slowly, cautiously, Grace began to forge bonds, with Karen, with some of the girls she worked with in her new job at the children's center, even with Cora Budds.

Cora was a mass of contradictions. Violent, moody and uneducated, she could certainly be a bully, as Grace had learned to her cost on her second night at Bedford. But Cora Budds was also a loyal friend and devoted mother. After Grace's suicide attempt, Cora's maternal side took over. It was Cora, more even than Karen Willis, who had led the campaign to change their fellow prisoners' minds about Grace Brookstein. When a group of women at the children's center froze Grace out, refusing to talk to her or even eat in the same room, it was Cora who confronted them.

'Give the bitch a chance. She din' steal nuthin'. You kidding me? She wouldn't know how.'

'She's rich, Cora.'

'She ain't even a mom. How'd she get a job in here? The warden's showing her favors.'

Cora Budds said, 'Lemme tell you something. The warden wanted her dead. Tha's why he sent her to me. But I'm tellin' yous, Grace is okay. She ain't the way they made her out to be in court and on TV. Just give her a chance.'

Slowly, grudgingly, the women began to include Grace in their conversations. Winning their acceptance, and later their affection, meant more to Grace than she could express. Society had labeled the women of Bedford Hills as criminals, as outcasts. Now, for the first time, Grace wondered if perhaps it was *society* that was criminal, for casting them out in the first place. Grace had lived the American Dream all her life. The fantasy of wealth, freedom and the pursuit of happiness had been her reality since the day she was born. Here, at Bedford Hills, she witnessed the flip side of that golden coin: the hopelessness of poverty, the unbreakable cycle of fractured families, poor education, drugs and crime, the iron grip of gang culture.

141

It's all just a lottery. Prison was these women's destiny, the same way wealth and luxury was mine.

Until someone stole it from me.

Grace was luckier than most inmates. She had something rare and priceless, something that other girls at Bedford would have given their eyeteeth for: a sense of purpose. Here, in jail, Grace finally had something to *do*, other than shop for designer clothes or plan her next dinner party. She had to find out what really happened at Quorum. It wasn't about freedom. It was about justice. About truth.

If Grace had to pick one word to describe how her first year in prison made her feel, it would have been *liberating*. That, perhaps, was the greatest irony of all.

From nine till three every day, Grace worked at the children's center. The work was rewarding and fun. Kids came in daily to spend time with their mothers, and though the bond between parent and child was usually obvious, both sides sometimes struggled to fill the hours in such an artificial environment. Grace's job was to make that easier by providing some structure: story time, reading lessons, art classes, anything that moms and kids could enjoy together without having to think too hard about where they were and why. The children's center was the only place at Bedford Hills where inmates were allowed to dress in 'outside' clothing, provided for them by the Sisters of Mercy. Sister Theresa, who ran the facility, made a strong case to Warden McIntosh. 'The children are frightened by the uniforms. It's tough enough rebuilding maternal relationships without making Mommy *look* like a stranger.'

Grace loved the feel of ordinary cotton against her skin. She loved the cheerful routine of the work: planning activities, laying tables with jars of paint, brushes and paper, playing games with the kids that she remembered from her own childhood. Most of all, she loved the kids themselves. When Lenny was alive, she'd never felt the desire to have children. But now that he was gone, it was as if a switch had flipped inside her. All her natural, maternal feelings came flooding out.

Working at the center, Grace was aware of a feeling of inner peace, a sort of low hum of contentment that followed her everywhere. It was the only place she could shut out thoughts of Lenny, and John Merrivale, and how he had betrayed them. In her simple cotton blouse and long wool skirt, it was hard to distinguish Grace from the nuns who ran the center. It occurred to her that prison life was not so unlike the world of the convent: enclosed, ordered, the days made up of a repeated series of simple, satisfying tasks. At the children's center, Grace felt the same deep peace of a nun fulfilling her vocation. Except that she had not found God. Hers was a mission of a different kind.

The only downside to Grace's work at the center came in the form of Lisa Halliday. Another A-Wing lifer, Lisa had been sent to Bedford Hills after an armed robbery that left a store clerk permanently paralyzed. An aggressive bull dyke with close-shaven blond hair and a livid scar across her chin, Lisa Halliday was viewed as a leader by the prison's white inmates, a small but vocal minority. Inmate leaders played an important role in the running of any prison, something Warden McIntosh understood only too well. He had given Lisa Halliday a cushy work detail, and the job at the children's center had appeased her for a while. Until Grace Brookstein showed up. Lisa Halliday made no secret of her loathing for Grace, whom she considered to be Cora Budds's 'pet' and a traitor to the white girls at Bedford. Not to mention a stuck-up bitch who'd somehow gotten the warden wrapped around her little finger. Lisa never missed an opportunity to bully Grace, or to try to get her into trouble.

The real work of Grace's days began after three, when she was allowed two hours in the prison library. Davey Buccola had promised to help her, but Grace had heard nothing from Davey in months. Impatient to make some progress, she devoted all her free time to researching Quorum. There was a lot to learn. Following Davey's advice, she had started at the beginning. She read about the stock market, what it was and how it worked. She discovered for the first time what a hedge fund actually *did* – it had never occurred to her to ask Lenny. She researched endless articles on the economy. In the past, terms like *credit crunch* and *bailout* had washed over her. Grace had no idea what they actually meant. Now she made it her business to know. She wanted to understand why companies like Lehman Brothers had failed. Why so many people had lost their jobs and their homes because of Quorum. The first few months were like painting the background to a huge canvas. Only once she'd finished the sky and the stormy sea could Grace begin work on the ship itself: the fraud that had brought her here. That, of course, was the most intricate, difficult part of the picture.

The main problem with hedge funds, Grace learned, was that they operated behind a veil of secrecy. Top managers like Lenny never gave away their investment strategies, let alone specific details about individual trades. And that was perfectly legal.

Karen Willis asked Grace, 'So how did people know what they were buying into? If it was all such a big secret.'

'They didn't,' said Grace. 'They looked at past performance and took a bet on future performance.'

'Like betting on a horse, you mean?'

'I suppose so. Yes.'

'Kind of a big risk, don't you think?'

'That depends on how much you trust the manager.'

People had trusted Lenny. They had trusted Quorum.

But something had gone terribly wrong. The more she studied the press reports, the more Grace understood why the FBI had failed so singularly in their attempts to trace the missing money. With so much secrecy and funds passing between countless different accounts, onshore, offshore, all over the planet, it was like combing a beach for a specific grain of sand. Shares were sold before they had been bought, creating 'phantom' profits that were then leveraged, multiplied three, four, ten times before being reinvested in derivative structures so complicated they made Grace's eyes water.

Davey Buccola finally came to visit her. From the look on his face, Grace could tell he had news. She could barely contain her excitement.

'It was John Merrivale, wasn't it? He stole the money. I knew it.'

'I don't know who stole the money.'

Grace's face fell. 'Oh.'

'My investigation took a different turn.'

Davey's expression looked sober, his lips pressed together in a grim line. Grace's stomach began to churn.

'What do you mean? What sort of a turn.'

Davey thought, *When I walked in here, she looked so happy. I'm about to blow her world apart. And what if I'm wrong?* Then he thought, *I'm not wrong.* He leaned across the table and took Grace's hand.

'Mrs Brookstein.'

'Grace.'

'Grace. I'm sorry to have to tell you this. But I believe your husband was murdered.'

'I'm sorry?' The room began to spin. Grace clutched the table for support.

'Lenny didn't kill himself.'

145

'I know that. It was an accident. The storm . . .' Her words trailed off into silence.

'It wasn't an accident. I spent months looking into Merrivale's activities at Quorum,' said Davey, 'but I found I was chasing my tail. So I decided to look at your husband instead. I went back over his disappearance, the investigation, what happened on Nantucket the day of the storm. Finally I looked at the autopsy.'

Grace swallowed. 'Go on.'

'It was a shambles. A joke. Death by drowning was assumed because the cadaver was washed up and because there was water in the lungs. When all this Quorum shit came to light, they ruled suicide because they figured there was a motive. But water in the lungs doesn't necessarily mean the person drowned.'

'It doesn't?'

'That body had been in the water for over a month. Of course the lungs were saturated. The question you need to ask yourself in a death like this is, how did the person *get* into the water in the first place, and was he alive or dead when he got there.'

'So you think . . .'

'I think your husband was dead before he hit the water. There was no blood in the lungs. Drowning at sea, in a heavy storm like that . . . the pressure of so much water entering the lungs so suddenly would almost certainly cause a hemorrhage.'

'*Almost* certainly?'

'It wasn't just the lungs. There were other signs, the bruises to the torso. Scratches on the fingers and upper arms that could have been indicative of a struggle. And the way the head was severed. I saw the pictures. Just look at the vertebrae. That wasn't *fish*. Not unless the fish had a guillotine. Or a meat cleaver.'

146

Grace put her hand over her mouth and retched.

'Oh, shit, I'm sorry. I didn't mean to be so graphic. Are you okay?'

Grace shook her head. She would never be okay again. She took a deep breath, struggling to control her emotions.

'Why didn't any of this come out at the inquest?'

'Some of it did. The bruising was mentioned, but dismissed. No one wanted to see the truth. Not at that time. You have to remember, your husband was the most hated man in America. Maybe it was just easier to think of him as a suicide, a coward, rather than a victim?'

'*Easier?*' Grace's head was spinning. It was all too much to take in.

Davey said, 'I wanted to tell you first. I know it's a hell of a shock, but this is actually good news. I think we have enough here to ask to have the inquest reopened, Grace. It would be the first step toward launching a murder investigation.'

Grace was silent for a long time. At last she said, 'No. I don't want the police involved.'

'But, Grace . . .'

'No.'

Someone had killed Lenny. Butchered him like an animal and tossed him into the waves. What use were the police, or the courts, or the whole corrupt, disgusting so-called justice system? *What justice was there for Lenny, or for me? America damned us both, for no better reason than that it was 'easier.' They let Lenny's killer walk away and left me here to rot. Well, damn America. The time for justice is past.*

Davey was confused. 'What *do* you want me to do?'

'I want you to find out who did it. If it was John Merrivale or someone else. I want to know who killed my husband. I want to know how he did it, and why. I want to know everything and I want to be sure. I'm not interested in reasonable doubt.'

Davey said, 'Okay. And then?'

'And then we'll think about next steps.'

And then I'm going to kill him.

After lights-out, Grace lay awake, her mind racing.

Whoever murdered Lenny had to have been on Nantucket the day of the storm. It could have been a stranger. But she knew that was unlikely. *It was someone close to us. It had to be. Someone close to Quorum. To the missing money.*

She thought back to the vacation, to their houseguests.

Connie and Michael.

Honor and Jack.

Maria and Andrew.

Caroline and John.

The Quorum family. Except they weren't family. They weren't friends. All of them had abandoned Grace in her hour of need.

One of them had killed Lenny.

Grace no longer wanted justice. She wanted vengeance. She would *have* vengeance.

That night, Grace Brookstein began planning her escape.

Chapter Thirteen

Karen Willis rubbed her eyes. It was two in the morning and Grace Brookstein was climbing into her bed.

'Grace? What is it? Are you sick?'

Grace shook her head. Beneath the blanket, the two of them huddled together for warmth. Karen felt the softness of Grace's breasts against her back. The smell of her skin, the soft caress of her breath. Instinctively, she slid a hand under Grace's nightdress, reaching for the silky wetness between her thighs.

'I love you.' Karen pressed her lips to Grace's. For a few glorious seconds, Grace responded, kissing her back. Then she pulled away.

'I'm sorry. I . . . I can't.'

Grace felt torn. Part of her was tempted to accept the comfort Karen was offering. After all, Lenny was gone. And Grace loved Karen, too, in a way. But she knew it wasn't right. She didn't love Karen in *that* way. Not really. Even if she had, it would have been wrong to raise her hopes. Especially considering what she was about to tell her.

Karen looked anguished. How could she have been so

149

stupid? She'd misread the signals. 'Oh God. Are you angry with me?'

'No. Not at all. Why would I be?'

'I would never have made a move if I hadn't thought . . . I mean, you came into my bed.'

'I know. I'm sorry. Look, it was my fault,' said Grace. 'I needed to talk to you. I need your advice.'

'My advice?'

'Uh-huh. I'm going to escape.'

It was the break in the tension Karen needed. She laughed so hard she almost woke Cora.

Grace didn't get it. 'What's so funny?'

'Oh, Grace! You can't be serious!'

'I'm deadly serious.'

'Honey, it's impossible. No one's ever escaped from Bedford Hills.'

Grace shrugged. 'There's a first time for everything, right?'

'Not for this.' Karen wasn't laughing anymore. 'You actually mean it, don't you? You're out of your mind Grace. Have you looked outside lately? There are nine barbed-wire fences between us and freedom, all of them electrified. There are guards and dogs and cameras and guns.'

'I know all that.'

'Then you're not thinking clearly. Look, even if you found some way to escape – which you won't, because it's impossible – you have one of the most recognizable faces in America. How far do you think you'll get?'

Grace ran a hand over her broken nose. 'I'm not so recognizable anymore. I don't look the way I used to. Anyway, I can disguise myself.'

'When they catch you, they'll shoot you. No questions asked.'

'I know that, too. It's a risk I'm prepared to take.'

Karen stroked Grace's cheek in the darkness. This was

madness. No one escaped from Bedford Hills. If Grace tried it, she'd be killed for sure. Even if, by some miracle, she were captured alive, it still meant Karen would never see her again. Grace would be transferred to solitary. Sent out of state. Locked up in some secret CIA holding pen never to be heard of again.

'Don't do this, Grace. Please. I don't want to lose you.'

Grace saw Karen's eyes well up. Leaning forward, she kissed her full on the mouth. It was a passionate, lingering kiss. A kiss to be remembered by. A kiss good-bye.

'I have to do it, Karen.'

'No you don't. Why?'

'Because Lenny was murdered, okay?'

Karen sat up. '*Whaaat?* Says who?'

'Davey Buccola. He found evidence, stuff that was suppressed at the inquest.'

So Buccola put her up to this. I'll kill him.

'I have to find out who killed my husband.'

'But, Grace – '

'I'm going to find him. And then I'm going to kill him.'

Grace waited for the outrage, the shock, but it never came. Instead Karen put her arms around her and hugged her tightly. Karen remembered Billy, her sister's boyfriend. How *right* it had felt when that bullet hit him between the eyes. Despite everything that had happened since, she had never regretted what she'd done. She did not want to lose Grace. But she understood.

'I assume you have a plan?'

'Actually, that's what I wanted to talk to you about . . .'

Sister Agnes watched Grace Brookstein clearing away a jigsaw puzzle and offered up a silent prayer to the Lord:

Thank You for bringing me this lost soul, Jesus. Thank You for allowing me to be the vessel of Your redeeming grace.

Sister Agnes had only been Sister Agnes for five years. Before that, she was Tracey Grainger, a lonely, unpopular teenage girl from Frenchtown, New Jersey. Tracey Grainger had fallen in love with a local boy named Gordon Hicks. Gordon had told her he loved her and Tracey had believed him. When Gordon got her pregnant, then promptly abandoned her, Tracey went home and swallowed as many pills as she could find. The baby did not survive.

Neither did Tracey Grainger.

The girl who woke up from that overdose in a grimly sterile hospital bed, clutching her stomach and weeping with guilt, was not the same girl whom Gordon Hicks had so peremptorily dumped. She was not the same straight-C student who had disappointed her parents since the day she was born. She was not the same socially awkward, unlovable tenth grader whom no one invited to prom. This girl was an entirely new person. A person loved by God. A person of value. A person whose sins had been forgiven, who would one day become one with Jesus at the right hand of the Father. If anyone believed in the power of redemption, it was Sister Agnes. God had redeemed her. He had saved her life. Now, in His infinite love and mercy, He had redeemed Grace Brookstein, too. And He had allowed *her*, Sister Agnes, to play a small part in the miracle.

Only this morning, Grace told her, 'I feel so fulfilled here, Sister. Working with these children. With you. It's like I've been given a second chance at life.'

What a warm glow of satisfaction those words had given her! Sister Agnes hoped she was not guilty of the mortal sin of pride. She must remember that it was God who had transformed Grace, not her. And yet Sister Agnes couldn't help but feel that her friendship *had* contributed to some of the changes in Grace.

Grace had changed Sister Agnes, too. A nun's life could

be lonely. Most of the other Sisters of Mercy were old enough to be Sister Agnes's mother, if not her grandmother. Over the last few months she had come to cherish the easy friendship she seemed to have developed with Grace Brookstein. The shared glances. The smiles. The trust.

Grace put the puzzle pieces back into their box then stacked it neatly on the shelf. Sister Agnes smiled warmly.

'Thank you, Grace. I can finish up here. I know you want to get to the library.'

'That's all right,' said Grace cheerfully. 'I'm happy to help. Oh, by the way, that modeling clay that we ordered last week? We need to return it.'

'Do we? Why?'

'I opened seven or eight of the crates this morning, and the stuff inside had completely dried out. I tried soaking it in water but it just ended up all slimy. It'll have to go back.'

What a pain, thought Sister Agnes. It had taken her the better part of a day to stack those crates in the children's center storeroom with Sister Theresa. Now she'd have to lug the stupid things back out again.

'I e-mailed the delivery company,' said Grace. 'They're coming to pick them up on Tuesday at four o'clock.'

'Tuesday?' Sister Agnes looked pained. 'Oh, Grace, it was kind of you to arrange it. But I can't supervise a pickup on Tuesday, I'm afraid. A delegation from the department of corrections will be here for a tour. Sister Theresa and I have our quarterly budget meeting with them afterward. We'll be out all afternoon.'

'Oh.' Grace looked disappointed. Then she suddenly brightened. 'Perhaps I could do it?'

Sister Agnes frowned. 'I don't know about that, Grace.'

Inmates in the A-Wing were not supposed to help with pickups or deliveries. The warden considered it a potential security risk. But Grace had come so far in her rehabilitation.

Sister Agnes would hate to give her the impression that she wasn't trusted.

Grace said, 'The children have already waited weeks. It seems a shame to delay things even further.'

'Those crates are heavy, Grace,' Sister Agnes said awkwardly. 'It's a two-person job.'

'Cora can help me.'

'Cora Budds?' This idea was going from bad to worse.

'She has KP duty on Tuesdays but she's usually finished by three.'

Grace looked so hopeful, so eager to please. Sister Agnes wavered. *What harm can it do? Just this once.*

'Well, I suppose . . . if you're sure you and Cora can handle it . . .'

Grace smiled. 'Loading a delivery truck? Yes, Sister. I think we can manage that.'

Her heart was pounding so loudly she was surprised Sister Agnes couldn't hear it. She was a sweet, kind woman and Grace felt bad deceiving her. But it couldn't be helped.

It was starting.

Grace Brookstein's planned escape attempt rapidly became the worst-kept secret at Bedford Hills. The idea was simple: The delivery truck would arrive at the children's center. Grace and Cora Budds would begin loading up the crates of clay. While Cora distracted the driver, Grace would go back into the storeroom, empty one of the crates and hide herself inside it. Cora would complete the loading on her own, making sure that the lid of Grace's crate was not fully sealed, to allow her some air, and that it was hidden well back among the others.

It was the next part of the plan that was the wild card. Everything rested on the security check. Trucks came in and out of Bedford Hills every day, delivering everything from toilet paper to detergent to food. The prison was equipped with state-of-the-art security systems. As well as manual searches, the guards used sniffer dogs and even infrared scanners to spot-check vehicles, in addition to the CCTV cameras that were everywhere at Bedford. Typically, the more thorough searches took place on the way *in* to the prison. There was less emphasis on what might be going out. But *all* searches were at the guards' discretion. If they didn't like the look of a driver, or a vehicle, or if they just felt like it for whatever reason, they could hold people up four hours, X-raying every square inch of their car or person. Grace hoped that on a cold January night, the guards' appetite for hauling out crate after crate of children's modeling clay would be low. But she wouldn't know until they got to the checkpoint.

Once the truck was waved through, if it was waved through, and they drove clear of Bedford, Grace would climb out of the crate and make her way to the rear doors. As soon as the driver stopped at a junction, she would open the door of the truck and jump to freedom.

Easy.

'It's not going to work.'

Karen leaned across the table and helped herself to Grace's watery mashed potatoes. They were at lunch, a few days before the breakout was supposed to take place.

'Thanks for the vote of confidence.'

'Have you thought about what you're gonna do if you *do* make it out of here?'

Grace had thought of little else. When she fantasized about her escape, she pictured herself as the hunter, unmasking Lenny's killer, wreaking her revenge. But the reality was that *she* would also be hunted down. If she were going to survive, she'd need food, shelter, money and a disguise. She had no idea how she was going to obtain any of them.

155

'What about friends on the outside. Is there anybody you can trust? Anyone who'll cover for you?'

Grace shook her head. 'No. No one.'

There was one person she trusted. Davey Buccola. Davey was working on new information, checking out the alibis for everyone who'd stayed with Grace and Lenny on Nantucket the day Lenny died. If Grace turned to anyone on the outside, it would be him. But she wasn't about to tell Karen that.

'In that case, we need to fix you up with a survival pack from here.'

'A survival pack?'

'Sure. You'll need a new identity. A few new identities, so you can keep moving. Driver's licenses, credit cards, some cash. You won't get very far as Grace Brookstein.'

'Where am I going to get a driver's license from, Karen? Or a credit card. It's impossible.'

'Said the woman who figures she's going to escape from Bedford Hills! Don't sweat the small stuff, Grace. Leave that to me.'

Karen had warned Grace that she would need to let 'a few of the girls' in on the escape plan in order to get what they needed in such a short space of time. To Grace's horror, 'a few of the girls' turned out to be almost every inmate at Bedford. Forging a credit card and a driver's license was no mean feat. Karen was forced to corral help from all over the prison. Inmates in the warden's office, the library, and the computer room typed, Photoshopped and laminated for days, all of them risking their own paroles and futures for a chance to help Grace and be part of the Great Escape. The only people who *didn't* know about the plan were the guards and Lisa Halliday.

It was debatable whether Lisa would have snitched on Grace – powerful inmates could attack their rivals with impunity but selling out another prisoner was still considered taboo. Still Karen wasn't prepared to risk it.

Grace was grateful for everyone's help, but she was nervous. 'Too many people know.'

'They're not "people,"' Karen told her. 'They're your friends. You can trust them.'

Trust. It was a word from another life, another planet.

Tuesday morning dawned gray and cold. Grace had barely slept. All night long, the voices haunted her:

Lenny: *Whatever happens, Grace, I love you.*

John Merrivale: *Don't worry, Grace. Just do what Frank Hammond tells you and you'll be fine.*

Karen: *When they catch you, they'll shoot you, no questions asked.*

Grace didn't touch her oatmeal at breakfast.

'You need your strength,' Cora Budds told her. 'Eat somethin'.'

'I can't. I'll throw up.'

The big black woman narrowed her eyes. 'I ain't asking you, Grace. I'm tellin' you. You better get it together, girl. I'm putting my hide on the line for you today. We all are. Now eat.'

She's right. I can do this. I have to do it.

Grace ate.

'Are you sure you're all right, Grace? Perhaps you should go and lie down.'

It was noon at the children's center. The delegation of senior prison officials was due to arrive at twelve-thirty. The morning had been spent tidying up desks and toys, putting up fresh artwork, and generally ensuring that the facility looked its very best. If the delegation was impressed, they might raise the budget. Or at least not slash it. Grace had

157

worked diligently as usual, but Sister Agnes was worried about her. Her complexion had been green when she arrived for work this morning. Now it had faded to sickly off-white. A moment ago, reaching up to a high shelf to rearrange some books, she'd become dizzy and almost fainted.

'I'm fine, Sister.'

'I don't think you are fine. The infirmary ought to take a look at you.'

'No!' Grace felt her throat go dry with panic. *You can't send me to the infirmary. Not today. What if they keep me all afternoon?* She remembered what Cora said to her at breakfast. She had to pull herself together. 'I'm a little dehydrated, that's all. Perhaps I could have a glass of water?'

Sister Agnes went to fetch the water. While she was gone Grace pinched her cheeks and took some deep, calming breaths. By the time the nun returned, she looked slightly better.

From the far corner of the room, Lisa Halliday watched the scene with suspicion. 'What's up with Lady Brookstein?' she asked one of the mothers, a young black woman who hadn't been at Bedford long. 'She's been acting weird as shit all morning, even by her standards.'

'Wouldn't you be if you was gonna bust out of here?' said the girl. One look at Lisa's face told her she'd screwed up big-time. But by then it was too late.

'What'd you say?'

'Nothing. I was just . . . I don't know what I'm talking about. It's just some crazy rumors.'

Lisa Halliday put her face within an inch of the girl's. 'Tell me.'

'Please. I . . . I shouldn'ta said nuthin'. Cora'll kill me.'

'Tell me everything or I'll make sure the warden never lets you see your kid again.'

'Please, Lisa.'

'You think I can't do it?'

The girl thought about her son, Tyrone. He was three years old, as cute and chubby as a puppy. He'd be here in a half hour, snuggling up to her, drawing pictures for her to keep in her cell.

She started to talk.

Hannah Denzel knitted her beetle brows into one long, angry caterpillar as she led the VIPs down the hall to the children's center

'This way, ladies and gentlemen.'

Denny did not like showing 'delegations' around Bedford Hills. Today's self-important posse of politicians and police officers was as bad as all the others: the do-gooder prison visitors, the priests, the social workers, the therapists, the nuns, the whole goddamn army of meddlesome outsiders who infested her territory twice a year with their clipboards and recommendations. None of them seemed to realize that these women were vermin. That they were at Bedford Hills to be punished, not saved. It made Denny sick.

The group 'oohed' and 'aahed' over the children's center, scattering among the pristine workstations and play areas. Warden McIntosh stood watching them like a proud father. Then his face changed. Grace Brookstein was hovering by one of the bookcases looking pale and ill. *Damn it*. He'd completely forgotten about Grace. The last thing he needed was to have his most notorious prisoner distracting the group's attention from the jewel in Bedford's crown.

He whispered in Hannah Denzel's ear. 'Get her out of here. Quietly. She's a distraction.'

The prison guard's cruel eyes lit up. 'Yes, sir.' This was more like it. Walking over to Grace, she grabbed her roughly by the arm. 'Let's go, Brookstein. Back to your cell.'

'My cell? But I-I can't,' Grace stammered. 'I'm working.'

159

'Not anymore you're not. Move it.'

Grace opened her mouth to protest but no sound came out. Panic rose up in her throat like vomit.

'Is something the matter?' Sister Agnes glided over. 'Can I help?'

'No,' snapped Denny, pushing Grace toward the door. She resented the Sisters of Mercy's presence at Bedford Hills. Sister Agnes should back the fuck off to her rosary and leave the inmates to the professionals. 'Warden wants this one on lockdown. And he *doesn't* want a scene.'

Grace looked pleadingly at Sister Agnes. *Help me!*

The nun smiled kindly at her friend. 'Don't look so woebegone, Grace. You could do with a little rest. Enjoy your afternoon off. We'll still be here tomorrow.'

Yes. And now so will I, thought Grace. She could have wept.

It was three forty-five before Lisa Halliday was able to get out of the children's center. That slave-driving do-gooder Sister Theresa had given her a list of chores as long as her police record. Sprinting to the warden's office, she marched up to the reception desk.

'I need to see the warden,' she panted. 'It's urgent.'

The receptionist looked at the surly bull dyke in front of her and stiffened. 'Warden McIntosh can't see anybody today. He has a delegation – '

'Like I said. It's urgent.'

'I'm sorry,' the girl repeated. 'He's not here.'

'Well, where is he?'

The receptionist's tone got frostier. 'Out. He's in meetings all afternoon. Is it something I can help you with?'

'No,' Lisa said rudely. 'I want the organ grinder, not the friggin' monkey.' She had to see the warden and she had to see him alone. If word got out that she was the fink

160

who'd sold out Grace Brookstein, she'd be finished at Bedford Hills.

'Then there's nothing I can do.'

Lisa sank her great bulk down onto one of the hard chairs lining the wall.

'Fine. I'll wait.'

Cora Budds left her job in the kitchen at ten of four and hurried over to the children's center as arranged. Two mothers were saying good-bye to their kids while a single, bored guard looked on.

Cora asked one of the mothers, 'Where's Grace?'

'In lockdown. Denny dragged her off hours ago. She didn't look well.'

Cora thought, *I bet she didn't. That's it, then. If Grace is in lockdown, the whole plan goes up in smoke.*

She walked into the storeroom alone. *Maybe it's for the best.*

Grace sat on her bunk, staring into space. She was too drained to cry. It was over. God knew when she'd have a chance to try again. Maybe not for years. Years in which whoever killed Lenny would be out there, free, happy, unpunished. The thought was unbearable.

Mindlessly, she looked at the clock on the wall: 3:55 . . . 4:00 . . . 4:05 . . . The truck would be there by now. Cora would be loading it, alone, wondering what had happened.

At 4:08, Grace heard the jangle of keys in the lock. Karen's shift must have ended early. At least *she'd* be pleased the escape plan had failed. The door swung open.

'Get up.' Denny's eyes blazed with spite. She'd been brooding all day over Sister Agnes's words to Grace. *Enjoy your afternoon off.* As if this were some sort of summer camp! There were no *afternoons off* at Bedford Hills. 'You

161

missed four hours of work detail this afternoon, you sneaky little bitch. Thought you were on vacation, did you? A free pass?'

Grace said meekly, 'No, ma'am.'

'Good. Because there are no fucking vacations in A Wing. Not while I'm in charge. You can make up those work hours, starting right now. Get your ass over to the children's center and start scrubbing the floors.'

'Yes, ma'am.'

'When you've finished, do it again. And you can forget about eating tonight. You stay on that floor, scrubbing, till I come for you, understand?'

'Yes, ma'am.'

'MOVE!'

Grace bolted out of the cell and started running down the corridor. Denny watched her go, a slow smile of satisfaction spreading across her face.

She had no idea that Grace was running for her life.

Cora Budds had almost finished loading the crates.

The truck driver grumbled, 'I thought there was gonna be two of yous? I'da brought another guy if I'd known.'

Cora shrugged. 'Life's a bitch, ain't it?' It was already dark in the cramped courtyard backing on to the children's center storeroom. The temperature was below zero, but the biting wind made it feel even colder. The boxes were small, about two feet square. Looking at them, Cora couldn't imagine how Grace had ever thought she was gonna squeeze herself inside one. They were also heavy. Their weight, combined with the finger-numbing cold, made the work slow going.

'Sorry I'm late.'

Grace stood shivering in the lamplight. Still in her skirt and thin cotton, she was ridiculously underdressed for the winter evening. The wind sliced into her skin like razor blades.

162

Cora Budds's eyes widened in surprise but she said nothing.

The driver looked pissed. 'Are you kidding me? This is your number two? She couldn't lift a cup of coffee, never mind a crate of clay.'

'Sure she can,' said Cora. 'You can leave it to us now.'

'Fine by me.' The driver climbed back into the welcoming warmth of the cab. 'One of you ladies give me the nod when you're done.'

Back in the storeroom, Cora and Grace worked quickly. Sister Agnes or one of the guards could come back any minute. Cora pulled Grace's documents out of the pocket in her jumpsuit, stuffing them into Grace's bra. There were four fake IDs with matching credit cards, a slip of paper with an anonymous Hotmail address on it and a small wad of cash.

'Karen has a friend on the outside who'll wire you more money with Western Union when you need it. Just e-mail an amount, the zip code you're in, and the initials of the fake ID you're using, and this person will do the rest. Take this, too.' She handed Grace a silver stiletto. 'You never know.'

Grace stared at the blade in her palm for a second, hesitating, then slipped it into her shoe. Cora pried open the lid of one of the crates, emptying its contents at lightning speed. Somehow the box looked even smaller when it was empty.

Cora said, 'I don' think it's possible, Grace. A cat couldn't fit in there.'

Grace smiled. 'It's possible. I was a gymnast when I was younger. Watch.'

Cora watched in awe as Grace climbed into the box, ass first, folding her tiny limbs around herself like a double-jointed spider. 'Girl, that looks painful.' She winced. 'You sure you're okay?'

'It's not exactly first-class travel, but I'll live. Try the lid. Am I in?'

Cora tried it. Easy. About an inch to spare. She levered it open again. 'You're in. I'm gonna load the rest of 'em now. I'll put you three rows back, so you're hidden at the checkpoint, but leave the lid loose so you got some air.'

'Thanks.'

'Sit tight till you get through the checkpoint. Once you're outta here, soon as the truck stops, you jump.'

'Got it. Thanks, Cora. For everything.'

Good luck, Amazing Grace.

Cora Budds replaced the lid and carried Grace out into the darkness.

Warden McIntosh eyed Lisa Halliday suspiciously.

'This had better not be some sort of scam.'

'It ain't.'

'Grace Brookstein is in lockdown. She's been in her cell since lunchtime. Besides, A-Wing prisoners never work on deliveries. Sister Agnes knows the policy.'

'Sister Agnes don't know her pussy from her paternoster.'

'That's enough!' the warden snapped. 'I won't have you disrespecting our voluntary staff.'

'Look. You don't wanna check the truck? Fine. Don't check it. Jus' don' say I didn't warn you.'

Warden McIntosh did not want to check the truck. It had been a long day. He wanted to finish up his paperwork and get home to his wife. But he knew he had no choice.

'All right, Lisa. Leave it with me.'

The darkness was disorienting. Grace heard the rear doors of the truck slam shut. For a moment fear gripped her: *I'm trapped!* But then she relaxed, forcing herself to take slow, even breaths. It was uncomfortable, coiled inside the crate like a marionette, but she could bear the position. The cold, on the other hand, was debilitating. Limb by limb, Grace felt

164

her body start to go numb. Her head ached violently, as if she'd just sunk her teeth into an ice cube.

The engine rumbled to life. *We're moving.* Soon, all Grace could hear was the beating of her own heart. She said a silent prayer:

Please God, don't let them check all the boxes.

The thud was so loud, the driver heard it through his blaring Bruce Springsteen CD. One of the crates must have come loose.

'What the fuck?' Slamming on the brakes, he climbed out of the cab. *Dumb-ass fucking dykes. How hard is it to stack a bunch of boxes? All they had to do was put 'em one on top of another.*

Grace heard the rear door open. Rays from a flashlight seeped through the crack above her head, where Cora had left the lid loose. She held her breath

'Goddamn it.'

Crates scraped noisily across the metal floor of the truck. The next thing Grace knew, her own box was moving. *Oh God, no! He'll see me.* But the driver didn't see her. Instead, pulling Grace's crate forward, he noticed the loose lid and banged it shut with his fist. Then he lifted another box and piled it on top of Grace's. The rear door slammed. Grace felt the lurch of the truck as it pulled away.

Cold beads of sweat broke out all over Grace's body.

She had no air.

I'm going to suffocate.

Chapter Fourteen

Warden McIntosh stormed into the children's center. All the kids had gone home. A lone inmate was clearing away the last of the toys.

'You alone here?'

'Yes, sir. I'm waiting for Sister Agnes to come back and lock up.'

'There was a pickup scheduled for four P.M. today. Did that happen?'

'I think so, sir. Cora Budds was in the storeroom.'

'What about Grace Brookstein? Have you seen her in here this afternoon?'

'No, sir. Cora tol' me she's in lockdown.'

Warden McIntosh relaxed. *Lisa Halliday had gotten it wrong. Grapevine information was often unreliable at Bedford.* Still, protocols had to be followed. He picked up the phone on Sister Agnes's desk.

I'm going to die!

Grace was already hyperventilating. As she felt the truck stop, her hopes soared. They must be at the checkpoint. She tried to scream.

'Help! Somebody help me!'

For weeks, she had dreaded this moment, terrified that the guards would discover her. Now she was terrified that they wouldn't. Without air, she would die in this box long before the truck reached the depot

'Help!' She was yelling as loudly as she could, but her lungs didn't seem to be working properly. The words came out soft and breathy, muffled by the crates above and to the side of her. The guards heard nothing.

'What's this lot, then?'

The driver handed over his paperwork. 'Modeling clay. About two tons of the stuff.'

'All right. Let's take a look.'

The two guards began opening the first row of boxes.

Please! I'm here!

Grace knew in that moment that she didn't want to die. Not yet. Not like this.

I have to find Lenny's murderer first. I have to make them pay.

She started to feel dizzy. Aware she was beginning to lose consciousness, she called out again.

One of the guards stopped. 'Did you hear anything?'

His companion shook his head. 'Only my teeth chattering. It's friggin' cold out here, man. Come on, man, let's get this over with.' Pulling forward another crate, he dumped it on the ground, opened it, and checked inside. He did the same with another. Then another. As he was opening the fourth, the driver pleaded, 'Come on, you guys, give me a break, wouldya? You know how long this shit took to load? I got a six-hour drive ahead a me and I'm freezing my ass off.'

The guards looked at each other. They could hear the distant ringing of a telephone, back inside their warm, comfortable surveillance tower.

'Okay. You're good to go.' They signed the driver's papers and handed them back to him. 'Drive safe.'

Sixty seconds later, the truck was cruising out through the prison gates.

Grace Brookstein was still inside.

Grace awoke to the sound of the engine gaining speed. Relief overwhelmed her.

I can breathe! I'm alive.

One of the guards must have loosened the lid of her crate! *Why didn't they find me? It's a miracle. Someone up there must be looking out for me. Maybe it's Lenny, come back as my guardian angel?*

For a few seconds she felt euphoric. *I made it out of Bedford. I did it!* But reality soon reasserted itself. She was a long way from being home free. Uncurling herself slowly and painfully like an arthritic jack-in-the-box, Grace pushed up the lid and climbed out of her cramped hiding place. The rear of the truck was freezing and pitch-dark. It took a minute for the circulation to return to her legs. As soon as she felt strong enough, she began to stumble forward, hands stretched out in front of her like a zombie, feeling for the truck's rear door. After what felt like an eternity, her fingers stumbled upon a handle. It was stiff. She couldn't move it. Just as she was wondering whether the driver had double-locked the doors from the outside so she wouldn't be able to open them, the handle suddenly shifted.

It all happened in an instant. The rear door flew open with such force Grace was pulled along with it. Suddenly she was outside, clinging on for dear life, her shins banging agonizingly against the bumper as she dangled one-handed above the ground. They were on an empty, unlit road, moving at incredible speed. *How fast? Fifty miles an hour? Sixty?* Grace tried to calculate her chances of survival if she fell. Before she came up with an answer, the road forked into a hairpin turn. The driver swung a sharp left. Grace felt the door handle slip from her grasp, as if it someone had dipped it in butter. Next thing she knew, she was flying through the air like a rag doll, hurtling toward the trees. The last thing she heard was the thud of her own skull hitting the ground.

Then nothing.

Warden McIntosh yelled at Hannah Denzel.

'Why the hell did you send her back to the center? Who gave you the authority?'

Denny bristled. If Grace Brookstein really *had* escaped, she was damned if she was going to take the blame. This was the warden's problem. 'I *have* the authority, sir. Work details on A-Wing are my responsibility. The delegation had left, and Grace had unfinished work. Who gave the Sisters authority to have A-Wing inmates supervise pickups?'

The two guards from the North Gate checkpoint were also in the warden's office. Warden McIntosh quizzed them. 'You're certain Grace Brookstein wasn't on that truck? You checked every crate?'

From the look on McIntosh's face, the guards figured honesty was probably not the best policy. 'Every crate. The truck was clean.'

Warden McIntosh's head was throbbing. *Then where the hell is she?* He turned back to Hannah Denzel. 'I want Cora Budds and Karen Willis in here right now. In the meantime, alert all police units. I want that truck found, stopped, and searched.' He looked at the two guards ominously. 'If you guys have fucked up, I'll have both your heads on a plate.'

'Yes, sir.' But everyone in the room knew that the first head to roll would be the warden's.

* * *

Grace opened her eyes slowly. Beneath her was a blanket of deep undergrowth. Springy and prickly like an old straw mattress, it must have broken her fall. Her head was filled with a loud whirring.

No. It's not in my head. It's overhead. Choppers.

They're looking for me.

She had no idea how long she'd been unconscious. Minutes? Hours? What she did know was that she was freezing cold, so cold that it was hard to move. She also knew that she was in grave danger. In the short time she'd been inside the truck, they could not have gotten more than a few miles away from Bedford Hills. She had to put some distance between herself and the prison.

Gingerly, Grace got to her feet. By some miracle, nothing seemed to be broken. Gradually her eyes acclimatized to the darkness and she could make out the shadows around her. She was standing in woodland just a few feet from a quiet country road. *Not quiet. Silent.* A single twig cracking beneath her feet sounded as loud as a thunderclap.

I have to get out of here.

Her left side was bruised and stiff, but she found she could walk without too much trouble. To her right, the tree line jutted up into a steep escarpment. From the top of the hill, Grace heard the dim rumble of traffic.

The police will be patrolling the main road. If I go up there, I triple my chances of being caught.

If I don't go up there, I won't get a ride out of here.

She started to climb.

At the top of the hill someone had planted a row of poplar trees, presumably as a sound barrier. Grace squatted low behind them, trying to get her breath. The climb had exhausted her. The road was busy, almost as if it were rush hour. Grace wondered again how late it was, but there was no time to dwell on that now. Brushing the icy leaves off of her skirt, she stepped out onto the side of the road and stuck out her thumb, the way she'd seen people do on TV.

I wonder how long it'll take for someone to stop. If I don't get inside soon, I could die of hypothermia.

A squad car screamed out of the darkness, blue lights flashing, sirens blaring. Instinctively Grace leaped back for the cover of the trees, twisting her ankle on the icy hard ground. It was agony but she didn't dare cry out, holding her breath in the darkness, waiting for the police car to slow or pull over. It didn't. After a few seconds the dying wail of the sirens faded to nothing. Grace crawled back out to the roadside.

Standing there, thumb out, stamping her feet against the subzero temperatures, Grace started to sway. She'd barely eaten all day, and the fall from the truck had left her weak and dizzy. Lights from the cars' headlamps began to merge into one solid orange glow. In Grace's frozen, confused state, it looked warm and welcoming. Half conscious, she staggered toward it. The deafening blare of a truck horn brought her back to her senses.

'Are you outta your mind, lady?'

A man had stopped. Pulled over onto the hard shoulder, he was talking to Grace out of the driver's-side window. Middle-aged, with a thick black mustache and dark eyes that sat flat on his face, he looked like he might be part Asian, but it was tough to be sure in the darkness. He was driving a light blue van with TOMMY'S YARD SERVICES written on the side in bold black lettering.

'Don't you have a coat?'

Grace shook her head. Pretty soon her whole body was shaking, racked with cold and exhaustion. The man reached over and opened the passenger door.

'Get in.'

BOOK TWO

Chapter Fifteen

Detective Mitch Connors returned to his desk in a pensive mood.

Is this a good thing, or a bad thing?

Tall, blond, athletic and altogether too big for his glass-walled office, Mitch Connors looked more like a football pro than a cop. Sinking into his uncomfortable chair (Helen had bought him the damn thing two years ago, for his back pain. It had won a bunch of design awards, apparently, and cost a small fortune, so he couldn't throw it away, but Mitch had always hated it), he stretched out his legs and tried to think.

Do I really want this case?

On the one hand, his boss had just handed him what would, in a few short hours, become the biggest, most high-profile investigation in the country. Late last night, Grace Brookstein had pulled off a dramatic escape from maximum-security prison. It would be Mitch Connors's job to find her, apprehend her and haul her thieving, designer-clad ass back to jail.

His boss said, 'You're the best, Mitch. I wouldn't put you on this if you weren't.' And Mitch had felt a warm glow.

But now he felt something else. Something bad. For the life of him, Mitch couldn't remember what it was.

He blamed the chair. It was so torturous, no wonder he couldn't concentrate. *Ergonomic, my ass. I figure Helen bought it on purpose to torment me. To pay me back for all the shit I put her through.* Then he thought, *That's bullshit, Connors, and you know it.*

Helen wasn't like that. She was an angel. Saint Helen of Pittsburgh, patron saint of tolerance.

And you drove her away.

Mitch Connors had grown up in Pittsburgh. He was born in the well-to-do suburb of Monroeville, where his mom was a local beauty queen. She married Mitch's dad, an inventor, when she was nineteen. Mitch arrived a year later and the couple's happiness was complete.

For about six months.

Mitch's father was a brilliant inventor . . . by night. By day, he was a traveling encyclopedia salesman. Mitch used to go on trips with him. The little boy would watch in awe as his dad scammed one housewife after another.

'Do you know the average cost of a college education, ma'am?'

Pete Connors was standing on the front steps of a dilapidated house in Genette, Pennsylvania, wearing a suit and tie and shiny black shoes, his trilby hat held respectfully in one hand. He was a handsome man. Mitch thought he looked like Frank Sinatra. The woman standing at the door in a stained housecoat was fat, depressed and defeated. Hungry kids ran around her feet like rats.

'No, sir. Can't say I do.'

The door was closing. Pete Connors stepped forward. 'Let me tell you. It's fifteen hundred dollars. Fifteen *hundred* dollars. Can you imagine that?'

She couldn't imagine.

'But what if I were to tell you that for as little as one dollar a week – that's right, *one* dollar – you can give your child the gift of that same education right here at home?'

'I never really thought about – '

'Of course you didn't! You're a busy woman. You have bills, responsibilities. You don't have time to sit down and read studies like this one.' At a given signal, Mitch would run forward and hand his father a laminated sheaf of papers with the words *Educational Research* printed on the front. 'Studies that prove that kids who have an encyclopedia in the house are more than *six times* more likely to go into white-collar jobs?'

'Well, I – '

'How'd you like for this little guy here to grow up and be a lawyer, huh?' Pete Connors slipped one of the dirty-faced children a boiled candy. 'For as little as one dollar a day, you can make that happen, ma'am.'

He was like a whirlwind. A force of nature. Some women he would bulldoze. Others he would charm and cajole. Others still he would take upstairs to perform some 'secret' sales technique that Mitch was never allowed to see. It always took around fifteen minutes, and it always worked. 'Those Pennsylvania women!' Mitch's dad would joke afterward. 'They're hungry for knowledge, all right. You ain't never *seen* a woman hungrier for knowledge than that one, Mitchy!'

After every sale, they would drive to the nearest small town or rest stop and Pete Connors would buy his son an enormous ice-cream sundae. Mitch would return home to his mother full of excitement and wonder, chocolate sauce smeared all over his face. *'Dad was amazing. You shoulda seen what Dad did! Guess how many we sold, Mom. Go on, guess!'*

Mitch could never understand why his mother never

wanted to guess. Why she looked at his dad with such bitterness and disappointment. Later – too late – he understood. She could have borne the infidelity. It was the recklessness she couldn't forgive. Pete Connors was a natural salesman, but he was also a dreamer, who regularly blew his earnings investing in one crackpot invention after another. Mitch remembered some of them. There was the vacuum cleaner you didn't have to push. That was going to make them millions. Then there was the mini-refrigerator for your car. The running shoes that massaged the ball of your foot. The clothes rack that got out creases. Mitch would watch his father work on each new design during weekends and late into the night. Whenever he finished a prototype, he would 'unveil' it in the living room in front of Mitch's mom.

'Whaddaya think, Lucy?' he'd ask hopefully, his face alight with pride and anticipation, like a little boy's. The tragedy was, Pete Connors loved his wife. He needed her approval so badly. If she'd given it, just once, perhaps things would've turned out differently. But her response was always the same.

'How much d'you blow this time?'

'Jeez, Lucy. Give me a break, would you? I'm an ideas man. You knew that when you married me.'

'Yeah? Well, here's an idea for you, Pete. How about we make our mortgage this month?'

Mitch's mom used to say that the only thing his father could ever economize on was the truth.

By Mitch's sixth birthday, they'd moved out of the Monroeville house. The new place was a condo in Murraysville. Next it was Millvale, an area full of old mill-workers' tenements. By the time Mitch was twelve, they were in the Hill District, Pittsburgh's Harlem, a boarded-up, drug-riddled hell bordering the prosperous downtown. Too poor to divorce, his parents 'separated.' Within a month, his mom had a new boyfriend. Eventually they moved to Florida, to a nice house with palm trees in the front yard. Mitch decided to stay with his dad.

Pete Connors was excited. 'This is great, Mitchy! It'll be like old times, just the two of us. We'll have poker nights. Sleep late on Sundays. Get some pretty girls over here, huh? Shake things up a bit!'

There were girls. Some of them were even pretty, but those ones were paid for. Pete Connors's Frank Sinatra days were long gone. He looked like what he was, a tired old roué long past his sell-by date. It broke Mitch's heart. As Mitch grew older, his father began to get jealous of his son's good looks. At seventeen, Mitch had his mother's blond hair and blue eyes and his father's long legs and strong, masculine features. He'd also inherited Pete's gift of gab.

'I'm just home for the summer, helping out my old man. I'm off to biz school in the fall . . .'

'My car? Oh, yeah, I sold it. My little cousin got sick. Leukemia. She's only six, poor kid. I wanted to help out with her medical bills.'

Women lapped it up.

Helen Brunner was different. She was twenty-five years old, a redheaded, green-eyed goddess, and she worked for a veterans' charity that provided impoverished ex-servicemen with meals and helped them out at home. Mitch never knew how his father had convinced Helen's charity that he'd been in the navy. Pete Connors couldn't even swim. Pictures of boats made him nauseous. In any event, Helen started showing up at the apartment three times a week. Pete was crazy about her.

'I bet she's a virgin. You can tell. Just thinking about that untouched ginger bush makes me horny.'

Mitch hated it when his dad spoke that way. About any woman, but especially about Helen. It was embarrassing.

'Twenty bucks says I fuck her before you do.'

'*Dad!* Don't be stupid. Neither of us is going to fuck her.'

'Speak for yourself, kiddo. She wants it. Take it from someone who knows. They all want it.'

Helen Brunner didn't want it. At least, not from a drunken alleged ex-midshipman old enough to be her father. Mitch, on the other hand . . . now, he was something else. Helen had been raised a Christian. She believed in abstinence. But Mitch Connors was testing her faith to the limits.

Lead me not into temptation. Watching Mitch move around the cramped apartment, feeling his eyes surreptitiously sweep over her body as she did the dishes or made the beds, it seemed to Helen that the Lord had led her *right* into temptation. Mitch felt the same way. He started to make lists.

Reasons not to sleep with Helen:

She's a nice girl.

You'll probably get struck by a thunderbolt halfway through.

If God doesn't smite you dead, Dad will.

Then one day Helen walked into the laundry room to find Mitch standing in his boxer shorts.

Helen said a silent prayer. *Deliver me from evil.*

So did Mitch. *Forgive me, Father, for I am about to sin.*

The sex was incredible. They did it on top of the washing machine, in the shower, on the floor in the living room and, finally, in Pete Connors's bed. Afterward, Mitch lay slumped back on the pillows, replete with happiness. He tried to feel guilty but he couldn't. He was in love.

Helen sat bolt upright.

'Don't tell me you want it *again*?' Mitch groaned.

'No. I heard something. I think it's your father!'

Helen was in her clothes in a flash. Rushing into the kitchen, she started scrubbing pots. Mitch, whose lower body suddenly seemed to have developed advanced Parkinson's, stumbled around the bedroom in blind panic. The front door opened.

'Mitch?'

Shit. There was nothing else for it. Stark naked, Mitch dived into the built-in closet, pulling the door closed behind him. At the back of the closet, against the wall, was a trapdoor leading into a crawl space in the roof. Mitch had barely managed to squeeze his six-foot frame through it when he heard Pete Connors's footsteps in the bedroom.

'MITCH!' It was a roar. The old man wasn't stupid. The combination of Helen's flushed, guilty face and the rumpled sheets must have given them away. Mitch heard the front door open and close. Helen, sensibly, had made a run for it. How Mitch wished he were with her!

The closet door opened. A shaft of light appeared under the trapdoor to the crawl space. Mitch held his breath. There was a pause. Shirts being ruffled on hangers. Then the closet door closed.

Thank you, God. I swear I will never screw a woman in my father's bed ever again.

Pete Connors's footsteps receded. Then, suddenly, they stopped. Mitch's heart did the same. *Hey, c'mon, God! We had a deal!*

The closet door opened again. Then the door to the crawl space. As Pete Connors looked down at his naked son, an unmistakably fishy waft of sex hit him in the face.

'Hey, Dad. I don't suppose you know where I could find a towel?'

Two minutes later, Mitch was out on the street. He never saw his father alive again.

'I want to get married, Mitch.'

Helen and Mitch had been living together for three years.

Now almost twenty-one, Mitch was making good money tending bar. Helen had cut back on her charity work to do three days a week as a trainee librarian, but her heart wasn't in it. She was pushing thirty and she wanted to have a child.

'Why?'

'*Why?* Is that a serious question? Because we're living in mortal sin, that's why.'

Mitch grinned. 'I know. Hasn't it been fun so far?'

'Mitchell! I'm not kidding around. I want to have a baby. I want to make a commitment, to start a family, to do this right. Isn't that what you want, too?'

'Sure it is, baby.'

But the truth was, Mitch didn't know what he wanted. Growing up watching his parents rip each other apart had put him off the idea of marriage for life. He loved Helen, that wasn't the problem. Or maybe it *was* the problem. Being with someone so good, so perfect, made him feel uneasy. He had too much of his father in him. A natural-born scammer, flirting was in Mitch's blood. *Sooner or later I'll let her down. She'll learn to hate me, to despise me for my weakness.* Helen was the mother ship, but Mitch needed lifeboats: other girls who he could keep as backup should Helen see the light and realize she could do a whole lot better than a barman from Pittsburgh.

'Next year,' he told her. 'Once Dad's come around to the idea.' He said the same thing the following year, and the year after that. Then, in the space of a month, two seismic events took place that were to change Mitch's life changed forever.

First, Helen left him.

Then his father was murdered.

Two weeks after Helen Brunner walked out on Mitch, Pete Connors was stabbed to death outside his apartment. He lost his life for a fake Rolex watch, a cheap, nine-karat gold wedding ring and twenty-three dollars in cash. Mitch's mom flew in for the funeral. Lucy Connors looked glamorous and suntanned and not remotely grief-stricken. Then again, why should she?

She hugged Mitch tightly. 'You okay, sweetie? No offense, but you look like hell.'

'I'm fine.'

I'm not fine. I should have been there. I abandoned him, and now he's dead, and I never got to say I was sorry. I never told him how much I loved him.

'Try not to be too upset. I know it sounds harsh, but if this hadn't happened, the booze would have gotten him soon enough.'

'It does sound harsh.'

'I saw the autopsy report, Mitch. I know what I'm talking about. Your father's liver was like a pickled walnut.'

'Jesus, Mom!'

'I'm sorry, honey, but it's the truth. Your father didn't want to live.'

'Maybe not. But he sure as hell didn't want some deranged junkie to stick a steak knife in his heart. He didn't ask for that! He didn't deserve that.' Mitch's mother raised an eyebrow as if to say, *That's a moot point,* but she let him finish. 'And what about the police? What the hell have they been doing? They just let whoever killed Dad walk free. Like his life didn't mean anything at all.'

'I'm sure they've done all they can, Mitch.'

'Bullshit.'

It was bullshit. The Pittsburgh police had done the bare minimum, grudgingly completing the paperwork on Pete Connors's murder without lifting a finger to attempt to track down his killer. Mitch made a bunch of complaints, all of them politely ignored. That's when it dawned on him.

People like my dad don't matter. In the end, he was no different from those poor housewives he used to scam with promises of a better life and white-collar jobs. There's no justice for people like that. The underclass. No one cares what happens to them.

Two weeks after his father's funeral, Mitch telephoned Helen.

'I've made some decisions.'

'Uh-huh?' Her voice sounded weary.

'I'm going to become a cop. A detective.'

It wasn't what she'd been expecting. 'Oh.'

'Not here, though. I need to get away from Pittsburgh. Start afresh. I thought maybe New York.'

'That's great Mitch. Good luck.' Helen hung up.

Ten seconds later, Mitch called her back.

'I was hoping you'd consider coming with me. We'd get married first, obviously. I thought we could – '

'When? When would we get married?'

'As soon as you like. Tomorrow?'

Six weeks later they moved to New York as man and wife. Seven weeks after that, Helen was pregnant.

They called their little girl Celeste, because she was a gift from the heavens. Helen delighted in motherhood, wandering around their minuscule Queens apartment cuddling her daughter for hours on end. Mitch loved the baby, too, with her shock of black hair and inquisitive, intelligent gray eyes. But he was working long hours, first training, then out on the streets. Often, by the time he got home, Celeste was asleep in her crib and Helen was passed out on the couch, exhausted. Imperceptibly, as the months and years passed, Mitch found it harder and harder to pierce the cocoon of love enveloping his wife and daughter.

He got promoted and moved them to a bigger place, expecting that this would make Helen happy. It didn't.

'We never see you, Mitch.'

'Sure you do. Come on, honey, don't exaggerate.'

'I'm not exaggerating. The other day I heard Sally-Ann ask Celeste if she *had* a daddy.'

Mitch said angrily, 'That's ridiculous. Who's Sally-Ann anyway?'

Helen gave him a withering look. 'She's your daughter's best friend. Sally-Ann Meyer? She and Celeste have been joined at the hip for the last two years, Mitch.'

'Really?'

'Really.'

Mitch felt bad. He wanted to spend more time at home. The problem, as he told Helen, was that the bad guys never took a vacation. Muggers, junkies, gang leaders, rapists, every day they walked the streets of the city, preying on the vulnerable, the helpless, the poor. *Preying on people like my father.* Being a detective was more than Mitch's job. It was his vocation, the same way that being a mother was Helen's. And he was great at it.

The divorce came like a bolt from the blue. Mitch got home one night expecting to find his supper on the table. Instead he found a sheaf of legal papers. Helen and Celeste were gone. In hindsight, he realized the writing had been on the wall for a long time. Ever since the economy imploded, crime in the city had been steadily rising. Then Quorum collapsed, unemployment in New York spiked, and overnight a bad situation got twenty times worse. Mitch Connors was on the front line of a war. He couldn't just lay down his gun and be home in time for dinner.

Well, maybe he could. But he didn't. By the time he realized the toll his dedication had taken on his marriage, it was too late.

The NYPD had become Mitch Connors's life. But that didn't mean he loved it. Guys joined the force for different reasons, not all of them laudable. Some reveled in the authority that the badge and the gun gave them. *Power trippers.* They were the worst. Others were looking for a sense of camaraderie. To those guys, the NYPD was like a softball team or a fraternity. It filled a void in their life that marriage, family and civilian friendships couldn't fill. Mitch Connors understood those guys, but didn't count himself among their number. He hadn't become a cop to make friends, or to lord it over his fellow citizens. He'd joined up as a form of atonement for his father's death. And because he still believed he could make a difference.

Whoever killed Mitch's father had gotten away with it. That was wrong. Guilty people deserved to be punished. As for guilty *rich* people, educated people like Grace and Lenny Brookstein, they were the worst of all.

Mitch stood up, kicking Helen's torture chair out of his way. *There was a problem with him taking this case. A downside. Now, what the hell was it?*

At last it came to him. *Of course. The FBI would be involved . . .*

It had been two years since the Brooksteins' audacious fraud first came to light, but as the whole of America knew, the stolen Quorum billions were still missing in action. Harry Bain, the FBI's debonair assistant director in New York, ran the task force set up to find the Quorum cash, and he'd come up with a big fat zero. Bain's agents had interviewed Grace Brookstein numerous times in prison, but she'd stuck like glue to her story. According to her, she knew nothing about the money and neither did her dear departed husband.

Like most NYPD men, Mitch deeply distrusted the FBI. With Grace Brookstein on the run, it was inevitable that Harry Bain would try to start poking his Harvard-educated nose into Mitch's case, asking questions, tampering with witnesses, pulling rank. As Mitch's boss so eloquently put it, 'Bain'll be all over your ass like a bad case of herpes. You better be prepared to fight him off.'

Mitch was prepared.

The money is Harry Bain's problem. Grace Brookstein is mine.

Maybe, if he caught Grace and became a national hero, Helen would take him back. Was that what he really wanted? He didn't know anymore. Maybe he wasn't cut out for marriage.

It was time to get to work.

Chapter Sixteen

As she climbed into the van, the warm air hit Grace like a punch.

Her fingers and toes throbbed painfully as her circulation began to return. It was good to be off the road, but she knew she could trust no one. How long till the news of her escape became public knowledge? Hours? A day at most. Perhaps it was on the radio already? They would issue a new Photofit . . .

'Where you headed?'

It was a good question. Where was she headed?

Grace looked at the compass on the dashboard. 'North.'

Her 'plan,' if you could call it that, was to meet up with Davey Buccola in three weeks' time. They had a rendezvous arranged in Manhattan – Times Square. It was Davey who had convinced Grace not to go after John Merrivale as soon as she got out. 'Don't risk blowing your cover till we know all there is to know.' Davey was convinced he was close to proving who had killed Lenny. 'Just a few more weeks. Trust me.' He'd proposed both the time and the place of their meeting. His theory was that Times Square was *so* public, *so* obvious, no one would think to look for Grace there.

'Even if someone were to recognize you, they'll assume they made a mistake. And hopefully by then, they won't recognize you. You'll have had time to work on how you look.'

Grace would have liked to meet sooner, but Davey was adamant. 'Not till I have more to tell you. Till I'm certain. Every meeting's a risk. We need to make it count.'

In the meantime, Grace would find a safe place to lie low, get her head together and, of course, start working on a decent disguise. She already looked completely different from the woman America remembered from her trial. No one who knew Grace in her glory days as the queen of Wall Street would have recognized her now. The broken nose, the dull complexion, the short, lank hair and pain-deadened eyes; they would all help protect her in the first few hours and days. But ultimately, Grace knew, they wouldn't be enough. She would have to keep changing, daily, weekly, like a chameleon.

It wasn't just her looks that had to evolve. *I'll have to change on the inside, too.* Successful con artists, like successful actors, learned how to *become* someone else. They projected a confidence, a believability, that worked better than any mask or wig or hair dye. Grace had repeated the mantra endlessly in the days leading up to her escape:

Grace Brookstein is dead.

My name is Lizzie Woolley.

I'm a twenty-eight-year-old architect from Wisconsin.

'North, huh?'

The driver's voice brought Grace back to reality. 'How far north?'

Grace hesitated.

'I only ask because you ain't got no case or nothing. And you look like you're dressed for Florida.' He chuckled. Grace noticed the way he stared at her bare legs. Instinctively she crossed them, pulling her skirt lower.

'I left in a hurry. My . . . my sister's been taken ill.'

It was such an obvious lie, Grace blushed. The driver didn't seem to notice. 'What's your name, sweetheart?'

'Lizzie.'

'Pretty name. You're a real pretty girl, Lizzie. I guess you already know that, huh?'

Grace pulled at the top of her blouse, looking for another button to do up, but there wasn't one. This guy was giving her the creeps.

Without warning, he swerved to the side of the road, bringing the van to a sudden halt. Grace jumped.

'Sorry. I gotta take a leak.' Unclicking his seat belt, he jumped out.

Grace watched him disappear behind the back of the van. Her mind was racing.

Should I get out? Run? No, that was crazy. She needed a ride and she'd gotten one. She'd let him take her fifty miles or so, then get out near a small town somewhere. *I can't afford to get spooked by every guy who hits on me. That's what men do, right? He's okay.*

Two minutes later, the driver returned. He was carrying a thermos and a Tupperware container full of sandwiches. He must have gotten them from the back of the van.

'Hungry?'

Grace's stomach gave an audible rumble. She was starving.

'Yes.'

He turned on the ignition and pulled back onto the road. 'Well, go on, then, Lizzie. Knock yourself out. I already ate, but my wife always packs me extra.'

So he's married. Instantly, Grace relaxed.

'Thank you. Thank you very much.'

She started to eat.

Grace woke up in the back of the van with her face pressed to the floor. Her wool skirt had been pushed up around her hips and her panties yanked down around her ankles. The driver was on top of her. His hand was between her legs.

'That's right, Lizzie. Nice and wide now. Open up for Daddy.'

Grace groaned. She tried to move, but her body felt as if it were made of lead. With the added weight of the driver on top of her, it was impossible. With his free hand he forced his swollen penis inside her.

'No!' Grace didn't know if she'd said the word aloud or in her head. It made no difference. The man kept thrusting, deeper, harder. There was nothing frenzied about his movements, though. He was taking things slow. Enjoying himself. Grace felt his hands move upward, clawing under her bra until he found her breasts.

'How about those titties?' He was whispering in her ear, taunting her. Grace could feel the prickle of his mustache against her cheek. 'You awake now, Lizzie, are you? I feel you stirring down there.' Another thrust. 'How does it feel, baby? Is it good to get fucked? I'll bet it is. Well don't worry, Lizzie. We got all night.'

He continued to rape her. Unable to move, Grace tried to think. *He must have drugged me. The flask. He must have slipped something into the tea.* She wondered how late it was and where they were now. Were they still near Bedford, or had hours passed? She couldn't hear any traffic.

We're probably somewhere secluded. Woodland. Where no one will hear me scream.

What would he do when he'd finished with her? Throw her out into the woods? Kill her? Slowly the thick fog in Grace's head began to clear. In his eagerness to get inside her, the driver had left her clothes on, even her shoes.

My shoes . . .

His movements were getting faster now as he built to a climax. Grace gritted her teeth, waiting for him to come, but he suddenly stopped, pulling out of her and flipping her over onto her back like a rag doll. Looking up at his face, into those flat Asian eyes dancing with sadistic pleasure, Grace knew: *He's going to kill me.*

The rape was just foreplay.

'Open your mouth,' he ordered her.

Grace lifted her legs in the air, spreading them wide then wrapping them around his back, pulling him back inside her. 'Make me.' She gazed into his eyes, her pupils dilating with excitement.

He smiled. 'Well, well, well. So you *do* like it, little Lizzie. Even better. This is going to be quite an evening.'

He started fucking her again, faster this time. Grace tightened her grip around his waist. Inside her left shoe she began to move her toes till she could feel Cora's stiletto.

'Yeah! That's it, baby!'

Grace felt the muscles stiffen across his shoulders and back. He started to ejaculate, then suddenly pulled out of her. Holding his grotesque, twitching penis in one hand, he knelt over her, pulling her mouth open with his other hand. Grace felt the hot spray of his semen on her tongue, down her throat. She gagged. He was laughing, closing his eyes, lost in sexual pleasure. *This is it. This is my chance.* Arching her back, with one single, fluid movement, Grace pulled off her shoe, grabbed the knife, flicked it open, and plunged it into between his shoulder blades.

For a split second the driver remained kneeling, a look of shock and bewilderment on his face. Then he fell forward, silently, the blade still stuck in his back like the key in a windup toy. It took all of Grace's strength to wriggle out from under him and remove the knife. Blood spurted from the wound like water from a faucet.

Grace rolled him onto his side. He was trying to talk to her, mouthing words, but all Grace could hear was a bloody gurgle. She kicked him hard in the crotch. He already *looked* incapacitated but you could never be too sure. After rifling his pockets for cash and anything else of value, she hurriedly pulled on her underwear and straightened her clothes, making sure she still had Karen's 'survival package' of documents. Then she went around to the front of the van and took the car keys, as well as the thick, lumberjack jacket the man had been wearing when he picked her up.

Ready.

Walking back to the rear of the van, Grace opened the door. The driver was still alive, but barely. Underneath him the pool of blood was growing bigger, like a deep red puddle. When he saw the knife in Grace's hand, his eyes widened.

'No!' he gurgled. 'Please . . .'

Her intention had been to finish the job. To drive the knife in to his heart, in and in and in and in, like his sick, rapist's dick, until he was dead. But watching him beg for mercy, hearing him plead so pathetically for his life, Grace changed her mind.

Why let him die quickly? He doesn't deserve it.

I'll leave the bastard where he is. Let him bleed to death, slowly and alone.

Grace flipped the blade shut, turned and ran.

It was two hours before Grace reached the outskirts of the nearest small town. The road signs proclaimed it to be Richardsville in Putnam County. Dawn was breaking, a faint strand of burnt-orange light forcing its way through the black night sky. At intervals during her long walk, she'd heard the distinct, insectlike whirring of choppers overhead. *They're hunting for me already.* She wondered if they'd found the van driver? If they were close? Adrenaline coursed through her bruised body, along with a torrent of other, conflicting emotions: Disgust. Terror. Pain. Rage. She'd been raped. She could still feel the evil man inside her, hurting her, violating her. She had also just killed a man. Thinking about the fear he would feel as the life drained out of him, alone in those dreadful woods, Grace recognized another, unfamiliar emotion in the maelstrom: hatred. She was not sorry for what she'd done. But all her feelings and thoughts were eclipsed by one, overriding sensation: exhaustion.

She needed to sleep.

The Up All Night Motel looked like something out of the opening credits of a horror movie. Out front, a flickering, cracked neon sign promised LUXURY INDIVIDUAL BATHROOMS and COLOR TV IN EVERY ROOM! Inside, the oldest man Grace had ever seen snored quietly at the reception desk. His gnarled face was crisscrossed with lines and his body looked ancient and shrunken. He reminded Grace of someone. *Yoda*.

'Excuse me.'

He jerked awake.

'Help ya?'

'I'd like a room, please.'

Yoda looked Grace up and down. She felt her stomach turn to water. *Does he recognize me?* She was so nervous she was sure her teeth were chattering, though she could conceivably pass that off as cold. She'd tried to make her voice sound firm and authoritative when she asked for the room, but it came out a frightened quaver. *Can he see I've been attacked? Can he smell that bastard on me? Maybe I shouldn't stay here? I should keep moving*. But she knew she was too exhausted to go on.

The old man, however, seemed more irritated than interested by her presence. After a long pause he grumbled, 'Foller me,' and led her down a long, cheerless corridor. At the end was a numberless white door. 'This do for ya?'

There was a single bed, made up with cheap, polyester sheets, floral curtains and a coffee-colored carpet splattered with miscellaneous stains. In the far corner, a tiny television was nailed to the wall. Next to it, the door to the 'luxury individual bathroom' stood open, revealing a luxury individual toilet with no seat or lid and a luxury individual shower with mold growing between the tiles.

'This is fine. How much do I owe you?'

'How long you stayin'?'

'I'm not sure.' Suddenly conscious of her disheveled appearance and the fact that she had no luggage with her, Grace blurted out, 'I had a fight with my boyfriend. I left in kind of a hurry.'

Yoda shrugged, bored.

'Twenty dollars for tonight.'

Grace pressed a bill into his hand and he left. Locking the door behind him, Grace drew the curtains closed. She took off all her clothes and walked into the bathroom. Only then did she sink to her knees, lean over the toilet, and vomit. When her stomach was empty, she stood up and stepped into the shower. Under the weak, lukewarm jets of water, she scrubbed at herself with the used bar of soap until her skin bled. She could still feel the man's filthy hands on her breasts, his revolting, rapist's seed on her face, in her mouth. There'd been two bottles of drinking water in the back of the van that she'd used to clean herself up as best she could a few hours ago, so as not to arouse suspicion. On the long walk here she had forced herself to focus on the shower awaiting her, on being clean. But she knew now she would never be clean again.

Drying herself off, she retched again, but there was nothing left inside her to throw up. She moved into the bedroom and sank down on the bed. It was warm in the room. Leaning back against the cheap foam pillow, Grace flicked on the TV. Her own face stared back at her. Or rather, her face as it had once been, long, long ago.

So it's public already. At least they're using an old picture. I'll have to do something about a disguise first thing in the morning, before they release a new one.

The newscaster was talking.

'*In breaking news, Grace Brookstein is reported to have absconded from a maximum-security correctional facility in upstate New York. Brookstein, widow of the billionaire con man Leonard Brookstein . . .*'

The report went on but Grace didn't hear it. She felt more tired than she could ever remember. It had been the longest twenty-four hours of her life. Sleep caressed her like the softest of cashmere blankets. She closed her eyes and let it take her.

Gavin Williams was screaming.

'Are you blind? This is it! The breakthrough we've been praying for. Grace will lead us straight to the money!'

Gavin Williams, Harry Bain and John Merrivale were having a working breakfast at Quorum's old offices. It was the morning after Grace's escape and the news was all over the TV and newspapers.

Harry Bain shook his head. 'I doubt that. Even assuming she knows where it is . . .'

'She knows where it is.'

'Even if she does, she won't get that far. She's got the entire NYPD looking for her. My guess is she'll be back behind bars by nightfall. Either that or some trigger-happy cop will have shot her.'

'No! We can't let that happen!' It was unlike Williams to lose control, but he looked close to tears. 'Grace Brookstein remains the key to this case. We must take control. We must insist the NYPD hand the investigation over to the Bureau.'

Harry Bain laughed. 'Oh, yeah. I'll insist. I'm sure the chief of police will love that.'

Gavin Williams looked to John Merrivale for support. But of course John just stared at his shoes, like the coward that he was. Furious, Williams got up and stormed out.

Merrivale said, 'I know it's not my p-place to say so. But I think perhaps the stress of this case is becoming too much for Agent Williams.'

Harry Bain agreed. 'You're right. I'm having him transferred. Grace Brookstein has become an obsession. It's clouding his judgment. Her escape is a distraction, and we can't afford distractions.'

'Exactly.'

John Merrivale breathed a sigh of relief.

He wouldn't rest completely easily until Grace was captured. Or, better yet, shot. News of her escape had shaken him deeply. But today's meeting was reassuring. With Gavin Williams out of the picture, it would be even easier to lead Bain and his men in the wrong direction. Eventually they'd run out of energy, or money, or both, and call off the investigation. Then finally he would be free. Free to leave New York, to leave Caroline. A life without chains! In the end it would all be worth it.

'D-do you really think they'll find her quickly?'

Harry Bain said, 'I'm sure of it. She's *Grace Brookstein,* for God's sake. Where's she gonna hide?'

In her dreams Grace heard knocking, faint but rapid and insistent, like a woodpecker in the distance. The noise grew louder, closer. She woke up.

There's someone at the door!

Jumping out of bed, she grabbed her switchblade and wrapped the bedsheet around her, stumbling toward the sound in the darkness.

'Who is it?'

''S me.'

Yoda. Grace put down the knife and opened the door a crack.

'You stayin' another night?'

The light from the corridor was blinding. Grace blinked. 'I'm sorry?'

'I said, you stayin' another night? It's noon. Changeover's twelve-thirty. You ain't staying, you gotta vacate the room by then.'

'Oh. No. I'm staying.'

'Twenty dollars.'

Grace pulled a second bill out of the wad Karen had given her and handed it to the old man. He took it wordlessly, scuttling back to his reception desk like a decrepit beetle.

Twelve o'clock! Jesus. I must have been out like a light. Grace opened the curtains, then closed them again. Far too bright. Splashing cold water on her face, she pulled on her clothes – they stank of that bastard but they were all she had. She would buy new ones today. The TV was still on from last night. Grace turned up the volume. This time the news report was on the economy. But a few moments later her face was back on-screen again, this time a mug shot from the day they brought her to Bedford. *It still looks nothing like me.*

The anchorwoman was talking. '*With Grace Brookstein now missing for over seventeen hours, the police appear to have no concrete leads. With me is Detective Mitchell Connors of the NYPD, the man leading the investigation into Brookstein's escape. Detective, people are already saying that you and your men are running out of ideas. Do you feel that's a fair statement?*'

An attractive blond cop responded by video link.

'*No, Nancy, I don't believe it is. We're pursuing a number of different avenues. This investigation is only hours old. It's our belief that the prisoner will be apprehended swiftly and we're working toward that conclusion.*'

Grace studied the cop's face. Detective Mitchell Connors looked like he'd been sketched by a cartoonist at Marvel Comics, all square jaw and steady, blue-eyed gaze. Physically

198

he reminded Grace of a rougher-around-the-edges version of her brother-in-law Jack Warner. But his expression was nothing like Jack's. If anything, it was more like Lenny's. *It's his eyes. He has kind eyes.*

He was still talking. '*Grace Brookstein and her husband brought extraordinary suffering to thousands of people, particularly here in New York. Believe me, Nancy, no one wants to see this convicted felon back behind bars more than I do. Make no mistake. We will find her.*'

Grace switched off the television.

Detective Connors might have kind eyes, but he's my enemy.

She mustn't forget it.

That afternoon, Grace walked into town. It was all she could do to stop her teeth from chattering, knowing that her face was all over the news, that at any moment, someone might recognize her and turn her in to the authorities. But she couldn't hide out at the motel forever. She needed supplies, and she needed to get out of Richardsville. Karen and Cora had both warned her of the dangers of staying in one place too long.

With the van driver's bulky jacket pulled tightly around her, Grace kept her head down as she walked the aisles of a Walmart. At the checkout, her heart was pounding so violently she thought she might faint. Happily the sullen teenager manning the register seemed more interested in the chip on one of her acrylic nails than in the nervous customer or her purchases.

'Eighty-eight dollazs yer total; cash 'r credit?'

'Cash.'

'Thangshaveaniceday.'

The girl didn't even look up.

By the time Grace returned to her room at the Up All

Night, it was almost four P.M. Locking the door, she emptied her Walmart bags onto the bed: hair dye, scissors, makeup, disinfectant, underwear, a three-pack of Haines T-shirts, jeans, a beanie hat, and a gray carry-all gym bag.

She got to work.

The old man at the reception desk studied the picture in his newspaper. His eyes weren't what they used to be.

Could it be?

This girl's nose was different. And the hair. Still, there was definitely a resemblance. And she *had* arrived in the middle of the night, with no suitcase. He looked at the paper again. The cop on the TV said to report anything suspicious, no matter how trivial.

The old man picked up the phone.

Grace looked at herself in the cracked bathroom mirror. Except it wasn't herself. It was someone else, the first of her four new identities. *Lizzie Woolley.*

Hello, Lizzie.

Carefully cleaning up all traces of dye and picking every lock of severed hair off the floor, Grace dropped them into the empty Walmart bag along with the discarded bottle of Nice 'n Easy and her old clothes, tied the bag by the handles, and stuffed it into her carry-all. She dressed quickly. The clean clothes felt wonderful. For a moment Grace thought back to her old life and smiled. She could never have imagined back then that the day would come when a pair of Walmart jeans would feel like the last word in luxury! She'd already spent two-thirds of the cash Karen and Cora had given her. Pretty soon she would have to make e-mail contact with Karen's mysterious 'friend' and ask for more. Cora had assured her that getting cash from Western Union was anonymous and easy. All you had to do was show up at one of their hundreds of thousands of locations, show your (fake) ID, and take the money. 'It's how every illegal immigrant in this country makes rent, honey. It's their business not to ask questions.' Even so, Grace hoped she wouldn't have to do it too often.

She'd checked the bus timetable earlier. The next bus to the city left at 6:15 P.M.

Plenty of time.

The old man knocked on the door.

No answer. Officer McInley, Richardsville's finest – Richardsville's *only* – looked pissed. 'I thought you said she was definitely here?'

Officer McInley knew the minute Old Man Murdoch called that it'd be some stupid-ass wild-goose chase. Grace Brookstein, staying at the Up All Night? Yeah, right. She was probably sharing a room with Kermit the Frog and Herman Munster. Everyone in Richardsville knew that Murdoch had lost his marbles years ago.

'She's here, all right? Saw her come in wi' my own two eyes and she ain't come out again. Muz be sleepin'.'

Unhooking the master key from his belt loop, the old man unlocked the door.

'Miss?'

The room was empty. Not just empty but pristine. The bed was made, the surfaces wiped clean. It looked as if no one had stayed there in weeks.

Officer McInley rolled his eyes.

'She wuz here, I tell ya! Last two nights. I swear to God. Musta 'scaped out the winda.'

'Uh-huh.' *On a flying monkey.* 'Well if you see her again, you be sure and let us know.'

Chapter Seventeen

Maria Preston floated into the sixth-floor Caprice restaurant in Hong Kong's Four Seasons Hotel. In a chiffon caftan, dripping in newly bought pearls from the Guangzhou City jewelry district, she waved the newspaper excitedly at her husband.

'Have you seen this, Andy?'

'Seen what, my love?'

'Grace Brookstein's escaped from prison!'

Andrew Preston went white. 'Escaped? What do you mean she's escaped? That's not possible.' Snatching the paper, he read the front-page story.

A major police operation was under way last night in New York after convicted con artist Grace Brookstein apparently broke out of a maximum-security facility in Westchester County. Brookstein, one of the most notorious women in America, is believed to have stolen upward of $70 billion in a conspiracy masterminded by her late husband, Leonard . . .

'Can you believe it?' Maria giggled as she poured herself a large glass of fresh orange juice. '*Escaped from jail.* It's like something out of *Desperate Housewives.* Next thing you know she'll wake up in the shower with amnesia and the last twenty years will never have happened! Do you think they'll catch her?'

Andrew was too stunned to speak. This was a disaster. A catastrophe. Just when he thought the whole nightmare was behind him, Grace had to pull a stunt like this and reopen old wounds. Maria seemed to think it was some sort of joke. But then why wouldn't she? She had no idea of the stress he'd been under. As long as she had money to spend – this trip to Hong Kong alone had cost over $40,000, not including the astronomical sums Maria had 'saved' on pearl jewelry – she was happy. What was it to her if Andrew hadn't slept properly in over a year? If he lay in their bed in the $12,000-a-night presidential suite overlooking Victoria Harbor and Kowloon Bay, bent double with stomach cramps and crippling migraines, haunted by nightmares involving Lenny Brookstein and the scarred, terrifying face of a man named Donald Anthony Le Bron? Had it not been for Maria, he would never have done what he did. Never have betrayed a friend, never have become a thief, never have had cause to associate with the likes of Le Bron. And yet he couldn't tell her. He just couldn't.

Most distressing of all was the alopecia. Since last Christmas, Andrew's hair had started falling out in clumps, like a dog with mange. He panicked. *I'm falling to pieces. Literally. It's the beginning of the end.*

Thank God it was John Merrivale who had to deal with the FBI day in, day out, and not him. The stress would have finished him off. Andrew could hear John's voice in his head now, repeating the mantra: *'Just stick to the story and you'll be f-fine. We both will.'*

So far, they had. But Grace's escape could change everything.

'Andy, are you listening to me? I said, do you think they'll catch her?'

'Yes. I'm sure they'll catch her.' *They have to.*

'What will happen to her then, do you think?'

'I don't know. They'll take her back to jail, I suppose.'

Andrew thought about Grace Brookstein, the sweet, naive child he'd known for all those years. Poor Grace. She was the only truly innocent victim in all of this. Unfortunately, that was what happened to pure little lambs. They got slaughtered.

Maria sipped her orange juice contentedly. 'Don't look so miserable, Andy. Anyone would think it was you the police were after. Now give me back the newspaper, would you? There's a gorgeous Balenciaga dress in the fashion pages. I'm thinking of having it copied.'

Jack Warner saw the news on television. He was in a bar with Fred Farrell, his campaign manager, discussing his re-election strategy. When he saw Grace's face on the TV screen, he choked on his pistachios.

'Holy mother of God. Can you believe this?'

Fred Farrell couldn't. People didn't break out of places like Bedford Hills. Not in real life. Especially not petite, blond trophy wives like Grace Brookstein.

'You'll have to make a statement.'

Fred Farrell's brilliant political mind was already whirring. This was not a good time for the Quorum scandal to come back and haunt them. Grace would probably be caught within a few hours, but the renewed media interest in the Brookstein case could last for months. Jack must not be dragged into it.

'I'll write you something. In the meantime, go home and lay low.'

Jack Warner went home. During the hour-long drive to Westchester, he composed his thoughts. Fred Farrell didn't know the half of it. He knew about the gambling debts, and

Lenny Brookstein's refusal to pay them. But Jack Warner had other skeletons in his closet besides gambling. Explosive secrets that could destroy him and put an end to all his political hopes.

Lenny knew the truth. But Lenny's dead, burning in hell, where he belongs.

The question was, had he taken his knowledge with him to his watery grave? Or had he shared what he knew with his beloved wife? While Grace was safely under lock and key, it didn't matter. But now she was out, running for her life. A loose cannon, with nothing to lose.

I can't let that bitch destroy me. I won't.

Honor ran out to the driveway to meet him. Her eyes were red and swollen. It was obvious she'd been crying. 'Oh, Jack! Have you seen the news?'

'Of course I've seen it.' He bundled her indoors. The press could show up at any minute. 'For God's sake, pull yourself together. Why are you crying?'

Honor didn't know. She'd always envied Grace. Resented her. Hated her even. Even so, her baby sister's conviction troubled her. Grace was no more capable of perpetrating a sophisticated fraud than she was of changing a tire or filling out a tax return. Honor knew that better than anyone. *I should have spoken up for her in court. Or at least visited her in prison. But I didn't. I did what Jack told me to. I always do what Jack tells me to.*

'They said on the news that someone might shoot her. That she's in more danger from the public than she is from the police.'

'So?' Jack wasn't interested in Grace's problems. He was interested in his own. 'Fred's writing me a statement. Until then, I want you and the kids to stay in the house. Don't talk to anyone about Grace. Do you understand?'

Honor nodded.

'If she tries to contact you, you must inform me immediately. Not the police. Me.'

'Yes, Jack.'

He started up the stairs. Honor called after him. 'Jack? Why do you think she did it?'

'What do you mean?'

'I mean why did she escape? She must have known the danger she was putting herself in. Not to mention blowing any chance of an appeal. It just seems so . . . reckless. So out of character.'

Jack Warner shrugged. 'Maybe she's changed. Prison does change people, you know.'

So does politics, thought Honor. She looked at herself in the hall mirror and shivered. She did not recognize the person she'd become.

'Escaped? Good God.'

Michael Gray had spent the day on his new boat, an anniversary present from Connie. He didn't hear the news till they sat down to dinner that evening.

'I know. I wouldn't have thought she had it in her. Stowed away in a delivery truck, if you can believe that. So much for "maximum security."'

Michael looked pained. 'Do you think we should . . . I don't know, try to help her in some way?'

Connie's eyes widened. '*Help her?* Whatever do you mean? How can we possibly help her? More to the point, *why* should we help her, after what she's done?'

Michael Gray loved his wife, and deferred to her opinions about her own sister. But he'd never felt comfortable about the collective washing of hands and turning of backs that had followed Grace's trial. It hadn't felt right at the time. Now, somehow, it felt less right than ever.

So much had changed since that fateful trip to Nantucket

a year and a half ago. Back then, Lenny and Grace had had everything – a perfect marriage, a fortune – and he and Connie had nothing. Michael Gray had not forgotten the darkness of those days. Losing his job at Lehman was like losing a parent. Lehman Brothers had been much more than an employer. It had given Michael his identity, his self-worth. When the company failed, it felt like a death. But Michael had had no time to mourn. He'd been plunged into one crisis after another, watching his savings disappear, then the house. Worst of all was the distance that began to grow between him and Connie. Michael Gray felt he could have borne anything with his wife's support. But with each blow, Connie withdrew from him further. Even the way she looked at him in those days, so *disappointed,* so *disgusted,* almost as if what had happened were his fault, as if she blamed him for their suffering . . . the memory could still cause him to break out in a cold sweat.

All that was only eighteen months ago, yet it felt like another lifetime. Since then, they'd lived through Quorum's collapse, Lenny's death, Grace's arrest, the trial . . . and now this. It was surreal. As Grace's fortunes had declined, so some invisible string seemed to pull Michael and Connie's lives upward, out of the mire and back into the warmth of the sun. Michael got a job with a boutique advisory firm. The salary wasn't great but he had equity. More important, he had a reason to get out of bed in the mornings again. You couldn't put a price on that. Connie became less distant and more loving. The disappointment was gone. In its place was the old familiar look of love, that unique combination of trust, lust and respect that made Michael feel he could move mountains. He loved her so much.

She's my strength and my weakness. I'd die for her and I'd kill for her. And she knows it.

But the best was yet to come. A few months after Grace

began her sentence at Bedford Hills, Connie was called to a meeting by her attorney. Apparently some distant, elderly relative had left her something in her will. Michael was expecting a few shares, or perhaps a piece of jewelry.

In fact, his wife had been left $15 million.

That night she made love to him with a passion Michael hadn't known in her since before they married. He made a joke. 'I guess being a woman of means suits you, honey.'

Connie beamed. 'I guess it does. Let's buy a new house, Mike. This place holds too many painful memories.'

'Hey, come on. It holds some good memories, too, doesn't it? This is where the kids were born. Do you really want to leave?'

Connie didn't hesitate. 'Yes. I want a new start. For all of us. No looking back.'

They sold the house.

'I can't believe you'd seriously want to help Grace? Where did that spring from?'

They were in the formal sitting room of their new town house. Connie had gone all out for their first Christmas, decorating the entire house in silver and white. A traditionalist, she refused to take down any of the decorations till Twelfth Night. Michael felt like he was coming home to Santa's grotto.

'I don't know. Nowhere specific. We have so much, that's all.'

'And Grace doesn't?' Connie laughed bitterly. Whenever the conversation turned to Grace or Lenny, her anger seemed to re-emerge, like a caged demon unleashed. 'That Quorum money is out there somewhere, Mike. The FBI is convinced little Gracie knows where it is. Who are we to say different?'

Mike wanted to say, *Her family,* but he didn't. He was too afraid.

Connie saw the fear in his eyes and felt her own fear subside.

Good. He's not going to force the issue. He loves me too much.

Connie was puzzled by her sister's escape. The Grace she knew would never have had the chutzpah to plan anything so daring, never mind see it through and outfox the police into the bargain. Deep down Connie knew that Grace had had nothing to do with stealing the Quorum billions.

It's not the money she's after. It's something else.

The truth, perhaps?

Mike still had no idea about Connie's affair with Lenny Brookstein. Nor had he questioned her mysterious inheritance. *He's so trusting. Just like Grace.* Connie wanted it to stay that way.

Wrapping her arms around Michael's neck, she whispered, 'I want us to be happy, darling. To put the past behind us. Don't you?'

'Of course I do, my darling.' He hugged her back fiercely.

'So no more talk about helping Grace. That chapter in our lives is closed forever.'

Chapter Eighteen

Being in New York again, experiencing the sights and smells, was a homecoming of sorts for Grace. She felt safer in the city. Her new look helped, too: cropped, chocolate-brown hair, dark makeup, baggy, mannish clothes. One of the girls at Bedford had told her that altering one's walk could dramatically change people's perceptions. Grace had spent hours perfecting a longer-strided, less girlish gait. It was still unnerving, catching sight of her 'old' face whenever she passed a television or a newsstand. But as the days passed, she grew more confident that the combination of her disguise and the crowded anonymity of the city would protect her, for a while at least.

Her second day in the city, she'd braved a hole-in-the-wall Internet café and sent a message to the Hotmail address Karen had given her using the specified code: '200011209LW.' Grace hoped this meant 'please send $2,000 to zip code 11209 in New York in the name of Lizzie Woolley,' but she still felt certain that something would go wrong. Was $2,000 too much to ask for or too little? She realized belatedly she had no idea how much money Karen's friend had, or was willing to send her. On the other hand, she didn't want to have to risk doing this every other week, not with half the country's police departments out searching for her.

In fact, the pickup had been as smooth as Cora told her it would be. There was a Western Union outlet in the pharmacy on the corner. A fat, depressed man in his midforties had glanced at Grace's ID and, not even bothering to make eye contact, still less examine her features, handed her an envelope full of cash and a printed receipt. 'There you go, Ms. Woolley. Have a nice day.'

Grace began to focus less on being captured and more on her impending meeting with Davey Buccola. Davey had been researching the alibis of everyone she and Lenny had invited to Nantucket that fateful weekend. It still didn't seem fully real to Grace, the idea that the Prestons or the Merrivales or even one of her own sisters could have done such a terrible thing – stolen all that money, killed Lenny, caused her to be imprisoned and gotten away with it. But what other explanation was there? She hoped that when she saw Davey's research in black and white, it would make things clearer. Everything depended on that meeting.

Alone in her tiny studio room, Grace pulled a stack of newspaper clippings out of the desk drawer and arranged them on the bed. There they were: Honor and Jack, Connie and Mike, Andrew and Maria and, of course, John and Caroline. Among them, those eight faces held the keys to the truth. Next to them, set slightly apart, Grace placed a ninth picture: Detective Mitchell Connors, the man whose job it was to catch her. He was definitely attractive. Grace found herself wondering if he was married, and if he loved his wife as much as she had loved Lenny.

He would catch her eventually, of course. Her luck wouldn't hold out forever. But eventually didn't matter to Grace. What mattered was doing what she had set out to do.

Closing her eyes, she spoke to Lenny, her words half promise, half prayer:

I'll do it, my darling. I'll do it for both of us. I'll find out who took you away from me and I'll make them pay, I promise.

She slept and grew strong.

'More tea, Detective? My husband should be back any minute.'

Honor Warner was visibly nervous. Mitch noticed the way her hands shook as she lifted the silver teakettle from its tray. Hot brown liquid spilled all over the white upholstered coffee table.

'No thank you, Mrs Warner. It was really you I came to see. Has your sister made any attempt to contact you since her escape?'

'Contact me? No. Absolutely not. If Grace had called, I'd have let the police know immediately.'

Mitch cocked his head to one side and smiled engagingly. 'Would you? Why's that?'

He was intrigued by this woman. She was Grace Brookstein's sister. At one time, by all accounts, the two women had been very close. They even looked alike. Yet when Grace fell from grace, Honor Warner had vanished into the ether.

'What do you mean? I don't understand.'

'Only that Grace is your sister,' Mitch explained. 'It would be understandable for you to want to help her. It wouldn't be wrong.'

This seemed to throw Honor completely. She looked around her, as if searching the room for a means of escape. Or perhaps she was scanning it for hidden microphones or cameras? Did she think she was being watched? Eventually she said, 'Grace made a lot of enemies, Detective. She's in

212

greater danger out of prison than she is inside. I'm thinking of her safety.'

Mitch fought back a smile. *Like hell you are.*

'You didn't go to the trial.'

'No.'

'As I understand it, you never visited your sister in Bedford Hills either.'

'No.'

'Why was that?'

'I . . . my husband . . . we felt it was for the best. Jack's worked so hard to get to where he is today. For voters to associate him with Quorum . . . well. You understand.'

Mitch made no effort to hide his disgust. He understood perfectly.

Reading his thoughts, Honor said defensively, 'My husband has done a lot of good for his constituents, Detective. A *lot* of good. Is it right that he should be tainted by Lenny Brookstein's greed? Grace made her own choices. I'm worried about her, but . . .' She left the sentence hanging.

Mitch got to his feet.

'Thank you, Mrs Warner. I'll see myself out.'

It was the same story with Connie Gray.

'My youngest sister has never learned to take responsibility for her actions, Detective Connors. Grace believes she's *entitled* to wealth, to beauty, to happiness, to freedom. No matter what the cost to others. So in answer to your question, no, I don't feel sorry for her. And I certainly haven't heard from her. Nor do I expect to.'

With friends like Grace Brookstein's, who needed enemies?

Talking to Grace's compassionless, embittered sister, Mitch almost felt sorry for the woman whose greed had brought New York to its knees. Connie's anger was like a physical presence in the room, emanating from her body

213

like heat from a radiator. The atmosphere was stifling.

'Is there anyone else you can think of? Anyone Grace might call, or lean on? An old school friend perhaps? Or a childhood beau?'

Connie shook her head regally. 'No one. When Grace married Lenny, she got swept up into his world completely.'

'You sound disapproving.'

'Lenny and I . . . Let's just say we weren't close. I always thought he and Grace were a mismatch. In any event, there are no old friends. John Merrivale supported Grace for a while, I believe, until Caroline got him to see sense. Poor John.'

'Why "poor John"?'

'Oh, come on, Detective. You've met him. He worshipped Lenny. He was his bag carrier for years.'

'He was more than that, surely?'

'John? No! Never!' Connie laughed cruelly. 'The media paint him as some sort of financial wizard, *a key Quorum insider.* It's farcical! He wasn't even a partner, after the best part of twenty years. Lenny used him. So did Grace. Even now he's stuck cleaning up the mess at Quorum. No wonder your colleagues at the FBI haven't found that money. Talk about the blind leading the blind.'

The press conference was openly hostile. People wanted answers and Mitch Connors didn't have them.

It was almost a week now since Grace Brookstein's dramatic escape from Bedford Hills and pressure was mounting on Mitch and his team to report some progress. The media seemed to have gotten it into their heads that the NYPD was withholding information. Mitch smiled. *If only that were true!* The truth was, he had nothing. Grace Brookstein had walked out of that jail and vanished into thin air like David friggin' Blaine. She had contacted no one, not family, not friends. Yesterday, in a move that had been widely and correctly interpreted as desperation, the NYPD put out a $200,000 reward for anyone who provided information leading to Grace's capture. It was a mistake. Within two hours, Mitch's team had received over eight hundred calls. Apparently Grace Brookstein had been spotted everywhere from New York to Nova Scotia. A couple of leads looked like they might pan out, but both ended up coming to nothing. Mitch felt like a kid trying to catch hold of bubbles, not knowing which way to turn and destroying everything he touched. And to think, he'd thought this case would be a slam dunk.

'That's it for today, folks. Thanks.'

The grumbling press pack dispersed. Mitch crawled back to his office to hide, but it seemed there was to be no respite today. Detective Lieutenant Henry Dubray was no oil painting at the best of times. Today, squatting in Mitch's torture chair like a giant toad, he looked even worse than usual. His skin was blotchy and drink-ravaged, and the whites of his eyes were as yellow as sunflowers. The pressure of the Brookstein case was taking its toll on all of them.

'Give me some good news, Mitch.'

'The Knicks won last night.'

'I'm serious.'

'So am I. It was a great game. You didn't watch?'

Mitch smiled. Dubray didn't.

'I'm sorry, boss. I don't know what to tell you. We got nothing.'

'We're running out of time, Mitch.'

'I know.'

Dubray left. There was nothing left to say. Both men knew the reality. If Mitch didn't come up with a solid lead in the next twenty-four hours, he'd be taken off the case. Demoted, certainly. Maybe even fired. Mitch tried not to think about Celeste, and the expensive private school Helen wanted him to pay for. In that moment he hated Grace Brookstein.

He stared at the whiteboard on the wall of his office. Grace's picture was in the middle. Radiating outward from it, like the points of a star, were various groups of other photos: Bedford Hills inmates and staff; Grace's family and friends; Quorum connections; members of the public who'd called in with the most promising leads. *How could so many sources lead to nothing?*

The phone rang.

'Call for you on line one, Detective Connors.'

'Who is it?'

'Grace Brookstein.'

Mitch gave a mirthless laugh. 'Yeah, thanks, Stella. I'm not in the mood for crank callers.'

He hung up. Thirty seconds later, the phone rang again.

'Stella, I told you, I got enough problems without – '

'Good morning, Detective Connors. This is Grace Brookstein speaking.'

Mitch froze. After listening to hours of recordings of Grace's court testimony, he'd have recognized her voice anywhere. He waved frantically to his colleagues in the outer office. 'It's her,' he mouthed. 'Trace the call.'

He made a conscious effort to speak slowly. He couldn't show his excitement. More important, he had to keep her talking. 'Hello, Ms Brookstein. What can I do for you?'

'You can listen to me.'

The voice was the same as the one in the court recordings, but the tone was different. Harder, more determined.

'I'm listening.'

'My husband and I were framed. I never stole any money and neither did Lenny.'

Mitch paused, trying to keep her on the line.

216

'Why are you telling me this, Ms Brookstein? I'm not a jury. Your conviction has nothing to do with me.'

'It's *Mrs* Brookstein. I'm a widow, Detective, not a divorcée.'

You're a fool. You should never have made this call. Just keep talking.

'I'm telling you because you look like a good man. An honest man.'

The compliment surprised Mitch. 'Thank you.'

'You look like a man who would want to know the truth. Are you?'

Actually I'm a man who wants to keep you on the line for the next ten seconds. Nine . . . eight . . .

'You know, Mrs Brookstein, the best thing you could do right now would be to turn yourself in.' *Six . . . five . . .*

Grace laughed. 'Please, Detective. Don't insult my intelligence. I have to go now.'

'No. Wait! I can help you. If you are innocent, as you say you are, there are legal channels – '

Click.

The line went dead. Mitch looked hopefully at the guys on the other side of the glass, but the shake of their heads told him what he already knew.

'Two more seconds and we'd've had her.'

Mitch sank into his chair and put his head in his hands. Immediately, the phone rang again. Mitch leaped on it like a jilted lover, willing it to be her. 'Grace?'

A man's voice answered. 'Detective Connors?'

Mitch felt the hope drain out of him like blood from a severed vein. 'Speaking.'

'Detective, my name is John Rodville. I'm the head of admissions at the Putnam Medical Center.'

'Uh-huh.' Mitch said wearily. The name meant nothing to him.

'We have a patient here, brought in last week with a knife wound to the back. He was in a coma till this morning. We didn't think he'd make it. But he pulled through.'

'That's terrific, Mr Rodville. I'm happy for him.'

Mitch was on the point of hanging up when the man said cheerily, 'Yeah, I thought you might be. Especially since he just identified his attacker as Grace Brookstein.'

Chapter Nineteen

Mitch burst into the intensive-care unit.

'Detective Connors. I'm here to see Tommy Burns.' He flashed his badge at the staff nurse

'Right this way, Detective.'

The head of admissions had filled Mitch in on the van driver's story. According to Tommy Burns, he was a freelance gardener who'd happened to pick up a hitchhiker a couple miles outside of Bedford last Tuesday night. The woman went by the name of Lizzie. Tommy drove her about forty miles north before she suddenly pulled a knife on him, forced him into the woods, stabbed and robbed him, leaving him for dead.

'Some local kids found him. They were out hunting. A few more hours and he'd have bled to death for sure.'

'And he believes this Lizzie who attacked him was actually Grace Brookstein?'

'He seems certain of it. A few hours after he came to, he asked to have the TV turned on. Brookstein's face came on the news and he went crazy. We had to sedate him. He wants to talk to you but he's still very weak, so go easy. His wife and kids haven't even seen him yet.'

Mitch thought, *Wife and kids. The poor bastard's a family man. But of course Grace Brookstein didn't care about that. She picked him up, used him to get what she wanted, then left him to die in the woods, alone.* Painful memories of his dad's murder came flooding back to him. Pete Connors's killer would never be caught. But Grace Brookstein sure as hell would be. Men like Tommy Burns deserved justice. They deserved to be protected.

Mitch approached Tommy Burns's bed full of compassion.

When he left the hospital fifteen minutes later, he found himself wishing Grace Brookstein had finished the job. Tommy Burns was about as likable as a bad case of hemorrhoids. He was also a rotten liar.

'Jesus, Detective, I already *told* you. I was the Good Samaritan, okay? I saw a chick in trouble and I did the right thing. One minute we was driving along, listening to the radio, nice as pie. The next minute, *bam*! The bitch has a knife to my throat. I never stood a chance.'

Mitch wanted to believe him. Badly. Right now Tommy Burns was the only witness he had. But he didn't believe him. Something about the guy wasn't right.

'Let's go back to when you first picked her up, shall we, Mr Burns? You said she looked like she was in trouble?'

'She was half dressed. It was freezing out there, snowing. She had this thin blouse on. You could see right through it.' A half smile flickered across his face at the memory. Just then a pretty young nurse came in to refill the water pitcher. Mitch Connors watched Tommy Burns follow her lustfully with his eyes as she turned and left the room. A light went on in Mitch's brain.

'You didn't think to ask her why she was dressed like that on a freezing winter's night?'

'Nope. Why should I? None o' my business.'

'I suppose not. Still, out of curiosity . . .'

220

'I'm not a curious person.'

'Yes. I can see that.'

Tommy Burns's eyes narrowed. Something about Mitch's tone gave him the feeling he was being mocked. 'What d'you mean by that?'

'I don't mean anything by it. I'm simply agreeing with you that you lack curiosity. For example, you don't seem to have asked yourself why, after going to all the trouble of trying to murder you, this woman didn't finish the job.'

Tommy Burns became agitated. 'Hey now. Don't you go givin' me no "this woman" bullshit. It was Grace Brookstein. I saw her on the TV, plain as day. You catch her, I'll be wanting that two-hundred-thousand-dollar reward.'

'Fine,' said Mitch. 'Let's say it *was* Grace Brookstein who attacked you.'

'It was.'

'If it were me, I'd still be asking myself that question: "Why did she let me live? Why didn't she finish the job?" But then again, you see, I *am* a curious person. We detectives usually are.'

Tommy considered this. 'I guess she thought she had. Finished the job, I mean. We were out in the middle of nowhere. Probably figured I'd die slow.'

Mitch pounced. 'Really? Why do you think she would want you to die slowly?'

''Scuse me?'

'According to you, her motive was theft. She needed a ride and she needed money. That being the case, I could understand her wanting you dead. She wouldn't want witnesses, right?'

'Right.'

'But what reason would she have to make you suffer? To prolong your agony?'

'What reason? Hell, *I* don't know. She's a woman, ain't she? They're all fucked-up bitches.'

Mitch nodded slowly. 'You're right. I mean, if a *man* had done this, he'd have taken the van, right?'

'Huh?' Tommy Burns looked well and truly confused.

'Once he'd gotten rid of *you*, he could have used the vehicle to get another forty, fifty, a hundred miles away from the crime scene before he dumped it somewhere. That'd be the smart thing to do, wouldn't it?'

'I guess it would.'

'But women aren't as smart as us, are they?'

'Damn right they ain't.'

Mitch leaned forward conspiratorially. 'We both know what women are good for, don't we, Tommy? And it isn't their powers of reasoning!'

Tommy smiled stupidly. *Now* the cop was talking his language . . .

'Tell me, Tommy, do you regularly pick up hitchhikers?'

'Sometimes.'

'Are many of them as attractive as Grace Brookstein?'

'No, sir. Not many.'

'Or as good in the sack?'

'No, sir!' Tommy Burns grinned. 'She was something else.'

It was a full five seconds before he realized his mistake. The smile wilted. 'Hey now, don't you go putting words in my mouth! I didn't . . . I mean . . . I'm the victim here,' he stammered. 'I'm the goddamn victim!'

It was late by the time Mitch got home that night. If you could call the shitty two-bedroom rental that was all he could afford since Helen left him 'home.' Helen got everything when they split: Celeste, the house, even the dog, Snoopy. *My dog.* Mitch could understand the things that drove men to hate women. Men like Tommy Burns. It would be easy to slip down that path. He had to guard against it himself sometimes.

It had been quite a day. The press conference, a phone call from Grace Brookstein herself, and finally Tommy Burns. Burns was Mitch's first, real, concrete lead. Mitch knew he ought to feel elated. Instead he felt uneasy.

After Tommy Burns's slip of the tongue this afternoon, they'd come to an understanding: Mitch would look no further into a possible sexual assault of Grace Brookstein. In return, Tommy would forget about the $200,000 reward and would tell Mitch everything he could remember from that night: Grace's clothing, her demeanor, anything at all she might have said or done that could shed light on her plans. Tommy's van had been sent to forensics. When Mitch spoke to them a few hours ago, they'd been hopeful. It should provide a treasure trove of new evidence.

So why do I feel like crap?

Mitch had walked into that hospital this afternoon full of righteous rage and loathing. Grace Brookstein was a criminal, a heartless thief and would-be killer who had violently attacked an innocent family man. Except that if Tommy Burns was an innocent family man, Mitch Connors was Big Bird. The e-mail finally came through after midnight. Mitch had run a check on Tommy Burns's record. Sure enough, he had a string of sexual-assault convictions stretching back almost twenty years. Two rape charges had been thrown out for lack of evidence. *So much for the Good Samaritan.*

Something had happened in that van. Burns was a sexual predator and Grace had defended herself. In this case, at least, that made her the victim. Mitch suddenly realized, *I don't want her to be the victim. I want her to be the bad guy.* Usually he was unequivocal about his cases, and the people he brought to justice. To Mitch, they were all paler versions of whoever had killed his father: bad men, men who deserved to be brought down. But already, this case felt different. Part of him hated Grace for her crimes. Her greed and lack of remorse were well documented. But another part of him pitied her. Pitied her for having to deal with the likes of Tommy Burns. Pitied her for having that pair of heartless vultures for sisters.

Mitch closed his eyes and tried to imagine how Grace Brookstein must have felt in Burns's van. Alone, on the run, already desperate, and the first man she trusted turned out to be a psychotic pervert. Burns wasn't a big guy but he was strong, and presumably determined. Grace must have shown great courage to fight him off like that.

What would her next move have been?

She wouldn't hitch another ride. Not if Burns had just raped her. She'd take off on foot. Which means she couldn't have gotten far that night. A couple of miles maybe. Five tops.

Pulling out a map, Mitch pinpointed the spot where Burns's van was abandoned. With a red Sharpie, he drew a circle around the van at a five-mile radius.

There was only one town inside the circle.

The old man waved his frail arms excitedly. Mitch Connors fought back the urge to laugh. *He looks like Yoda having a seizure . . .*

'I told 'em! I told 'em she wuz here, but they jus' pooh-poohed me. Reckon an old man like me don't know what he saw. Dead of night she shows up, *dead of night*. No suitcase! I told 'em. I said, she din' have no case. That ain't right. But did anybody listen to me? No, sir.'

It turned out Richardsville only had the one motel. When Mitch called and mentioned Grace Brookstein's name, the proprietor of the Up All Night had gone ballistic. *Yes, Grace had been there. He'd already told the police. Didn't those bozos speak to each other?*

224

'I hope you gonna fire that officer. McInley. Arrogant little piece of *S-H-I-T*, 'scuse my language, Detective. But I told 'em.'

Mitch turned to the technician sweeping the room for prints. The technician shook his head. 'Clean as a whistle, boss. Sorry. If she was here, she did a good job covering her tracks.'

The old man looked like his grizzled head might explode. 'What do you mean "*If* she wuz here"? Ain't no *if*. She wuz *here*! How many more times do I gotta tell you people? Grace. Brookstein. Wuz. Here.'

'I'm sure she was, sir,' said Mitch. *But she's not here now. Another dead end.*

'How's about my reward? Man on the TV said two hundred thousan' dollars.'

'We'll be in touch.'

There were messages waiting for Mitch back at the station.

'Your wife called,' the sergeant on the desk told him.

'Ex-wife,' Mitch corrected her.

'Whatever. She was yelling something about your kid's school play. She wasn't a happy camper.'

Mitch groaned. *Damn it. Celeste's play. Was that today?* Mitch had sworn up and down he'd be there, but with all the excitement of the last forty-eight hours, he'd totally forgotten. *I'm the worst father in the world* and *the worst cop. Someone should give me a medal.* Guiltily he began punching his old home number into his cell when the desk sergeant interrupted him.

'One more thing, sir. A guy was here earlier. He said he had information about Grace Brookstein; said he knew her. He wanted to talk to you but he wouldn't wait.'

'Well, did you get his details?'

She shook her head. 'He wouldn't tell me anything. He

225

said he'd wait for you in this bar until six.' She handed Mitch a dirty piece of paper with an address scrawled on it.

Mitch sighed. It was probably another crank. On the other hand the bar was only a couple of blocks away. And anything was preferable to facing Helen's wrath, or hearing the disappointment in Celeste's voice.

The clock on the wall said ten of six.

At six o'clock exactly, Mitch walked into the bar just as a good-looking, dark-haired man with a hawklike nose was walking out. When Mitch saw there were no other customers, he ran back onto the street and caught up with him.

'Hey. Was it you who wanted to see me? I'm Detective Connors.'

The dark-haired man looked at his watch. 'You're late.'

Mitch was irritated. *Who does this dickhead think he is?* 'Look, buddy, I don't have time for games, okay? Do you have information for me or don't you?'

'You know, you might want to be a little more polite to me. Your ass is on the line, Connors, and I can save it. For a price, of course. I know where Grace Brookstein's going to be at noon tomorrow. If you're nice to me – real nice – I'll take you to her.'

Celeste Connors cried herself to sleep that night.

Her daddy never called.

Chapter Twenty

Davey Buccola paced his hotel room like a caged tiger. His suite at the Paramount on Times Square was luxurious. Frette bed linen, sleek modern furniture, $500 cashmere blankets draped casually over the back of the armchair. Davey thought, *This'd be an impressive place to bring a woman.*

Unfortunately, he wasn't with a woman. He was with a bunch of cops. And they were starting to make him nervous.

'Stand still, please, Mr Buccola. We need to check your wire.'

Davey lit a cigarette, his third in as many minutes.

'Again?'

'Yes. Again.' Mitch Connors was in a pissy mood. 'You want to see that two hundred grand, Mr Buccola, I suggest you cooperate.'

Davey thought, *He's probably nervous, too. Doesn't want anything to go wrong.*

Davey felt bad, doing the dirty on Grace Brookstein. He'd always liked her. What's more, he was convinced she was innocent of the crimes she'd been convicted of. But $200,000 . . . *two hundred thousand* . . . He tried to rationalize the decision to himself. He was protecting Grace. This way she would be captured unharmed. He hadn't told Connors or any of the cops about the information he'd uncovered, either. Later, once Grace was safe, he'd use it to launch an appeal against her conviction and reopen the inquest into Lenny's death. *Either that or sell it. What would* Vanity Fair *pay for a scoop like this?* If he was lucky, he might double his reward money!

Of course, deep down, Davey Buccola knew the truth. He was betraying an innocent woman for money, the same way everybody else had betrayed her. It wasn't $200,000. It was thirty pieces of silver.

'Mr Buccola. Are you with us?'

Davey looked up, startled. Mitch Connors was shouting at him again.

'We only have an hour. Let's run through the plan one more time.'

Grace dipped her donut into the hot black coffee and took a big, satisfying bite.

Delicious.

She and Lenny used to have the finest chefs on staff at all their homes, ready to prepare lobster thermidor or whip up a Gruyère soufflé at any hour of the day or night. But not until this week had Grace tasted a Dunkin' Donut. She couldn't imagine how she'd ever lived without them.

The week had been full of new experiences. The familiarity she felt when she first came back to New York had been replaced by a sort of delighted wonder. It was the same city she'd lived in, on and off, for her entire life. And yet it was completely different. *This* New York, the New York of the ordinary people, of the poor, was like another planet to Grace, with its subway trains, its dirty buses, its donut shops, its walk-ups and shared bathrooms and television sets with

228

wire coat hangers jammed into the top. Lenny had always told Grace it was terrible to be poor. 'Poverty is the most degrading, most soul-destroying state into which the human soul can sink.' Grace disagreed. True, she had never been poor before, but then Lenny had never been to prison. Grace had. She knew what 'soul-destroying' meant. She knew what it was to be degraded, to be robbed of one's humanity. Poverty didn't come close.

By all objective standards, the hotel in Queens where Grace had been staying was a dump – dirty, cramped, with depressing mustard-colored walls and linoleum floors. But Grace had come to enjoy the smells of fried onions wafting up from the hot-dog stand outside her window, and the ridiculous arguments between the couple across the hall. It made her feel less alone. As if she were part of something.

Getting dressed this morning, preparing for her meeting with Davey, she actually thought, *I'll be sorry to leave here.* But she knew couldn't stay. For one thing, it wasn't safe. She had to keep moving. More important, the time had come to begin her mission. Armed with Davey's information, she could at last begin her journey. Today, her vengeance would take flight.

She had dressed simply for their rendezvous. Jeans, sneakers, a black polo-neck sweater and a down jacket, her beanie hat pulled low over her newly darkened hair. The jeans already felt a little tighter on the waist than they had in Richardsville. Grace was gaining weight, a side effect of her newfound donut addiction. Swallowing the dregs of her coffee, she looked at her watch. *Eleven o'clock.*

She headed for the subway.

Mitch Connors hadn't slept. The plan was simple. Davey had arranged to meet Grace at noon exactly, in front of Toys 'R' Us on Times Square. At that time of day the New

York landmark should be crawling with shoppers looking for a bargain in the winter sales, as well as the usual back-pack-laden hordes of tourists. Mitch had positioned two men behind Davey, inside the store, another two at the entrance to the subway, and six more scattered throughout the crowd. All ten would be in plainclothes, wired and armed. Mitch wasn't expecting any trouble, but after the way Grace had dealt with that scumbag Tommy Burns, he wasn't taking any chances. As soon as Davey saw Grace in the crowd, he would use his hidden mike to alert the cops, who would close in around her. Once she reached Davey and shook his hand, that was the signal to move in and grab her. *Easy.*

Mitch himself would be watching the proceedings from the Paramount Hotel. His face had been all over the news for weeks. If Grace saw him, she'd know something was up.

Davey Buccola lit another cigarette. Eleven forty-five. Time to go downstairs. Davey looked on in alarm as one of the cops checked his gun before slipping it back into the holster under his jacket.

'What's that for? You aren't going to hurt her, are you?'

The cop looked at Davey like something he'd just scraped off of his shoe. He'd given them good information but he was a snitch. Nobody liked a snitch. 'I'm sure Mrs Brookstein would be touched by your concern. Are you ready?'

Davey nodded. *Two hundred grand. My own place.*

'I'm ready. Let's go.'

Ten to twelve.

'Do you see her?'

Davey Buccola stamped his feet against the cold. Resisting the urge to put his hand to his ear – he hated wires – he murmured, 'Negative. Not yet.'

Times Square was even more crowded than he'd expected. Toys 'R' Us was jammed. Half of New York was out of work, but people would rather starve than see their kids go without the latest Hannah Montana doll or Special Agent Oso flashlight. *Sad, really,* Davey reflected.

The woman opposite Grace was staring. Grace felt her stomach flip over.

'Hey.'

The train was crowded, but no one was talking. The woman's voice rang out like a foghorn.

'Hey! I'm talking to you.'

Grace looked up. She felt the blood rush to her face. *She recognizes me. Oh God. She's going to say something. They'll turn on me. The whole train will turn on me, they'll rip me to shreds!*

'You done with your paper?'

Paper? Grace looked down. There was a *New York Post* in her lap. She had no idea how it had gotten there. Wordlessly, she handed it over.

'Thanks.'

Suddenly the train jerked to a halt. The lights flickered, then went out. Everybody groaned. The lights came on again. Grace looked at her watch. *Five to twelve.*

'Forget it,' the man next to her said genially. 'Wherever you're going, you're going to be late.'

A voice came over the address system. 'We apologize for the inconvenience. Due to some electrical problems, we expect a short delay.'

No! Not today. Why today?

Grace took a deep breath. She couldn't draw attention to herself by appearing jittery. Besides, it was okay. They said a short delay. Davey would wait.

* * *

As he stared out of the window Mitch's heart sank.

She's not coming.

He'd been so sure this was it. So certain. The clock on the wall taunted him. Ten after twelve. What could have gone wrong? Had Buccola had a change of heart and tipped her off? Had Grace realized she couldn't trust him? Or maybe it was worse than that. Maybe something had happened to her. An accident. Someone had recognized her and taken the law into his own hands.

'I think I see her.'

Buccola's voice sounded crackly in Mitch's earpiece.

'You *think*? Don't you know?'

Buccola didn't answer.

'Well, where?' Mitch couldn't hide his excitement.

'She just came out of the subway. I didn't get a good look at her face. It might not be her.'

'Danny, Luca. Did you guys see anything?'

Two of Mitch's men were right outside the subway, checking out every woman who emerged.

'Nope.'

'Nothing.'

Jesus. 'What was she wearing, Davey?'

'Jeans. Dark coat. A hat . . . I think. Shit.'

'What?'

'I lost her.'

'You *lost* her? Well, was she heading toward you? Did she see you?'

'Forget it. It wasn't her.'

Grace darted out of the subway onto the street. She was late. Very late. Would Davey have waited this long? God, she hoped so. He was taking a big risk agreeing to meet her at all.

She pushed forward into the crowds, head down. The multicolored lettering of the Toys 'R' Us store called to her from across the square. Grace headed toward it, scanning the throng for her friend's familiar face.

Officer Luca Bonnetti was disappointed. So much for being part of the big show. Grace Brookstein had obviously made other plans.

Still, getting paid to eye up women wasn't the worst way to spend a morning. A cute brunette in a hurry brushed past him.

'Hey, babe. How you doin'?'

He tapped her on the ass, but she hurried on.

'What is your *problem,* Bonnetti?' His partner was mad. 'We're supposed to be looking for America's most wanted, not harassing members of the public.'

'Aw, lighten up, Danny. She was cute. And in case you haven't figured it out, Lady Brookstein ain't coming.'

Grace's heart was pounding. *Asshole.*

After what that bastard van driver had done to her, the thought of a man touching her or even looking at her sexually made her want to scream to the top of her lungs. But she couldn't scream. She couldn't stop and yell at the guy to get his stinking hands off of her. She had to be invisible, to melt into the crowd.

Where the hell is Davey?

Just as she thought the words, she saw him. He was standing a few feet in front of the store. She walked toward him, smiling. Sensing her smile, Davey looked up. That's when Grace noticed.

'It's her! I see her. She's heading over. Jeans, dark jacket. Beanie.'

Mitch asked the cops in the square, 'Have you got her?'

'Yes, sir. We see her. Closing in.'

*   *   *

Grace's mind raced.

He said he'd have the file with him. The evidence. Why didn't he bring it?

Something was wrong. It wasn't just the file. It was Davey's face. It had guilt written all over it. Just then, two men brushed past Grace, heading toward Toys 'R' Us. Some sixth sense made her slow her pace.

Cops. It's a setup.

There was no time to think. Acting on instinct, she whipped off her hat and stuffed it into her coat pocket. A group of foreign schoolchildren was heading in the opposite direction, back toward the subway. Grace slipped in among them, another small dark fish entering the safety of the shoal.

The men clutched at their earpieces. Up in the hotel room, Mitch Connors was yelling bloody murder.

'Where is she? WHERE IS SHE?'

'I don't know.' Davey Buccola was confused. 'She was coming right for me and then she . . . she disappeared.'

Mitch could have wept.

'Spread out, all of you. Keep looking. She's in that crowd.'

He couldn't take it any longer. He ran out of the hotel room and headed for the stairs.

From the sixth floor of the Paramount, Mitch had had a bird's-eye view of the square below. Now, running outside at street level, he could barely see three feet in front of his nose. There were people everywhere, jostling their bulky shopping bags, pushing their kids' strollers across his path.

Jeans, dark jacket, beanie hat. She's here. She must be.

He pushed into the heaving mass of bodies.

* * *

234

Grace was almost at the subway. The stone steps beckoned her, promising safety, escape. *Just a few more seconds. A few more steps!*

She glanced to her right. A man in a Yankees cap was looking around him frantically, muttering to himself. *One of the cops. How many are there?* The man was heading straight for Grace's group. Now he was stopping their tour guide, asking him something. *I have to break away.*

Suddenly Grace saw the sleazeball who had pawed her earlier. He was still hanging around the entrance to the subway. On closer inspection she could see he was a young Italian, attractive, if you liked assholes. Not that Grace would have cared if he looked like Quasimodo. She walked in his direction.

Mitch held his breath. *There she is!* The crowd moved almost imperceptibly and he saw her, not fifteen feet away from where he was standing. She was tiny, maybe five feet tall, in jeans and a dark coat and she had almost reached the subway. Mitch broke into a run.

'Hey, buddy! Look where you're going.'

'Slow down, jerk.'

Mitch ran on blindly, knocking pedestrians off their feet. As Grace reached the steps Mitch made a lunge for her, rugby-tackling her to the ground, facedown. She screamed but it was too late. Blood gushed from her nose. Mitch snapped a pair of handcuffs on her wrists. It was over.

'Grace Brookstein, you're under arrest. You have the right to remain silent. You have the right to an attorney.' Turning her over, he pulled the beanie hat up to get a better look at her face. 'Oh Jesus.'

A terrified blond stared back at him.

Mitch had never seen her before in his life.

*　　*　　*

Luca Bonnetti couldn't believe his luck.

'Hey, sexy. You're back.'

'I'm back.' The gorgeous brunette stood up on tiptoes, wrapped her arms around his neck, and started kissing him passionately. Luca returned the favor. This time he got both hands on her ass.

Out of the corner of her eye, Grace saw the cop with the Yankee hat, still talking to the tour guide. *He's probably describing me.* If she looked like she were part of a couple, it would throw them off the scent. This bozo could be her cover till she got safely on a train. Then she'd jump off at the next station and lose him.

She broke off the kiss and smiled at him. 'Wanna take a ride with me?'

Luca grinned. 'Do I ever!'

'He's busy.' Another man, older, with a thick, salt-and-pepper mustache, had appeared out of nowhere and looked daggers at Grace. 'He's busy.'

Luca Bonnetti protested. 'No, I'm not. Give me a break, Danny, would you?'

'Give *you* a break?' The man turned to Grace. 'Look, lady, we're NYPD and we're on a job. So get the hell out of here before I book you for soliciting.'

Grace felt the bile rise up in her throat. *He's one of them.* Her legs started to shake. She ran.

It took Mitch a few moments to react.

He was apologizing to the young woman whose nose he'd just broken when the girl tore past him, two steps at a time. Turning back to the woman, Mitch started removing her handcuffs when he saw it: a gray woolen beanie hat sticking out of the girl's coat pocket.

'Stop!' he yelled. 'Police!'

*   *   *

Grace was on the platform. Behind her, she could hear the shouting.

'Police! Let me through!'

The train was packed. Grace tried to force her way into a car but a man pushed her back. 'Use your eyes, lady. There's no room here. Move down.'

'Police!'

The shouts were getting louder. Grace looked back over her shoulder. It was him. Detective Connors. She recognized his face from the TV reports.

The next car was also full. People had started moving back, waiting for the next train. There was no space on this one. The electric doors whooshed shut. It was too late. The train started to move away.

'Grace Brookstein! Stay where you are. You're under arrest!'

Grace heard her name. So did everybody else. Suddenly hundreds of pairs of eyes were swiveling around, scanning the platform. *Grace Brookstein? Where? Is she here?*

Mitch Connors was sprinting along the platform, faster than the train. He ran past the first car. Then the second. As he reached the third the crowds parted. Mitch and Grace were face-to-face.

Grace looked into Mitch's eyes and Mitch looked into hers. The hunter and the prey. For a moment something passed between them. Mutual respect. Affection, even. But only for a moment.

The train was gaining speed. Safe in the warmth of the carriage, Grace turned away from the window.

Mitch Connors stood on the platform and watched her disappear into the dark oblivion of the tunnel.

Back at the station, Lieutenant Dubray lost it.

'What the fuck? How could you lose her like that? *How?*'

'I don't know, sir.' Mitch sighed.

He tried to look on the bright side. They knew more than they did forty-eight hours ago. They knew Grace was still in New York. They knew she was a brunette now and that she'd gained weight. Tomorrow they'd issue a new Photofit picture to the media.

Thanks to Luca Bonnetti, the NYPD's crack surveillance team had managed to gather one other new piece of information.

America's most wanted woman was a terrific kisser.

Chapter Twenty-One

For three days, Grace lay low. She found a new place to stay, another studio, this time in Brooklyn. Where the room in Queens had been shabby but welcoming, this place could only be described as squalid. Grace didn't care. She drew the curtains, locked the door and crawled into bed. Depression washed over her in slow, lapping waves.

This is worse than prison. This is hell.

In prison, Grace had had Karen and Cora. There was Sister Agnes and the kids at the center. Visits from Davey Buccola. *Davey.* Grace ought to be used to betrayal by now but what Davey had done shocked her to the core. She'd really believed he was on her side. More important, he'd held the key to all her hopes of finding Lenny's killer. Grace had put her faith in another human being for the last time. *The only person I trust is gone forever, betrayed and murdered for his money.*

The way she felt now, Grace wouldn't have trusted her own shadow.

She wept. When she could cry no more, she got dressed. For the first time in three days, she went out.

* * *

It was a crazy risk. Insane. But Grace didn't care.

Cypress Hills Cemetery in Brooklyn overlooked Jamaica Bay. It was nondenominational, although much of its upkeep in recent years had been funded by Jewish charities. Grace remembered the outcry when Lenny's remains were buried there.

'That son of a bitch betrayed the Jewish community. We trusted him because he was one of us. Now he wants to rest among us? No way.'

Eli Silfen, head of the Beth Olom Benevolent Fund, was particularly strident. 'A memorial to Lenny Brookstein? At Cypress Hills? Over my dead body.'

But Rabbi Geller had stood firm. A soft-spoken, deeply spiritual man, Rabbi Geller had known Lenny for most of his life.

'Actually, Eli, it will be over his. This is a religion of forgiveness. Of mercy. It's for God to judge, not man.'

Grace had never forgotten the rabbi's compassion. She wished he were here now as she picked her way through the gravestones and angel statues, her breath white in the freezing winter air. The cemetery was huge. Tens of thousands of graves, maybe more, stretching as far as the eye could see. *I'll never find it. Not without help.*

An elderly groundskeeper was tending to a plot a few yards away. Grace approached him.

'Excuse me. I was wondering, are there any . . . any notable people buried here?' It seemed safer than asking outright.

The old man laughed, revealing a mouthful of rotten teeth.

'Any? How long've you got. It's like *People* magazine down there.' He banged the frozen earth with his hoe, cackling again at his own joke. 'We got Mae West. Jackie Robinson. We got some bad pennies, too. Wild Bill Lovett. Know who that is?'

Grace didn't.

'He was a gangster. A killer. Leader of the White Hand Gang.'

'I'm sorry. I don't know much about criminals,' said Grace, forgetting that officially at least, she *was* one.

'We got one criminal here I'll bet you know about. Leonard Brookstein. Mr Quorum. You'd heard of him, ain't you?'

Grace blushed. 'Yes. Yes, I have. Do you know where he's buried?'

'Sure do.'

He started to walk. Grace kept pace with him for almost ten minutes, the two of them like a pair of drill sergeants inspecting a parade ground of silent, wintry dead, the gravestones standing to attention like soldiers. Eventually they reached the top of a hill. Grace froze. Less than two hundred yards ahead, two armed policemen stood yawning beside a simple white stone. Or at least, it had once been simple and white. Even from here Grace could see it had been covered with graffiti, bloodred messages of hate that no one had bothered to erase. *Of course there are cops here! They're probably waiting for me to make a stupid mistake. Like this.*

'What's the matter?' asked the groundskeeper. 'We ain't there yet, you know.'

'I know, I . . . I've changed my mind.' Grace's heart was pounding. 'I don't feel well. Thank you for your help.'

He looked at her strangely, studying her features as if for the first time. Hoping to distract him, Grace hurriedly pressed a twenty into his arthritis-stiff hand, then turned and fled back down the hill.

She didn't stop running till she reached the subway, slipping into a nearby café to catch her breath and collect herself. How could people deface a man's grave? What sort of a person did that? She'd been too far away to read any of the graffiti, but she could imagine the poisonous things that had

241

been written. Her eyes brimmed with tears. None of them knew Lenny. What a decent, loving, generous man he had been. Sometimes even Grace felt that that man was slipping away from her. That the reality of who Lenny was had already been lost, crushed beneath a mountain of lies and envy and loathing. People called him wicked, but it was a lie.

You weren't wicked, my darling. It's this world that's wicked. Wicked and greedy and corrupt.

In that moment Grace realized that she had a choice. She could give up. Turn herself in, accept the rotten hand of lies that life had dealt her. Or she could fight.

Rabbi Geller's words came back to her: *It's for God to judge. Not man.* Perhaps Grace should leave the crushing of her enemies to God? Let him right the wrongs the world had done to her, and to her darling Lenny?

Perhaps not.

Grace knew what her next move would be.

Davey Buccola fumbled with the key to his hotel room. He was very, very drunk.

When Grace slipped through his fingers, so did the money. He'd betrayed her, and she knew it, and it had all been for nothing. Too depressed to face going home to his mother's house, Davey had hung around the city, spending what was left of his savings on strippers and booze.

'Stupidfugginthing.' He tried the key again twice, before it dawned on him: *I'm on the wrong floor.* As he staggered back down the hall to the elevator, the walls lunged toward him and the floor moved up and down, up and down, like a ship on the high seas. Davey remembered the fun house at the Atlantic City amusement park his dad used to take him to as a kid. He felt nauseous. It was a relief to step into the elevator.

'What floor?'

The woman had her back to him. Even in his drunken state, the PI in Davey took note of her long auburn hair and shiny black trench coat. Or was it two trench coats?

'What floor?' she asked again. Davey couldn't remember.

'Third,' he guessed. The woman reached forward and pressed a button.

Then she pressed a gun into the small of Davey's back.

'Make a move and I will kill you.'

Up in his hotel room, Davey sat on the edge of the bed, stone-cold sober.

'I know how it looks. But I can explain.'

Grace raised the gun and pointed it directly at his head. 'I'm listening.'

Getting hold of a gun was a lot easier than Grace had thought it would be. She'd assumed it would be a complicated, dangerous process, but turned out you could buy them on the street. Like chestnuts. She'd noticed the man loitering in the alleyway, exchanging money with neighborhood kids in what Grace assumed must be drug deals. Yesterday afternoon she walked right up to him.

'I need a gun. Do you know anyone who can help me?'

The guy looked Grace over. With her shaven head and baggy masculine clothes, he put her down as a dyke, probably fresh out of prison. He wasn't a fan of carpet munchers, as a rule. On the other hand, she certainly wasn't a cop, and he could use the money.

'That depends. How much you payin'?'

They agreed on a price that was twice what the pistol was worth. He instantly regretted not having held out for more.

As Grace walked away, he called after her: 'D'you know how to use that thing?'

Grace stopped, thought about it, shook her head.

'Fifty bucks, I'll give you a private lesson. I'll even throw in some ammo, how's that?'

'Twenty,' Grace was amazed to hear herself saying.

'Thirty-five. Tha's my final offer.'

'Deal.'

'Oh God, Grace, please! Don't shoot!'

Davey Buccola was sobbing. Grace felt oddly detached. It was almost distasteful, listening to him beg for his life, rivers of tears and mucus streaming down his contorted, terrified face. As if any words of his could change her decision.

'Give me the file.'

'The file?'

'The information you promised me. The information you were going to give me in Times Square, remember? Before you got greedy and decided to turn me in for two hundred grand. '

'It wasn't like that, Grace. I was trying to protect you.'

Grace moved her index finger over the trigger. 'One more lie out of your mouth and I swear to God I will blow your head off.'

Davey whimpered with fear. She meant it. This was not the Grace Brookstein he'd met at Bedford Hills. This was a totally different person. Cold. Ruthless. Reckless.

'There *is* a file, isn't there, Davey? I hope for your sake you weren't lying about that as well.'

'No, no, it's here. I have it.'

He'd missed out on the reward, but Davey had still hoped to find a bidder for his gold mine of secrets. So far no magazine editors had taken his call, but he was working on it. He reached under the bed.

'Stop!' Grace commanded.

Davey froze.

'Keep your hands where I can see them. On top of your head.'

Davey did as he was asked.

'Good. Now walk into the middle of the room and kneel down.'

Davey felt his stomach turn to liquid. *Oh God. The classic execution pose. She's going to put a bullet in the back of my neck.*

'Please, Grace . . .'

'Be quiet!' Cautiously, keeping the gun trained on Davey, Grace squatted down on her haunches and reached under the bed herself. She pulled out a brown manila folder.

'Is this it?'

Davey nodded. 'Once you were safe, I was going to take it to a lawyer, I swear to God! I would have helped you launch an appeal.'

Grace pressed the folder to her chest like a lover. Then she released the safety catch on the gun. 'Have you shown this to anyone? The police, or the press?'

Davey shook his head vehemently. 'No one. The only people that know this exists are you and I.'

It was the right answer. Grace smiled. Davey felt relieved. *She's going to let me live.*

Grace picked up a pillow from the bed. Holding it in front of the gun, she said coolly, 'You betrayed me. Do you know what the punishment is for traitors, Davey?'

Before he could answer, he heard the muffled sound of the shot, followed by a warm, wet sensation in his lower body.

After that, there was nothing.

Mitch Connors surveyed the scene. The hotel maid who made the call had such poor English, and was so terrified and hysterical, he hadn't known what to expect. But it definitely wasn't this.

Despite himself, Mitch burst out laughing.

'It's not funny!'

Davey Buccola was in the middle of the room, naked and trussed up like a chicken with the cord from the window blinds. *Literally* like a chicken. After he's passed out some-one – Grace – had tarred and feathered him. Feathers from the hotel pillows had been stuck to his limbs with hair gel, and the word *traitor* written across his forehead in permanent marker. The same permanent marker, Mitch presumed, that was sticking out of Davey's asshole now like a poultry ther-mometer.

'From where I'm standing buddy, it is a *little* funny.' Mitch was starting to like Grace more and more.

A single bullet was lodged in the wall next to the window. Below it, in a pile on the floor, lay Davey's soiled clothes. Buccola must have been so terrified when Grace fired the shot into the pillow, he'd lost control of his bowels.

'She's psychotic!' Davey sobbed. 'She could have killed me! I want police protection.'

'Yeah, and I want Gisele Bundchen to lick whipped cream off my balls but it ain't gonna happen,' said Mitch wryly. 'Untie him, somebody, would you? If I have to look at that ass crack for one more second, I'm gonna need some serious therapy. I may never eat chicken again.'

'Shouldn't we take some pictures first, boss? Document the crime scene?'

'Who for?' Mitch laughed even harder. 'Colonel Sanders?'

'You're not taking this seriously!' Davey Buccola did his best to sound indignant, not an easy thing to do with a Sharpie stuck up your ass. 'Grace Brookstein threatened me at gunpoint. That's armed robbery! Don't you care?'

'About you, Buccola? No, I don't care And what do you mean "armed robbery"? Robbery of what? What did she steal?'

Davey hesitated.

'Either you tell me, or I'm gonna leave you here like this.'

'If I tell you, with you give me police protection?'

Mitch walked toward the door.

'Wait!' Davey yelped. 'Okay, okay. There was a file. Information about her husband's death. We think . . . we believe that Lenny Brookstein was murdered.'

'*What?*'

'I was working with Grace. Investigating the case. That's why she broke out of Bedford. She doesn't care about the money. All she wants is to find who killed her husband. Who set her up. She wants vengeance.'

Mitch could understand about wanting vengeance. He thought back to the day Grace had called him. '*I didn't steal any money, Detective. I was framed and so was my husband.*' *Was it possible?*

'Why the hell didn't you tell me this earlier?' he shouted. But as soon as he'd said the words, he knew the answer: 'You were going to sell the information, weren't you? You greedy little shit.'

Davey Buccola was silent.

'So you gave her this file?'

'I had to! She had a gun . . .'

'You have a copy, right? Tell me you have a copy.'

Less than three miles away, Grace lay in a bathtub, rereading Davey's information for the hundredth time.

Suddenly she sat bolt upright. There it was, in black and white.

I know who killed Lenny.

At last, the hunt was on.

Chapter Twenty-Two

Andrew Preston walked down Wall Street with a familiar feeling of tightness in his chest. Maria was in the throes of a new affair. He knew the signs by now. The bedside drawer stuffed with receipts from La Perla. The Brazilian bikini wax she booked *after* their Hong Kong trip, not before. This morning, he'd even walked in on her singing *La Traviata* in the shower.

If only I didn't love her so much. None of this would have happened.

It was five-thirty, and the street was already crowded with traders and secretarial staff on their way home. Since he'd started his new job in the M&A division at Lazard, Andrew often worked till nine or ten at night. But this was a Thursday: gym night. Andrew's doctor had emphasized how vital it was for him to exercise regularly. 'Nothing combats stress like a good game of racquetball. No point being a big swinging dick on Wall Street if your heart gives out at forty-five, you know what I'm saying?'

Andrew knew what his doctor was saying. Although he couldn't help but question the judgment of anyone who perceived him, Andrew Preston, as a 'big swinging dick.'

Maria certainly didn't. Whatever he achieved, however much money he made, it was never enough. Andrew's vintage Aston Martin DB5 was parked in an underground garage, four buildings down from his office. The rates were extortionate, but driving to work was one of the few small luxuries he allowed himself. Mindful of his heart, he took the stairs to P4 instead of the elevator, pressed the unlock button on his remote, and jumped into the driver's seat.

'Hello, Andrew.'

He was so shocked he almost screamed. Grace Brookstein was crouched low in the backseat. She was holding a gun and smiling.

'Long time no see.'

Mitch Connors couldn't believe his ears.

'Sir, with all due respect, this is bullshit. We *have* to reopen the investigation into Leonard Brookstein's death. If we don't, and it came out later that we'd suppressed this evidence . . .'

When Mitch finally untrussed Davey Buccola, the red-faced PI had handed him a USB chip. The information it contained was so explosive, Mitch had printed it out and taken it straight to his boss.

'No one's suppressing anything.' Lieutenant Dubray snapped the file shut. 'Frankly, Mitch, I don't understand why you're so hot to start a new investigation when you're making such a mess of the one you're on now. Grace Brookstein's made a fool of you. She's made a fool of this entire department.'

'I know, sir. But if her husband *was* murdered, and the inquest criminally mishandled, there's been a major miscarriage of justice.'

Dubray scoffed. 'Justice? Give me a break. Lenny Brookstein was an asshole, Mitch, okay? A rich, greedy

249

asshole who took this city for a ride. If someone *did* whack the old man, they did the world a favor. Nobody cares, least of all me.'

Mitch was silent. Was Dubray for real? The whole investigation into Lenny Brookstein's death had been a sham. The coroner ruled suicide, because America had already passed judgment on its once beloved son. Lenny Brookstein was a thief, a greedy liar who'd raped the poor and stolen from his own fund.

But what if America was wrong? About Lenny *and* Grace.

From the very beginning of the investigation, Mitch had had conflicting feelings about Grace Brookstein. The initial, knee-jerk hatred he shared with the rest of America had rapidly been replaced by a combination of pity and, he might as well admit it, respect. Grace was brave, determined and resourceful, qualities that Mitch had always viewed as predominantly male. Yet when he'd finally seen Grace Brookstein in the flesh, fleetingly, the day her subway train pulled away at Times Square, the face staring back at him was all woman: vulnerable, compassionate, kind. In other circumstances, another life, Mitch could picture himself falling for her. *I could save her. We could save each other.* He dragged himself back to reality.

'Suppose Leonard Brookstein was innocent.'

Dubray's eyes widened. 'Excuse me?'

'I said suppose he was innocent. Suppose someone else took that money.'

'Like who? The tooth fairy?'

'How about Andrew Preston? No disrespect, sir, but have you *read* Buccola's file? Preston had been embezzling funds for years.'

Dubray waved a hand dismissively. 'Petty cash. Besides, all the Quorum guys were interviewed up the wazoo at the time. I know the feds aren't always the sharpest knives in the drawer, but do you really think Harry Bain wouldn't have caught on by now if one of them had that cash? Your PI's barking up the wrong tree.'

'Maybe,' Mitch conceded. 'But shouldn't we at least check out Buccola's leads? The more I look at the Quorum case, the more it stinks.'

'So stop looking at it. Do your job. Find Grace Brookstein and get her back in jail where she belongs.'

Back in his office, Mitch turned off his phone and closed the doors. *Did* Grace Brookstein belong in jail? He wasn't so sure anymore. He tried to push the thought down, to strangle it. But it wouldn't stop growing, forcing its way up into the sunlight of his consciousness like a weed.

It's a put-up job. The inquest, the trial, whole thing. It's all been staged, like a scripted reality show.

Dubray wasn't interested in the truth. Neither were the Massachusetts cops who'd investigated Lenny Brookstein's death, or the coroner, or the media, or even the FBI. The Quorum fraud was a movie and America had already cast its villains: Grace and Lenny Brookstein. No one wanted an alternative ending. Not when they'd paid so dearly for their seats, and were already halfway through their popcorn.

Dubray had told him to forget Buccola's information: 'Delete it, shred it, burn it, I don't care. Lenny Brookstein's dead and buried.' But Mitch knew he couldn't do that.

That information would lead him to the truth.

With a little luck, it would also lead him to Grace Brookstein.

Andrew Preston gritted his teeth. If he was going to die, he would try to do it with courage. 'Everything I did, I did for Maria. You must believe that, Grace.'

Grace tightened the cord around his wrists. They'd driven

out to New Jersey, to an abandoned barn off the 287 Freeway. Outside it was dark and a starting to rain. A cold drizzle dripped through the holes in the barn's roof, soaking Andrew's shirt. The post he was tied to pressed painfully into his back.

'Don't tell me what I must believe. Just answer my questions. How much did you steal from Lenny?'

'I didn't steal from Lenny.'

The hard metal butt of the gun slammed into the bridge of Andrew's nose. He screamed in pain.

'Don't lie to me! I have proof. One more lie and I will shoot you in the head. Do you believe me?'

Andrew Preston nodded. He believed her. If this had been the old Grace, he would have appealed to her compassion. But the old Grace was clearly dead and gone. Andrew Preston had no doubt that the woman in front of him would put a bullet through his brain without hesitation.

'How much?'

'About three million altogether. Over a number of years. But I wasn't lying. I didn't steal from Lenny. I took the money from Quorum. It was always my intention to pay it back eventually.'

'But you didn't.'

'No. I couldn't. Maria's debts . . .' He started to cry. 'She spent so much she started going to loan sharks. It's an illness with her, Grace. An addiction. She can't help herself. I had no idea how bad things had gotten. Then one day some people came to the house. Violent people. Killers. I wouldn't have cared for myself, but they were threatening to hurt Maria. They showed me pictures.' He shuddered. 'I won't forget those images as long as I live.'

Grace thought of Lenny's bloated, headless corpse lying on a slab in the morgue.

'So you stole from the fund and Lenny found out?'

Andrew hung his head. 'Yes. I thought I'd covered my tracks. The SEC was investigating us but they never caught on. I guess Lenny was smarter than all of them.'

'And that's why you killed him? So you could keep stealing, keep paying off these gangsters?'

Andrew looked at her with genuine surprise. '*Killed* him? No way did I kill him. I stole from Quorum and that was wrong. But I would never have hurt Lenny. He was a good friend to me.'

'Please!' Grace laughed bitterly. 'Lenny knew what you'd done. He and John were discussing it in Nantucket. You were scared he was going to fire you, or turn you over to the authorities, so you killed him.' She released the safety catch on the gun. Her hand was shaking. 'I don't believe you only took three million. You took all of it. You stole all those billions and made it look like it was Lenny.'

'That's not true.'

'You killed him! I know it was you!' Grace was hysterical

Andrew Preston closed his eyes. At least it would be a quick death.

I wonder if Maria will miss me?

Mitch Connors lay on his bed, reading. Davey Buccola was a bottom-feeder, but he was a meticulous bottom-feeder. His report was diligently researched. Of course, a lot of the information was hearsay, based on unofficial interviews with staff at the coroner's office or the Nantucket coast guard. Less than half of it would have stood up in court. But the overall picture it painted, of a wealthy man surrounded by false friends, parasites and hangers-on, rang horribly true.

Mitch imagined Grace reading it. If it made *him* sick, how would she feel, wading through the sticky web of half-truths, greed and deception spun by her nearest and dearest? No wonder she hadn't turned to any of them when she broke out of Bedford. With friends like the Brooksteins had, who needed enemies?

The only problem with the information was that there was so much of it. Too many people had had the motive and the opportunity to do away with Lenny Brookstein. Mitch thought, *Grace is following these leads, just like I am. Where would she go first?*

Andrew Preston opened his eyes. He'd been waiting for Grace to shoot him, but so far the expected bullet hadn't come. He was surprised to see her cheeks were wet with tears.

'I want you to admit it,' she sobbed. 'I want you to say you're sorry.'

'Grace. I *am* sorry for what I did. But I didn't kill Lenny and that's the honest truth. I was in New York the day he died. Remember?'

'I know you were. And I know what you were doing there. You were paying off a hit man.' Grace reached into a rucksack and pulled out a photograph. 'Donald Anthony Le Bron. I suppose you're going to tell me you don't recognize him?'

Andrew's face drained of color.

'No. I recognize him. And you're right, he is a hit man. He works for a Dominican gang known as the DDP. It stands for Dominicans Don't Play, which is something of an understatement, as it turns out.' He laughed nervously. 'And yes, I did hire Le Bron. But not to kill Lenny.'

Grace hesitated. 'Go on.'

'They said they were debt collectors. "Legitimate businessmen," that's how they described themselves. They came to the house and showed me pictures of women being raped and mutilated. They said Maria would be next. Then a month before the Quorum Ball, one of them showed up at the office. He brought a severed finger, wrapped in kitchen towel.'

Andrew closed his eyes at the memory. 'I'd paid off what Maria owed by then, but they still came back for more. They wanted interest, hundreds of thousands. It was never going to end. I couldn't go to the police, in case they found out about the money I'd stolen from Quorum. So I contacted Le Bron. He and his people took care of it.'

Grace tried to take this in. When she'd read the file entry about Andrew's embezzlement and learned of his contacts with the New York gang, she was sure she'd found her man. It all made sense: the thefts Lenny had discovered were the tip of the iceberg. In reality, Andrew must have been siphoning off billions from Quorum's coffers, cooking the books to make it look like Lenny was the thief. Then he'd hired a professional hit man to murder Lenny, and stood by and watched while Grace took the blame. But listening to Andrew talk, watching the horror on his face as he remembered the threats made to Maria, she was convinced he was telling her the truth.

Andrew Preston was not Lenny's killer.

It was a crushing blow.

'Lenny was like a father to me, Grace, and I betrayed him. I'll carry the guilt of that with me till the day I die. But I never wanted him dead. Not like Jack Warner.'

Grace had read Davey's file on Jack, too. She knew about the gambling debts and Lenny's refusal to pay them. But it hardly amounted to a motive for murder. Besides, Jack's alibi was rock solid. The coast guard had rescued him miles away from where Lenny's boat was found.

'Jack was mad at Lenny. I know that.'

'Mad?' Andrew looked surprised. 'He *hated* him, Grace. Lenny had Warner over a barrel. He knew all of his dirty little secrets. Everyone in the Senate knew that Jack Warner was Quorum's puppet, that he voted however Lenny Brookstein told him to vote. Lenny squeezed Jack like a wet rag. The guy couldn't breathe.'

Grace looked disbelieving. 'I'm sure it wasn't like that. Lenny would never have blackmailed Jack. He would never have blackmailed anyone.'

Andrew Preston smiled. It was a flash of the old Grace. Unquestioning, adoring, convinced that Lenny could do no wrong. Not that he blamed her. Andrew knew better than anyone what it was like to love someone so much you would defend them against all reason.

'Grace,' he said gently, 'whatever happened to Lenny, it happened at sea and it happened on the day of the storm. Jack was also out on the water that day, remember?'

Grace remembered. Like Michael Gray, Jack Warner was an expert sailor. *Expert enough to somehow board Lenny's boat and kill him? To dump him overboard and make it look like an accident?* It was possible.

'Try to find a lady called Jasmine,' said Andrew. 'That's the best advice I can give you. She might make you see things in a different light.'

Mitch had gone to the Prestons' apartment on impulse. He'd hoped to quiz Andrew about his alleged embezzlement from Quorum, but was met instead by a hysterical Maria. It was almost midnight, and Andrew hadn't called. No one had seen him since he left the office at five. She'd called the police but no one took her seriously. Mitch did. 'Let me pour you a brandy, Mrs Preston.'

Had Grace taken the law into her own hands? By now, she would know that Andrew had been stealing from Lenny. What if she'd abducted him? Or worse? If Grace got it into her head that Andrew was behind Lenny's death, there was no telling what she might be capable of.

When the apartment door opened and Andrew Preston walked in, Mitch was at least as relieved as Maria. Andrew's shirt was bloodied and his nose badly bruised, but he seemed calm. Unlike his wife, who flung herself melodramatically into his arms.

'Oh, Andy, Andy! What happened? I've been out of my mind. Where have you been?'

'At the hospital. I'm fine, Maria. I had a slight accident, that's all.'

'What sort of accident?'

'Ridiculous really. I slipped and fell in the rain and landed flat on my face on the sidewalk. I would have called, but I was stuck in the ER for hours. You know what those places are like. I didn't want to worry you, darling.'

'Well you did worry me. The police are here.'

Maria gestured toward Mitch. Andrew Preston recognized him from the TV reports as the guy who was looking for Grace. He did his best to sound nonchalant. 'My goodness. Does one errant husband warrant a search party these days? I'm sorry if I've caused any trouble, Detective.'

'Not at all, Mr Preston. I actually came to talk with you about another matter, but it can wait. I'm glad to see you home safe. Look, this is probably going to sound like a ridiculous question. But I don't suppose Grace Brookstein has tried to contact you by any chance. In the last forty-eight hours?'

Andrew looked puzzled. 'Grace? Contact me? No. Why on earth would she do that?'

'No reason,' said Mitch. 'I'll see myself out.'

Later, in bed, Andrew watched his wife sleep. *I love you so much, my angel.* He'd been touched by Maria's concern when he got home. Perhaps things were going to be all right between them after all?

He'd considered telling Detective Connors the truth about Grace and what had happened that afternoon. But only for a moment. Grace had spared his life and forgiven him his sins. The least he could do was return the favor.

If Lenny really had been murdered, Andrew wished Grace luck in finding his killer. Whatever the world might think, Lenny Brookstein had been a good man. Reaching across the bed for Maria, Andrew pulled her close, inhaling the heady scent of her body. The faint whiff of aftershave he detected as well brought tears to his eyes.

Andrew Preston never wore aftershave.

Chapter Twenty-Three

Jasmine Delevigne admired her naked body in the mirror. She was twenty-four years old, with smooth café au lait skin, long, slender legs and a new set of perfect silicone breasts, a birthday present from a powerful client. Cupping them lovingly in her hands, Jasmine thought, *No. He's more than a client. He's my lover. I adore him.*

It was unlike Jasmine to get attached to the men who paid to share her bed. The daughter of a French businessman and a Persian princess, Jasmine Delevigne didn't need the money she earned as a hooker. She did it for the thrill. Just knowing that rich, powerful men, men with beautiful wives and even more beautiful mistresses, found her irresistible, so intoxicating that they would *pay* for the privilege of bedding her, gave Jasmine an incredible high. It was years since she'd dipped into her trust fund. Her Fifth Avenue apartment, her vintage MG convertible, her wardrobe full of couture dresses and thousand-dollar-a-pair shoes; Jasmine's perfect body had paid for them all. Other people might call her a whore. People like her father, who lavished all his attention on Jasmine's mother and never noticed his daughter's efforts to please him. But Jasmine didn't care what they thought.

I'm a feminist. I fuck who I like, when I like, because I like. I answer to no one.

She wandered into her dressing room and picked out some underwear. Chocolate-brown, silk La Perla panties and a matching camisole. *Classy and feminine. Just how he likes it.* It had been weeks since Jasmine had seen him and she was excited. There were others, of course. All her clients were good-looking, successful men, and all of them were good in bed. Jasmine Delevigne was the best, and she only worked with the best. But none of the other men had gotten to her the way that he did.

The buzzer rang.

He's early. He wants this as much as I do.

Jasmine opened the door coolly, like the princess that she was.

'Hello, darling.'

He grabbed her by the throat. 'Take your fucking clothes off. Now.'

Jasmine's pupils dilated with excitement. *I've missed you so much.*

'Please! No!'

Gavin Williams tightened the knots around Grace Brookstein's wrists. Then he lifted the cane and brought it down hard across the backs of her legs. Two livid red welts joined the others. Gavin Williams smiled.

'I'll ask you again, Grace. Where is the money?'

She was crying. Begging. Lenny Brookstein's wife, his most treasured possession, was begging *him,* Gavin Williams, for mercy. But Gavin Williams would show no mercy.

Let the sinners be consumed out of the earth, and let the wicked be no more.

He felt himself getting hard. He lifted the cane again.

'Excuse me, sir? Are you okay?'

Gavin Williams's fantasy evaporated. He was back at his desk at the SIBL, the Science, Industry and Business Library on Madison Avenue. The librarian was standing over him. *Stupid, meddlesome bitch. Why couldn't she mind her own business?*

'I'm fine.'

'Are you sure? You look very flushed. Would you like me to open a window or something?'

'No,' Gavin snapped. The old woman got the point and returned to her seat.

It was ridiculous, being forced to work in a public library. After Harry Bain had summarily dismissed him from the Quorum task force, Gavin's bureau chief had insisted that he take a paid leave of absence.

'You're stressed out, Agent Williams. You need some time off. Happens to all of us.'

It happens to weak idiots like you, you mean. Not to me.

'I'm fine. I'm ready for service.'

'Take the vacation, Gavin, okay? We'll call you in a couple of months.'

A couple of months? Gavin knew what was going on. John Merrivale had been conspiring against him. Poisoning the well. *They all think I'm crazy. Obsessive. But I'll show them. When Grace Brookstein leads me to that money, they'll be eating their words. I'm close. I can feel it.*

Gavin Williams pulled an antiseptic wipe out of his briefcase and started cleaning the spot where the librarian's fingers had touched his desk. Then he closed his eyes and tried to recapture his fantasy: Grace Brookstein, at his mercy, tied up like an animal.

It was no use. She was gone.

'Sir, take a look at this.'

Mitch leaned over the younger detective's computer screen.

'You asked me to do some digging on Senator Warner. This e-mail just came in from vice squad.'

Mitch read the e-mail.

'No one ever followed this up?'

'It appears not, sir. Senator Warner's a big supporter of NYPD causes.'

I'll bet he is.

'This is all off-the-record. My buddy in vice was doing me a favor. I told him we'd handle it sensitively.'

'Do you have an address for the girl?'

'Yes, sir. It's a pretty swanky address, too.' The detective clicked to another window. 'Do you think maybe we should send a female officer out there first? We don't want to spook her.'

Jack Warner sat in the back of his limousine, feeling the adrenaline course through his veins. Being with Jasmine again, touching her, fucking her, gorging himself on her body . . . it was the best feeling in the world. Knowing that the whole of America idolized him as a Christian conservative, a walking embodiment of righteousness and family values, only added to the thrill. Jack remembered Fred Farrell's advice to him, about his gambling.

'I get it. It's a turn-on. All this risk. But is it as much of a turn-on as being the next president of the United States? That's what you have to ask yourself, Jack. You could lose everything.'

Ah, yes. But that was the thrill, wasn't it? Knowing you could lose everything. Fred Farrell knew about the gambling and the extramarital flings. But he didn't know about Jasmine. Only one person had ever known about Jasmine.

And that person was a rotting, worm-eaten corpse by the name of Lenny Brookstein.

*   *   *

Jasmine Delevigne poured tea from a silver pot into two porcelain cups. She handed one of them to the policewoman.

The officer, a nerdy, pale young woman with short black hair and thick plastic-framed glasses, looked around the sumptuous apartment and thought, *I'm in the wrong business.*

'Sugar?'

'Oh. No, thank you. You have a beautiful place.'

'Thanks. I've worked hard for it.' Jasmine leaned back on the Ralph Lauren suede couch and crossed her long legs demurely. 'So. You want to know about Senator Warner?'

When the female cop had showed up unannounced, asking questions about Jack and his relationship to Leonard Brookstein, Jasmine's first reaction was panic. Her second was loyalty. Jasmine loved Jack. She couldn't betray him. But it was her third reaction, self-interest, that eventually won the day. This could be her chance to pry Jack away from his wife at last. He only stayed with Honor because she was necessary to his political ambitions. It stood to reason that if those political ambitions were to die, then so would his marriage.

'How long have the two of you known each other?'

Jasmine took a sip of tea. 'Socially, about five years. We've been lovers for three. Cookie?'

This girl's a piece of work.

'No, thank you. You say "lovers?"'

'You're right. I should probably clarify. Senator Warner is a client of mine. He pays for my services.' She spoke without a hint of shame. 'Nevertheless, I would characterize our relationship as a love match. We adore each other.'

'I see. So Senator Warner confides in you?'

'Absolutely.'

'I wonder, did he ever talk to you about Lenny Brookstein?'

'He did. Lenny knew about us. He was the only one who knew.'

'Jack told him?'

'No! God, no. He found out somehow. Lenny Brookstein was blackmailing Jack. He was a vicious, bullying man and he made Jack's life hell. When I heard he'd killed himself, I was pleased. It couldn't have happened to a nicer guy.'

The policewoman sat up, startled by the girl's bluntness. Jasmine noticed the reaction.

'I'm sorry.' She shrugged. 'I could lie about it, but I don't see the point. I hated Lenny Brookstein. Jack and I both did. He was a manipulator and a fake.'

'Ms Delevigne, in your opinion, did Senator Warner hate Lenny Brookstein enough to want to have him killed? Or to kill him himself?'

Jasmine smiled. The policewoman thought, *Even her teeth are perfect.*

'Did he hate him enough? Absolutely. Lenny was threatening to destroy everything Jack had ever worked for. He would force Jack to swing votes in Quorum's favor, back when they were rewriting all that hedge fund legislation, you remember?' The policewoman nodded. 'Every time Lenny would tell Jack, "This is it, one more vote and you're off the hook." But every time he would come back for more, squeezing and squeezing.' Jasmine shook her head angrily. 'Jack hated Lenny Brookstein with good reason. But he didn't kill him.'

'You sound sure of that.'

'I am sure. Jack was supposed to be out sailing that day, you see. The day of the storm, when Lenny Brookstein went missing.'

The policewoman looked at her notes. 'That's right. He did go sailing. The Nantucket coast guard rescued him, six miles off Sankaty Head. He returned to the Brookstein estate at around . . . six o'clock that night.'

'The coast guard didn't rescue Jack. At least, not in the way you mean.'

'I'm sorry?' The policewoman frowned. 'I don't follow.'

'Jack never took the boat out. He was with me all day, in a beachside cottage in Siasconset. The coast guard covered for him.'

'You mean the coast guard helped Senator Warner to give a false alibi? They *lied*?'

Jasmine laughed, a low, sensual vibration that brought her whole body to life. 'Don't look so shocked. It happens all the time. Senator Warner's a powerful man. People scratch Jack's back so that he'll scratch theirs. I'd have thought, in your profession, you'd be used to that sort of thing. I certainly am in mine.'

Jasmine politely showed the officer to the door. As she left, Jasmine asked her, 'So the police think Lenny Brookstein might have been murdered? I've been following the case but I hadn't heard anything about murder.'

'It's a possibility we're considering.'

'Do you think that means things will come out now? About me and Jack?' Jasmine cocked her head to one side, hopefully. The policewoman thought, *So that's it. She wants people to know. She's hoping to force the senator's hand so he'll leave his wife.*

'I don't know, Ms Delevigne. That's not for me to say.'

Jasmine leaned forward conspiratorially. 'My money's on his mistress. That woman is as hard as nails.'

The policewoman smiled. 'I think you must be mistaken. Mr Brookstein didn't have a mistress.'

'Sure he did. Connie Gray, his sister-in-law. They were lovers till Lenny abandoned her and went crawling back to his wife. Didn't you know?'

Chapter Twenty-Four

'Police! Open the door, Ms Delevigne.'

Jasmine sighed. *Again? What do they want this time?*

She opened the door.

'Hey, I know you, don't I?'

Downstairs in the lobby, Grace locked the door of the ladies' room. Removing her black wig and eyeglasses, she stepped out of her police uniform, folded it neatly and placed it in the toilet cistern. Only after she'd replaced the lid of the cistern and straightened her own clothes did she collapse onto the floor and cry.

No. Not Lenny. Not my Lenny.

With my own sister?

He couldn't.

She cast her mind back. Lenny and Connie had always gotten along. They were kindred spirits in a way, both tough, both ambitious. *The opposite of me.* She remembered the pair of them dancing at the Quorum Ball, deep in conversation. Connie arguing with Lenny on the beach in Nantucket, then storming off in tears. *I thought he was comforting her, because of Michael. Because of all the money they'd lost. How could I have been so blind?*

Grace didn't care about Connie. Her sisters were long since dead to her. But Lenny! Grace's memory of their marriage, of Lenny's love for her, was the one true thing she had left in this world. Without that, there was no hope, no meaning, no point to any of it. Without that love, the anguish was unbearable. She cried out to the heavens.

'Oh, Lenny. Tell me it isn't true!'

But Grace heard nothing, only the echo of her own words in the silence.

Jasmine smiled at the hunky blond cop. Usually she only went for wealthy men. But in Detective Mitch Connors's case, she might be persuaded to make an exception.

'I'd like to talk about your relationship with Senator Warner.'

'Certainly. Although I'm not sure how much more I can help you. I already told your colleague everything I know.'

Mitch frowned 'My colleague?'

'Yes. She was just here.'

She?

'She was asking me all about Jack, and what happened on Nantucket the weekend that Lenny Brookstein disappeared. Didn't you send her?'

Mitch's mouth went dry. He bolted for the elevator, pounding his fist on the call button. It seemed to take forever.

Should I wait, or take the stairs?

Fuck it.

He pushed open the emergency exit door and bounded down the stairs, three at a time. Bursting into the lobby, he looked around. *Empty.* He ran out to the street, frantically looking to the left and right. Fifth Avenue was busy. The street was choked with afternoon traffic and the sidewalk was full of people. Mitch weaved among them holding out his badge like a talisman, grabbing every petite woman he came across, scanning the features of every woman he passed.

It was no good.

Grace Brookstein was gone.

Chapter Twenty-Five

As soon as he realized Grace had given him the slip, Mitch sprinted back up to Jasmine's apartment. 'What did you tell her? I want to know everything, word for word.'

It was quite a conversation. Mitch was used to hearing Lenny Brookstein derided as a fraud and a coward. But in all of the media's vitriolic portrayals, there had never been so much as a whisper about his sleeping around. As for a full-blown affair, with his wife's sister? It just seemed so out of character.

No wonder 'the policewoman' had left in such a hurry.

Mitch tried to figure out what Grace's next move would be. After so many weeks on the case, he was starting to feel as if he *was* in her head, almost as if they were psychically connected in some way. It was weird. Technically they barely knew each other. *Didn't* know each other. Yet there were times when Mitch felt closer to Grace Brookstein than he had to any of his past lovers, even Helen.

Her first instinct, he felt sure, would be to head straight to Connie's house for a confrontation. But then what? Would common sense kick in? Showing up at her sister's place would be insanely risky. On the other hand, Grace *had* robbed Davey

Buccola at gunpoint. Her appetite for risk seemed to be growing by the day.

Mitch had interviewed both Grace's sisters immediately after her escape from Bedford. It was routine procedure to contact family, just in case a suspect tried to make contact. He remembered the way that both Honor and Connie had washed their hands of Grace like a pair of Lady Macbeths, abandoning her utterly in her time of need. Fair-weather friends were bad enough, but Grace seemed to have been cursed by fair-weather family.

If Lenny really *had* traded a looker like Grace for an ice maiden like Connie Gray, he must have needed his head read. Mitch thought back to his encounter with Grace on the subway at Times Square. He'd come so close to catching her that day, but it wasn't his disappointment that he remembered. It was the look on Grace's face, that haunting combination of vulnerability and strength. Despite her exhaustion and the baggy, drab clothes she was wearing, there was something uniquely compelling about her. In some ways, she reminded Mitch of Helen, back in the early, happy days of their marriage. Both women had an inner beauty, an innate femininity that drew men to them like moths to a flame. Connie Gray was the exact opposite. Connie's features might be regular and her figure toned and trim, but she was about as feminine as a sumo wrestler. *Maybe that's what Lenny wanted. A tranny version of his wife?* Now that really would be sick.

Michael Gray answered the door.

'Detective. This is a surprise.'

Mitch thought the same thing everyone thought when they met Michael. *You're a straight-up, old-fashioned, decent man. You're too good for these people.*

'Do you have news about Grace?'

270

'Nothing concrete. We're pursuing some new lines of inquiry. I wondered if I might speak with your wife again?'

'Of course. I'll see if I can find her.'

'It's all right, Mike. I'm here.'

Connie appeared in the entryway. Mitch thought, *Maybe I was a little harsh*. In a pretty, floral-print dress, her blond hair drawn back in an Alice band, she looked a lot more attractive than he remembered her. Behind her, an adorable towheaded boy was pushing a wooden train along the floor. Through double doors to Mitch's right, an older, darker boy was practicing the piano. The whole thing looked like a scene from a Currier and Ives print. *Too good to be true?*

Connie led Mitch into a study where they could be alone. Mitch noticed two first-edition Steinbecks in the bookcase, and what looked like an early Kandinsky on the walnut-paneled wall. The Grays' money troubles were evidently behind them.

Connie saw him admiring the painting. 'It was a present.'

'A very generous one.'

'Yes.' Connie smiled sweetly but didn't elaborate. 'How can I help you, Detective?'

Mitch decided to go for the direct approach.

'How long were you and Lenny Brookstein lovers?'

Blood rushed to Connie's face, then drained from it. She contemplated denying the affair but thought better of it. *He obviously knows. Lying now will only anger him.*

'Not long. A few months. It was over before Nantucket. Before he died.'

'Who ended it?'

Connie picked up a silk cushion and dug her nails into the fabric. 'He did.'

'That upset you?'

A vein in Connie's temple throbbed visibly. 'A little. At the time. As you can imagine, Detective, this is not a chapter

271

of my life story of which I'm particularly proud. Michael has no idea. Nor does Grace.'

She does now.

'You lied to the police about your relationship.'

'I didn't lie. I concealed. I didn't see the point in dredging it all up. I still don't.'

Mitch thought of Lenny's body, or what was left of it, dredged up from the bottom of the ocean. Did Connie have a hand in his death? The woman scorned? She had a cast-iron alibi for the day of the storm. Scores of people had seen the three Knowles sisters lunching together at the Cliffside Beach Club. But she could have orchestrated things behind the scenes.

'What is it that you weren't proud of, exactly? The affair? Or the fact that Lenny dumped you and went running back to Grace?' Mitch was trying to hit a nerve. If he succeeded in shaking Connie out of her queenly self-control, she might let something slip. 'It must have been humiliating, being rejected for your little sister.'

'I'll tell you what was humiliating, Detective. Lenny's ridiculous *obsession* with Grace. That was humiliating. For an intelligent, dynamic man like that to saddle himself with a half-witted child of a wife? It was laughable. It was pathetic.' The spleen dripped off Connie's tongue like venom. 'Everybody thought so, not just me. Oh, we all paid homage, of course, fawned over the loving couple. But that marriage was a running joke.'

'You loved him, didn't you?'

'No.'

'You loved him, but *he* loved your sister.'

'He was obsessed with my sister. There's a difference.'

'Bullshit. Grace was the love of his life. You couldn't forgive either of them for that, could you, Connie?'

Reaching into her purse, Connie took out and lit a cigarette.

272

She inhaled deeply and said, 'Let me tell you something, Detective. The only love of Lenny Brookstein's life was Lenny Brookstein. If you don't know that, you don't know the man at all.'

'But you knew him. You abased yourself, prostituted yourself for his pleasure, then got tossed aside like a used rag.'

'That's not true.'

'Admit it. You threw yourself at the guy's feet!'

The muscles in Connie's jaw visibly tightened. For a moment Mitch thought she was finally going to lose it. But she reined in her temper. Stubbing out her cigarette, she said calmly, 'You're quite wrong. If you must know, I hated Lenny Brookstein. Hated him.'

'Is that why you had him killed?'

Connie burst out laughing. 'Oh, dear! Is that what all this has been about, Detective?' She wiped away tears of mirth. 'You found out about my affair with Lenny, and all of a sudden I'm the jilted lover, off on some murderous rampage? It's a little simplistic, don't you think?'

Mitch was angry. 'I'll tell you what I think. I think you were there that weekend because you wanted revenge.'

'Yes indeed. And I *got* revenge.' Standing up, Connie walked over to the painting Mitch had admired earlier, lifted it off the wall and handed it to him. 'A gift from my dear departed brother-in-law. A fake, as it happens. Like him. But a pretty addition to the room, I'm sure you'll agree. I wanted it, so I made Lenny give it to me. I made Lenny give me a lot of things.'

'You were blackmailing him? Threatening to tell Grace about the two of you?'

'Blackmailing him? Not at all.' The suggestion seemed to surprise her. 'I simply collected what I was owed.' Walking around the room, admiring its array of rare books and objets d'art, Connie smiled contentedly to herself. 'Michael, bless

273

his heart, thinks I bought this house with inheritance money. He actually believes that a rich old aunt left me fifteen million dollars.'

'Lenny gave you the money?'

'Who else? He wrote the check in Nantucket, two days before he died. Thank God I cashed it promptly. A couple more weeks and that money would have been seized by Quorum's administrators. As it was . . .' She smiled smugly, leaving the sentence hanging. 'I can say with my hand on my heart, Detective, that Lenny Brookstein's death was a grievous blow to me. But not because I *adored* him. I am nobody's victim. I leave that to my sister. She's so *good* at it, you see.'

Later that night, Mitch lay awake thinking about Connie and Grace, and about the man both women had loved. Lenny Brookstein was an enigma. He was not the caricature of evil that the press had made him out to be, of that much Mitch was sure. But neither was he the saint of his wife's imagination. What he appeared to be was a mess of contradictions. Generous and mean. Loyal and vengeful. Devoted and unfaithful. Brilliant at business, but unable to tell a friend from a foe.

Had Lenny Brookstein really stolen all that money?

He was capable of it. But had he done it?

If so, the poor bastard never got to enjoy it. Someone had seen to that with a meat cleaver. Someone Lenny Brookstein knew and trusted.

Buccola had provided some tantalizing leads, but all of them had wound up as dead ends: Andrew Preston, Jack Warner, Connie Gray. It was time to take another look at John Merrivale.

Mitch fell asleep dreaming of stormy seas, Kandinsky paintings, and Grace Brookstein's haunting face.

Chapter Twenty-Six

The nausea came in waves.

At first Grace tried to ignore it. She was under stress. She wasn't eating properly. After Jasmine Delevigne had told her about Connie and Lenny, she ran back to her miserable room, crawled into bed, and stayed there for two days. This was worse than Davey Buccola's betrayal, worse than being sent to Bedford, worse even than being raped. She only got out of bed to use the toilet and to vomit. The vomiting was getting worse, both more frequent and more violent. She was getting sick.

It's probably a virus. I'm depressed. My immune system's low.

After forty-eight hours of unbearable nausea, Grace finally dragged herself to the Duane Reade on the corner. With a baseball cap pulled low over her eyes and a muffler covering the bottom half her face, she mumbled her symptoms to the pharmacist.

'Uh-huh. When was your last period?'

The question caught Grace by surprise. 'My period?'

'Is there a chance you could be pregnant, sugar?'

Grace tried to block out the sounds and images, but they

kept coming: The van driver's face, his cruel, flat black eyes, his voice taunting her. *Don't worry, Lizzie, we've got all night.*

'No.'

'You're quite sure?'

'I'm positive. There's no chance.'

Grace bought a pregnancy test.

Ten minutes later, sitting on the broken toilet she shared with three other tenants, Grace peed on the stick for the requisite five seconds, mentally chiding herself for wasting fifteen bucks.

This is ridiculous. I'm late because I'm exhausted.

Two pink lines appeared in the results window. Grace's palms began to sweat. *It must be a faulty test.* She ran back to the pharmacy and wasted another fifteen bucks. Then another. Each time the white plastic stick taunted her, its pink lines dancing in front of her eyes like the elephants in *Dumbo*.

Positive. Positive. Positive.

Congratulations! You are pregnant.

Grace felt dizzy. She slumped back on the bed and closed her eyes. Somehow, over these past three weeks, she'd managed to block out the rape. As if she knew instinctively that to let it in, to think about it, would destroy her. But now there could be no more hiding. It was here, inside her, growing and alive like some unwanted alien, a parasite consuming her from the inside out.

I have to get rid of it. Now.

A doctor was out of the question. Grace was already using the third of the fake driver's licenses Karen had made for her at Bedford. This week Grace was Linda Reynolds, a waitress from Illinois. The cards were good enough to fool sales assistants and hotel desk clerks, who only glanced at them for a second. But Grace couldn't risk showing them to some doctor's officious assistant who might take a good, long look.

I'll have to do this myself.

Some of the girls in prison had talked about backstreet abortions, appalling, gruesome horror stories involving coat hangers and hemorrhages. Remembering them, Grace started to shake.

I can't. I can't go through with it.

There has to be another way.

In a quiet corner of Queens Public Library, Grace sat at a computer. A quick Google search told her what she needed to know.

. . . ingestion may cause gastrointestinal upset, spontaneous abortion, seizures, coma, disseminated intravascular coagulation, hepatic and renal injury and death.

Spontaneous abortion . . .

There was a health-food store that sold herbs a few blocks away.

Grace headed there.

'The Romans used to use this, you know.' The clerk at the store was in a chatty mood. 'It was a common herb for cooking. Of course, what you have here is the essential oil.' She passed Grace a thumb-size glass bottle. 'You can't cook with this. Not unless it's a stew for your mother-in-law and you're trying to kill her!' Grace forced a smile. 'But a few drops in the tub? Amazing. Your troubles will melt away.'

If only. 'How much do I owe you?'

'That'll be fifteen dollars and twenty-two cents.' The clerk dropped the bottle into a paper bag and handed it to Grace. Suddenly her face changed. 'Do I know you from someplace? Your face looks familiar.'

Grace pushed a twenty-dollar bill into her hand. 'I don't think so.'

'No, I do. I'm sure I do. I never forget a face.'

'Keep the change.'

Grace snatched the bag and ran out of the store. The clerk watched her go. It was terrible the way people in this city lived their lives in such a rush. She seemed like such a nice girl, too. Hopefully the oil would help relax her.

I'm sure I know her from somewhere.

Mitch Connors met John Merrivale for lunch at a restaurant in midtown Manhattan.

'Thanks for meeting me.'

John Merrivale stood up and smiled graciously. Mitch was struck by how slight he was. Everything about him seemed faint, from his colorless skin and watery gray eyes to his thin, reedy voice and limp handshake. *He's more ghost than man.*

'N-not at all, Detective. I'm happy to help, if I can. I assume this is about G-Grace?'

'Actually it's about Lenny.'

The gracious smile faded. 'Oh?'

'I'd like to get a better understanding of your relationship with him.'

'My relationship? I fail to see how my r-relationship with Lenny is of any relevance.'

Mitch thought, *That touched a nerve.* Aloud he said, 'We're trying to build as complete a picture as we can of the Brooksteins' life before Grace was imprisoned. We're hoping it might help us to predict her movements now.'

'I see.' John sat down warily.

'Shall we order?'

Mitch opted for a steak and salad. John perused the menu for an inordinate amount of time before deciding on the quiche. *Weak and insipid, like him,* thought Mitch. But there had to be more to John Merrivale than that. You didn't get to the top of the food chain at an institution like

Quorum unless you had a tough side. Or at least some serious smarts.

'You knew the Brooksteins as well as anyone,' Mitch began. 'Grace even stayed with you and your wife during her trial, I believe?'

'That's correct.'

'And you paid for her defense.'

Merrivale looked uncomfortable. 'I did. Lenny was my b-best friend. It was what he would have wanted.'

'But you never visited her in jail. Never contacted her again, in fact. Why was that?'

'Try to understand, Detective. I believed in Grace for as long as I c-could. Just like I believed in L-Lenny. But there came a point when I had to face the truth. They both l-let me down. I lost everything when Quorum collapsed. My g-good name, my savings, my l-life's work. I know there were others who suffered more than I did. And I'm d-devoting all my time now to trying to help those p-p-people.'

'You're talking about the FBI investigation?'

'Yes.' John nodded earnestly. 'I'm still trying to m-make sense of it all myself.'

Mitch thought, *Everything he says makes sense. So why don't I believe him?*

The food arrived. Mitch devoured his steak hungrily. He watched John Merrivale pick at his quiche Lorraine, taking tiny bites, like a bird. When they'd finished eating, Mitch changed tack. 'If you had to hazard a guess, where do you think Grace might be headed?'

'I have no idea.'

'Perhaps Lenny talked to you about some of the places he used to take her?'

'No. Never.'

'Somewhere romantic, somewhere that might have had significance for them as a couple . . .'

279

'I've told you,' said John tersely. 'Lenny didn't talk to me about things like that.'

'Really?' Mitch feigned surprise. 'I thought you said he was your best friend?'

'He was.'

'Your best friend never talked to you about his marriage? The most important thing in his life?'

'Grace wasn't the most important thing in Lenny's life,' John snapped. '*I* was.' Catching the look on Mitch's face, he blushed and began to backtrack. 'Well, not me p-personally. Quorum. Our work t-together. *That's* what Lenny lived for.'

It was too late. The damage was done. Mitch thought, *He sounds just like Connie Gray. Like a jealous lover.* The hairs on Mitch's forearms began to stand on end.

'Remind me, Mr Merrivale. Where were you the day of the storm on Nantucket? The day that Lenny Brookstein went missing.'

John blinked twice. 'I was in Boston on business. It was a prearranged trip. I flew out early and I was gone all day. All my statements are in the file, if you'd like to check them.'

'Thank you,' said Mitch. 'I'll do that.'

It was only later, after he'd paid the check and John Merrivale had returned to work, that it struck him.

He didn't stammer.

When I asked him for his alibi that day, his speech was perfect.

Grace lay back on the bed, the little bottle of oil in her hand. It smelled heady and comforting, like rosemary wafting on a warm summer breeze.

The label said: WARNING: TOXIC. DO NOT INGEST.

Grace thought about the bastard who had raped her.

She thought about the innocent life inside her.

She thought about Lenny. When she closed her eyes, she could hear his voice.

What about children? I suppose you'll want to be a mother?

And her own. *Not really. I'm happy as we are. There's nothing missing.*

Lying on the bed, Grace realized that she had sacrificed motherhood for Lenny. She'd sacrificed everything for him, for their love, and she was still sacrificing. How could he have betrayed her with Connie? *How?* She felt angry and humiliated. She tried to hate him, to let go of his memory, but she couldn't.

It's no use. I still love him. I'll always love him.

She opened the bottle and swallowed the bitter liquid.

I wonder how long it will take.

'You okay in there, lady?'

The super was knocking on Grace's door.

'Do you need a doctor?'

Grace couldn't hear him. Pain tore through her body like a giant razor blade, slicing into her flesh, her nerves. She screamed. Blood poured out of her. Her limbs began to shake and dance as the seizure took hold of her body, contorting her arms and legs like a sadistic puppeteer.

The super unlocked the door. 'Jesus Christ. I'm calling an ambulance!'

Grace didn't hear him. She was deafened by the sound of her own screams.

Chapter Twenty-Seven

She heard voices.

'Linda? Linda!'

'Still no response. She's flatlining.'

'Shock her again.'

Grace wondered, *Who's Linda?* She felt the weight of the paddles pressing on her ribs, then an indescribable pain, like a kebab skewer being driven into her heart.

She fainted.

She was in a pale green room with a gray, checkered ceiling. There were needles in her arms. Someone was talking to her. A nurse.

'Linda?'

Grace remembered. She'd had to abandon Lizzie Woolley and move on to another of her fake identities. *I'm Linda Reynolds. I'm a thirty-two-year-old waitress from Chicago.*

'Welcome back.' The nurse smiled. 'Do you know where you are, Linda?'

'Hospital.' Grace's throat was so dry and sore, the word was barely audible. 'Water.'

'Sure.' The nurse pressed a call button. 'Just hold on a

couple more minutes. The doctor will know whether it's safe for you to drink right now. He's on his way. Is there anyone else I can call for you, honey? A relative or a friend?'

Grace shook her head. *Nobody.*

She fell back to sleep.

She was in East Hampton at a July Fourth party. She was six years old. Her father had scooped her up in his arms and placed her on his shoulders. Grace felt like a princess in her powder-blue, ruffled party dress, with red, white, and blue ribbons in her blond hair.

One of her dad's friends called out to them. 'Hey, Cooper. Who's that gorgeous young lady you're with?'

'Only the prettiest girl in New York.' Cooper Knowles grinned. 'When you get married, Gracie, it'll be to a king. You'll have the world at your feet, my angel. The world at your feet!' He tugged on her new blue party shoes. Grace laughed.

The laugh turned into Lenny's laugh. They were on the terrace at their home in Palm Beach. Lenny was reading the newspaper.

'Look at this, Gracie.' He chuckled. 'You see what they're calling me. "Leonard Brookstein, King of Wall Street!" How does it feel to be married to a king?'

'It feels wonderful, my darling. I love you.'

'I love you, too.'

'Linda. LINDA.'

The spell was broken.

'This is Dr Brewer. He's on our psychiatric team. He's just gonna have a little chat with you, okay?'

Days passed. Doctors and psychiatrists came and went. DIY abortions were a dime a dozen, sadly, but Linda Reynolds's case was unusual enough to attract attention.

'Pennyroyal poisoning? What the fuck is that?'

'Some crazy herb. Women used it for abortions in medieval times. But it's gruesome. Ingesting the essential oil can cause renal failure, acute uterine hemorrhage. Seizures.'

The doctors told Grace it was a miracle she had lived. The pennyroyal had done its job of killing her baby, but her liver would be permanently weakened. Grace didn't care. She tried to cry for the baby, to feel sad for it, but she couldn't even do that. She knew if she looked back, she would crumble. All that mattered was that she was alive, recovering, growing stronger. She could feel it in her body. Soon she would be able to get out of here. Her work was not yet done.

In the hospital corridor, Juan Benitez whispered to his friend José Gallo.

'Es ella. Estoy seguro.'

José poked his head around the door of Grace's room. 'No way.'

Juan and José were both janitors. Not much exciting ever happened during their workdays, mopping the hospital halls. But that was no reason for Juan to go making things up.

'Ella es horrible. Ugly,' said José. 'Grace Brookstein *era hermosa.'*

Juan was insistent. *'Les digo que, es ella. Quieres que la recompesa o no?'*

José thought about it. He *did* want the reward. Badly. But he and his family were all in the States illegally. He didn't want to be the guy who called the NYPD out on a wild-goose chase.

He looked at the patient again. With her newly shorn, peroxide-blond hair, her pain-lined face and cold, listless eyes, she had none of the radiance of the beautiful young woman he'd seen on TV. And yet there was a resemblance . . .

* * *

284

The doctors had told Grace she could walk around the room if she felt up to it. The electrolyte drip had been removed from her arm. Gingerly, Grace swung her feet to the floor. After a week in bed, her legs felt like Jell-O. The pennyroyal had given her seizures, one of which had torn a muscle in her calf. She hobbled to the window.

In the parking lot below, a young couple was taking their newborn baby home. The father was wrestling with a car seat, a look of terrified anxiety on his face, while his wife calmly looked on, rocking the child in her arms. Grace smiled sadly.

What a lovely, normal, happy family. I'll never have that.

There was no time to dwell on her wistfulness. A police car pulled into the lot, then another, then another. Suddenly there were cops everywhere, swarming into the building like termites. Grace felt her heart rate jump. *Are they looking for me?*

A blond head emerged from one of the squad cars. Even before he looked up, Grace recognized his stocky, footballer player's physique. *Mitch Connors. So they* are *here for me.*

Adrenaline coursed through her body.

Think! There must be a way out.

Mitch Connors got into the elevator. He was so tense he could hardly breathe. As if the prospect of finally catching Grace weren't overwhelming enough, he'd spent the last three days looking into John Merrivale's cover story for the day Lenny Brookstein disappeared. He had so much to tell her. So much still to do.

'Seal off all exits and entrances. I want guys on the emergency stairs, in the kitchens, the laundry, everywhere.'

'Excuse me!' A furious chief resident stuck her arm in the elevator just as the doors were closing. In her early fifties with short gray hair and a steely don't-fuck-with-me expression, she gave Mitch a piece of her mind. 'What the hell is going on here? This is a hospital. Who gave you permission to come storming in here like this?'

Mitch flashed her his badge, simultaneously pressing the button for the sixth floor. He should have alerted the hospital authorities, but with a tip this good, there was no time for niceties. 'Sorry, lady. We have good information that Grace Brookstein is in the building. If you'll excuse me . . .'

'I won't excuse you! I don't care if Elvis Presley's in the building. My job is to save lives. You have no authority . . . hey! Get out of there!' Turning around, the chief resident saw four uniformed cops pushing open the swing doors to the OR. Seizing his chance, Mitch physically pushed her out of the elevator. The last thing he saw as the elevator doors closed was the furious doctor running toward him, shaking her fist like a cartoon villain.

Grace had better be here. If she wasn't, he was in big trouble.

'Linda Reynolds. Which room is she in?'

The staff nurse on the desk hesitated. 'We're not supposed to give out patients' room numbers. Are you a family member?'

Mitch flashed his badge. 'Yeah. I'm her uncle Mitchell. Where is she?'

'Six-oh-five,' said the nurse. 'It's at the end of the hallway on your right.'

Mitch was already running. He burst into the room, gun drawn. 'Police! You're under arrest!'

A terrified orderly put his hands in the air.

'Jesus! What did I do?'

'Where is she? Grace.' The man looked blank. Mitch corrected himself. 'I mean Linda. The patient. Where did she go, damn it?'

'Bathroom,' the orderly stammered. 'Three doors down. She'll be right back.'

Grace looked at the grate covering the ventilation shaft. It was two feet square. *The same size as the crate I escaped from jail in.*

As she climbed onto the toilet seat, then up onto the cistern, tears of pain filled her eyes. Her left calf was in agony. She bit down hard on her lip to stop herself from screaming and reached up with both hands. Dislodging the grate was easy. As she pushed it aside, a shower of dust fell into her eyes, temporarily blinding her, but there was no time to stop and recover. Digging her nails into the ceiling, Grace hauled herself up, squeezing her tiny frame into the ventilation shaft like dough into a pasta maker. Carefully, she replaced the grate behind her. Dust still stung her eyes like acid, but it didn't matter. Ahead of her was nothing but darkness. Inch by inch, she pulled herself forward into the void.

Mitch walked into the ladies' room. There were three cubicles, all of them empty.

He turned to leave, then stopped. Walking into the middle cubicle, he ran his finger across the top of the toilet seat. The dust was as thick as sugar icing. Mitch traced a letter G and looked up. *Could a human being fit in there?*

Back in the corridor, he yelled into his radio.

'I need to see plans of the ventilation system. Blueprints. Where do those tunnels go?'

The chief resident stepped out of the elevator and pointed at Mitch. 'There! In the blue shirt.' Three burly security guards rushed toward him. Seconds later Mitch found himself being manhandled toward the emergency stairs while the resident looked on, arms folded, smiling with satisfaction. *Talk about a ballbuster.*

'For God's sake! I'm a police officer. Do you *realize* what I could do to you guys for this? Let me go.'

The biggest of the guards murmured, 'You kidding, right? Do *you* realize what *she* could do to us if we let go of your ass? Trust me, Officer. You ain't got no idea.'

Grace's vision was clearing. She saw light, faint rays at first, but they gradually got stronger. The tunnel forked left and right. The light was coming from the left.

Grace moved toward it.

'I swear to God, if we've lost her because of this *bullshit*, I will personally see to it they don't let you loose on a patient again with so much as a Band-Aid.'

It had taken fifteen minutes for Mitch's boss, Lieutenant Dubray, to fax the necessary warrants and consents to the hospital. Only once she had them in her hands did the chief resident order her heavies to let Mitch out of her office.

'Don't try to scare me, Detective.' She laughed. 'Haven't you embarrassed yourself enough for one day?'

Mitch was about to hit back when one of his subordinates burst in.

'Blueprints,' he panted, unrolling paper onto the desk.

Grace looked down through the grille. The room was empty. This time it was tougher to wrench the ventilation panel free. Squeezed into the shaft like raw meat in a sausage skin, she was having a tough time getting any traction. Finally, with sweat from her efforts pouring down her back and chest, Grace pulled out the grille and eased herself down into the room below. The light was so bright it took a few seconds to get her bearings. She looked around.

I'm in an X-ray room.

She wondered how long it would be before the technician

showed up with the next patient. *Do they always leave the lights on, or did someone just step out for a minute?* Voices outside the door answered her question. Two men were talking. Grace watched their shadows grow larger. *They're coming in!*

Mitch studied the blueprints. The ventilation shaft had nine grilles on the sixth floor, each of them a potential exit. Mitch dispatched men to each one. The bad news was he'd lost fifteen minutes. The good news was there was no way out of the building, nor could somebody crawl between floors. It was a case of 'what goes up must come down.'

'What's the closest exit to that ladies' room?'

The officer traced the tunnel with his finger.

'That would be . . . right here. X-ray and MRI room.'

Mitch started running.

The grille in the X-ray-room ceiling was still hanging open. Grace hadn't bothered to try to cover her tracks. *She knows she's running out of time.*

'I don't understand it,' said the technician. 'I've been here the whole time. I stepped out for literally thirty seconds. But if she got in here while I was gone, she'd have had to come past our reception desk. Liza would have seen her for sure.'

'Hmm. So would my men,' said Mitch. He scratched his head. 'Is there any other way out of here?'

'No.'

'No service elevator? Fire stairs? No window?'

'No. Look around you, Detective. This is it.'

Mitch looked around. The technician was right. The room was a smooth box, empty apart from the humming X-ray machine and the circular MRI tube. *Nowhere to run, nowhere to hide.* Then suddenly he saw it. In the corner. A laundry hamper, full of used scrubs.

289

Heart pounding, Mitch dived in, pulling out used scrubs like a starving man hunting for food scraps in a Dumpster. In seconds, the floor was littered with blue hospital gowns and face masks. But no sign of Grace.

He tried to keep the disappointment out of his voice.

'Okay. So she must have gone back into the shaft. Where's the next exit?'

Grace waited till they'd gone. Then, releasing the locked muscles in her arms and legs where she'd pressed herself flat against the top of the MRI tube, she fell into the body of the machine, bruising her ribs painfully. She'd outwitted Mitch Connors for now. But how much time had that bought her? A minute? Three? Five? Despair washed over her.

The whole hospital's surrounded. I'm never going to get out.

She contemplated giving up. Before she knew about Connie, and Lenny's betrayal, she'd never questioned *why* she kept running, *why* she kept fighting. It was all for Lenny. She had to clear his name, to honor his memory. Now, for the first time, Grace realized that wasn't enough anymore. She needed another, better reason. She needed to fight for herself. She needed to save her own life.

Easing herself out of the machine, she stood up.

I can't give up. I won't.

She picked up a set of scrubs from the pile on the floor and pulled them on.

Grace walked slowly toward the fire stairs, trying not to limp. *I have to get off this floor. Make it to ground level and try and bluff my way out of here.*

The X-ray-department receptionist watched her pass but said nothing. With her blue paper hat pulled low and a surgical mask over her face, she could have been anyone. Beyond reception, two cops stood by the swing doors. Grace waited with her heart in her mouth for one of them to ask her for ID, but they, too, let her pass. She was almost at the emergency exit door. Just a few more paces.

'Hey. Hey, you! In the blue.'

Grace kept walking.

'HEY!' The voice got louder. 'Stop!'

Keep going. Don't look back.

'You can't go out of there. It's . . .'

Grace opened the door.

' . . . alarmed.'

Sirens whooped. Bells, shrill and deafening, rang in Grace's ears. For a moment she panicked, frozen. In a few seconds, the stairwell would be crawling with cops. *I'll never make it down six floors. There's no time.*

She looked up and started to run.

Mitch's radio crackled. 'She's on the east fire stairs. Sixth floor.'

His heart leaped. 'Cover every exit.'

'Already done, sir.'

'Tell all units, you can draw your weapons but *do not fire*. Understand? No shooting.'

'Sir.'

There was no way out of the building. Outside the hospital, the media had already begun to arrive. Mitch knew none of his men would have leaked the story, but it was tough to send a hundred cops into a major New York City hospital without people getting curious. TV crews scrambled to set up their equipment, eager to capture the drama as it unfolded. Mitch thought, *They're probably hoping for a shoot-out. How much would the first shots of Grace Brookstein's dead body be worth?*

He wished he could protect her. That he could stop her from running. Keep her safe, with him.

He headed for the roof.

Grace looked around her. *This is it. The end of the road.*

If only Manhattan's skyline were like a Spider-Man movie, where the next building over was always a short jump away. In real life, the eight-story hospital was sandwiched between two twenty-story towers. The only way down from the roof was via the fire stairs Grace had just come up, or an identical set of stairs on the western side of the building.

Unless, of course, you jumped.

Bolting both sets of fire doors behind her, Grace crawled on her hands and knees over to the edge of the rooftop, making her way around the perimeter. She peered over the edge of the rooftop. In a movie, there would have been a handy dumpster to break her fall. Or a truck full of feather pillows that just happened to have pulled up at a red light. No such luck.

She heard the door to the east stairs start rattling. A few seconds later, the other door followed suit. *They're coming.*

Tears filled Grace's eyes. They would catch her. They would send her back to jail. She would never know the truth.

In that moment, as the rattling of the doors grew louder, it became clear.

She had nothing left to live for.

The door burst open, sending the metal bolt clattering. Mitch shot out onto the concrete like a ball from a cannon. He looked up just in time to see a flash of blue disappearing over the edge of the rooftop.

'Grace! NO!'

He was too late.

BOOK THREE

Chapter Twenty-Eight

Mitch put a hand over his mouth. There was an audible gasp from the crowds gathered below, then screams.

I've just chased an innocent woman to her death.

Why hadn't Grace waited? If he'd only had a chance to talk to her. To tell her he believed in her. That he knew Lenny hadn't killed himself. That he knew she was innocent. That he was starting to fall in love with her.

He couldn't bear to look, yet he knew he had to. Behind him, a stream of cops had filed onto the rooftop, all with guns drawn. Mitch walked forward slowly to the spot where the blue flash had disappeared. Squatting down on his haunches, he took a deep, fortifying breath and looked down, bracing himself for the sight of Grace's bloodied, broken corpse.

The sidewalk was empty.

'What the . . .'

The roof jutted out about two feet beyond the outer walls of the hospital building, like stiff white icing spilling over the edge of a wedding cake. Lying on his belly, Mitch reached under the ledge. His fingers grasped at the air. Nothing. He inched farther forward, like a snake, till his torso dangled perilously over the edge of the building. The crowd gasped again. Suddenly Mitch felt a small, cold hand in his.

Perched on a window ledge no more than eight inches wide, Grace looked up into Mitch's eyes and gave him a sad, defeated smile.

'Detective Connors. We must stop meeting like this.'

The sensational footage of Grace Brookstein's capture was aired around the globe. Overnight, Mitch Connors of the NYPD went from bumbling cop to national hero. Speculation was rife as to where America's most wanted fugitive was being held. Would Grace be sent back to Bedford Hills? Or to a different, secret, more secure location? Would there be another trial? The hunt for Grace Brookstein had cost the U.S. taxpayer millions of dollars. Surely some stiffening of Grace's original sentence was called for?

Behind the scenes, an interagency battle raged. Everyone wanted access to Grace. Mitch Connors's view was that possession was nine-tenths of the law.

'We've got her and we're not handing her over to the FBI, or anyone else, till *we're* done questioning her.'

But the FBI's Harry Bain wasn't the only one on Mitch's case. His own superiors in the police department seemed eager to wash their hands of Grace as soon as possible. Detective Lieutenant Dubray agreed.

'She's not our problem anymore.'

Mitch dug his heels in. 'I have a right to question her for forty-eight hours.'

'Don't lecture me about your "rights," Connors. And don't be so fucking naive. This case is political dynamite and you know it. Grace Brookstein's a walking embodiment of everything this country's trying to forget. This goes all the way to the top. The president himself has told his advisers that Grace's face on the news is bad for business, bad for jobs, bad for Brand America.'

'"Brand America"? Come on, sir.'

Mitch fought his corner, but he knew time was running out. Soon Grace would be taken away from him, and his chance to help her would be gone. Whatever other feelings he had, or thought he had, for her, he had to put them aside. All that mattered now was the truth. *I have to get her to trust me.*

Grace studied Mitch's features intently. *He seems genuine. But then my track record as a judge of character is hardly exemplary.*

'So you're saying you want to help me?'

'Yes. I want to help you. I'm the only one who wants to help you, Grace. But I can't if you don't talk to me.'

Grace looked at him skeptically.

'I read Buccola's file,' said Mitch. 'I believe that Lenny was murdered. I believe that you were both set up. But I need your help to prove it.'

'If you know Lenny was murdered, why haven't you reopened the investigation into his death?'

'I tried to. I was blocked. My superiors were more interested in capturing you than in finding out the truth about Quorum, or what may have happened on that boat.'

'But you're different. That's what you want me to believe, right? That you're a lone warrior for truth.'

'Look, I don't blame you for distrusting me. But I don't have time to convince you. In a few hours, the powers that be are gonna take you away from here. We may never get another opportunity to speak to each other. This is our last chance, *your* last chance. Tell me what you know.'

'What I know?' Grace laughed bitterly. 'I don't know anything anymore. Everything I thought I knew turned out to be a lie. I thought I was rich, but it turned out I had nothing. I thought the courts would protect the innocent, but they sent me to jail. I thought my friends and family loved me, but they were nothing but a pack of vultures. I thought Lenny died in an accident. I thought he was a faithful husband. I thought . . . I thought he loved me.'

Tears rolled down her cheeks. Without thinking, Mitch walked around the interview table and put his arms around her. She was so tiny, so vulnerable. He was overwhelmed with an urge to protect her, to rescue her.

'I'm sure Lenny loved you,' he whispered, stroking her newly shorn, white-blond hair. 'People have affairs. They're weak. They make mistakes.'

He told her how close he'd come to catching her at Jasmine Delevigne's apartment.

'Was that why you tried to kill yourself? Because of Connie and Lenny?'

'No!' Grace said hotly. 'And I didn't try to kill myself. I – ' She broke off. She wanted to tell him about the abortion, about the rape, about all of it, but she didn't have the words.

Mitch said, 'He broke it off with Connie, you know. Before he died. Your sister was blackmailing Lenny, threatening to tell you about their affair. He'd already paid fifteen million into an offshore account for her, but Connie was squeezing him for more.'

'Was she? How do you know?'

'She told me herself. Bragged about it, if you must know. The point is, Lenny was desperate not to hurt you, Grace. Not to lose you. He regretted what happened, I'm sure of it.'

Grace closed her eyes and succumbed to the comfort of Mitch's arms around her. It had been so long since she'd had intimate contact with another human being. So long since she'd felt kindness, warmth, affection. *That's all this is,* she told herself firmly. *Affection. A moment's break in the battle.* In another life, another world, things might have been different. As it was . . .

There was a knock on the door.

'Sorry, boss.' The officer was hesitant. He liked Mitch and hated being the bearer of bad news. 'Dubray says you've got five minutes. We got orders direct from Washington. The prisoner's being transferred out of state.'

When he'd gone, Mitch clasped Grace's hand. There *was* a connection between them. He could see she felt it, too. 'Talk to me.'

Grace told him everything she knew. When she was done, Mitch said, 'You realize who's left, don't you? If Andrew Preston and Jack Warner and your sister Connie are all innocent?'

Grace sighed. 'John Merrivale. But it wasn't him.'

'You sound very sure.'

'I suspected John from the beginning. I know he set me up at my trial, and who knows, maybe he took that money. But he couldn't have killed Lenny.'

'Why not?'

'He was in Boston the day Lenny took the boat out. Davey checked out his alibi months ago.'

'Yes, so did I.' Mitch looked thoughtful. He remembered his lunch with John Merrivale, the way his speech impediment had magically disappeared when he spoke about the day Lenny Brookstein disappeared. 'Still. There's something not right about that man.'

Grace stared blankly at the door. Mitch thought, *She doesn't care anymore. She's given up.* When she spoke, there was neither fear nor curiosity in her voice. 'Do you know where they're taking me?'

'No. But I'll find out.' Once again Mitch found himself

gripped with the urge to rescue her. What was it about this woman that brought out his inner knight in shining armor? 'I'll do my best to help you, Grace. Get you a decent lawyer, begin an appeal.'

'I don't want any of that.'

'But you have to . . .'

She looked him in the eye. 'If you want to help me, find out who murdered my husband. I don't think you'll ever be able to clear his name of the Quorum fraud. But I'd like people to know Lenny wasn't a coward. That he didn't kill himself.'

'I'll try. But, Grace, even if I succeed, Lenny's dead. You're alive. You have your whole life ahead of you. You *must* get a new lawyer. You must appeal.'

The officer reappeared, along with two more armed officers and a dour-faced man in a suit. *CIA? FBI?* 'Time to go.'

Grace stood up. Impulsively, she kissed Mitch on the cheek. 'Forget about me.'

Mitch watched the men take her away. After she'd gone, he stood in the empty interview room for a long time.

Forget about you.

If only I could.

Chapter Twenty-Nine

Maria Preston tossed back her long mane of chestnut hair and admired her reflection in the rearview mirror. She had the skin of a woman ten years younger, and she knew it. This afternoon, her creamy-white complexion was flushed and glowing, a testament to the three hours she'd just spent in bed with her lover. What a *joy* it was to be with a man who appreciated her! Maria had been with scores of men, many of them more technically proficient at lovemaking than her current paramour, and almost all of them more physic-ally attractive. But woman could not live on six-pack abs alone. There came a point in her life when she needed more. *Power.* Maria Preston's lover was a powerful man, a man of influence. Not like Andrew.

Poor Andy. He wasn't a bad husband. In the last couple of years, he'd finally started making the sort of money that could give Maria the lifestyle she deserved. Wealth was the one thing she'd thought she wanted all these years. But now that she finally had it, it bored her. *He* bored her, sexually, intellectually and every other way. She realized now that however much money Andrew made, he would always be an accountant. And as long as she stayed with him, *she* would always be an accountant's wife. *Maria Carmine! An accountant's wife!* The very idea was preposterous, an affront to nature. The only wonder was that it had taken her so long to see it. A free spirit like Maria should not be trapped in such a banal marriage, like lesser mortals. It was like trying to freeze a volcano or to flood a desert.

Applying a fresh slick of bright red Dior lipstick, Maria reflected on her destiny. *I was born to be a great man's wife. His muse.*

Now, at last, she would be.

She'd finally figured it out: a way for her lover to leave his wife, to be free of all the pressures weighing him down and to run away with her. Maria, in her brilliance, had solved all their problems. She would leave Andrew and start afresh. Her lover had been overjoyed when she told him the plan last week. He'd still been excited about it when they met today, making love to her with a passionate intensity unusual even for him.

Maria smiled at her reflection in the rearview mirror and laughed. 'You're not just a pretty face!'

She was on her way back to the city from Sag Harbor. It was a schlep to get out there, two hours on a good day, three in rush hour, but Maria's lover couldn't risk being seen with her in Manhattan, and besides, the American Hotel on Main Street was so quaint and charming with its white portico and cheery, striped awning, it was worth the trip. Turning onto Scuttle Hole Road, Maria noticed Nancy's Cake Shop up ahead, one of her favorite haunts, its window display enticingly crammed with cupcakes of every color and flavor. All that sex had given her quite an appetite. *Why not?*

She pulled over and turned off the engine, humming happily to herself as she opened the driver's-side door.

Nancy Robertson was out back in the kitchen when she heard the explosion. Her heart racing, she ran into the store. Thank God no one was in there! The room was destroyed. Every window was shattered, shards of glass mingling with the buttercream icing stuck to the walls. Outside on the street, all that was left of Maria Preston's Bentley was a twisted hulk of burning metal.

Mitch Connors was at the playground with his daughter. It was the first Saturday he hadn't worked in months. Helen was reluctant to let him have Celeste.

'You can't just swan in and out of her life when it suits you, Mitch. Do you have any idea how disappointed she was when you didn't show up for her school play? You couldn't even be bothered to call her and explain.'

Guilt made Mitch lash out. 'Explain what? I'm working, Helen. I'm paying for that roof over both your heads. Besides, I'm not asking your permission to see her. It's my weekend.'

Now, watching Celeste kick her skinny legs as he pushed her on the swing, he regretted losing his temper. He wasn't in love with Helen anymore. But there was no denying she was a great mom. He, on the other hand, was a lousy father. He liked to tell himself that he spent *quality time* with his daughter, but he knew it was a crock. Mitch loved Celeste, but the truth was he barely knew her. Even now, when he hadn't seen her for weeks, he couldn't switch off work. His thoughts kept drifting back to Grace Brookstein: where she was being held, and how on earth he was going to keep his promise to her. No one wanted to know about his theories of foul play in Lenny Brookstein's death. Two days ago, Dubray spelled it out for him in black and white.

'Let it go, Mitch. You're a good detective, but you've gotten way too personally involved on this one. Besides, I've got a new case for you. Teen homicide, junkie, no leads. Right up your alley.'

'Can you give it to someone else? All I need is a little more time to look into this stuff, a few weeks at most.'

'No, I can't *give it to someone else*. You don't get to choose your assignments, Mitch. You are on the Brady homicide as of right now. And if I catch you wasting one more minute of department time on this Brookstein bullshit, believe me, I will have you suspended so fast you won't know what hit you. I won't tell you again. Drop it.'

Drop it.

Forget about me.

Maybe next, someone would tell him to stop exhaling carbon dioxide or sleeping with his eyes shut.

His cell phone rang. It was Carl, a buddy from work.

'You anywhere near a TV, man?'

'Nope. Why?'

'There's been a car bombing in Long Island. Looks like a Mafia job. The victim's the wife of one of those Quorum guys you keep talking about. Preston.'

Mitch stopped pushing the swing.

'Maria Preston?'

'Daddy! Higher!'

'She's dead?'

'Very dead. Nothing left of her, apparently.'

'Dadd*eeee*.'

'You gotta watch this, man, it's all over the news.'

Mitch hung up and started running to his car. He had to get to a TV.

A woman ran after him. 'Sir? Excuse me. Sir!'

Mitch turned around.

The woman pointed to Celeste, sitting forlornly on the stationary swing. Mitch had forgotten all about her.

*   *   *

John Merrivale was late. He hated being late. Hurrying into his office, he sat down and started pulling open drawers, looking for papers while his computer fired up.

'You all right, John?' Harry Bain put his head around the door.

'F-fine, thank you. Sorry I'm late in this morning. The p-press keep badgering me for a statement about Maria Preston.'

'Poor woman. Terrible thing. You expect car bombs in Beirut or Gaza, but not in Sag Harbor. She was a friend of yours, wasn't she?'

John looked irritated. 'No, not really. Her husband was a c-c-colleague. But the media hear the word *Quorum* and I'm their f-first call. I wish to God they'd leave me be.'

Harry Bain frowned. It seemed an oddly detached, clinical response to such an awful tragedy. But then he never had figured out John Merrivale. He let it go.

'Are you still all set for Mustique?'

'Of course.'

The task force had discovered that one of Lenny's family trusts, Brookstein Dependents in Guernsey, had made a number of payments to a financier called Jacob Rees. The FBI was interested in what had become of that money, but so far Mr Rees's business managers in New York had been less than co-operative. John Merrivale was planning a surprise visit to the great man's Mustique estate. Jake Rees's mansion was less than a mile down the beach from Lenny's own (now seized) compound, and the two men had once vacationed together.

'I guess if you have to spend years of your life chasing a money trail, there are worse places to go, right?'

John forced a smile. 'I suppose there are.'

'How long do you think you'll be gone?'

'A day or so, I hope. It may take longer if Jake's not immediately r-receptive.'

'Well, if you need any help, you know where I am.' Harry Bain walked back to his own office. John Merrivale breathed a sigh of relief.

You're in the home stretch now, John. The hard part is over.

It was all coming together at last. Grace was back behind bars. Whispers had already started around the office that the Bureau was growing tired of throwing good money after bad and that Harry Bain's Quorum task force might soon be quietly disbanded. John had suffered a terrible moment of panic last week when the prospect of exposure had suddenly loomed from a *most* unexpected quarter. But now that, too, was over.

In a few days, he'd be on an airplane.

At last.

The Maria Preston murder case had been given to an old rival of Mitch's from his own precinct, an overweight family man in his fifties named Donald Falke. With his tonsure of white hair, big belly and full, salt-and-pepper beard, Detective Falke's nickname on the force was Santa. Not that Don's cases called for much ho-ho-ho-ing. An NYPD lifer, Don Falke specialized in Mob killings.

He told Mitch, 'The media's getting folks all stirred up about terrorism. It's bullshit. If this was a terror attack, I'm Dolly Parton. This wasn't al-Qaeda. It was Al Capone. It's got Mafia written all over it.'

'What makes you so sure?'

Don Falke's eyes narrowed. 'Experience. What makes you so interested? This ain't your case, Connors.'

'What if it wasn't a Mob hit? What if Maria Preston knew something? Something about Quorum, maybe. Something important enough to make someone to want to kill her.'

'We looked into all that,' said Don dismissively. 'This had

nothing to do with Quorum, okay? Definitively. *Someone* didn't kill her; this was a sophisticated car bomb, not a knife or a gun. It's a classic Casa Nostra MO.'

'Do you know who invented the car bomb, Don?'

Falke rolled his eyes. 'I don't got time for a history lesson, Connors. I have a murder to solve. Now if you'll excuse me . . .'

'It was a guy named Buda. Mario Buda. He was an Italian anarchist back in 1920.'

'What'd I tell you? Italian.'

'It was a hot day in September . . .'

'Jesus, Mitch.'

' . . . this guy, Buda, parks his horse and wagon on the corner of Wall Street and Broad, across the street from J.P. Morgan's offices. He gets out and wanders into the crowd. Twelve o'clock, all the bankers are heading out for lunch, right? You can hear the bells of Trinity Church ringing.'

'Very poetic.'

'Then *boom,* the horse and cart are blown to bits. It's mayhem, dead bodies everywhere, rubble, shrapnel. Right on Wall Street. Nineteen twenty. Two hundred people were wounded. Forty killed. *Not* including old J.P. himself, I might add. He was the intended target, but he was in Scotland at the time.'

Don Falke had humored him long enough. 'Where are you going with this, Mitch?'

'The car bomb was invented by one lone, ignorant immigrant with a grudge against rich Wall Street bankers.'

'So?'

'So it was a hundred-odd years ago, but the principle's the same. Why does this have to be Mafia? Any idiot with a grudge could have strapped some Semtex to that car. Some fruit loop might have linked Maria in his addled brain with Quorum or Lenny Brookstein.'

Don Falke laughed. 'Dubray's right. You *are* obsessed. This doesn't have a fuckin' thing to do with Lenny Brookstein, okay? I think you need to go and lie down.'

'I want to interview Andrew Preston.'

Donald Falke finally lost his temper. 'Over my dead body. Now you listen to me, Connors. Stay the fuck away from my case. I'm serious.'

'Why, Don? Are you worried I might uncover something inconvenient?'

'If I hear you've been within ten miles of Andrew Preston, I'm going to go to Dubray and he is going to fire your ass. Drop it.'

Drop it. Mitch was starting to feel like a naughty Labrador retriever with his jaws around some other dog's stick. He left Donald Falke's office and walked straight to his car.

It had been a month since Mitch last visited the Prestons' midtown apartment. He remembered it as an expensive piece of real estate, an enormous five-bedroom pad in a tony, well-maintained building. But what had struck him most about it was how *little* it struck him. Everything about Andrew and Maria's home was bland, from the nondescript street outside to the dutifully tasteful cream-and-brown decor inside. Mitch couldn't imagine having that much money to spend and wasting it on something so *safe*. Maria Preston had been an irritating woman. Mitch loathed drama queens. But at least she'd had some color to her. Some life. She must have felt entombed in that apartment. As if she'd been cut and pasted into a page from the Pottery Barn catalog, laminated for all eternity onto a cream B&B Italia sofa and left there to rot.

Turning onto the Preston's block, Mitch slowed. Uniformed beat cops were in the process of having the street cordoned off. Mitch pulled up at the same time as two ambulances and a fleet of squad cars.

'What's with the circus? What going on?' He flashed his badge.

'It's Maria Preston's husband, sir.'

'What about him?'

'Looks like he hanged himself, sir. About an hour ago. They're cutting him down now.'

Chapter Thirty

Upstairs, paramedics leaned over Andrew Preston's body, pumping the chest. Mitch could tell instantly that it was hopeless. They were just going through the motions.

'Crime-scene guys got here yet?'

One of the medics shook his head. 'You're the first. Detective Falke is on his way.'

'Any note?'

'Yeah. Through there.'

The medic gestured toward the living room. The window was open. On the tasteful oak coffee table, between the two tasteful beige suede armchairs, a piece of paper fluttered in the breeze, pinned down by a heavy glass ashtray. Without bothering to put on gloves, Mitch moved the ashtray and picked it up. In neat, cursive handwriting, Andrew Preston had written seven words.

It was my fault. Forgive me, Maria.

'What the FUCK are you DOING?'

Mitch jumped, dropping the note. Detective Lieutenant Dubray's voice boomed off the walls like an angry giant's. 'Are you out of your mind?'

Mitch opened his mouth to explain himself, then closed

it again. What could he say? He knew he shouldn't be here. Still less should he be messing with another detective's crime scene. Dubray was incandescent with rage.

'That's evidence tampering! Do you understand how serious that is? I could have you thrown off the force. I *should* have you thrown off the force.'

'I'm sorry. I needed to talk to Andrew Preston.'

'You're a little late for that.'

'Yeah. So I see. Look, sir, I would have waited for Falke, but I knew he'd be obstructive. He probably wouldn't even have let me see the note.'

'Of course he wouldn't! And why the fuck should he? This is *not your case,* Mitch.'

'But, sir, he's not even asking the obvious questions. Like what was Maria Preston doing in Sag Harbor anyway. And who knew she was gonna be there.'

'Don called me half an hour ago. He told me you were poking your nose in, rambling about Lenny goddamn Brookstein. He thinks you've lost it . . .'

'Oh, come on, sir. You know Don Falke's always had it in for me.'

'I think you've lost it, too. I'm sorry, Mitch. But you've gone too far this time. You're on suspension until further notice.'

'Sir!'

'Consider yourself on indefinite leave until you hear from me otherwise. And don't look so goddamn hard done by. You're lucky you aren't fired. If I didn't know how much Helen and Celeste count on that paycheck, I wouldn't think twice. Now get out of here, before I change my mind.'

On his way home, Mitch passed the bar where he'd first met with Davey Buccola. He went inside and ordered a scotch. 'Keep 'em coming,' he told the barman.

'Bad day?'

Mitch shrugged. *Bad year. Bad life.* Part of him wished he had never laid eyes on Davey Buccola. If it hadn't been for Davey's ferretlike digging into Lenny Brookstein's death, none of this would have happened. Mitch would have arrested Grace and been done with it. Moved on to the next case, like everyone wanted him to. Maybe even made captain.

Instead, here he was, alone, suspended from duty, all because of Buccola's file and the promise he'd made Grace. *Grace.* Mitch wondered again where she was. No one would tell him anything. He imagined her being interrogated, locked in solitary confinement, sleep-deprived. He thought about her sad eyes, her courage, her surprising sense of humor, even in the direst of situations, and hoped her spirit hadn't already been broken.

Through the whiskey haze, Grace's words floated back to him.

Forget about me.

It was much too late for that. Mitch realized that in the last two months, he'd barely thought about Helen. Grace had taken her place in his subconscious, his dreams. Now it was Grace he was letting down, Grace he was failing. Just as he'd failed Helen and Celeste. Just as he'd failed his father. *I've disappointed everyone I ever loved. I let them all down.*

Fuck suspension. Fuck toeing the line. And fuck giving up.

Tomorrow Mitch would take a flight to Nantucket Island. The truth couldn't wait.

Chapter Thirty-One

Mitch couldn't understand it.

You have all the money in the world. You can go anywhere you like – Miami Beach, Barbados, Hawaii, Paris. Why the hell would you buy a house in this dump?

Clearly, Lenny Brookstein didn't have the best judgment in the world. He'd had a beautiful wife who adored him, but had chosen to shack up with an ugly mistress who loathed him. His so-called friends were about as trustworthy as a bunch of used car salesmen. But this took the cake. As far as Mitch could see, Nantucket had nothing to recommend it. With its gray, clapboard houses and rain-swept, desolate beaches, it was the sort of place that could make anyone depressed.

'What do people *do* here?' he asked the pharmacist at Congdon's on Main Street, one of the few stores that kept its doors open off-season.

'Some people paint. Or write.'

Write what? Suicide notes? Leonard Cohen lyrics?

'Some people fish. It's pretty quiet in March.'

This was an understatement. The guesthouse in Union Street where Mitch was staying was as silent as the grave.

The only noise in the evenings was the heavy *tick, tick* of an antique grandfather clock in the parlor. A couple more weeks of this and Mitch would end up like the Jack Nicholson character in *The Shining*.

But it wouldn't take two weeks. Within twenty-four hours of his arrival, word went around the island that a strange guy was in town, asking questions about Leonard Brookstein. Instinctively, collectively, the islanders clammed up. Felicia Torrez, Grace and Lenny's cook up at the Cliff Road estate, now worked at Company of the Cauldron, the only high-end restaurant that catered to locals outside of the summer months. Mitch went to find her there.

'I'm trying to get a clearer picture of the events in the days leading up to the storm, back in the summer of 2009. You were living at the Brooksteins' home at that time?'

Silence.

'How long had you been in their employ?'

More silence.

'Look, ma'am, this is not an official investigation, okay? You don't need to be nervous. Did you notice any tension among any of the houseguests that particular weekend?'

At first he thought she had poor English. Then he wondered if she was mute, or deaf, or both. Whatever it was, Felicia was about as forthcoming as a clam that had swallowed some Superglue. Mitch tried the housekeeper, the maid, the gardener. It was always the same story.

'I don't remember.'

'I didn't see anything.'

'I did my job and went home.'

Tomorrow he would head down to the harbor and talk to the fishermen. Some of them must have been out on the water that day. But he didn't hold out much hope. *It's like they're all part of some secret club, like the Masons or something.* But it made no sense. Lenny Brookstein was

314

already dead. What did they think they were protecting him from?

Hannah Coffin called to her husband.

'Tristram! Come see this.'

'In a minute.'

The Coffins worked at the Wauwinet Hotel, a five-star retreat in one of the quietest, least-populated parts of the island. Like all the big hotels, they were closed through the spring months, but kept a skeleton staff to work on maintenance and repairs. Hannah and her husband acted as caretakers, overseeing the off-season staff. It was a job with a lot of downtime, which Tristram Coffin spent tinkering with his Ducati motorbike, and Hannah spent watching daytime television.

'Tristram!'

'I'm *busy*, honey.' Tristram Coffin sighed. *Just buy the damn earrings already, or the super-duper potato peeler, or the* Greatest Hits of Neil Diamond, *or whatever it is they're selling! You don't need my opinion.*

'It's important. Come on in here.'

Reluctantly, he put down his wrench and wandered into the living room of their modest ground-floor apartment. As usual, the television was on.

'Do you remember that guy?'

Hannah pointed at the screen. A man was being interviewed about Maria Preston's murder. The story was getting juicier by the day. It now looked as if the husband had done it, hired a Mob hit man to kill his wife because he suspected her of having an affair. Hannah Coffin was particularly interested in the murder because Maria Preston had stayed at the Wauwinet once.

Tristram studied the man's face.

'He looks familiar.'

'He *is* familiar!' said Hannah triumphantly. 'Where's that cop staying? The one that's been asking all the questions about Lenny Brookstein?'

'Union Street. Why?'

'I'm gonna call him, that's why.'

Tristram looked disapproving. 'Come on, honey. You don't want to get involved.'

'Oh yes I do.' Heaving her two-hundred-pound frame up off the couch, Hannah lumbered toward the phone. 'I know where I've seen that guy before. And *when*.'

'Are you sure?'

Mitch felt like pinching himself. If he weren't scared of putting his back out, he'd have picked Hannah Coffin up in his arms and kissed her.

'One hundred percent. They checked in here together. It was the day of the storm. Him and Maria Preston.'

'And they stayed . . .'

'All afternoon, like I told you. I'll write it down for you if you like. Make a statement. He was on TV, acting like he hardly knew her. But he knew her all right. *Intimately*, if you know what I'm saying.'

Mitch knew what she was saying. He was due at the harbor in half an hour, but this called for a change of plans. He headed for the airport.

Nantucket airport was little more than a shed, a simple L-shaped shingle structure with a pitched roof, one-half of which was designated 'Departures' and the other half 'Arrivals.' As single- and twin-engine Cessnas landed, passengers got out and helped the pilot unload luggage onto the tarmac. In the departure lounge, 'security' consisted of a gray-bearded old man named Jo who glanced at the locals' bags before waving them through with a cheery smile and a 'See you at the Improv Friday night. Baptist church, don't be late now.'

Mitch marched up to the desk of Cape Air.

'I'd like to see your passenger records, please. I'm interested in all flights in and out of the island on June twelfth, 2009.'

The girl at the desk rolled her eyes. 'And you are?'

'Police.'

'Darlene?' she called over her shoulder. 'I got another one here. Wants those June twelfth records. Can you take him?'

An old woman in a tweed skirt emerged from the office. She wore her snow-white hair tied back in a neat bun, and a pair of pince-nez glasses perched on the end of her nose, like Little Red Riding Hood's grandmother.

Mitch looked puzzled. 'Another one? Has someone else been asking to look at your passenger lists?'

'They have indeed. Darlene Winter.' She shook Mitch's big, bearlike hand with her thin, wrinkled one. 'You policemen are like buses. Never there when you need one, then suddenly you all show up at once. Come on back.'

Mitch followed Darlene into an office that was as neat and orderly as she was. There was a computer in one corner, but she led him to a desk on the other side of the room. A big brown leather book lay open. It looked like an antique Bible, or an enormous visitors' book from some medieval Scottish castle.

'All our records are computerized, of course,' Darlene told Mitch. 'That's the law. But we like to do things the old-fashioned way around here. We keep a daily logbook of our flights as well, handwritten. I suspect I already know what you're looking for.'

She pointed to a familiar name, beautifully rendered in italics and black ink.

'He caught the six-ten A.M. to Boston, along with five

other passengers. Landed at six fifty-eight. Whatever he was doing that day it looked like he changed his mind, because at seven twenty-five' – she flipped a page – 'he boarded an eight-seater right back to the island. This is his landing record, right here. June twelfth, eight-oh-five A.M. Flight 27 from Logan. John. H. Merrivale.'

Mitch ran his finger across the paper.

So Hannah Coffin wasn't a fantasist. John Merrivale really could have been at the Wauwinet that day, shacked up with Maria Preston.

According to Hannah, the pair of them hadn't arrived at the hotel until early afternoon. A full five hours after John got back to the island, after setting up his alibi. More than enough time to sail out to Lenny Brookstein's boat, get aboard and murder him.

'You mentioned someone else had asked to see this. Another cop?'

'That's right. FBI, I think he said he was, but he came off as more of a military man. Very brusque. A little rude, if you must know. He had one of those army haircuts, you know. Much too short.'

'You don't remember his name?'

The old woman furrowed her brow. 'William,' she said eventually. 'William someone-or-other I think it was. Went straight to the same page. June twelfth. John Merrivale. Is this Mr Merrivale in some sort of trouble?'

Not yet, thought Mitch. Then he thought, *Who the hell is William?*

The guard looked at the mud-spattered sedan and its lone occupant. He'd expected an armored vehicle, or even a convoy of some sort. Not a middle-aged man in a dirty family car. *This guy looks like her dad coming to pick her up after a sleepover.*

318

The camp outside Dillwyn in rural Virginia was a top secret OGA facility. OGA stood for 'Other Government Agency,' which typically meant CIA, although the Dillwyn camp provided a temporary 'home' for a variety of non-military prisoners considered too disruptive or dangerous to be returned to a mainstream correctional facility. Some were terror suspects. Others suspected spies. A few were classified as 'politically sensitive.' But none of the inmates at Dillwyn was more 'sensitive' than the one this man had come to see. The prisoner was being transferred to an FBI holding cell in Fairfax. *In a sedan, apparently.*

'Papers, please.'

The gray-haired man handed over his credentials. For a few moments there was a tense pause while the guard leafed through them. But everything was in order, as he knew it would be.

'Okay, go on through. They're expecting you.'

Grace stood in the center of her six-by-eight-foot cell. Planting her legs in a wide stance, she stretched out her arms, focusing on her breathing as she lunged forward into warrior 2 pose.

She'd been at Dillwyn almost two weeks, locked for twenty-two hours a day in a spare, windowless box. With no one to talk to, no human interaction of any kind, yoga had been her salvation. She spent hours going through a series of poses, energizing her body and focusing her mind and breathing, staving off despair.

I'm alive. I'm strong. I won't be here forever.

But would she? Hours, days and nights had already merged into one, long, unbroken stretch of nothing. The lights in Grace's cell were permanently set on dim. Meals were pushed through a tray in the door at regular six-hour intervals, but there was nothing to distinguish breakfast from lunch or lunch from supper.

They're trying to break me. Make me crazy so they can lock me up in a mental institution and throw away the key.

It wasn't working. Yet. Between yoga sessions, Grace would lie on her bunk, close her eyes and try to conjure up an image of Lenny's face. He was the reason she was living, after all, the reason she kept fighting. At Bedford Hills, and later when she was on the run, she'd found it easy to summon his kind, loving features at will. Grace talked to Lenny the way that other people might pray to God. His presence was a great comfort to her. But here, in this awful, mind-numbing place, she was distressed to find that his image was fading. Suddenly she could no longer remember the exact sound of his voice, or the look in his eyes when he made love to her. He was slipping away. Grace couldn't shake the feeling that once he was totally gone, her sanity would disappear with him.

The one face she could conjure, ironically, was Mitch Connors's. A few nights ago, for the first time in many months, she had an erotic dream, one in which Mitch was the lead actor. She woke up feeling embarrassed, guilty even, but talked herself out of it. *You can't help what you feel when you're unconscious. Besides, at least it proves I'm alive. I'm still a woman, still a human being.*

The door of the cell opened. Grace startled. It wasn't time for her daily exercise. The guard said brusquely, 'Come with me. You're being transferred.'

They were the first words anyone had spoken to her in over a week. It took Grace a moment to unearth her voice.

'Where?'

The guard didn't answer. Instead he slapped handcuffs on her wrists. Grace followed him mutely along a maze of corridors, trying to contain her elation.

This is it. I'm getting out of here. I knew they couldn't keep me here forever.

She wondered if Mitch Connors had had a hand in her

release, and was curious as to where they were taking her. Wherever it was, it couldn't be worse than this place. The guard punched a seven-digit code into a heavy metal door. It swung open. Grace followed him outside into a courtyard.

'Hello again, Grace.' Gavin Williams smiled. 'We've a long journey ahead of us. Shall we get going?'

The country roads were rough and rutted. Each bump and jolt tore through Grace's frayed nerves like a razor. Williams was a madman. She thought back to the last two times they met – once at the morgue, when he'd grabbed her like an animal – and once in the infirmary at Bedford. That second time Grace was sure he meant to harm her. The feral hatred in his eyes . . . she would never forget it. Of course, she had been heavily sedated at the time.

'Where are you taking me?'

Without taking his eyes off the road, Gavin Williams took his right hand off the steering wheel and slapped Grace hard across the cheek.

'Do not speak unless I tell you to.'

In mute shock, Grace put her free hand up to her throbbing cheek. Her right hand was cuffed to the passenger door. The handcuffs chafed painfully against her wrist. She sat as still as she could, trying not to move against the metal. Gavin Williams began talking, mumbling to himself like a junkie.

'I thought things would be different at the FBI. But of course they weren't. The cancer is everywhere: ignorance, stupidity. That's why the Lord sent me. He blessed me with the gifts of intelligence, of wisdom. He gave me courage to act.'

Grace felt her heart rate quicken. *I have to get out of here.* Since they left Dillwyn, they seemed to have been driving deeper and deeper into the wilderness. It was a sinister landscape. On either side of the unmade road lay dense thickets of stinking sumac, broken only by an occasional black walnut tree. Darkness was closing in.

'Of course Bain trusted him. They all did. He was smarter than Bain. Smarter than Brookstein, too. But he wasn't smart enough for me.'

I have to engage him. Keep him talking till I figure out what to do.

'Who wasn't smart enough?' Grace braced for another slap, but this time Williams seemed eager to talk.

'Merrivale, of course,' he spat contemptuously. 'He tried to humiliate me. In Geneva. He'd been there before with *Lenny*. Got Bain to throw me off the task force. But my work wasn't done yet. I uncovered his secret.' John smiled. Madness blazed in his eyes.

'What was his secret?'

Gavin Williams laughed. 'He killed your husband, my dear. Didn't you know?'

Grace sat in silence. Williams kept talking.

'John flew to Boston on the day of the storm. But of course, the police were too lazy to check the Cape Air records. I had to do it myself. As soon as Merrivale landed, he turned around and caught the next plane back. He took a helicopter out to Lenny's boat. This was early, mind you, before the bad weather set in. They had a couple of drinks – your husband's was drugged, of course – and then dear John did the deed. Lenny was decapitated, by the way. Not cleanly either. Merrivale must have gone at him like he was a tree stump, hacking away. Did your investigator boyfriend tell you that?' He was taunting her, delighting in her horror like a kitten playing with a mouse before the kill.

Grace felt dizzy.

'It was John who took the money, diverting all those funds from Quorum. After he dispatched your old man, he got *you*

322

out of the way – that was the easy part – then buddied up with that brainless popinjay Harry Bain.' Gavin parodied Harry Bain's gravelly baritone: '"John's our key asset in this investigation. You must stop alienating him, Gavin." Fool! All this time the truth was right under his nose. Stinking, like your husband's corpse. But Harry couldn't see it.'

Grace tried to process what Gavin Williams had just told her. Clearly the man was unhinged. And yet she knew in her bones he was telling the truth about John. He *had* checked those flight records. It was John who stole the money, John who killed Lenny, John who stage-managed her trial and sabotaged the investigation. Her instincts had been right all along. Why hadn't she trusted them?

The good news was, if Williams knew the truth about John, it stood to reason he must also know that she was innocent. That she and Lenny had never stolen anything. That they were victims. *He's not abducting me. He's rescuing me!*

She opened her mouth to thank him, but she never got the chance.

Leaning over, Gavin Williams punched her so hard, she blacked out.

She was wet. Soaking wet. Gavin Williams was pouring a bottle of ice-cold water over her head. She was still in the car. The a/c had been turned up full blast. Grace shivered with cold.

Williams pushed her seat back as far as it would go, then climbed on top of her. Grace screamed and struggled, waiting for the inevitable, but Williams didn't try to rape her. Instead he pinned down her legs with his forearm so she couldn't move, closed his eyes and began reciting what sounded like some bizarre form of liturgy.

'The wicked shall gnash with his teeth and melt away . . .

the desire of the wicked shall perish . . . even in darkness, light dawns for the righteous . . . Lord, deliver me from evil . . .'

'I'm innocent,' Grace pleaded. 'You know I am.'

'You are guilty!' spat Gavin, his face grotesquely contorted with hatred and lunacy. 'All of you – you, your disgusting husband, Merrivale. You're all the same, you rich parasites, you bankers, thinking yourselves so much better than the rest of us. Better than *me*. You're vermin. Depraved, sick vermin. But don't despair. I have been sent to cleanse you.' Reaching across to the driver's seat, he grabbed a second water bottle, emptying it over Grace's head.

'I baptize you with water for repentance.' The liquid was freezing. Grace shut her eyes and gasped for breath. When she opened her eyes, she saw Williams unscrewing a plastic gas can. Slowly, he began to pour a snail's trail of the viscous liquid over Grace's clothes and hair. 'But a second baptism is at hand. A baptism by fire. The winnowing fork is in the hand of the Lord. He will clear his threshing floor, gathering his wheat into the barn.' Gavin's voice grew louder, more excited. He climbed off Grace, flinging open the passenger door, and clambering to safety. Grace's arm was still handcuffed to the door. As it swung open she roared in agony, feeling her shoulder joint dislocate. Williams was still incanting. 'He will burn the chaff with unquenchable fire.' Reaching into his pocket, he pulled out a book of matches.

Grace didn't think. On instinct, she propelled herself forward, kicking Williams hard in the groin. He bellowed in pain, dropping the matches.

'You bitch!' He ran at her like a maddened bull, throwing himself back into the car, hands clawing her face, fingernails gouging deep, bloody grooves in the skin. Grace sank her teeth into his arm. Gavin yelped and let go of her for a moment, but his anger was stronger than his pain. *I must*

324

destroy her. I must rid America of the wicked, cut out the cancerous scourge of greed before it devours us all.

'Repent!' His hands gripped Grace's cheek like a vise. He was trying to press his thumbs into her eyeballs. Grace felt her skull fill with blood. The pain in her shoulder was so excruciating she was surprised she hadn't passed out. 'Repent, sinful daughter of Eve!'

'You repent, asshole!'

With all her remaining strength, Grace brought her free arm down hard in a karate-chop motion on the back of Gavin Williams's neck. She heard a crack, like a snapping branch. Williams's hands went slack, a toy robot whose batteries just died. As he slid to the floor of the car, his head dangled from his torso at an absurd angle, like a flower on the end of a broken stem. His eyes were still open, frozen for all eternity in an expression not of hatred, but of intense surprise.

With her free arm, Grace got hold of the lapel of his jacket and pulled the slumped corpse toward her. It was slow work, but eventually he was close enough for Grace to reach into his jacket pocket. Inside, glinting like nuggets of gold in a stream, were the keys to her handcuffs.

The cuffs opened easily, but moving her arm was agony. Grace screamed as she staggered out of the car, tears of pain coursing down her cheeks, mingling with the blood from where Williams had scratched her. She'd seen girls dislocate their shoulders during her gymnast days, and knew what to do. Slumped down in the mud, leaning back against the side of the car, she gritted her teeth.

One. Two . . . three.

The pain was indescribable. But the relief was instant and sweet. Grace savored it. She laughed, the deep, heartfelt laugh of the survivor. When her strength had returned, she went over to Williams's body, retrieving his wallet and everything else he had of value. Then she stood up, lit a match, and tossed it into the sedan. She watching the flames engulf Gavin Williams's body, and stood there, warming herself in their heat. It felt good.

She was alive.

She was free.

But her work wasn't over.

Chapter Thirty-Two

Caroline Merrivale sat down at her dressing table, pulled back her hair and slathered Crème de la Mer moisturizer over her face. At forty, she still had the skin of a woman half her age, which pleased her. Caroline had never been a classic beauty, not like the Grace Brooksteins of this world. But she had style and presence, she dressed well, and she knew how to take care of herself.

She wondered what she would do with the rest of the day. John had left early for the airport. Harry Bain was sending him to Mustique of all places, in search of another piece of the giant Quorum jigsaw puzzle. But not before Caroline had forced him to have sex with her, photographing him in a series of humiliating and graphic poses. Dominating John was always a pleasure, but today she'd enjoyed it more than usual. In recent weeks, Caroline had noticed a change in her pathetic, milquetoast of a husband, a growing confidence that made her uneasy. He practically skipped out of the house in the mornings, excited to get to work. He'd even taken to telling her things about his day – *as if she were interested!* – 'Harry Bain said so-and-so,' or 'the agency were delighted with my work on such-and-such.'

Caroline had deliberately waited until this morning to teach John a lesson. He'd been full of this trip to Mustique for days, and she wanted the bursting of his bubble to have as much impact as possible. When he got home, she would tell him flat out: he'd acted as the FBI's unpaid lackey for long enough. It was time to get back to work, start a fund of his own and bring in some more money. Billy Joel's estate in East Hampton was up for sale after his third divorce. Caroline had had her eye on that house for years.

'Mrs Caroline?' Cecilia, the Merrivales' housekeeper, knocked nervously on her employers' bedroom door. 'Is a gennelman downstairs to see you.'

Caroline turned and glared. Naked from the waist up, with a thick white layer of cream on her face, she looked like a Maori warrior minus the tattoos. 'Do I look like I'm ready to receive guests?' she snarled.

Cecilia tried to avert her gaze from her boss's nipples, large and dark and repellent, like two rotting mushrooms. 'He ask for Mr John. Is from police. He said he will wait.'

Meanwhile, downstairs, Mitch looked around the Merrivales' sumptuous living room. The most striking object in it was probably the solid gold Louis XV carriage clock over the mantel. It was vulgar and hideous, but it must have cost a fortune. But everything about the room bespoke serious money: the heavy, brushed-silk drapes, the antique French furniture, the Persian rugs, the Ming vases. *This is what they had left after the Quorum fraud wiped them out? How much did they have before?*

It didn't matter now anyway. Armed with Hannah Coffin's testimony and a copy of the airline records, as well as Buccola's evidence of foul play to Lenny's body, Mitch had enough to bring John Merrivale in. Of course, a confession would seal the deal. Push it from a solid circumstantial case to a guaranteed conviction. Mitch pictured the expression on

Dubray's face when he told him. The groveling apology. His triumphant reinstatement and promotion to captain. Better still would be Grace's smile. How happy he, Mitch Connors, would make her, and how grateful she'd be. *Oh, Mitch, you're incredible. How can I ever make it up to you?* He'd get her a lawyer. She'd appeal her sentence and –

'This had better be important.'

In a stark gray kimono, with her black bobbed hair slicked back and her face bare of makeup, Caroline Merrivale looked even harder than usual. She reminded Mitch of a prison matron. Anna Wintour meets Cruella de Vil.

'I don't appreciate uninvited guests at eight-thirty in the morning.'

'I need to speak to your husband. Urgently.'

'He's not here. Was that all?'

Christ, she's disdainful. Mitch stiffened. 'No, it's not all. I need to know where he is. Like I said, it's urgent.'

Caroline Merrivale yawned. 'I have no idea where he is. Gretchen, John's secretary, keeps his diary. She'll be here at ten, I believe. Or is it eleven? Now, if you'll excuse me.'

'Take one more step and I will arrest you.' Mitch stood up and grabbed Caroline by the wrist. She swung around, laughing.

'Arrest me? For what? Let go of me, you fool.'

'Not until you tell me where your husband is.'

Caroline tried to shake him off, but Mitch tightened his grip. As he did so he noticed her chin jut forward defiantly and her pupils start to dilate. He thought, *This is turning her on. She likes power games.* Although physically she repulsed him, he forced himself to pull her closer, dropping his voice to a whisper.

'Don't make me hurt you. I'll give you one last chance. Where. Is. John?'

Caroline ran her eyes lasciviously over Mitch's butch,

masculine physique. Here was a man she could respect. A man who was worth giving in to.

'He's at Newark Airport.' She breathed huskily. 'He's on his way to Mustique.'

Mitch drove like a madman. Pulling up outside departures, he leaped out of the car, leaving the engine running. An official yelled at him.

'Hey! HEY! You can't leave your car there, man.'

Ignoring him, Mitch kept running and didn't stop till he got to the Delta desk.

'Flight 64 to St. Lucia,' he panted.

'I'm sorry, sir. Boarding's completed.'

'Well, reopen it.' Mitch pushed his police badge across the desk.

'I'll go get my supervisor.'

An older woman with thick, black-framed glasses emerged from a back office. 'How can I help you?'

'There's a passenger on Flight 64. J. Merrivale. I need to speak to him. I need him off the plane.'

'I'm sorry, sir. Flight 64 already left. Two minutes ago.'

Mitch groaned and put his head in his hands.

'Let's have a look, though. What did you say the passenger's name was?'

'Merrivale. John.'

The woman typed something into her computer. 'If need be, we can alert the cabin crew and ground staff. They can hold him until – ' She broke off.

'What?' asked Mitch.

'Are you sure it was this flight? There's no J. Merrivale on the passenger list.' She spun the screen around so Mitch could see it.

He had a bad feeling about this.

* * *

'What do you mean he's dead?'

The director of the FBI lost his temper. 'What do you mean "what do I mean"? He's dead! What part of "dead" do you not understand, Harry?'

Harry Bain held the phone away from his ear and waited for Ashton Kutcher to jump out from behind the door. He was being 'punk'd.' He had to be.

'But, sir, Gavin Williams is on leave. He has been for over a month.'

'Yeah, well, that's not what he told the guys at Dillwyn. He said he was personally authorized by you to transfer Grace Brookstein to our Fairfax facility. They faxed me the documents, Harry. I'm looking at your signature right now.'

'This is crazy! I never authorized anything. Williams was obsessed with Grace Brookstein. He had this weird, personal thing going on with her. That's why we let him go.'

'Jesus *Christ*!' roared the director. 'Do you have any idea what a stinking mess this is?'

Harry Bain did have some idea. The staff at the OGA prison had released Grace Brookstein into Gavin Williams's custody last night. The two of them were last seen driving out of Dillwyn at around five P.M. At five A.M. this morning, the burned-out shell of Williams's car had been discovered in a remote part of rural Virginia with Gavin's remains inside. Or as Harry's boss put it, 'his barbecued remains.' Grace Brookstein herself had vanished.

'What's happening with the search effort? Is there anything my guys can do to help?'

'We're all over it. We got helicopters up, tracker dogs, you name it. I was gonna say "she won't get far" but after last time . . .'

'I take it the media don't know yet?'

'No one knows. And we're gonna keep it that way. No one knew she was at Dillwyn in the first place, thank God.'

Harry Bain thought, *Except Gavin Williams*. How long would it take for a persistent reporter to uncover the truth? Long enough for them to find Grace? He was reminded of Lady Bracknell's famous line in *The Importance of Being Earnest*. To lose Grace Brookstein once may be regarded as misfortune. To lose her twice looked like carelessness.

He hung up, wondering under what circumstances it might be possible to salvage his career, and was searching through his desk drawer for some aspirin when a disheveled blond man burst into his office. Harry reached for his gun.

'Easy.' Mitch put his hands in the air. 'We're on the same side, remember?'

Harry Bain didn't remember. The NYPD had been nothing but obstructive with his guys since the day Grace escaped. Even after they captured her, Mitch Connors had done all that he could to block their access to her.

'What do you want, Connors?'

Mitch got straight to the point. 'John Merrivale did not catch his flight to St. Lucia this morning.'

'How do you know?'

'I went to the airport. Checked the passenger lists. I've been doing a lot of that lately.'

Harry Bain shrugged. 'So he missed his flight.'

'No. You don't understand. He never intended to catch that plane. He's not going to Mustique.'

'Why would you think that?'

'Because I believe Merrivale has left the country to avoid being prosecuted for murder.'

'Murder?' This conversation was starting to become surreal. 'Whose murder?'

'Leonard Brookstein's.'

Harry Bain laughed, then stopped laughing. Connors was serious.

'I believe that John Merrivale was responsible for the theft of billions of dollars from the Quorum Hedge Fund. I believe he's known where that money has been hidden all along. I believe he is on his way to retrieve it now.'

Harry had heard rumors that the NYPD's erstwhile wonder boy had gone off the rails. There was a 90 per cent chance the guy was a crackpot.

That meant there was a 10 percent chance he could be onto something.

Harry Bain pointed to the chair opposite him. 'Sit down. You've got fifteen minutes. Convince me.'

Mitch didn't take a breath. Starting with Davey Buccola's information, he told Harry Bain everything he knew about what might have happened the day that Lenny Brookstein's boat went missing. He talked about evidence of violence to the corpse; about Lenny's affair with his sister-in-law; about his strained relationships with all of his so-called friends, and their various motives for wanting him dead. He talked about Andrew Preston's debts and his obsessive love for his adulterous wife, about Jack Warner's love affair with a hooker, and Connie Gray's blatant attempts at blackmail. Finally, he talked about John Merrivale: Grace's suspicions that John had deliberately sabotaged her trial; the lies John had told police; his faked alibi; his affair with Maria Preston, whom he claimed barely to have known.

Fifteen minutes passed, then twenty, then thirty. Harry Bain listened and said nothing. When Mitch finished, he asked only one question.

'How much did Grace Brookstein know about all this?'

'Up to the part about Merrivale, she knew everything,' said Mitch. 'I only figured it out myself in the last forty-eight hours.'

He told Harry Bain about Grace outsmarting him and his men at Times Square, about her humiliation of Buccola after he'd betrayed her, about her rape and abortion and her determination to clear her husband's name at all costs. 'I'll tell you something about Grace Brookstein. She's smart. She's courageous. And she's resourceful as hell.'

'Sounds like you admire her,' said Bain.

'I do.'

'Like her?'

'Yes, I like her.' Mitch smiled. *I like her too much for my own good.* 'The real Grace, not the monster they paint on TV. But at this moment I'm happy she's locked up somewhere. She's safer that way.'

Harry Bain looked uncomfortable. Mitch Connors had risked a lot coming here, to a rival agency, an agency that theoretically supported John Merrivale, and laying his cards on the table. On the other hand, he was a maverick. He'd already broken every rule in the book to get the information he had. His own department had suspended him. *Is this really the sort of man I can afford to trust right now?*

Bain made a decision. 'There's something you ought to know.'

Mitch listened openmouthed. *Was it possible? Grace had escaped? She'd killed a man?* His first thought was for her safety. If those helicopters found her, they would shoot first and ask questions later. Everything about Grace Brookstein's case had been a cover-up, so why not her death? Mitch could imagine the headlines now. Grace had slipped in the shower. She'd succumbed to a rare virus. Who would know? Who would care?

'The dead guy, the one who faked your signature on his authorization papers. What did you say his name was?'

'Williams. Gavin Williams.'

Alarm bells went off in Mitch's head. Nantucket. The woman at the airport. *William, he said his name was . . . he had one of those army haircuts . . . went to the same page, June twelfth, John Merrivale . . .*

'How did he wear his hair?'

Bain looked confused.

'Gavin Williams. His hair. Was it long, dark, light, was he bald?'

'He was gray-haired. Always wore a crew cut. What the hell has that got to do with anything?'

Mitch sprang to his feet. 'He knew. He knew about John Merrivale! He was the guy in Nantucket asking questions, just a day or so before me. Gavin Williams knew John flew back to the island, that he'd lied about his alibi. He must have suspected he was involved in Lenny's death.'

Bain let the significance of this sink in.

'Do you think he told Grace?'

'I have no idea,' said Mitch. 'You're the one that knew him. But if he did, and your helicopters don't find her, at least we know where she's headed.'

'We do?'

'Sure. Find John Merrivale and you've found Grace Brookstein. She's on her way to kill him.'

Chapter Thirty-Three

John Merrivale did not like flying. Pulling down the window shade, he tried to focus on the jet's luxurious interior, and not the fact that he was thirty thousand feet over the Atlantic Ocean in a hurtling metal box with wings.

Taking in the soft leather couches, cashmere-covered cushions and inlaid walnut table set with a pair of crystal flutes and a dainty silver bowl of caviar, he thought, *It's wasted on me*. Perhaps that was the greatest irony in all of this. John Merrivale didn't care about money. He never had. John Merrivale wasn't interested in things. The truth was, things bored him. Bespoke suits, sports cars, private planes, yachts, mansions. It was women who lusted after all that, the accoutrements of wealth, the status symbols. With Caroline it was real estate. Maria had been more of a magpie, a bauble whore, salivating over anything and everything that sparkled.

Poor Maria. Killing her had never been part of the plan. But she'd put him in an impossible situation. By threatening to tell Andrew about their affair, she'd put everything at risk.

For two years now, the delicate balance of mutual dependency between John and Andrew Preston had protected both of them. If Lenny had been Quorum's head, its brain and its nerve center, Andrew and John had been the fund's left and right hands. John brought money in. Andrew paid it out to investors. Keeping the SEC, and later the FBI, in the dark had been a simple matter of each of them covering for the other.

Of course, the scale of their respective crimes varied wildly. *I'm like a hippo on a seesaw with an ant.* Andrew's thefts – $600,000 here, a million there – were small. As for his reverse engineering of financial statements, 'spinning' the fund's accounts to make it look more profitable than it actually was . . . every hedge fund on Wall Street did that. Compared with what John had done, Andrew Preston's 'crimes' were laughably insignificant.

The truth was that Andrew could have gone to Harry Bain at any time and spilled the beans about both of them in return for a plea deal. John Merrivale understood that only too well. The beauty was that Andrew didn't. Desperate as he was to keep Maria in trinkets, and in his bed, his terror of exposure kept him silent. The poor man was even grateful to John for covering for him with Bain. 'I don't know how to thank you, John,' he would say, groveling, and John would reply graciously, 'It's n-nothing, Andrew. What good will it do to pick open old wounds?'

It was pathetic, really. Andrew Preston had no idea how many cards he held. Just like he had no idea what was going on between his drama-loving slut of a wife and his friend John Merrivale. Andrew's ignorance had been John's saving grace. Until Maria threatened to shatter it.

'I'm going to tell Andrew about us. We can finally be together, my darling. If he kicks up a fuss, I'll tell him I'm going to go to the police and report him. He was stealing from Quorum for years, you know.'

It was a terrible shame. After so many years of humiliation and hell with Caroline, Maria had been a lifesaver for

John. She made him feel like a functioning, sexual male again. More than that, she made him feel desirable. Powerful. If only she'd kept her mouth shut and her legs open, he would never have had to take such drastic action. But she'd left him no choice. Once Andrew knew that John had betrayed him, he'd tell the FBI everything. Without Maria, he would have nothing left to lose.

Silly girl. Did she really think I wanted to marry her? For us to run away together?

In a few hours, John Merrivale would be landing in paradise, reunited with the love of his life. But it wasn't Maria Preston.

He hadn't intended things to be so rushed at the end. The original plan was to wait until public interest in Quorum had faded, then to slip quietly away. But events had overtaken him. First came Grace's escape and recapture, both of which put Quorum firmly back in the headlines. Then the Maria situation had gotten out of control. John hadn't been prepared for the storm of media interest in her murder. Having the press sniffing around him made him nervous, and when Andrew offed himself, it started to get worse. Predictably, Maria's death had destroyed poor Andrew. He was so deranged with grief that he seemed to blame himself for what happened, for not having protected her. Sooner or later someone – a whiz kid at the FBI perhaps, or a dogged journalist – would start putting two and two together. That psychopath Gavin Williams had already come dangerously close to uncovering the truth. That threat had been neutralized, but there would be others. It was time to get out.

Scooping up some caviar in a little silver spoon, John dolloped it onto a blini and swallowed.

Disgusting.

There was only one true luxury in life: freedom. As a boy, John had been imprisoned by his ugliness and his parents' stifling ambition. As a man, he'd been subjugated by his evil, sadistic wife. Now, for the first time in his life, John Merrivale was going to taste freedom, with his love by his side.

He closed his eyes, lost in the bliss of anticipated pleasure.

Chapter Thirty-Four

Three weeks later

Grace clung to the rail of the fishing boat, wondering if it was physically possible for her to throw up a seventh time.

The waves off the coast of Mombasa, Kenya, were vast and terrifying. From a distance each looked like the giant, grimacing mouth of a cobra, rearing up, jaws wide, ready to strike. Up close they were simply walls of water, gray, angry, and destructive, mercilessly pounding the rickety wooden trawler. For the first few hours, Grace was afraid she might die. Later, once the seasickness really took hold, she was afraid she might *not* die. Lying exhausted on her simple wooden bunk, she wondered what possessed people to get into a boat for fun.

Eventually the ocean calmed. Out on deck, a blazing African sun shimmered in a sky so blue and cloudless it looked like something from a cartoon. Grace watched the three young Kenyan men lower their nets into the water. There was a simple beauty about the way they worked, silently passing the heavy nets between them, muscles rippling with effort beneath their shiny black skin. When they first set sail, Grace had willed them to hurry. She'd paid eight thousand shillings for her passage, almost a thousand U.S. dollars, a fortune to men like these, and she expected a speedy crossing. Now, if it hadn't been for the nausea, she would almost have enjoyed the trip.

She felt as if she'd been running forever. After she left Gavin Williams smoking in his automotive funeral pyre, she'd hitchhiked to Portsmouth, Virginia. Knowing that the cash from Williams's wallet would not last long, she'd taken a risk and sent an uncoded e-mail to Karen's friend, asking for new supplies, money and a fake ID good enough to fool the staff at nearby Norfolk airport. For three days Grace lay low at her motel praying for a package to arrive and anxiously scanning the news channels for word of her escape, or of Gavin Williams's murder. None came. The powers that be must have hoped they'd find her before she caused them any more embarrassment. By the end of the third day, she was starting to despair that her e-mail had been intercepted when the motel owner informed her that a FedEx envelope had arrived. 'Linda Reynolds. That's you, right?'

Grace's heart soared. One day, when all this was over, she would repay her debt to Karen's mysterious contact, this stranger who had risked so much to help her. Right now, though, she had work to do. Her first call was to Mitch Connors.

'Grace! Thank God you're alive. Did Williams hurt you? Where are you?'

The sound of his voice made Grace smile.

'Sorry. Can't tell you. But I'm fine.'

'Listen, Grace, I know about John Merrivale.'

'It's true, then? John killed Lenny?'

Mitch sighed. 'It's looking that way, yes. We think he was behind the fraud, too. He's been hoodwinking the FBI this whole time. But for God's sake, don't do anything stupid,

341

okay? Everyone knows now – the FBI, the CIA. John'll get what's coming to him just as soon as they bring him in.'

'Bring him in? He's missing?'

In the silence that followed, Grace could hear Mitch kicking himself. *What the hell did I say that for?* 'Grace, honey, I'm on your side. You know that.'

Grace blushed. Lenny used to call her 'honey.' She couldn't decide if she liked hearing the endearment from Mitch or resented it.

'But you have to let justice take its course. Turn yourself in. Let the feds deal with Merrivale. Grace . . . Grace?'

After she hung up, Grace sat on her motel bed for a long time, thinking.

So John was on the run now. A fugitive. *Like me.*

Everyone was looking for him, that's what Mitch said. But not because he'd murdered Lenny. No one gave a damn about that. Because they thought he'd taken the money. The stupid money, that was all that mattered to the FBI. Not right and wrong. Not *justice*. America had forgotten what justice meant. If it ever really knew.

Grace closed her eyes. She tried to put herself in John Merrivale's shoes.

Where would I go? With the whole world looking for me. Where would I hide?

A few minutes later, Grace opened her eyes. *Of course.*

She picked up the phone. 'I'd like you to send a cab please. Norfolk International Airport. Uh-huh. As soon as you can get one here.'

Back on the fishing boat, listening to the soft lapping of the waves as the warm African sun kissed her face, Grace smiled to herself again, thinking about her revelation in that grimy Virginia motel room and how it had brought her here, halfway across the world. Or perhaps *revelation* was the wrong word?

342

Memory. It was a memory that had told her where John Merrivale would run, a memory that made her certain of where he was now. The memory was so sweet, Grace closed her eyes and savored it again . . .

It was the month before she and Lenny got married. They were in France, in a charming little *bastide* Lenny had rented in the hilltop town of Ramatuelle, a ten-minute drive from Saint-Tropez.

Grace sighed. 'I never want to leave here. It's enchanting.'

They were having dinner with Marie La Classe, Lenny's French real estate broker, and John and Caroline Merrivale.

'Don't you find a bit quiet?' said Caroline. She'd been lobbying since the start of the vacation for the four of them to move into Le Byblos, or better yet have Lenny's yacht sail up from Sardinia so they could lord it over the smaller boats in the harbor. What was the point in coming all the way to Saint-Tropez and spending the entire week stranded up a mountain in a dull little village no one had ever heard of?

'S-some people like the quiet,' John ventured timidly. Caroline shot him a thunderous look.

'It makes me feel like the princess in a tower,' Grace gushed, beaming at Lenny, who beamed back. 'Like I'm stranded on the most beautiful island and no one can reach me.'

''Ave you ever been to Madagascar?'

They all turned to look at Marie.

'All the culture of France, combined with the natural beauty of Africa, encapsulated in a single, unspoiled island. I grew up there.'

'It sounds magical,' said Grace.

'It is. You would love it. The wildlife, the scenery, the view from Fort Dauphin is one of the wonders of the world. *Je vous assure.*'

'I'll tell you something else about Madagascar.' Lenny

343

grinned that naughty, schoolboy grin of his, stabbing a piece of perfectly cooked lobster tail with his fork. 'It's a crook's paradise. No extradition treaty with the United States. Did you know that, Marie?'

Marie smiled politely. 'I did not.'

Caroline said, 'Well, if John ever robs a bank, we'll move there. In the meantime, I, for one, am pining for a bit of civilization. Who's on for a trip to Les Caves after dinner?'

The property was in Antananarivo, on a hilly, cobbled street that might have been lifted brick by brick from Ramatuelle. With its two-foot-thick stone walls and imposing turrets, it was more like a small castle than a house. A retreat, in every sense of the word.

Lenny looked at Grace. 'Is this the one?'

They'd been in Madagascar less than two days, with Marie La Classe acting as their tour guide, and already Grace had fallen in love. They both had.

'This is the one.'

Lenny pulled out a checkbook, wrote a check for 10 percent more than the asking price and handed it to Marie. He turned to Grace and smiled. 'Happy one-month anniversary, Gracie.'

Grace had been so happy, she'd danced in the street.

They called the house 'Le Cocon' – the cocoon. They planned to retire there.

John Merrivale wasn't well. His doctor prescribed antide-pressants and a month of total peace.

'Here.' Lenny pressed the keys to Le Cocon into his hands. 'Take as long as you need. There's a housekeeper, Madame Thomas, in permanent residence. She'll wash and cook for you, but otherwise you'll be alone.'

John was touched, but the idea wasn't practical. 'I c-can't just disappear to Madagascar. What about Quorum?'

344

'We'll be fine.'

'C-Caroline will never agree to it.'

'Leave Caroline to me.'

When he returned to New York six weeks later, John was a new man. He showed Lenny and Grace the photographs. Himself, strolling the cobbled streets of Upper Town in Antananarivo, relaxing in the hot springs of Antsirabe, trekking through the rain forest at Ranomafana.

Of course, his happiness didn't last. Caroline made sure of that. But Grace would never forget the look of childlike wonder on John's face when he spoke of Madagascar. He even approached Lenny privately about buying Le Cocon.

'Name your price.'

Lenny smiled. 'Sorry, buddy. Any house but that one. The guest suite will always have your name on it. But she's not for sale.'

Grace called to the fishermen. *'Combien de temps encore?'*

'Environ deux heures. Trois peut-être. Vous allez bien?'

Grace *wasn't* doing fine. But she would be once they got there. Reaching into the knapsack she never let out of her sight, she fingered Gavin Williams's gun lovingly, stroking it the way a child might a teddy bear. She wondered how long it would take her to track John down once they got to the island. Le Cocon had been sold when Quorum was liquidated. The buyer was a Dutch Internet entrepreneur, a man named Jan Beerens.

I'll start with him.

Chapter Thirty-Five

Harry Bain turned to Mitch Connors. 'I hate this shithole.'

'Yeah, well. Don't we all.'

Mombasa *was* a shithole. Hot and dirty and soulless. Both Mitch and Harry were covered in bites from mosquitoes as big as hummingbirds, and the combined effect of the itching and the heat made sleep all but impossible. No wonder they'd begun to get short with each other. They'd been able to trace John Merrivale's movements as far as Kenya, but since they arrived in Kenya, the trail had gone stone cold. At this rate they might be stuck here for many more days, perhaps even weeks.

Mitch thought about Helen and his daughter, back in New York. It was shamefully long since he'd last seen Celeste. He didn't miss Helen anymore, but Celeste was a different story. He tried to push the little girl out of his mind, to focus all his mental energy on this case, but it was hard.

If Mitch and Harry Bain didn't find John Merrivale before Grace did, Grace would kill the guy for sure. Understandably, she'd lost all faith in the system. The whole notion of an appeal seemed laughable to her. Personally, Mitch couldn't have cared less if Merrivale got a bullet between the eyes.

But if Grace ended up with a murder charge against her, she would be beyond his or anybody's help.

There was a knock on the door of the hotel room. Mitch looked at Harry, as if to say, *Who the hell can that be? It's after midnight.* Both drew their weapons.

'Who is it?'

'It is I, Jonas. We met this morning at the airport. Please, you are letting me inside?'

Mitch grinned. The Kenyans might rob you blind, but they'd say 'please' and 'thank you' while they did it. As a nation, you couldn't fault them for politeness. Jonas Ndiaye was a pilot Mitch and Harry had interviewed earlier after a tip that Merrivale may have chartered a small plane to fly into Tanzania. But the trip had been another dead end. None of the pilots had recognized John's picture.

Mitch opened the door.

Jonas Ndiaye was thirty years old but looked younger. He had a naughty, boyish face, with no visible stubble, and a spiky, Westernized hairstyle glued into place with some sort of spray or gel. He reminded Mitch of a black Bart Simpson.

'I apologize with the late hour.'

'That's okay,' said Harry Bain. 'We weren't sleeping. What can we do for you, Jonas?'

'The question I am asking is what *I* can do for *you*? After you leave today, I am shaking my brains about that photograph. Yes indeed. I think you will be happy to give some dollars to me about the things I am knowing, yes, yes, I think so.' He flashed Harry an open, expectant smile. As if asking flat out for a bribe was the most normal, reasonable thing in the world. 'Tonight we are doing business, yes indeed! My memory is becoming alive.'

Wearily, Harry Bain unlocked his bedside drawer. He pulled out a wad of twenty-dollar bills, held together with a rubber band. You couldn't take a dump in Kenya without bribing somebody. Jonas Ndiaye's eyes widened. He stretched out a hand for the money, but Bain shook his head.

'What do you know?'

'The man in the photograph was traveling in my plane. Yes, it is true! Two weeks ago he came.'

'You took him to Tanzania?'

'No.' Jonas held out his hand again. Harry Bain peeled off five bills from the pile and handed them to him.

'Where?'

'The gentleman was wishing to fly to Madagascar.'

Harry looked at Mitch. *No extradition treaty.*

'I brought him to Antananarivo airport. He was talking about the wildlife. He will go there on safari, you see, to take many pictures and also to dive in the ocean. Now my memory has come back to me, I can tell you he was a charming gentleman. Very charming, the man in the photograph.'

Mitch asked, 'Did he tell you where he was staying? Or how long he intended to be on the island?'

Jonas smiled expectantly at Harry. More cash was exchanged.

'He did not.'

'Hey! Give me back that hundred, you son of a bitch.'

Jonas looked hurt. 'Please, sir, do not become agitated. The gentleman did not tell me his plans. But he did ask me some sights to recommend.'

'And?'

Another smile. Harry Bain's patience was fraying. 'Don't push it, kid.'

Mitch looked pointedly at his gun lying on the bedside table. The pilot decided not to push it.

'For diving, there is only one place and that is Nosy Tanikely.'

'Nosy *what*? What is that? A beach?'

348

'It as an island,' Jonas explained politely. 'A place of sanctuary for the wildlife of the ocean.'

'A marine reserve?'

'It is where the divers go. Your friend, the gentleman, was traveling with diving equipment.'

Harry Bain looked at Mitch and smiled. 'Thank you, Jonas. You've been a lot of help.'

'Yes, I am delighted to make this service to you. Now you are giving me some dollars for my transport, and I think it is the end of our business.'

Grace stood outside Le Cocon for a long time. She hadn't expected to feel emotional. After everything that had happened, she didn't believe she was capable of it anymore. But as she stood on the steep cobbled street, looking up at the thick stone walls that had once made her feel so protected, tears streamed down her cheeks.

She was surprised to learn that Mr Beerens was in residence. She'd assumed he bought Le Cocon on a whim, as Lenny had done, one of a fleet of vacation homes he thought about from time to time but rarely visited. She gave her name as Charlotte Le Clerc, and was even more surprised when Beerens agreed to see her.

'May I offer you a drink, Ms Le Clerc?'

Jan Beerens was middle-aged, fat and amiable, with thinning reddish-blond hair and brown eyes that twinkled when he smiled.

'Thank you. A glass of water would be great.' Grace struggled to maintain her composure. Inside, the house had not been changed at all. She hadn't realized that Beerens had bought it lock, stock and barrel, including her and Lenny's furniture and artwork. She even recognized the glasses, crystal tumblers she'd had shipped especially from Paris.

Grace's hair had grown out a little at Dillwyn and in the

weeks since her escape. In Mombasa, she's had it cut into a chin-length bob that she dyed a rich, mahogany brown. Catching sight of herself in the library mirror, she thought, *The only thing in this house I don't recognize is myself.*

'What brings you to Le Cocon? To Madagascar, for that matter. You are on vacation?'

'Sort of. I stayed here once, with a friend. Years ago.'

'You were a guest of the Brooksteins?'

'My friend was. It's actually a little awkward, but this friend of mine, he's been going through a hard time recently.'

Jan Beerens looked sympathetic. 'I'm sorry to hear that.'

'Thanks. He took off a few weeks ago and no one's heard from him since. I know he made it as far as Madagascar. I wondered if maybe, out of nostalgia or whatever, he'd stopped by the house.' She pulled out a picture. 'I don't suppose you've seen him?'

Beerens studied the picture for a long time. Grace's hopes soared, then plummeted when he handed it back to her.

'Sorry. I feel as if I recognize him from somewhere. But he hasn't been here.'

'You're quite sure?'

'Positive, I'm afraid. You're my first visitor in over a year. That's partly why I decided to sell. I adore the house and the island, but it's too isolated. I'm only here now to sign the papers, and to say my farewells. You're lucky you caught me.'

'Oh.' She didn't know why, but it made Grace feel sad that this kind, thoughtful man would be leaving Le Cocon. 'Who's the new owner? If you don't mind me asking.'

'Actually, it's all rather mysterious. I was approached by a lawyer in New York, and he's handled everything, but he's never divulged the name of his client. Whoever it was clearly knew the house intimately. This lawyer made a number of requests for specific pieces of furniture, carpets, that sort of thing. He's moving in on Monday, I believe.'

350

Grace's breathing quickened. She felt the hairs on her arms prick up. *Whoever it was knew the house intimately.*

Jan Beerens walked her to the door. 'I'll say this for Lenny Brookstein. He may have been a crook, but he'd have made a hell of an interior designer. I'm gonna miss this place. As for your friend, I'm sorry I couldn't be of more help.'

Grace shook his hand. 'Actually, you've been very helpful. Good-bye, Mr Beerens. Good luck.'

Harry Bain and Mitch Connors decided to split up. Madagascar was the size of Texas, and all they had to go on was what Jonas Ndiaye had told them.

Harry said, 'I'll stay in Antananarivo. I can interview staff at the airport, taxi drivers, real estate brokers. I'll talk to the managers of all the good local hotels. If he was here, some-one'll remember him, especially with that stammer.'

Mitch took a small plane to the north of the island. Nosy Tanikely was a tiny atoll in an extensive archipelago off Madagascar's northwest coast. A diver's paradise, there was nothing there but beach and ocean. For a roof over their heads, divers and sightseers alike had to go to nearby Nosy Be. It amused Mitch that the capital of Nosy Be was called 'Hellville.' If anywhere truly lived up to the brochure fantasy of paradise, with white sandy beaches and tranquil turquoise waters, it was this place. If you were going to spend the rest of your life on the run from U.S. authorities, this was the place to do it, all right. John Merrivale was nobody's fool.

Mitch went to every five-star hotel on the island. Every supermarket, drugstore, bar and car rental office.

'Have you seen this man?

'Are you certain? Look again. If we find him, there's a substantial reward.'

In Mombasa, that approach was bound to yield a response of some sort, even if not the truth. Here, nothing. The locals had not seen John Merrivale. As for the divers, Mitch got the impression that they saw themselves as a community, and that they might have protected one of their own from the police even if they *did* know something. Either way, after three days, the tan on Mitch's forearms had deepened from butterscotch to molasses, but he was nowhere nearer finding John, or Grace.

Harry Bain called. 'You got anything?'

'Nope. You?'

'A little. Jonas wasn't bullshitting. Two witnesses at the airport confirm seeing him. It looks like he spent two nights at the Hotel Sakamanga, then moved on. He was talking about going diving. Said he was "meeting a friend."'

'I'll stay up here till Monday,' said Mitch.

Harry Bain didn't ask the obvious question: *And then what?*

Pretty soon they would both have to head back to New York. It was a minor miracle that neither Grace's escape nor John Merrivale's disappearance had yet been reported in the media. But at some point, a statement would have to be made. There was music to be faced, and while Mitch could probably hope to be reinstated at the NYPD, Harry Bain knew that if he returned home empty-handed, his career was over.

'Keep me posted.' He hung up.

Grace's heart stopped.

Coming out of a grocery store, she saw him across the street. *The guy from the FBI! Gavin Williams's boss, the one who worked with John.* She ducked back into the store.

'*Vous avez oublié quelque chose, madame?*'

Is he looking for John, or for me?

'Madame?'

Grace blinked at the shopkeeper.

352

'Me? Oh, *non, j'ai toutes mes affaires*. I'm fine, thank you.'

She peered through the window.

The man had gone.

I must lay low. All I have to do is make it through the weekend. After Monday, I won't care anymore. He can haul me back to Super Max in leg irons.

Harry Bain received an anonymous tip. A note was left at his hotel.

The man you are looking for is no longer in this province. He is in Toliara. Talk to the rangers at Isalo National Park.

Harry tried to reach Mitch but his cell phone was switched off.

I'll go tomorrow.

When Mitch woke up on Sunday morning, he thought his head was going to explode. He wasn't sure whether to blame the whiskey, or the fact that during the night someone had surgically implanted a church bell into his cranium and was now ringing the damn thing at a hundred decibels.

He got up, staggered to the bathroom, threw up, felt better. Opening the white wooden shutters in his bedroom a crack, he flooded the room with laser-bright light. *Must be later than I thought.* He winced, closing the shutters and crawling back into bed.

This would be his last day on the archipelago. He ought to have been up at dawn, turning over every rock he could think of in hopes of one sighting of the elusive John Merrivale. But he knew it was hopeless.

He fell back to sleep, but his dreams were disturbing and fitful.

Church bells ringing. He was marrying Helen. *'Do you*

take this woman?' 'I do.' He lifted Helen's veil, except it wasn't Helen; it was Grace Brookstein. *'Forget about me.'*

He was on a beach, chasing John Merrivale. John turned a corner and disappeared. When Mitch reached the corner, it changed into Detective Lieutenant Dubray's office. Dubray's voice: *'This is not your case, Mitch. If it weren't for Celeste and Helen . . .'* Then Harry Bain walked in. *'He spent two nights at the Sakamanga. He said he was meeting a friend.'*

Mitch woke up with a start.

He said he was meeting a friend.

Could it be?

He picked up the phone. 'Harry Bain, please. Room sixteen.'

There was a pause on the other end of the line. 'Mr Bain checked out early this morning. He'll be back on Tuesday, same room. Can I leave a message?'

The bells in Mitch's head were still ringing, but the pitch had changed. They weren't church bells anymore. They were alarm bells.

I have to get back to the city.

Grace was already awake when the alarm went off.

Four A.M.

She pulled back the curtains in her cheap hotel room and looked down at the deserted street. According to weather.com, dawn would break in less than ten minutes. Right now it was pitch-dark outside, the buildings slick with the blackness of night, gleaming-dark, as if they'd been dipped in tar.

Grace dressed hurriedly. The backpack was light, but it contained everything she needed. She looked in the mirror.

For you, Lenny my darling.

It's all been for you.

Silently, she slipped out of the hotel and into the shadows.

Chapter Thirty-Six

The streets were deserted. Antananarivo slept. In a week's time, the dry season would begin and cold, mountain winds would once again grip the town. Tonight, though, the air was as thick as soup, heavy with threatened thunder. Grace moved like a wraith through the empty city, as silent and deadly as a virus.

Yesterday, she'd panicked. *What if he isn't there? What if it's not him, this mystery buyer? What if it isn't John?*

But now, as she climbed up the hill toward Le Cocon and the first rays of dawn pierced the stormy April sky, her doubts evaporated. He was here. John Merrivale was here. Her whole body was alive to his presence, like a shaman sensing an evil spirit.

She reached inside her jacket and touched the gun.

The time had come.

'I'm sorry, sir. The early flight to Antananarivo has been canceled.'

The girl at the check-in desk gave a careless little shrug of the shoulders, as if to say, *What can you do?* Mitch fought back the urge to vault over the desk and throttle her. Through gritted teeth, he asked, 'When will the next flight be?'

She looked at her computer screen.

'Nine o'clock. But everything will depend on the weather. If these storms continue, they might close the airport.'

You don't have to look so damn happy about it.

Why had John Merrivale come to Madagscar? Mitch and Harry had assumed it was because the island had no extradition treaty with the United States, that he'd be safe from the long arm of federal law. But what if that wasn't the only reason? He'd told the manager at his hotel that he was meeting 'a friend.' Perhaps John had a personal connection with the island? And who was this friend? Mitch's first thought was that it might be Grace herself. Had she contacted him somehow and persuaded him to meet? Perhaps, as two criminals on the run from the U.S. justice system, she'd convinced John that she was prepared to let bygones be bygones. If so, Mitch was certain, she was luring him into a death trap.

Mitch had called Caroline Merrivale. Woken her up.

'Has John ever been to Madagascar? Does he have any acquaintances there?'

Caroline's answer had hardened Mitch's hunch into a certainty. He knew where John was. He knew where Grace was headed. But could he get there in time to prevent the inevitable?

'I'd like a ticket for that flight, please. The nine o'clock.'

She looked at her screen again. 'Oh, dear. I'm afraid it's fully booked. Shall I put you on standby?'

Breathe deeply. Count to five.

'Sure.'

Mitch tried Harry Bain again.

On the floor next to Harry Bain's sleeping bag, his cell phone vibrated quietly. It was five A.M. at the Isalo National Park campsite. Outside, hikers were already warming cups of coffee over the breakfast campfire and checking the settings of their cameras. The big thing at Isalo was the birdlife. You could never get up too early to watch birds.

Unlike his fellow campers, Harry Bain had no interest in snapping a crested coua or catching a rainbow-plumed coraciidae feeding its young. He'd come to Toliara in search of the lesser-spotted Merrivale, but the whole thing had been another wild-goose chase. Whoever left him that note was either deliberately playing games with him or had gotten his signals crossed. The rangers at Isalo had the combined IQ of a dung beetle. None of them had seen John.

Harry Bain wanted to get back to Antananarivo last night, but he'd left it too late. Reluctantly, he'd settled in for a night's sleep in the park.

His phone buzzed five or six times, like a dying wasp, then fell silent. Thanks to his trusty foam earplugs, Harry Bain slept on, oblivious.

Grace slipped off her backpack. Inside were a length of rope, pliers, a stick of chalk, a square black piece of cloth and a Dictaphone tape recorder.

Tying a simple slipknot at one end of the rope, she threw it over the lowest part of Le Cocon's fortresslike outer wall, aiming for a metal rod that jutted out below one of the bathroom windows. Lassoing was harder than it looked. It took Grace more than ten minutes to snag the rod, minutes in which she looked anxiously over her shoulder for early-morning pedestrians. The dawn had broken slowly at first, but now daylight seemed to flood the alley, shining on Grace as aggressively as any police flashlight. Rubbing chalk onto her hands, she gripped the rope and began pulling herself up. The wall was as smooth as newly shaven skin and slick with moisture from the air. Even with her climbing shoes, it was tricky to get a firm grip. With every slip, every lost footing, the strain on Grace's triceps increased fivefold till her arms started to shake. Halfway up she thought desperately, *I'm not going to make it! I can't hold on!* She could feel the rope chafing against her palms, the sweat of her efforts washing away the chalk. She started to slide, imperceptibly at first, but then faster and more surely, back down toward the street.

Voices. Girls' voices, or young women. They were giggling, gossiping to one another in French. Grace couldn't make out what they were saying, but it didn't matter. Their conversation grew louder. *They'll be here any second! They'll see me!*

Grace looked up. There was another fifteen feet to the top of the wall. Her hands were still slipping, her feet scrabbling for purchase. The voices were even louder now. Gripping the rope, Grace forced herself to move upward. She had no energy left, yet somehow she kept going, powered by determination. It wasn't about saving herself. It was about destroying John Merrivale.

On the other side of that wall is the man who killed Lenny. The man who took everything from you. He's living in YOUR house, hiding in YOUR sanctuary, spending YOUR money.

Rage was like a turbocharger in Grace's chest, pulling her up, propelling her on. Her hands were bleeding now, blood mingling with the sweat on her palms as the rope lacerated her skin, but Grace felt nothing. She could see the top. She could touch it! Swinging her legs over to the other side of the wall, she pulled the rope up behind her. The girls were directly below her now, three of them. Dressed in supermarket uniforms, they were on their way to work. Grace waited for them to stop and point. The bottom of the rope was less than two feet from where they were walking. But they continued on their way, laughing and joking with one another. *Happy.* Grace felt a pang of envy mingled with her relief as she watched their backs disappear from sight.

Then she pulled up the rope, turned around, and lowered herself down into Le Cocon's courtyard garden.

Mitch looked out of the plane window. There was nothing to see but clouds, thick and gray and impenetrable. Next to him a young woman whimpered with fear as the aircraft bucked like a wild bull, juddering its way through the turbulent sky.

Mitch tried not to think about Grace, or John Merrivale, or what might already have happened back in Antananarivo. If this were New York, he'd radio the local police for backup, get them to deal with it. But the last thing he wanted was a bunch of trigger-happy Madagascans storming Le Cocon.

Where the hell was Harry Bain when you needed him?

Grace edged her way around the courtyard with her back to the wall. Le Cocon was a vast house, a maze of corridors and bedrooms and little hidden gardens and terraces. She would begin the search inside the house, but first she had to disable the security alarm, cameras and phone line.

Lenny used to complain about the archaic systems at Le Cocon. 'Have you seen the wires out there? It looks like something from a bad seventies sci-fi movie.' But he never got around to replacing them. Grace was banking on the fact that Jan Beerens wouldn't have gotten around to it either.

Edging toward the back kitchen door, she saw to her relief that he hadn't. One arthritic closed-circuit camera pointed toward the same old fuse box that had been there in her and Lenny's day. Approaching the camera from behind, Grace covered it with the black cloth she'd brought with her. Then, pulling out her pliers, she advanced toward the fuse box.

Mitch's plane hit the tarmac with a violent bump. The woman next to him made the sign of the cross and offered up a little prayer of thanks.

Mitch was not a religious man, but he, too, started to pray.

Don't let me be too late.

Harry Bain rubbed his eyes. For a moment he forgot where he was. He'd been in the middle of a wonderful dream. He was in New York at Sweetiepie, one of his favorite restaurants on Greenwich Avenue, salivating over a hot fudge sundae, when some A-hole started shaking him by the shoulders.

'Camp's packing up. If you want a ride to the airport, you better get up now.'

Madagascar. Isalo. John Bastard Merrivale.

Gloomily, he reached for his phone. The red message light flashed at him reproachfully. Harry flipped it open and hit the key for voice mail.

'You have . . . seven new messages.'

Seven?

He sat up and listened.

Grace leaned on the kitchen door. It opened immediately.

John must feel safe here. Like we did.

There were only two places in the world where she and Lenny had routinely left their doors unlocked: Madagascar and Nantucket. John had ruined the memory of both those places, poisoned them, like he poisoned everything he touched.

Hugging her hatred to her like a security blanket, Grace crossed the dark room. It was eerie. Above her head hung copper pots and pans, shadowy and immobile like a set of unloved puppets. In front of her the enormous triple-fronted cook's stove gleamed, pristine and untouched. Next to it, on the countertop, Grace noticed that someone had recently bought, unwrapped, and plugged in a basic microwave oven.

Its box could still be seen in the corner, propped on top of the trash can.

Typical. A single man moves into a house with a fully equipped gourmet kitchen and the first thing he does is buy himself a microwave.

Grace found herself wondering if John had used it yet, and if so, what he had prepared. She hoped it was delicious, whatever it was. It didn't seem right to eat a horrible last meal.

The inner kitchen door opened into a small flagstone pantry, which in turn led to stairs. These were originally the servants' stairs and they ran all the way from the cellar to the attic on the west side of the house. Grace drew her gun – it was Gavin Williams's gun but she thought of it as hers now – and started to climb.

The house was not just quiet. It was silent. Grace could hear her own breath, the soft rustle of her clothes as she moved, the creak of a water pipe. It was only a few days since she'd last been here, sitting in the library with the kindly Jan Beerens, but something seismic seemed to have happened to the place in the interim. It was more than just the absence of furniture and people. Beerens's staff had gone, and John had clearly moved in alone. It was as if the house itself had died. As if John's presence had forced all the life and the joy out of it, like albumen from a straw-blown egg. All that was left was the shell.

Suddenly a door slammed. The noise was so loud and so unexpected, Grace opened her mouth to scream, but stopped herself, stifling the sound with her hands. She'd almost reached the second floor, but the noise had come from below, at ground level. As quietly as she could, Grace turned around.

On this floor, the door from the servants' stairs opened into a large, marble-floored atrium. It was shaped like a pentagon, with five floor-to-ceiling archways giving onto various reception rooms. The library and the study faced inward, toward Le Cocon's small central courtyard, but the dining and living rooms opened onto the main garden, each with a set of French doors. Grace stepped cautiously into the atrium, looking around her, listening for a second sound, some sign to guide her. She felt a soft breath of wind on her face. The drawing-room doors were open to the garden. Grace took a step toward them, then stopped.

There he was.

She saw him from behind, walking out into the garden, still in his pajamas and bathrobe. He had a coffee mug in one hand and a book in the other, and he looked like any tourist on vacation. His red hair was unkempt, sticking up at strange angles from where he'd slept on it. Grace was struck by how small he looked. How slight. How *normal.* If one were to form a mental picture of a brutal murderer, it would not be this harmless, shambling, middle-aged man.

She had not seen John in the flesh since her trial. Her last memory of him was his pained face as she was led from the dock. *Don't worry,* he mouthed to her. Grace thought back to the terror of those first days in custody, the van ride to Bedford, being beaten to near death by Cora Budds. Back then, she'd still believed John Merrivale would rescue her. He was her friend, her only friend.

She released the safety catch on the gun.

'John.'

He didn't hear her. Grace moved closer, walking at first, then running.

'John!'

He turned around. At the sight of the gun, his face drained of color. The coffee mug fell from his hand, shattering into a thousand pieces on the paved stone of the terrace. Instinctively he moved to one side, covering his head with

362

his hands. As he did so, Grace saw for the first time that he was not alone.

Behind him, sprawled out in a lawn chair, was another man. The second man was turned three-quarters away from Grace, facing the garden rather than back toward the house. At first she could only see the top of his head and his slippered feet stretched out in front of him, but still a shiver of familiarity shot through her. Something about his posture, his body language . . . *I know you.*

She stood transfixed as the man slowly turned. Even before she saw his face, she knew. The languid, unconcerned way he moved, as if the commotion behind him, and John Merrivale's cowering terror, didn't bother him in the least. Grace had met only one man with that confidence. That total, unshakable sangfroid.

'Hello, Gracie.' Lenny Brookstein smiled. 'I've been waiting for you.'

Chapter Thirty-Seven

Grace watched her life flash before her eyes. Was this a dream? Or a nightmare? Part of her wanted to touch Lenny, to stick her hands in his sides like a doubting Thomas and prove that he was real. But something made her hesitate.

'I saw you! I saw your body.' She was shaking. 'I went to the morgue, for God's sake.'

'Why don't you put down the gun?' Lenny's voice sounded soothing. Hypnotic. 'We can talk.'

Grace was about to do as he asked when John Merrivale took a step toward her. Instinctively she swung the gun in his direction and stepped back, her finger hovering over the trigger. 'Don't move!' she shouted.

John stepped back.

'Sit down on that chair. Put your hands where I can see them.'

John did as he was asked, sinking down into the lawn chair beside Lenny's.

Grace looked at Lenny. 'You, too.'

Lenny raised an eyebrow, in admiration as much as surprise. He, too, put his hands on his lap. Keeping the pistol trained on the pair of them, Grace reached into her backpack and pulled out the Dictaphone. She pressed the record button and set it down on the ground between them.

'Talk,' she commanded.

Lenny couldn't take his eyes off Grace's face. *So beautiful. But she's changed. I suppose she had to. She's stronger. That sweet, trusting little girl could not have survived.*

'What do you want to know?'

'Everything. I want to know everything, Lenny. I want to know the truth.'

Lenny Brookstein started talking.

Chapter Thirty-Eight

'What you have to remember, Grace, is how long ago this all started. You were a tiny child when I founded Quorum. Four, maybe five years old. I'd had a couple of funds before that, made a little money, but I always knew Quorum would be different. I set out to rule the world and I did.'

Lenny looked at John Merrivale and smiled. John smiled back, a look of blind adoration on his face. Grace remembered that look from the old days. *He loves him. John's always loved Lenny. How could I have forgotten that?*

Lenny went on, warming to his theme. 'In the early days of the fund, it was a struggle. It was the beginning of the Nineties, the economy was in the tank, people were losing their jobs, their homes. No one wanted to invest. Remember now, I'd staked every cent I owned on Quorum. Every cent. If she went down I'd be back at the bottom. Poor again, in my forties. Penniless.' Lenny's face darkened. 'You can't imagine the fear, Gracie. How terrifying that was, coming from where I came from. The idea that I might have to go back, back to the dirt, the violence, the hunger. No. It wasn't going to happen to me.' His said this angrily, almost as if it

366

were Grace who had tried to bring him down. 'And thanks to John here, it didn't.'

John Merrivale flushed with pleasure, like a teenage girl being complimented by the high school quarterback. Grace listened in silence.

'I had a great model. Foolproof, actually. But at that time, a guy like me with no formal education was seen as way too much of a risk. I couldn't sell a dollar for ninety cents, but *this* guy' – he nodded at John – '*this* guy had the heads of those Swiss pension funds eating out of his hands like a flock of lambs. It was thanks to those early institutional investors that we rode out the storm. But it was the small investors that really made us what we became. The mom-and-pop stores, the little charities that gave us their money. You know Madoff and Sandford and all those guys, they were a bunch of snobs. If you didn't belong to the right golf club, or come from the right family, those bastards would turn your money away. Turn it away! That made me sick. Like, who the hell were they to tell ordinary people they can't get a taste of the good life? That the American Dream was closed to them? Quorum wasn't like that. We loved the little guy, and we made him rich, and he made *us* rich, for a long, long time. People always gloss over that part.'

Lenny's anger was back and growing. Grace had heard about as much self righteousness as she could stomach. 'Those people, those "little guys," she spat the words back at him, still feeling like she was talking to a ghost but unable to hold herself back any longer, 'they lost everything because of Quorum. *Everything*. Families were made destitute because of what you did. Charities closed their doors. People, young men with families, have killed themselves because of – '

'Cowards.' Lenny shook his head in disgust. 'Imagine killing yourself because you lost money? That's not tragic. It's pathetic. I'm sorry, Grace, but it is. You make an investment, you take a risk. No one forced them to give me their goddamn money.'

Grace was horrified by how much she wanted to shoot him. One squeeze of the trigger and she could stop him talking then and there. Stop this obese, heartless apparition, this ghost, destroying the Lenny she remembered, the Lenny she had loved, the Lenny she had believed in, had *needed* to believe in, her whole adult life. But as deeply as his words hurt her, she felt compelled to hear them. She had to know the truth.

'Anyway,' he went on, 'for years, it was good. Everyone was happy. Then, around 2000, things started to go wrong. That was the tech boom, the rise of the Internet, and it was a crazy time. Just crazy. Overnight, every business model, every investment strategy you ever knew, got turned on its head. Young kids, still in college some of 'em, were founding businesses that never made a red cent, then turning them around and selling them for billions of dollars in eighteen months flat. Everywhere you looked, people were launching rockets and everyone was trying to grab one by the tail. All the old dinosaurs like me. Pick the right start-up and hold the hell on for the ride.' Lenny's eyes lit up with excitement at the memory. 'That was around the time I met you, honey. The happiest time of my life. I've always loved you, you know.' He looked at Grace, his eyes welling with tears.

Grace thought, *He means it. He's insane. After everything he's done to me, he thinks he can talk about love?* Aloud she said only, 'Go on.'

Lenny shrugged. 'It's pretty straightforward after that. I made a lot of Internet investments, bought a bunch of speculative businesses, and I took a bath. Between 2001 and 2003 I must have lost' – he looked at John Merrivale for confirmation – '. . . I don't know. A lot. Ten billion.'

'At least,' said John.

'How is that possible?' Grace interrupted.

'How is it possible? You take a bet and you lose, that's how. We just took big bets.'

'I mean how come nobody knew about it?'

'Because I didn't tell them,' said Lenny. 'What am I, stupid? I was careful, Gracie. I covered my tracks. We got creative with our financial statements. It's easier than you might think, in a business as complex and diverse as Quorum, to make your assets look bigger than they are and to hide your liabilities. We stopped logging trades, destroyed a bunch of paper and computer records. We kept the funds we did have moving constantly, from one jurisdiction to another. The SEC sniffed around a bit in 2003 and 2005 but it never opened an official investigation.'

'So you lied. You lied to your investors, the "little guys" who'd trusted you. Just like you lied to me.'

'I was protecting them! And you!' Lenny shouted.

'Protecting *me*?' If it hadn't been happening to her, Grace might have laughed.

'Sure. Don't you see? As long as nobody panicked, as long as they all stuck with me, I could make that money back. I'd already started to do it, Grace. That's the fucking irony. All those destitute families you want me to cry over, *they're* the ones who got us all into this mess, not me! If they hadn't all tried to cash in at once, pulling their money out like a herd of frightened, stupid sheep following each other over a cliff . . .' He threw up his arms in despair. 'I could have made things right. I could have. But I never got the chance. After Bear went down, then Lehman, it was mayhem. Those bastards destroyed everything I'd ever worked for. They sank my ship, and I couldn't stop them. All I could do was make sure I didn't go down with them. I had to survive, Grace. I had to survive.

'John came up with the idea of the boat. We'd do it on

Nantucket, make it look like suicide. At first we thought I could just disappear, you know, missing presumed dead. But I couldn't leave anything to chance. Knowing the storm that would be unleashed at Quorum, I didn't want some vigilante out there looking for me. We had to have a body.'

Grace started to shiver. *The stump in the morgue. Davey Buccola's pictures. The severed head . . . He couldn't have!*

'You mean . . . you killed somebody?'

'He was a nobody. A homeless bum from the island, a lazy drunk. Trust me, he'd have been dead in a few months anyway the way he was treating his liver. I just speeded things up a little. Took him out on the boat, gave him a bottle of bourbon and left him to it. When he was passed out cold, I did what needed to be done.'

Grace put her hand over her mouth. She felt the vomit rise up inside her.

'Yeah. It wasn't pretty.' Lenny winced in distaste. 'But like I say, it had to be done. The cops would have to think that the corpse was me, so I had to . . . alter it. The hardest part was getting my wedding ring onto his finger. He was stiff by then and so fucking fat. Plus, of course, there was the storm. We hadn't figured on that. A couple of times I nearly did go overboard. I tell you, I've never been happier to see Graydon in my life.'

Graydon. Graydon Walker. It was a name from another life. Grace and Lenny's helicopter pilot, Graydon Walker, was a quiet, taciturn man. Grace had never really warmed to him. But like many of the longtime Brookstein staff, he was fanatically loyal to Lenny.

'Graydon took me to a quiet airstrip on the mainland. Des had the jet waiting, brought me straight here.' Desmond Montalbano was the pilot of their G5, a young, ambitious ex–fighter pilot with a taste for daredevilry. 'I knew Graydon would keep the secret but I wasn't sure about Des.'

Grace gasped. 'You didn't kill Des?'

'Kill him? Of course not.' Lenny sounded offended by the suggestion. 'I structured his compensation over thirty years. Made it worth his while to keep his trap shut. He's paid out of a trust in Jersey. That money's completely untraceable,' he added with a touch of pride.

'It's all completely untraceable,' said Grace bitterly. 'Who hid the rest of the money? You? John?'

Lenny smiled. 'Darling Grace. Haven't you figured it out yet? There *is* no "rest of the money."'

Grace looked at him blankly. 'What do you mean?'

'I mean this mythical seventy-plus billion everyone's so busy looking for. It doesn't exist. It never did exist.'

Grace waited for him to explain.

'Oh, Quorum was making money all right. We were trading. Up until the Internet losses we were doing well, perhaps twenty billion in our heyday. Never over seventy! In any event, by 2004, it was all gone.'

'*All* gone?'

'There was a few hundred million left. I was using that to pay dividends and cover occasional redemptions. And to bankroll our lifestyle, of course. I always wanted you to have the best, Grace.'

Grace thought about the nightmare of the past two years of her life. 'You wanted me to have the best?' she murmured.

'Yes. People think success is measured in wealth, but it's not. Not in America. It's measured in the *perception* of wealth. If people perceived me as wealthy and successful, they would continue to lend to me. And they did. Until Lehman went down. After that, everyone got jumpy. People started to do the math and I knew I had to create an exit strategy.

'I put some money aside for myself and John. We didn't need much. We always planned to live simply, didn't we?' John nodded. 'Madagascar's a simple island, Grace, you know

371

that. That's why you and I both loved it so much. You know, I'm so happy you're here, darling.' He stood up and threw his arms wide, as if expecting her to embrace him, 'It'll be like old times, the three of us together again. I've missed you, Gracie, more than you know. Won't you put the gun down? Let bygones be bygones?'

Grace laughed, a loud, joyless roar of a laugh. She laughed till her body shook and tears streamed down her face. Then she stood up and pointed the gun between Lenny's eyes.

'Bygones? *Bygones!* Have you totally lost your mind? You set me up! You stole and murdered and lied and cheated and you left *me* to take the fall. I went to the *morgue,* Lenny! I saw that corpse, that bloated hulk of the poor man you killed, and I wept. I wept because I thought it was you. I LOVED you!'

'And I loved you, Grace.'

'Stop it! Stop saying that! You left me for dead. Worse than dead. You had John rig my trial! They locked me up and threw away the key and you let it happen. You *made* it happen. My God. I believed in you, Lenny. I thought you were innocent.' She shook her head, bitterly. 'All this time, everything I've been through, it's all been for you. For your memory. The memory of who I thought you were. Do you know why I came here today?'

Lenny shook his head.

'To kill John. That's right. I was going to shoot him, because I thought he'd murdered you. I thought he'd stolen the money and framed you.'

'John? Betray me?' Lenny seemed to find this idea amusing. 'My dear girl. The entire world has betrayed me, and you single out the one man, the *only* man, whose loyalty has never been in question? That's priceless.'

'What about *my* loyalty, Lenny? *My* love? I'd have given anything for you, risked anything, suffered anything. Why didn't you trust me? You could have talked to me when things started going wrong at Quorum.'

'Talked to *you*? About business? Come on, Grace. You never looked at the price tag on anything in your life.'

It was true. Grace looked back at the naive, idiotic person she'd been back then and felt ashamed.

'Look, perhaps I should have trusted you, Gracie. Perhaps I should've.' For the first time, a look that might have been guilt passed briefly across Lenny's features. 'I did love you. But it's like I said. I had to survive. People wanted a scapegoat for their own stupidity. Quorum investors, America, the world. They wanted a sacrificial lamb to atone for their own greed. It was you or me, darling.' He shrugged.

'And you chose me.' Grace's finger caressed the trigger. 'You heartless son of a bitch.'

John Merrivale whimpered in fear. 'P-please, Grace.'

Lenny asked, 'What do you want me to say, Grace. That I'm sorry?'

Grace thought about it. 'Yes. I would like you to say you're sorry, Lenny. I'd like you to say you're sorry for that poor man you butchered. Sorry for the millions of people whose lives you destroyed. Sorry for me, for what you did to *me*. Say you're sorry. SAY IT!'

She was screaming now, hysterical. Lenny looked at her dispassionately, the way one might observe a rampaging animal in a zoo.

'No. I won't say it. Why should I? Because I'm not sorry, Grace. I'm not. And if I had a chance to do it all over again, I'd do it exactly the same way.'

Desperately, Grace searched his face for any sign of the man she remembered. Any hint of compassion, of remorse. But Lenny's eyes blazed with defiance.

'I'm a survivor, Grace. That's what I am. My father survived the Holocaust. He came to America with nothing but the shoes on his feet. And yes, he made a god-awful mess of his life, but that was only because he was poor. He survived, that's the point. He *had* a life, and he gave me life, and I devoted *my* life to escaping poverty. I wasn't going to make the mistakes he made! I wasn't going to be a second-class citizen, another poor little Jewish boy begging to be let into the goddamn country club. I owned the country club, okay? I owned it! I had all those preppy, protestant Walker Montgomery the Thirds begging *me* for acceptance. I even married one of their daughters.'

Grace winced. *Is that all I ever was to you? Cooper Knowles's daughter? A status symbol?*

'You expect me to apologize for surviving? For fighting to the end? Never! I came from nothing, Grace, from less than nothing. I built Quorum up out of *dust*.' He quivered with anger. 'What do you know about hard work? About prejudice? About poverty? About suffering?'

Grace thought about the grinding days at Bedford Hills. About living hand to mouth, on the run from the law, knowing the entire world was prejudiced against her, that not a soul on earth knew the truth. She thought about fighting off rapists, of bleeding half to death from a self-induced abortion, of slashing her wrists with the pin of a brooch. *What do I know about suffering? You'd be surprised.*

Lenny went on. 'You were the American princess. Life handed you everything on a plate and you took it, accepted it as your due, as your right. You never asked where it *came* from. You didn't care! So don't stand there and try to take the moral high ground with me. I'm sorry that you suffered, Grace. But someone had to. Maybe it was your turn.'

'My *turn*?'

'Yes. Don't look so horrified, darling. You made it out, didn't you? You learned to survive, yourself. I'm proud of you. You're here, you're alive, you're free. We all are. You wanted the truth and now you've got it. What more do you want?'

And that's when Grace knew for sure.

'Vengeance, Lenny. I want vengeance.'

The shot rang out, its echo bouncing off the high stone walls. Lenny touched his chest. Blood seeped through his fingers, soaking his white linen shirt. He looked up at Grace, surprised. John Merrivale screamed, 'NO!'

Another shot was fired, then another.

'Grace!'

Grace turned. Mitch Connors was running through the drawing room toward the garden, his blond hair stuck to his forehead with sweat, his gun drawn. 'Stop!' But she couldn't stop. John Merrivale had run into the house. Grace swung back to face Lenny but he was gone, too. *No!* Then she saw him, crawling toward the summerhouse on his hands and knees, a thick trail of blood staining the ground behind him. Grace took aim again. She raised her arm to shoot, but Mitch Connors ran past her, throwing his arms wide to make a human shield between Grace and Lenny.

'It's over, sweetheart. Stop, please. Put the gun down.'

Grace screamed, 'Get out of my way, Mitch. MOVE!'

'No. This isn't right, Grace. I know you want justice, but this isn't the way.'

Lenny was getting away. She couldn't bear it.

'Move, Mitch, I swear to God! I'll shoot.'

She heard a commotion inside the house. Doors slamming. Men running. Through Mitch's legs she saw Lenny had almost reached the safety of the summerhouse. Out of the corner of her eye she saw John Merrivale running out of the house screaming, waving a shotgun. The footsteps behind her grew louder. 'Police! Drop your weapons!' It was now or never.

Grace fired her gun for the last time. She watched in horror as Mitch pirouetted on the grass, the bullet tearing through his flesh. *Mitch!* She screamed but no sound came out. The razors were tearing at her, too, her side, her arms her legs. She was on the grass, bleeding. Sound faded. Grace opened her eyes to a silent ballet of running feet. Mitch was still, slumped on the lawn. She looked for Lenny but she couldn't see him, only the red haze of her own blood, blotting out the sun and the sky and the trees, falling, falling, heavy like thick velvet on the theater stage: her final curtain.

Chapter Thirty-Nine

New York, One Month Later

The woman in the hospital waiting room whispered to her daughter. 'Is it her?'

The daughter shook her head. 'I don't think so.' Normally she wouldn't have been so hesitant. She was a great one for all the gossip magazines and prided herself on being able to spot a celebrity from fifty yards. Sunglasses and head scarves didn't fool her. But in this case . . . The woman *did* look a bit like her. A lot like her, if you broke down her face feature by feature. The cupid's-bow lips, the child-like dimple in the chin, the wide-set eyes and delicate line of the nose. Yet somehow, put them all together, and her face looked . . . *less*. Less beautiful, less striking, less special. Combine this effect with the woman's drab clothes, the gray wool skirt and simple white blouse, and . . . no. No, it wasn't her.

'Mrs Richards?'

The girl's mother looked up. 'Yes?'

'You can go in now. Your husband's awake.'

Mother and daughter filed out of the waiting room. As they passed the look-alike woman, both stole surreptitious glances. Close up she looked even smaller. It was almost as if she projected anonymity, the same way that other people, stars, gave off charisma or sex appeal. 'Poor thing,' said the mother. 'She's like a little mouse. I wonder who she's visiting?'

Grace was glad when the women left. It was still only seven in the morning. She'd expected, and hoped, to find the waiting room empty. It was getting harder to be around people. Any people. Soon she would leave America for good. Find somewhere peaceful, a retreat where nobody knew or cared about her past. A monastery perhaps, in Spain or Greece, if they'd have her. *They'll have me. That's what they do, isn't it? Offer sanctuary to sinners, to criminals and the poor. I qualify on all three counts.* According to her new lawyer, she'd be entitled to federal compensation eventually. 'It could be a considerable sum of money. Not as much as you've been used to, perhaps, but certainly seven figures.'

Grace wasn't interested. Whatever the government gave her, she would send directly to Karen Willis and Cora Budds. She owed them her freedom, a debt that no amount of money could hope to repay. Besides, Grace had no use for money. All she wanted was to get away. But she couldn't leave yet. Not till she knew he was all right. Not till she had a chance to explain.

She touched the scar on her arm, from where the bullet had sliced into her. She had four similar scars, all on her right side, on her leg, hip and shoulder. *Lucky to be alive,* that's what the doctors said. And Grace had smiled and wondered, *Am I? Am I lucky?* It was amazing how quickly the body could heal. But the spirit was not so resilient.

Without Lenny, Grace Brookstein no longer knew what she was living for.

The story of the shoot-out at Le Cocon, and the sensational killing of John Merrivale and capture of Lenny Brookstein, had gripped the entire world. The Madagascan authorities made a token effort to prevent the Americans from flying Lenny back to the United States, but a personal phone call from the president, along with some promises of substantial U.S. investment in various Madagascan infrastructure projects, swiftly changed their minds.

Harry Bain briefed the local press. 'Mr Brookstein is returning to his home country of his own free will for urgent medical treatment. Once he recovers – if he recovers – his future will be determined by the U.S. Justice Department.' It was Bain who'd gotten hold of the local police and sent reinforcements to Le Cocon that day. Once he finally heard Mitch's messages, he got right on the phone to the chief of police in Antananarivo and filled him in on everything.

'It would have helped if you'd been honest with us about your presence in Madagascar in the first place,' the police chief said stiffly. 'We could have helped.' Harry Bain had had to grovel to get him to agree to send men up to the estate. But thank God he had. By the time they got there, Lenny Brookstein had been shot in the stomach and groin. Had Grace aimed a little higher, she would have severed his coronary artery and robbed America of its most sensationalistic and shocking trial since . . . well, since her own. As it was, after extensive surgery, Lenny survived. Before he knew where he was, the FBI had him heavily sedated and shipped back home on a military plane. It was over before you could say 'human-rights violation,' never mind 'miscarriage of justice.'

For two weeks it was unclear whether Mitch Connors would be so lucky. His life hung in the balance. Grace was terrified that it was a stray bullet of hers that had lodged itself in Mitch's spine, but the cops assured her it was John Merrivale who had almost killed him. When the police showed up, they screamed at him to drop his weapon but John continued firing indiscriminately, at Grace and at them. They'd had no choice but to take him out.

At first Grace was happy when she heard John was dead. But as the weeks passed, her happiness faded. What did it matter? What did any of it matter: John's death, Lenny's trial (for fraud and murder) and sentence of death by lethal injection, her own presidential pardon? None of it was going to bring her old life back, or help the people who'd been ruined by Quorum. None of it was going to make Mitch Connors get well, or bring Maria Preston, or Andrew, or that poor homeless soul from Nantucket back to life. The whole thing was so utterly, utterly pointless. Justice had become a mere word, letters on a page, empty of meaning. There could be no justice, no closure, no satisfying ending. The whole thing was a farce, a game. Grace herself has been pardoned, not because she was innocent, but because it was too much of an embarrassment for the authorities to admit she'd escaped from custody *twice,* and that it was *she,* not they, who had found Lenny and uncovered the truth about the Quorum fraud.

'I am convinced that Mrs Brookstein was as much a victim of her husband's duplicity as the millions of others who suffered at his hands,' said the president. And America applauded. 'Of course she was. Poor thing.' They had their villain now, their pound of flesh. Lenny Brookstein was being sent to Super Max in Colorado, the toughest prison in the land, home to the most dangerous Islamic terrorists and deranged child killers. The play was in its third act, and suddenly there was a vacancy for a convincing tragic heroine. Who better to fill it than Grace? After all, the show must go on.

A nurse tapped Grace on the shoulder.

'Good news. He's awake. Would you like to go in?'

*　　*　　*

380

Mitch looked pale and thin. Horribly thin. Grace tried not to look shocked. *He must have lost forty pounds.* When he saw her, he smiled.

'Hello, stranger.'

'Hello.'

There was so much to say, but in that moment Grace couldn't think of a single word. Instead she took Mitch's hand in hers and gently stroked it.

'They told me you testified against Lenny at the trial.'

'Yes. I didn't have to go in person. They let me give a statement.'

'He got the death penalty?'

She nodded.

'So your testimony must have helped.'

'I doubt it. He admitted everything anyway. Once they knew about the murder, the die was cast. I think he wanted people to know how clever he'd been. He didn't seem upset at the trial. It was almost as if he were enjoying himself.'

Mitch shook his head in disbelief. 'He still doesn't see himself as guilty, does he?'

'Not in the least.' She paused. 'They're executing him today, you know. He waived all his rights to appeal.'

For a few minutes they were both silent. Then Mitch said, 'I know this is going to sound like a ridiculous question. But do you still have any feelings for him? Knowing, you know, that he's going to die. Does it upset you?'

'Not really.' Grace looked thoughtful. 'It's not so much that I have no feelings *for him*. It's more that I have no feelings, period. I'm numb.'

Mitch squeezed her hand. 'It takes time, that's all. You've been through so much.'

'To tell you the truth, I don't know if I *want* to feel anymore. I want peace.'

She stared out of the window. It was late May, and spring

381

was in its last glorious flush, the trees on the sidewalk exploding with blossoms, the blue skies alive with birdsong and joy. Grace thought, *I'm happy that life goes on, that it's beautiful. But I can't be part of it anymore.*

'Do you know who called me the other day?'

Mitch shook his head. 'Who?'

'Honor. The FBI told her about Jack and Jasmine. He's decided not to seek another term as senator. They're getting a divorce.'

'She called *you* to tell you this?'

Grace laughed. 'I know. As if we could pick up where we left off. That's actually what she said to me. "Can't we be sisters again?" Connie and Mike moved to Europe, so I guess she feels alone. Lenny said something similar actually, in the garden at Le Cocon. He thought I was going to stay there with him and John. That the three of us could hide out in Madagascar together and live happily ever after. "Like old times," that's what he said.'

'Are you kidding me?' Mitch's eyes widened. 'What did you say?'

'I didn't say anything. I shot him.' Grace grinned, and Mitch remembered everything he loved about her. *She thinks she's dead inside but she's not. She's just hibernating.*

Grace stood up and moved toward the window. Mitch watched her, her graceful dancer's walk, the fluid ballet of her limbs. While he was the cop and she was the fugitive, he'd forced himself to keep a lid on his feelings. Now that it was all over, he could no longer hold them back. Longing hit him like a punch to the stomach.

I love her.

I want her.

I can make her happy.

'What?' Grace turned around and stared at him accusingly.

382

Mitch blushed. Had he spoken aloud? He must have. He propped himself up higher on the pillows. 'I'm in love with you, Grace. I'm sorry if that complicates things. But I am.'

Grace's face softened. She was fond of Mitch, after all. And he had risked his life to try to save hers. There was no reason to be angry with him. But love? No. She couldn't love again. Not after Lenny. Love was a fantasy. It didn't exist.

Mitch said, 'I think we should get married.'

Grace laughed out loud. 'Married?'

'Yes. Why not?'

Why not? Grace thought about Lenny. About their beautiful wedding on Nantucket, her happiness as a young bride, her hopes and dreams. They hadn't just been crushed. They'd been incinerated, annihilated, scorched to dust and ashes along with the trusting, happy girl she had once been.

By nightfall, Lenny would be dead.

Grace could no more marry again than fly to the moon.

'I will never get married again, Mitch. Never.'

Hearing her say the words, Mitch knew she meant them.

'I'm leaving.'

Mitch felt his stomach lurch. Panic gripped him. 'Leaving? What do you mean leaving? Leaving where? Leaving the room?'

'Leaving the country.'

'No you're not. You can't!'

'I have to.'

'But why? Where would you go?'

Leaning forward, Grace kissed him, just once, on the lips. It was a short kiss, not sexual, but loving, almost maternal. It made Mitch want to cry.

'I don't know where I'll go. Somewhere quiet and remote. Somewhere where I can live simply and in peace.'

'This is bullshit. You can live simply with me.' He took her face in his hands, willing her to listen to him, to love him, to let herself believe he loved her. 'I can do simple. You want simple, you should see my apartment. It's so simple they repossessed my furniture.'

Despite herself, Grace smiled. It was a tiny chink in her armor. Mitch jumped on it.

'You like that? Hell, if simple's what you're into, I'm your guy. I can even do flat broke. Cold Domino's pizza for breakfast? You got it. With a little more effort I can probably get them to cut off the electricity. We could sit in the dark under a blanket and hum.'

'Stop it.' Grace giggled.

Mitch brought her hand to his lips, kissing each of her fingers in turn. 'I tell you what. I'll forget about marriage if you forget about leaving the country. Just . . . say you'll have dinner with me when they let me out of here.'

Grace hesitated.

'C'mon! One lousy dinner. You owe me that much at least.'

It was true. She did owe him.

'All right. One dinner. But I can't promise you anything.'

Chapter Forty

Lenny Brookstein looked at the straps on the bed and felt his insides liquefy with fear. He told himself it wasn't death that frightened him. It was dying like this, on someone else's terms. But now that he was actually here, he realized what a self-delusion that was. *I don't want to die. I want to live.*

'No!' He panicked, trying to back out of the room. 'I . . . I can't do it! Help me!'

Strong, young male hands restrained him. 'Easy.'

He forced himself to calm down. The room was clean and white and sanitized, like a hospital. The three men inside it looked like doctors, with their blue scrubs and face masks and their clear plastic gloves. But they weren't here to heal him.

After all the years of struggle, in the end it had come to this. He would have appealed his sentence had there been even the slimmest hope of success, but Lenny was shrewd enough to know that there wasn't and too proud to play a game he could not win. Besides, what were ten more years of life in jail worth to him? He'd already lost ten pounds and he'd only been here a matter of weeks. You wouldn't give the food at Super Max to a dog.

Two of the doctors started to help him up onto the gurney but he shook them off angrily.

'I'll do it.'

He lay down on the gurney. The doctors fastened the straps. Lenny was embarrassed to find his legs were shaking. He had once controlled a business empire worth more than the gross national product of some countries. Now he was not even master of his own body.

He turned his head and saw the prison rabbi standing awkwardly in the corner of the room. 'What's he doing here? I said I didn't want anyone.'

The rabbi stepped forward. 'They're going to sedate you in a moment, Lenny. I wanted to give you a chance to pray with me. Or if there's anything you feel you'd like to say?'

'No.'

'It's not too late to repent of your sins. The Lord's forgiveness is infinite.'

Lenny closed his eyes. 'I have nothing to say.'

His felt the sharp prick of the IV in his arm. For a second the terror welled up again. He wanted to vomit, but his stomach was empty. His bowels, too, thank God. A few seconds later, the sedatives began to do their work. Lenny felt his heart rate slow, and a warm, sleepy feeling creep over him.

He thought about his mother. She was wearing the one pretty dress she owned, a floral, Liberty print, and she was dancing around the kitchen, and his father was drunk again and yelling at her, 'Rachel, get in here!' and then he staggered in and hit his mother and Lenny wanted to kill him . . .

He thought about the Quorum Ball. It was 1998 and he was untouchable, a god, watching Wall Street's lesser mortals compete with one another just to be near him, to touch his clothes or hear him speak. He wished his mother could have been there . . .

He thought about Grace, her trusting, innocent face, her glorious, naked body that had once been his delight. She was talking to him, singing in that sweet child's voice of hers: *I don't want children, Lenny. I'm so happy as we are. There's nothing missing,* and he opened his mouth to tell her he loved her, and there was nothing missing for him either, but then her face changed and she was old and sad and angry and she was pointing a gun at him, not just pointing but firing, over and over and over, *bang, bang, bang,* and John Merrivale was screaming *NO!* but the shots kept coming . . .

He was on the boat, exhausted, the ax still in his hand. He tried to stand but he couldn't; he was slipping everywhere. The deck was slick with blood and water from the storm and the boat was lurching, rocking wildly and he was sure he was going to go overboard. And he looked up and there was the chopper, fighting against the wind like a giant insect, and Graydon lowered the rope and he was climbing, hanging on for dear life, pulling himself up, up into the heavens, and Graydon was gone but his mother was there again, *Come on, Len, you can do it, darling. You can do anything you want to* . . . and he cried out, 'I'm coming, Ma! I'm coming! Wait for me!' and her arms were around him and he had never felt happier in his life.

The rabbi looked at the doctors. 'Is that it?'

'That's it,' said one. 'He's gone.'

'Not fair, is it? For a heartless butcher like him to die with a smile on his face? He should have suffered.'

The rabbi did not reply, but walked sadly away.

Epilogue

Grace walked out of the hospital and down the street. New York looked its most beautiful in the spring sunshine, as vibrant and alive as she had ever known it. The streets were thronged with people, rushing about the business of life as if it mattered. It was at once familiar and strange, like walking through a dream that she had had many times before.

She was alive. She was free. Grace understood that these things were supposed to make her happy. She wondered if they ever would.

Looking back over her shoulder at the hospital, she thought fondly of Mitch Connors. Mitch was a good man. A kind man. Grace had sensed that from the beginning. *In another life, a different dream, I could have loved him.* But that chance had passed, blown away like a feather in the wind. She knew she would never go back.

Would she really go abroad? Probably. Or perhaps she would simply fade away here, as she had before, disappear into the comforting anonymity of the city.

Turning the corner, Grace Brookstein walked toward the subway. The crowds on the sidewalk opened up to let her in, then closed around her like a womb.

She was gone.

Acknowledgments

My sincere thanks are due once again to the Sheldon family for their trust in me, their support and generosity. Also to my editors, May Chen, Wayne Brookes, and Sarah Ritherdon, and to everyone else at HarperCollins who has worked so hard on this book. To my agents, Luke and Mort Janklow and Tif Loehnis, and to everyone at Janklow & Nesbit: you are the best. And last but not least to my own family, especially my darling children, Sefi, Zac, and Theo, and my husband, Robin, who supports me in everything I do. I love you.

What's next?

Tell us the name of an author you love

| Tilly Bagshawe | Go ▶ |

and we'll find your next great book.

www.bookarmy.com